Partap Sharma is best known as the author of the play *A Touch of Brightness*, which has been produced in India, England and the USA. He has written four books of stories for children. *Days of the Turban* is his first novel.

Partap Sharma lives in India and is a leading documentary film maker and commentator.

DAYS OF THE TURBAN

PARTAP SHARMA

Futura

A Futura Book

Copyright © 1986 by Partap Sharma

First published in Great Britain in 1986 by
The Bodley Head, 32 Bedford Square, London WC1

This edition published in 1988 by
Futura Publications, a division of
Macdonald & Co (Publishers) Ltd
London & Sydney

The author and publishers wish to thank Blackwood, Pillans
and Wilson for permission to quote from *The Life of General
Dyer* by Ian Colvin.

ISBN 0 7088 3640 2

Reproduced, printed and bound in Great Britain by
Hazell Watson & Viney Limited
Member of BPCC plc
Aylesbury Bucks

Futura Publications
A Division of
Macdonald & Co (Publishers) Ltd
Greater London House
Hampstead Road
London NW1 7QX
A Pergamon Press plc company

The title owes its inspiration to the cockaded frontier-style turban but is a tribute to all turbans and the times they have seen.

Though this is a work of fiction set against a background of fact, the statements made by historically real persons are true in that they have been culled from their own speeches and sayings.

The bus will take you there. Now. But before, it was wild. Desolate. The backyard of Punjab. Here, in my village, the men carry guns and anger easily between their quotidian farming chores.

These are men of the far North born out of the fore-runners and morass of all civilizations that attacked India through the Himalayan passes. These are men born out of and into the war.

They carry their bloodshed lightly between jokes and daily lawful living. They are men and women of the earth, as basic as that—as quick to yield harvests of kindness and goodwill, as quick to dry up and turn sullen and destroy. These are my people.

To them this book is dedicated

Contents

Contents

1

• • •

The View From the Village

In the stodgy North Indian hamlet of Jagtara, twenty thousand rupees signified a lot and young Balbir, desperate for the money, had forged his father's signature on a cheque. Now as he hurried guiltily through the lanes he had begun to loathe, with the wad of currency notes hot in his pocket, he feared he might be too late. The local passport racketeer had told him clearly to make payment the week before.

'What can I do, Balbir?' shrugged Tarsem as he ran a hand over his crew-cut hair. 'You're too late. The others left Delhi yesterday. Here, you can see the telegram for yourself.'

Expecting to read a long complicated message, Balbir was unprepared to find just two words. Partly in disbelief, partly in anticipation, he mouthed each syllable as though it might crack open and reveal another. Then he hauled out the entire phrase.

'Happy birthday. It says happy birthday!' he exclaimed in surprise.

'That's the code,' Tarsem rubbed a thumb over the stubble on his chin. 'It means they left as planned, yesterday.'

'But where for?'

Tarsem cocked an eyebrow at him and said nothing.

Balbir didn't really know Tarsem. But he did know that Tarsem could usually be found in this enclosed yard each morning. Here, one of the hobbies that Tarsem indulged in was cooking. He cooked in the morning for the gluttony and discussions of the evening. Balbir detested Tarsem and hated the fact that he had no alternative but to deal with him. It made Balbir even more resentful of the restrictions that his family had imposed.

He looked at the three rolls of fat that coiled like a python round Tarsem's belly. And yet Tarsem, like many men in the village, had been a wrestler! Indeed, he had been a professional wrestler.

Tarsem yanked up his *tamba*, stuffed it in his crotch and settled his bulk on a low stool. He reached for a ladle. The stool tipped a little but he retained his balance. He knew how to shift his weight and retain a comfortable centre of gravity. He stirred the chicken curry with great concentration and said, 'If you join us, you could travel anyway. You'd make money.'

'I want to go out and stay out like . . . elder brother Raskaan.'

Tarsem grinned. The very mention of Raskaan had that effect on people who knew him. It was like reminding them of a good joke. Not only did the man have a peculiar name—Raskaan!—but his blithe absurdities endeared him even to his enemies. Who could take a clown seriously? And yet each one of his hare-brained schemes made money! There he was in Germany, a millionaire many times over, and that too in Deutsche Mark. No, no one could repeat Raskaan's escapade into wealth. He had a knack, even a genius perhaps, for turning the ridiculous into the practical. If he sat down on a stone and a snake were to slither out from under it, he would not waste time in fear but marvel at the creature and probably seize the opportunity to deprive it of its venom which he would surely sell to some laboratory. Raskaan was an oddity of nature, a startling quirk in the steady graph of dull premeditated business.

Balbir had grown up in the shadow of Raskaan's success, stunted for want of sunlight and spiky as a thorn-bush. He prickled with anticipation, anxious to protect himself even from those who sheltered him from the world. Indeed, that was his main grouse—that the family did not give him the freedom to grow.

Raskaan certainly would never help Balbir to leave the village. Balbir was hostage to the responsibilities that his elder brother had forsaken. Someone had to be on the land, someone had to stay with the ageing parents.

And Satyavan their cousin, their elder uncle's son, the one in direct line of succession to the patriarch, what of him? A chameleon if ever there was one. But dangerous. A peasant among peasants, a rich man among the rich, a chieftain's grandson among the feudal, the power behind the local political throne and yet so self-effacing that you hardly remembered when he had been present on the scene and you couldn't be sure when he withdrew. He watched others make mistakes and made sure he didn't make any. No wonder he was referred to as the sharpest henchman of the patriarch. He was an 'operator' beyond the dreams of Tarsem. Tarsem feared him and wished to emulate him and hated him. Just thinking of him made Tarsem break into sweat.

A bead of perspiration trickled down the hairline of Tarsem's chest, rolled over the folds of his stomach and vanished somewhere. The glistening sinuous movements were interrupted as he leaned back. His navel came into view and disgorged the perspiration. He swept the back of his hand over his belly as casually as a man might wipe his face. It *was* hot by the stove.

Tarsem looked directly at Balbir. 'You're educated. Connected. You've just got to put me in touch with your family's contacts.' He paused only a second before taking the leap. 'The arms and ammunition people in Europe.' Balbir was about to protest. 'No, Balbir, don't play the innocent with me. Your cousin Satyavan is there right now, making arrangements.'

'He's not in the gun trade.'

'I wouldn't be so sure,' Tarsem slurped a little gravy from the ladle and smacked his lips. 'The trouble is he won't have anything to do with me. He's a big shot. He's into politics. Me? I'm just a social-worker helping people get what they want. I don't turn up my nose at people because they have their own political views. I'm a businessman, clear and simple. Think about it. We could be partners. You'd be richer than Raskaan, more powerful than Satyavan—if that's what you want. Me? I'm happy just to fulfil a few big orders I have.'

Standing there Balbir felt altogether too lean and lanky. He longed for the day when he too might have a mature man's authoritative paunch. Squatting down quickly by the hissing gas-ring, he said guardedly, 'The family has its own stock of guns somewhere in Chamkalan. It's only three miles from here but the old man is there and won't let me nose around.'

'Don't tangle with your grandfather. You'll upset everything if you alert him.' Tarsem dropped a pinch of salt into the steam. 'Pass me the cloves. There. And the cardamom.'

Tarsem's chicken curry was as famous as Tarsem was notorious. Balbir dug among the packets of turmeric, garlic, aniseed, then located the cloves and cardamom beside a large sack of cement.

Tarsem grunted by way of thanks, then said, 'You're too . . . straightforward.'

'I don't understand.'

'You're too direct. I told you I'd take cash or kind. Twenty thousand rupees or one Light Machine Gun. And what do you do? You go straight to Satyavan and ask for a gun! What made you think he was just going to hand you an LMG? Now it will get to the old man, and you'd better have a good answer ready.'

Balbir said, 'I won't be here then. I'll be away. I've got the money.' He took out the wad of notes and held it across the singing, bubbling pot.

Tarsem tapped the ladle on the side of the pan and put it down but he didn't reach for the money. 'Everyone's gearing for action in Punjab. The police are out-gunned. President's rule has been declared. Punjab is now officially 'A Disturbed Area'. There are factions preparing to fight. Even within the Golden Temple they're preparing to kill each other. They're building barricades, bunkers, bringing in brick and mortar and sandbags. You're missing an opportunity. You can earn money by the shovelful. They're desperate for carbines and machine guns. With those kind of weapons, a few men can hold a fortification against thousands.'

'I don't want to discuss it.'

'Pity. But I'm patient. As for that wad—return it.'

'What? But—!'

'Return it to the bank, Balbir. Put it back in your father's account. Yes, I know what you did. Your father sent for me last night. He told me. He . . . he warned me.'

'How did he know so quickly? I only took it out yesterday. And the bank is miles away in Jalandhar.'

Tarsem sighed and stood up. 'You've been away too long in school and college. You've forgotten how it is in these parts. If you sneeze in the bazaar, your family will ask you the moment you step in the door whether you have a cold. They'll hear of it through some busybody.'

In a panic now, Balbir put the money away and retied the muffler round his head. He didn't like to wear a turban. That was old-fashioned. But here in the village he felt alienated by his better education and needed a token of conformity to rustic custom.

Tarsem took the pot off the stove with some cotton-waste from the motorcycle tool-kit. This was his favourite corner of the yard. He kept everything here—his Norton Dominator motorcycle, some tins of paint, a chair on which to hang his shirt and trousers, a bottle of Tarsem-made 'country', a double-barrelled gun, a packet of Red Lamp cigarettes, matches and all that a man might find immediately useful.

This corner was sheltered by the flooring of the *chabara* overhead, the room that is normally used for keeping farming implements but where Tarsem kept more bags of cement. In the evening, he would retire to this room with his chicken curry, his gun, cigarettes and matches for a drinking session with his friends. Till then the chicken curry would mature and Tarsem would see to the day's demands. He said, 'I think it was the Head Clerk of the bank, that fellow who still goes about wearing a solar topee, he rushed over to your father.'

'But it's none of his business!' Balbir almost shouted then controlled himself as he found his voice cracking.

'It is,' said Tarsem. 'He's match-making for the Bank Manager's son. You know they're trying to marry the boy to your sister. When the head clerk saw that twenty thousand rupees had been withdrawn, he was worried that it might be in preparation for a wedding. He came to ask your father. Your father was horrified, of course, but when he learnt that you had collected the money, he realized that you had forged his signature. He guessed you wanted it to pay me.' Tarsem assayed a kick at the stray dog that was sniffing towards the pail of buttermilk. 'Return it. Quietly. The bank doesn't know it was a forgery. Your family may punish you but they won't prosecute you. Put it back in the account. No one will bother.'

'My father's money is my money,' Balbir said.

Tarsem scratched at the rolls on his belly and muttered patronizingly, 'If you were earning, your money would still be your father's. But your father's money is his own. You know that's the way it has always been.'

Balbir didn't like that reprimand, especially since it came from Tarsem—wastrel, scoundrel, no-gooder, cement-monger, blackmarketeer. He retied his muffler again.

Tarsem levelled another kick at the dog which had sidled back. The dog yelped, whimpered, tucked his tail under and slunk away.

Tarsem's blubbery lips were wet as he muttered, 'There are other ways of going about it than what you did. You know that.'

Balbir nodded. Then said softly, 'But you'd get into real problems with my family if I helped you get the kind of guns you want.'

Tarsem's eyelids flickered for a moment. 'For that, I'd be prepared to take the risk. That would be worth it. But this,' he indicated the wad that was like a brick in Balbir's pocket, 'would be cheating your family, especially since your father has informed me about how you got the money. I don't cheat.'

Tarsem was not a big-time operator. He was, as they say, small fry. But he was big in the set-up of this area comprising several villages. Yet he was not big in the village of Jagtara itself or, let us say, he was as big or as little as any other villager here, for this was where he lived and here he was equally vulnerable. He loved the village. He was born here and chose to continue to live here.

Jagtara was a village, a proper village that had grown up over centuries accumulating to itself the human moss of an unmoving habitation. True, families came from neighbouring villages and settled here and one or two families from here drifted out within a radius of a few miles to another village with the same sort of character. But full knowledge of every branch of the family always preceded the family's arrival. These were villages composed of human beings who had come together for security against the elements and against the depredations of dacoits. These were villages that had grown over a huddle of human beings into a huddle of huts and houses.

There is the other kind of village that is first composed of buildings and then of human beings. That is the model kind set up by a government for political, administrative or territorial reasons and by an industry for business purposes. There, human beings are transplanted and the families are initially strangers to each other.

Jagtara was not a village of families but of generations. Like all such villages in the North, it had known its invasions and upheavals and catastrophes. If you dug into the mounds around the village you might find old bones and pottery. If you dug under the houses you might find older foundations and remnants of old implements. But Jagtara lacked a sense of its own history. If you asked, you would be directed to the oldest man who would dig merely into his own memory. Yet by piecing together scraps and shards and lingering tales, you could put together for any man there in a single day a genealogy of at least fifteen generations.

You would learn that Balbir's family were Muhiyals and once had lived in the mountains; fourteen generations ago his ancestor was one of the clansmen who fought against the invader Ahmed Shah Abdali and had been driven south to the vicinity of this village. That very same Ahmed Shah Abdali had desecrated the Golden Temple in Amritsar.

Among the Muhiyals are hindus, sikhs and even some muslims. Clan kinship goes beyond religion and pre-dates the advent of all religions.

Balbir's family was not uncommon to the region. Though they were brahmins by caste, as are all Muhiyals, they behaved primarily as Muhiyals and did not set themselves up as twice born and twice virtuous; they were farmers and fighters and had no use for the scriptural begging bowl and merely tolerated all rites and ceremonies. They were as fierce and as ignorant as the next and did not pretend to be otherwise. They were as generous and as hospitable as any rural family. And if you, with your sense of history, looked for some traditional justification for such martial behaviour in the thinking caste you might alight, in the past, on the sage Dronacharya who taught the arts of war.

Half of Balbir's relatives were in the armed forces and most of the rest were farmers.

So too the generational intricacies of the others in the village were known. Name any one, including Tarsem—they walked with their precursors in their train.

Therefore Tarsem was loathe to diddle anyone from the village or the surrounding villages. In fact, he was not a diddler at all. He openly conducted dealings aimed at enabling villagers to get what they wanted, even if the process entailed breaking a governmental or international law.

In Punjab a man could die for a diddle. Or less. Tarsem carried a gun because he was afraid he might be misunderstood to have diddled when he had only dealt. He also carried it as a precaution against fools and the long arm of the law. He expected never to have to use it.

But the sort of guns he sought, sophisticated, high calibre, rapid-firing weapons that could decimate large numbers, were for people who would actually use them. Though he was fascinated by the sleek, light, collapsible versatility of the latest development in carbines, he knew he could not with safety carry one. It would call too much attention to itself.

Till now Tarsem's sources had been limited to men who made duplicates in illegal factories. The country-made pistols, revolvers and guns were crude, unreliable and prone to all the defects of hand-crafted products. Now even these factories, some of them in Punjab, others in Jammu and Kashmir and a few across the border in Pakistan, were working overtime, but though they increased their quantity they could do nothing about the quality of their manufacture. And further towards Afghanistan there was pressure from the demands for weapons made by the rebels fighting Soviet Russia's forces. The American weapons that came into that market were absorbed like ink into blotting paper. Here in Punjab, Bhindranwale's fight for supremacy was only just beginning and the demand for accurate, effective weapons would grow. These were not dacoits who would make do with a few frightening devices; these were terrorists with political aims who hoped to increase their numbers by the successful use of guns, grenades, bombs and timed explosives for sabotage. Tarsem felt his future was opening up.

He said to Balbir, 'Come over in the evening. A friend of mine will be here. He'll tell you what's to be done.'

Balbir was now besieged. Everywhere he went, with the money burning like a block of coal in his pocket, he felt uncomfortable, holding it down sideways, fearing it would be noticed.

All through that straggly bazaar, he was aware of the shop-keepers' eyes. A bearded Jat farmhand looked up from his game of *chaukoni* and hesitated before casting his throw. Balbir stopped as though to merge into the gaggle of spectators. With a smart flick of the wrist, the man caught five of the six cowrie shells on the back of his hand. There were murmurings, comments, proverbs.

The Jat said, 'That's how you make money!' and winked at Balbir.

Balbir's pocket bulged.

At home, he sat down on the string-bed in the courtyard and draped a towel from the line, casually, across his thigh. He despised the village, its primitiveness, its slow pace, its seeming lack of enterprise. He was annoyed even with the rudimentary nature of the facilities around him. Little changed here; much was as it had been for centuries. Why had they sent him to boarding school and university among the sons of industrialists and professionals if they intended him to return and rot here? Of course, among the boys there had been the sons of other big zamindars and maharajas and nawabs, but they were all being prepared for a bigger world than that of their land-owning fathers. Balbir felt land-bound, land-locked. Suddenly he smiled remembering the schoolboy phrase, 'Gosh, I'm really landed with this!' And he shuddered to think that other boys like him even as far away as England had suffered enough to coin the usage. Balbir felt landed in the worst possible way with the land he would one day inherit.

His father bathed in the courtyard, bending down to work the hand-pump, behind the waist-high walls. Across, in the kitchen, his mother and his sister tittered.

'Balbir, O Balbiraa!' his father called.

This was it. Balbir knew this was it. But his father didn't look him in the face. He merely asked why the food hadn't been taken yet to the men in the fields. It was getting on to eleven o'clock, he said, you couldn't expect people to work if their stomachs were snarling at them. The morning is nearly gone, he shouted, working himself into a rage, most people have been about and done half the day's work and here the morsel of the labourer is being delayed because the women are gossiping and dawdling round the fire.

Balbir's mother leaned into the smoke and slapped another *roti* on the *tava*.

'*Your* meal is ready,' she replied with just a hint of good-humoured rebellion.

'Lahh!' his father exclaimed losing impetus. 'Is that any kind of an answer to make?'

Balbir meandered into the kitchen. His sister continued blowing through the piece of metal pipe, rekindling the dried cowdung in the grate. His mother patted the *peedi*, the low stool beside her and said, 'Sit down, son.'

Just then his father roared, 'Who, in God's name, has taken my towel from here?'

Balbir realized he was still holding the towel, inconspicuously, to his side. He felt the tears start into his eyes.

'Why, Billu!' his mother exclaimed, addressing Balbir by his pet name. He resented even that. He wasn't a baby any more. They didn't treat him like a grown-up.

'It's the smoke,' he said and took the towel outside to his father. Then it occurred to him that he had to hide the money somewhere. The bank in Jalandhar was forty miles away. Till he could return it, he had to hide it. It wouldn't do to get caught carrying it. His father might, even now, take the walking stick to him. He went quickly into the so-called sitting room which was really his father's room. He muttered a response to the greeting of old Parsini, the sweeper woman, who was down on her haunches swabbing the floor. He took the *chillum* from his father's *hookah* by the bed. But it was too early to re-plenish it with coal and tobacco. His father had not eaten yet.

There seemed not a private, untouched place where he could safely stow the money. He crossed from room to room, pausing by the beds with their rolled-up quilts, the alcoves with clothes hanging from pegs, the niches with lanterns and clay-lamps and misshapen candles that might be relit at nightfall because the electricity from the Bhakra Nangal Dam was constantly failing. Behind him, he was dimly aware of the scraping of the bucket as the sweeper woman pulled it along, and the slop and swish of the cloth as she cleaned. He looked into the vats containing lentils and gram and potatoes. He poked into the sack of *gur* and put one lump in his mouth savouring the sweet aroma of sugarcane. Then he undid the rectangle of tin covering the mouth of the storage bin on the other side of the wall. He peered into its depths. Wheat for the consumption of the house. He took the wad of notes from his pocket and thrust it deep into the swallowing grain. He needed time to think.

His father had dressed. Close-fitting pyjamas. Loose white shirt. Rough leather moccasins. Had taken his sturdy walking-stick from against the wall and crunched into the front room. His right leg was giving him trouble again.

His sister went in with a *thali* of food. He stopped her as she emerged out of the sounds of his father's chomping.

'Aadran, did he say anything? About me?'

'What could anyone say about *you*!' she laughed, stuck her tongue out at him and scurried into the kitchen.

'Aadran!' he called imperatively. But she was elder to him and paid no heed.

His mother had raked some embers out by the kitchen door. He prepared the *chillum* for the *hookah*. Inside him, like a searing bolt of lightning, the thought raced, not for the first time, 'Here I am, able to quote Byron, Shelley, Keats, Kalidas, Tagore, able to do trigonometry and calculus, able to conduct classroom experiments in chemistry and physics, and what am I being made to do? The chafing brainless chores of a peasant! I am just a begotten servant.'

'And what will we do,' said Aadran loudly in the kitchen, 'when Billu goes off to Germany and forgets all about us?'

'Don't you worry,' said Balbir sharply, 'I'll be back to see you properly married. I'll find you a husband who'll muffle your tongue and stop it from ringing like a bell.'

'Wah! Well said, son!' his mother laughed. 'But what'll you do there without your mother's cooking?'

'Oh he!' said Aadran, 'He'll find himself a *mem*. They all do! And he'll bring her back too. But she won't be able to sit on the floor and cook. She'll want an electric stove.'

'No, son, don't do that!' his mother wailed, still taunting him. 'She'll drink with her food and want to eat beef!'

They collapsed against each other with laughter.

Balbir took the *chillum* in to his father.

'What's all this nonsense, Balbireya?'

'Nothing, Papaji.'

'I could hear the women teasing you. Once a pigeon always a pigeon. They'll have you eating out of their hands. Travel is good for the mind, the mature mind and the strong body. It's a different matter that there's no muscle on your bone and you want to venture out. That's another matter entirely. But there's no harm in wanting to travel, if you have some place to go and something definite to do. When we had land near Nowshera and your grandfather's *dera* was in the village of Matala, I used to ride beyond Peshawar through the Khyber Pass, to the markets of Jalalabad and Sarobi. Beyond that lay Kabul from where the King of the Afghans ruled. I never had reason to go beyond Sarobi. But the other way, up north, I had been as far as Kunar and Asmar. To do that, you had to be hardy. And you had to have a good horse.'

Balbir's father thought for some time, sighed, reached for the turban beside him on the bed and placed it on his head without bothering to retie it properly.

'Your grandfather's horse was a wonder, Balbireya,' he said. 'You never saw Shaitaan. There is no horse even in Ferozepur today like him. He was a Mintgumery horse, raised and ridden by your grandfather from the best that his father had. You don't see any Mintgumery horses now, do you Balbireya?'

'No, Papaji. The custom of horses is going altogether. And Montgomery is in Pakistan. And Babaji is half blind.'

'I know. I know all that . . .' Balbir's father brooded with all the weight of his fifty-five years. Then roused himself and said, 'I know your grandfather is going blind. But don't you speak lightly of him—even with his cataract, and his hearing less and his face wrinkling like furrows in a field, he's got twice your strength yet, though he's eighty-four. And he could put two of you straight. I know you think I am joking. You don't live with him like your elder uncle does or his son Satyavan. You're lucky I'm easy on you and your Babaji is living in the village of Chamkalan. But that is only three miles from here and I've seen you tremble even when he farts, Billu, so don't be brave behind a man's back.'

Balbir's sister came in and took the empty *thali* away.

His father said, 'And, of course, I know Mintgumery is now in Pakistan. Didn't I come back through it all? In rags like a beggar who my own mother couldn't recognize, may God keep her soul! What I'm saying is, you should travel when you're fit for it. But why go so far away? And why go through Tarsem? And who is this fancy teacher who has taught you to say Montgomery instead of Mintgumery? I don't mind that. I'm not saying I mind that. But why talk strange? It only seems like you're putting on airs. You understand me? I don't mind at all if a man has travelled and then talks peculiar. But you're too young yet. Wait a little, Billuaa, and then travel.'

'I'm twenty-four, Papaji.'

His father chuckled, 'Sometimes I almost forget that you're a man now. All the more reason why we need you here.' He sighed. 'I shouldn't have listened to Raskaan about giving you all that fancy schooling. Too much education is not good. Just enough to read the newspapers and do the accounts—that's best. Otherwise everyone will be wanting to run away from work, real work. Did you milk the buffaloes this morning? No, some farmhand did. Did you chop the fodder? No, Kumhareya has been employed to do it. Did you water the fields? No, Raseela started the pump and stupidly destroyed a patch of mustard. Have you taken the food to the men? No, you're still here and you'll banter away the hours with the women in the kitchen.'

His father's voice had now risen to a roar. Balbir looked down, quivering with shame, anger, humiliation and uncertainty.

'A landowner's son,' his father said, 'must work the land or he's no good.'

With that he turned slowly on his heel and walked painfully through the huge doors that were always kept open during the day. At the steps he paused. Other villagers passing by greeted him but he was in no mood for niceties.

He looked again at Balbir and said more softly now, 'It was those educated men who ruined our peace and carved out Pakistan. Then they made Haryana and Punjab. Now maybe they'll start riots in the cause of Khalistan. Is this education, is this culture, that teaches man to misbehave with man? You understand me, Balbireya? We need you here. It's a fine village, our Jagtara. And everyone loves you. It may seem too small to your youth. But it's a fine village.'

When his father left, Balbir fled into the small adjoining room and fell on a patchwork quilt and wept. What they didn't understand was not that he wanted to go away but that he wanted to come back.

'I want to come back,' he said later that morning as he set down the packed food for the fieldhands, 'like Raskaan in a brand-new Mercedes bought just for the duration of my visit. I'd like to be wearing the latest style of suit, with a camera over my shoulder and dark glasses on my nose. I want to gift new tractors to all my relatives and maybe buy you a piece of land.'

'You will,' said the strapping young farmhand whose name was Uday Singh but who was called simply Kumhareya meaning that he was a potter's son. Other men were working farther out, in the fields. Here, by the cattle shed and the huge tanks into which water was being pumped from the well, the air was cooler and birds twittered in the soughing branches of the spreading trees. Kumhareya was a Jat. He was also a sikh. But like many Jats he had cropped his hair. His beard was a mere wisp.

'I want,' said Balbir, 'to bring back a lot of money and distribute sweets in the village. I won't mind the children making marks in the dust on my Mercedes. And, talking of dust, I'll have a tarred road made so that people don't have to walk about with their turban flaps over their noses.'

'That'll cost a lot of money,' Kumhareya panted as he chopped fodder with the hand-worked machine, swinging the bladed wheel down and round and up.

'Fifty thousand at most,' said Balbir over the chee-ack chee-ack of the chopping wheel.

'At least,' Kumhareya nodded.

'And I'd build myself a country residence for the times I come back to visit or maybe for my old age, a house here by the well.'

'What's wrong with this shed?'

'It's cold at night in the winter and hot in the summer.'

'But you sleep soundly. You prefer being here to at home with your elders.'

'They bother me. They won't admit it when I win an argument. They don't let me rest. I prefer being on my own.'

'Here you sleep deep,' Kumhareya snorted, 'so deep you don't even get up at five in the morning to milk the buffaloes. I have to come and do that.'

'I lie awake all night thinking and fall asleep in the morning. You can't imagine the house I will build, Kumhareya. It will have a generating set for electricity, to make sure there's always light. It will have a fridge and you can eat ice all day sitting under the trees. It will have a bathroom with a flushing commode. It will have a garden through which the water will flow as it goes to the fields.'

Kumhareya collected some fodder in a basket and took it across to the outdoor troughs where the buffaloes stood. He said, 'Raseela started the pump this morning and ruined the mustard. Then the pump stopped and he didn't know where to put the diesel.'

Annoyed at the implied rebuke, Balbir said, 'That's the trouble with people around here. They don't think beyond the day to day. There's no intelligent conversation.'

Suddenly Kumhareya stopped and looked at him. 'Do you really want to hear some intelligent conversation, Billu?'

'Don't you call me Billu. You're not an elder in my family. I am Balbir to you.'

'Right,' said Kumhareya with a laugh. 'And don't you go on calling me Kumhareya. I have a name too.'

Balbir stared at him in astonishment. He had never realized that Kumhareya might actually dislike being called that. It was as if a smith had baulked at being called Smith or a weaver had refused to be known as Weaver.

Kumhareya said, 'My name is Uday. Uday Singh. And if you want to meet some really lively minds, educated people, students, not just labourers like me, then come with me tomorrow.'

Balbir moved close to him. Kumhareya was shorter by a couple of inches. Looking down into his eyes, Balbir smirked, 'We all know about those two educated girls you go and meet on the sly. I followed you once all the way to the village of Maina and that ruin of a farmyard. The two girls came with books in their hands. One stayed outside to keep a look-out and one went in to be with you. I felt like barging in and surprising you. But then I thought, let poor Kumhareya have his fun.'

Under his tan, Kumhareya went a deep red. Then he grimaced, 'Yes, yes, that's all I am to you—poor Kumhareya.'

'I didn't mean it like that. Sorry. Uday.' Balbir almost laughed as he said it. It was strange to think that ordinary, average, hardworked, hardworking Kumhareya had space in his mind for ambition or resentment.

Kumhareya said, 'I'm not going to Maina tomorrow. I'm not meeting the girls.'

'Then who?'

'Just come. You'll see. I'm doing you a favour, only because you think you're so clever.'

'That's very cagey of you. All this last year, you've been secretive. You know what alerted me into following you that day?'

Kumhareya tried to be nonchalant. He thumped a buffalo on the rump and pushed her aside.

Balbir said, 'You weren't in the stinking knickers and shirt you always wear.'

'I keep my special clothes to wear for special people,' Kumhareya said moving away to refill the basket with fodder.

The bond between Balbir and Uday was not of the mind but of the heart. They were young men of about the same age. You might have thought it odd to see them together in an industrialized modern city. There, a difference in status creates vast barriers. But here, in a farming community, men of different backgrounds and varied means are thrown together. Man is a gregarious animal; friendship is an essential need.

And yet you would be right if you felt that it was not a wholly satisfying relationship for either of them. Uday could not always expect sympathy from Balbir and Balbir could not hope for complete understanding. It was, in a sense, a friendship forged by convenience and circumstances; it was a friendship liable to ebb and flow in accordance with the pressures exerted upon it. Perhaps that is why they kept secrets from each other, sharing them only when the cup of emotions overflowed. They might not have been friends had they had a choice in the matter. They were on an island; there was simply no one else.

Balbir laughed and said, 'When I have all that money I'll buy you a lot of special clothes so you can meet a lot of special people!'

Just then to their surprise, from the innards of the tractor trolley that was parked nearby, an earringed head raised itself and came into view. This was Jheera, the gaunt-faced opium smoker, therefore also known to the villagers as *Afeemchi*. 'And what will you give me, Balbireya,' he asked, 'when you have all that money?'

'A kick,' Balbir said, 'and I'll throw you in the hospital.'

'Lahh!' Jheera moaned. 'As if I'm ill!'

'Go to sleep, *Afeemchi*,' Kumhareya said, 'Dream your dreams and let Billu dream his.'

'I also need things,' Jheera protested.

'Of course,' Kumhareya said. 'Opium—to smoke, to eat and to drink. Where you get all that money I don't know!'

'I earn it,' Jheera said. 'Hard work first. This afterwards.'

He lay back in the trolley. Balbir went up to Kumhareya and whispered, 'Come on, who is this special person you want me to meet?'

'I didn't say person. I said special people. We'll go to Amritsar, to the Golden Temple.'

'What?'

'Why not? Just go and pay our respects.'

Balbir shrugged. 'Of course. Why not? But tell me, who do you want us to meet?'

'If you defeat me, you weak city-slicker!' Kumhareya shouted as he ran laughing to a fallow field. This was almost a ritual with them, as indeed it was with most able-bodied young men of the village. Wrestling took the place of games. The villages of Punjab and Haryana have always been the spawning ground of India's greatest wrestlers.

Balbir flung off his muffler, kicked off his shoes, stripped to his underwear and dashed after Kumhareya. Jheera peeked over the edge of the trolley, pained by all the sudden noise.

Kumhareya had thrown off his turban and shirt and was circling Balbir. Both clapped their hands against their thighs with great bravado and gave off warlike whoops and cries. Kumhareya kicked up a shower of earth. Balbir ducked and lunged. They grappled, twisted and broke free. Kumhareya preferred to use his legs. He always maintained they were the strongest part of his anatomy because he often sat for his father at the edge of the potting hole and spun the giant wooden wheel. Now he turned, fell on his hands and locked his legs round Balbir's neck, bringing him down like a tree.

'Bravo!' Jheera cried, sitting up in the trolley.

Levering his arm between Kumhareya's legs, one hand gripping the other wrist, Balbir prised them apart. Kumhareya recoiled like a spring, struggling to get up in time. But Balbir had hold of his foot and wrenched. Kumhareya rolled and struck out with the other foot. Balbir was now kneeling and braced. As Kumhareya wriggled up, he jumped butting him with his shoulder. In a trice he was astride Kumhareya's chest.

'*Wah! Shabashe*!' Jheera cried and, bravoing thus, climbed carefully off the trolley.

Kumhareya now slid about and slithered. He had to keep his shoulders off the ground. Once pinned that would signal the end of the bout. Balbir was using both hands to force him down.

Kumhareya knit his fingers, linking his hands between Balbir's arms and turned. Balbir crashed to one side. Kumhareya was free.

Jheera applauded from the side of the field. He had slumped down any which way but managed to sit cross-legged and his *tamba* was all awry. He was too absorbed or too far gone. Either way, he didn't care, and kept applauding helplessly while the combatants began again the ritual circling and threatening.

A Nihang, a member of the traditional army of the sikhs, in a dark blue turban with a dagger at his side and a gun in his hand, stopped at the other corner of the field then sauntered round to Jheera.

'What's happening?' he asked.

Jheera semaphored vaguely into the air.

The Nihang went to the tap of the tank below the pump, washed his face, came back and sat down in the shade of a tree to watch the fun.

The village headmaster cycling back from school looked, bumped over a stone, wobbled and stopped to adjust his trouser clips and wipe his forehead. He too decided that he might as well stop and watch.

Sikh and hindu fieldhands carrying bundles of sugarcane stopped.

The two young men were rolling over and over, sweating and picking up a great deal of earth.

At first only Jheera's encouragement was audible. Then the headmaster began offering expert academic advice which neither of the two understood.

'Balbir!' he would shout, 'The pincer grip! The pincer grip! Now the scissor hold, Kumhareya! Tiger stance, you dolt! Oh no, the fending fall now!'

Gradually the spectators drew into a tight little knot, exclaiming, commenting, arguing, joking. Every now and again the combatants would take a breather by the simple expedient of stalking each other aggressively at a safe distance. They were tired and wanting to get on to the finale of their accustomed practice which was to have a refreshing bath in the large tank with the pump jettisoning barrages of water on their prickling bodies. Followed by a tall tumbler of buttermilk. But there was no way of stopping with so many spectators enjoying themselves so much. Just then, the vigorous mutter of a tractor engine drew near.

Balbir's father, Khushi Ram, steered off the dust road, jounced over pit and drain, and drove into the field. He de-geared, braked, left the engine gargling, separated the two who had now locked in a last attempt to claim nominal victory, and gave them each a push that sent them sprawling.

'Mother-eating bastards!' he shouted, 'Have you nothing better to do with your time?'

Then he turned on the spectators whose laughter slowly died.

'Have you bought tickets? Or are you just scratching your arses on the ground?'

They dispersed sheepishly.

He looked at Balbir and seemed about to explode. 'You ... you criminal!' is what he said. And Balbir knew he was referring to the forgery and the twenty thousand rupees. But he was holding himself in. Why? On orders from the patriarch, from Babaji? That was the only feasible answer.

Like a flash of inspiration it came to him: he decided then and there that he would not return the money to the bank account in Jalandhar. No. He would use the money to go some-where, perhaps Bombay, and get away to Europe. After all, Tarsem was not the only operator in India. With the money to serve him, anything was possible. He almost smiled at his father.

'What are you grinning for, you idiot? I'll deal with you as soon as I've attended to V.P. Joshi. Don't look so startled. You know what it's all about. But we won't discuss it now. That stupid Head Clerk has just got off the bus from Jalandhar. He's taken leave for the day, to talk about Aadran's marriage ... and your antics!' Again he held himself in. Then he churned his way through the soft earth, twisting on his game leg slowly towards the tractor. Before mounting, he said, 'If you have anything of mine that you wish to return, come to the house as soon as you've washed that mud off yourself. That's what I came to tell you. You could go to jail, you know.'

He drove away.

As soon as they were alone bathing under the battering torrent that cascaded into the tank, Kumhareya said to Balbir, 'You've been up to some funny business. What was all that?'

Balbir shook some water out of his ear and said, 'In one hour from now I'll be on my way out of Punjab.'

'But ... we're going to Amritsar tomorrow, remember? You said you wanted to meet some—'

Balbir held Uday by the shoulders and said, 'I couldn't care a damn about Amritsar, Jalandhar, Jagtara, Chamkalan or the whole of Punjab. I owe it to myself to get out.'

Kumhareya nodded. Then he said with a rueful smile, 'Write to me sometimes.'

'Of course. But how will you read my letters?' Balbir couldn't help the taunt. It was the usual way between them.

'I have . . . a friend . . . who reads things for me.'

Balbir's eyes dilated, then lit up. 'Ah I get it. The girl in the village of Maina, the one with the cat eyes, she reads things for you! And she's beautiful! But what do you have that needs to be read?'

Kumhareya executed the two or three strokes that it was possible to swim in that tank. Then he laughed, 'I'm not as unimportant as you think. People write to me.'

Balbir shrugged, 'I could have read things for you.'

Kumhareya shook his head. 'Not these papers. This is different. She's one of us.'

Balbir raised a quizzical eyebrow. 'You mean she's a potter?'

'No. She's a sikh. Daughter of a *sardar*.'

Balbir's head seemed to spin, his heart sank as though to the pit of his stomach. He felt ill. It had never struck him that, with all the differences between them which lay covered under the blanket of friendship, there was this difference too and it was of consequence to Uday.

Balbir nodded slowly and looked down. Then holding his breath he ducked underwater and stayed there as long as he could. He felt he would burst with all the pressures around him.

At the house, his father was parrying the thrusts of V.P. Joshi, Head Clerk, Jalandhar Branch, Punjab Farmers' Cooperative Bank. This little man was something of a quidnunc in addition to being a marriage-broker. He cracked his knuckles, shifted forward uncomfortably against the constant swallow of the easy chair that had been set down for him, and said, 'Pandit Khushi Ram, you must at least tell me *why* your son forged your signature on the cheque.'

Balbir's father stared out of the open door as though contemplating the passing scene.

This unnerved the bank clerk. It distressed him to have to sit thus, discussing serious personal matters before a large open door. Villagers kept ambling in and out. Sometimes bullock carts went by creaking and rumbling, their wheels tumbling now and again into the drain. The man opposite was coaxing a buffalo out of his yard. And now Balbir's father seemed to be scanning a team of donkeys jogging along with their load of bricks. The Head Clerk made another attempt. He said, 'You can imagine my consternation, Panditji, when I learnt yesterday that you had drawn twenty thousand rupees. That's why I telephoned you. It seemed as though you had finalized Aadran's marriage somewhere else. But I knew you wouldn't do that without informing me. After all, the Manager's son is not a proposal we can easily overlook. Of course, yours is an old and respected family and you have every right to change your mind whenever you wish . . .'

'Of course,' Balbir's father said, startling the Head Clerk. But it was clear by the way he glowered out and massaged the thick crook of his walking-stick that he was distracted. He had merely interrupted automatically with a habitual assertion of his independence.

The Head Clerk adjusted his tie and thought how difficult it was to get any work done with these peasants. He tried another tack.

'It was my duty,' he said, 'to make that trunk call to you last evening.'

'Yes.'

'Otherwise you would not have known, even till now perhaps, that the money had been withdrawn.'

'That's obvious.'

Somehow this farmer fellow was getting argumentative. There was no disagreement between them but his voice was developing a querulous tone. Head Clerk V.P. Joshi knew how to blunt the edge of irritation. He had handled insubordination among his juniors. He uttered a glancing threat. He said, 'Forgery is a crime.'

Khushi Ram turned to him with a look of slow surprise and tapped his walking-stick on the ground.

'But I sent for the money,' he said. 'There was no forgery. I have made no complaint.'

'But, Panditji, you yourself said last evening on the phone that—'

'Balbir is my son,' Khushi Ram said with finality and placed his walking-stick on the bed beside him.

Aadran came in with a pot of pre-made tea and a cup and saucer on a wooden tray. She was properly demure before V.P. Joshi, said the customary, 'I touch your feet, ji,' and placed the tray on a stool beside his chair. She asked her father if he would like a glass. He never drank in a cup. But he wasn't too fond of either. He asked for a glass of milk. She retired respectfully. He turned his attention again to the passing scene. Two mounted constables from the Phillaur *chowki* rode by. They were probably hunting for extremists. Punjab was beginning to bloom with terrorists as though they were a newly-introduced cash crop!

He noted that the constables sat their saddles in the English style. He wondered if they taught their horses the *chaal*. It was by far the most comfortable pace for a long journey; you could drink a glass of milk while moving and not spill a drop. Or even a saucer of tea as Joshiji was doing just now. But he supposed if you sat your horse in the English style it was unlikely you would also teach him the Indian *chaal*. People would soon forget the *chaal*. Only the army and the police and a few Nihangs used horses these days. And a very few villagers. He wondered how his cousin's young mare was faring. His cousin had bought her just a few days ago, to hitch to a *tonga*, but she was terribly skittish and refused the shafts. At the first attempt she over-turned the tonga. His cousin Gopal would have to break her in. She was just about three years old.

V.P. Joshi slurped the last bit of tea from his saucer leaving the dregs in the cup. He said, 'About Aadran, Panditji, what have you thought?'

'Oh no, you know as well as I do that that cannot be my decision. We shall have to put it to her grandfather. He is the head of the family.'

'But as her father, do you give your consent?'

'Of course. But let us see what the old fellow says.'

V.P. Joshi sighed and relaxed. Aadran came in with a scalding tumbler of milk wrapped round with a piece of cloth. She handed it to her father and went in, perhaps no further than the inner door which always remained closed and from behind which she could eavesdrop on the future that was being planned for her.

After a discreet pause, V.P. Joshi asked, 'When shall we go?'

'Now, if you wish. Chamkalan is only three miles from here. I'll drive you there by tractor.'

Khushi Ram put down the tumbler of milk, stood up and moved painfully on his arthritic leg to the top of the steps. Just then he saw Balbir coming down the street.

He caressed the handle of his stick as though savouring the thought of clobbering Balbir with it but he said almost gently, 'Son, you know Mr Joshi is here. He doesn't seem to believe that

I asked you to withdraw the money. He thinks we're scuttling his plans for your sister's marriage. We wouldn't hurt your sister's future, would we? Now bring me the money so that he can see for himself that it is still with us. Go on, son.'

Balbir felt trapped.

V.P. Joshi was watching him closely as he donned his archaic solar topee.

Balbir nodded, brushed past his father and the clerk, and went in. He heard the clerk relax audibly.

Very well, thought Balbir, I shall show them the money but I shall hang on to it. They're obviously on their way out. By the time they're back, I shall be gone.

Outside, standing by the tractor, Head Clerk Joshi said by way of conversation while they waited, 'Our bank has financed the purchase of many tractors recently.'

'But it's a pity,' Khushi Ram said, 'that the government is now adding sales tax to the price. What's worse is that they no longer allow relatives abroad to gift you a tractor. My elder son Raskaan wants to send us a new one but we'd be stuck with the duties and taxes!'

Somehow another argument seemed to be brewing. V.P. Joshi fell back on some sound clichés. 'Punjab is the most prosperous state in the country. It flourishes while other regions are in the grip of famine. It can afford to pay taxes. The agricultural sector here is rich.'

'Sector-fector be damned! I don't understand the way you reason though you may be good at accounting in the bank.' Even while he said this, Khushi Ram wondered what was keeping Balbir. The longer he waited, the higher his blood pressure rose.

Inside, standing by the storage bin, Balbir noticed some grains of wheat on the floor. It gave him an uneasy feeling. He lifted the latch on the square of metal that was hinged to the wall. He swung open the hatch and looked inside, beyond the line of the wall. It was dark there but the light was sufficient to reveal the outline of a little mountain of grain. He had thrust the wad of money in no deeper than his wrist. He felt around for it. And he couldn't find it.

Outside, his father was yelling so loud that the locals gathered to listen. He was telling V.P. Joshi, 'It's the farmer who feeds you, and we will feed the entire country, but we must have tractors, water, electricity and fertilizers. If you take any of these things away now, you will be trying to reap the so-called prosperity of Punjab before it is ripe. Our tractor is shared by others in the village. We share the water too. We could do with more tractors. We could do with more wells. But there is a shortage now of diesel, kerosene, petrol. Most of the tubewells have been switched to electricity but they say there's not enough power coming from Bhakra Nangal. It's going to Haryana and Rajasthan. And the electricity people are often dissatisfied and on strike. When the electricity fails like that or is in short supply for months, there isn't enough water for the fields. We have no alternative. Everyone I know has sold his bullocks or keeps them only for churning out sugarcane juice. The Persian Wheels have been dismantled and discarded. When there is no water for the fields, the crop fails, and Punjab fails to do what it could. No wonder the Akali Dal is making political capital of the situation. Every Punjabi, whether he is sikh or hindu, wants more electricity, more water, but the Akali Dal is mixing this up with some purely religious demands on behalf of a section of sikhs so it ends up seeming to be a communal party that is out to drive a wedge between people of the same household. I mean, what has the carrying of *kirpans* on aeroplanes or the broadcast of the Gurbani over All India Radio or the management of *gurdwaras* got to do with a demand like more water and power from the Bhakra Dam? It is merely an attempt to sway the sikh vote against Indira Gandhi. Meanwhile that extremist fellow Bhindranwale is using fanaticism to take control of the Akali Dal. Tohra and Longowal are scared to speak out. Bhindranwale's terrorists are causing havoc, shooting all opponents.'

'Panditji, Panditji . . .' V.P. Joshi began but his voice trailed away as he looked nervously about him. It wasn't safe to rant against Bhindranwale in public. The majority might agree with what was said but there was always the danger that some lone dissenter might be seeking another notch on his pistol.

Inside the house, hearing the vociferous denunciation, Balbir's mother ran to her son. 'Billu!' she called. 'Go and stop your father from bursting a blood vessel.'

She stood where she was, astounded. Balbir had scooped out nearly half the grain in the bin. It lay like a castle of sand on the floor. And he was delving in and furiously flinging out more.

Outside, Balbir's father was saying, 'The only things I read are the newspapers and the news each morning is drenched in blood.'

An old sikh couldn't resist the urge to join in. He said, 'Panditji, what we need are more public meetings of protest against Bhindranwale and his terrorists. I attended one in Amritsar. It was addressed by Kuldip Nayyar and General Aurora—you know, the man who led the troops in the 1971 war.'

'Yes, yes, we must all do our bit,' said Khushi Ram thoughtfully. 'But some fault lies with the government too.'

One of the villagers called out from behind the knot of people. 'They say Bhindranwale was set up by Indira Gandhi and President Zail Singh in order to divide the Akali Dal.'

'Be that as it may,' said Khushi Ram gyrating slowly on his bad leg in the direction of the voice, 'but he has got out of hand. If someone employs a servant in good faith and he goes berserk and turns out to be a murderer, you cannot blame the employer. So it isn't her fault or Zail Singh's that Bhindranwale has shown himself to be a maniac in search of personal power at any cost. No, that is not what I started to say. What I was getting at is that the government machinery is so slow that sometimes it is a drag on the development of Punjab. That makes us all feel upset and rebellious. For instance, there is no fertilizer sometimes. They've made us all change to these new chemicals and they've become like mother's milk to a baby. The earth cries out for them. And when we can't get them, the soil is suddenly drained of its strength. Have you seen a strong man falling sick? He falls sick worse than someone who has been weak all his life. At any rate, he feels worse and it is a shameful sight to see. When such great earth dies it is a crime and when you see it happening to the fields you tilled and watered with your hands, it is a soul-breaking agony.'

Khushi Ram interrupted himself and called out for Balbir. He was beginning to twitch and quiver with impatience.

V.P. Joshi said, 'They say this fertilizer shortage will pass—'

'But meanwhile,' Khushi Ram turned on him and gradually his voice rose in volume, 'the fields will be dead! Do you hear what they are saying on the radio now? They say that scientists have discovered that cowdung is good manure! But, mothers' sons, didn't we know it for centuries and didn't we use it year after year till they said you must move with the times, nature is not a good enough provider, use the fertilizer we make? And now that people have bought their kerosene stoves, they've sprung a kerosene shortage and there are long queues of people wasting their time arguing and pleading for a drop outside the *bania* shops and the ration dealers. Then the radio tells you that scientists have discovered that cowdung is good as burning fuel!

They'll tell us next that a cow is good for milking. But I see the trick, Joshiji, I see the trick. No child of this house will ever be brought up on powdered milk. And we will grow everything we need. The only things we buy are salt and diesel for the tractor. So when there is no diesel available at the petrol pumps and people are sitting and sleeping in queues waiting for days, do I stop my son when he goes out with Jaggu Singh and twenty others onto the high road to stop a diesel tanker by force? No, I bless him in my heart and say nothing. They haul out the driver politely and take what diesel they need.'

'But that is robbery, Panditji!'

'That is progress, Joshiji. The progress of Punjab is built upon taking the bull by the horns. It is not robbery. There are too many middlemen and hoarders and agencies that rob the farmer. The farmer is a good man in a good season and a bad man in the bad because first and always he must farm. If we did not grow your food somehow or the other, you would starve the way some other states do. Ah, here's Balbir.'

Balbir came down the steps like a man in a trance. He had emptied out the whole bin. His face was ashen.

His father said, 'Give me the money, boy. You've kept us a long time.'

Balbir shook his head slowly, dazedly, from side to side.

His father scowled now. 'What's your problem, boy?'

'The ... the money ...' Balbir wet his lips and almost whispered. 'It's gone. Stolen. Someone stole it.'

'What?' His father's voice tore through the air like the neigh of a horse confronted by a wall of fire. The full horror of it seemed beyond his comprehension. 'What?!'

Almost by reflex his stick rose in the air, rearing up, beyond control. His son did not avoid it. He walked towards his father.

The thick stick struck Balbir across the head. He fell on the spot, writhing, the blood beginning to flow into the dust.

Khushi Ram turned and climbed into the driving seat of the tractor. V.P. Joshi wavered and then clambered onto the passenger seat above the mudguard. No one else moved.

Khushi Ram wove the tractor round the prone body of his son and drove on to Chamkalan.

2
◆◆◆

The Lion in His Den

The bank clerk's entire being had run cold when he saw the father strike the son. He shivered as the tractor jounced forward in the blazing sun.

He pushed back his solar topee that kept jiggling down over his eyes. And to think that he was being transported on robbed diesel!

And he thought of all that he was going through for his Manager's son and he hoped that the damned fool would be happy. And he hoped that the Manager would appreciate it.

They were passing fields of sugarcane interspersed with a few acres of dancing mustard flowers. Most of the land on both sides of the road belonged to the family. And there were considerable holdings beyond that: more land, orchards, houses, kilns, liquor shops, shops in the bazaars, entire streets of buildings, investments in various enterprises. It was a family worth marrying into, even though they were blunt villagers. These were the real home-grown *zamindars*, solid as the trees from which rogues may be hanged, with roots that reached into a pit deeper than rural history. They did not depend for their strength on benefactors and benediction.

Even doing them a favour was difficult. Most fathers would be delighted to have a daughter taken off their hands but this Khushi Ram seemed to expect you to grapple him for it.

He looked at the leathery face of the farmer bouncing on the driving seat. Apart from a slow lick with the tip of the tongue at the brush of moustache on his upper lip, the man betrayed no anxiety for his son or the money that was lost.

The bank clerk held onto his topee with one hand and said, 'You had told me that that account was for Aadran's marriage. Now it is depleted by twenty thousand.'

Khushi Ram did not take his eyes off the dusty road. 'We'll get it back. The old man will think of a way. He always does.'

The tractor swung down a ridge onto a track, towards the narrow lanes of Chamkalan.

If the village of Jagtara was old, Chamkalan was ancient. The streets of Jagtara could accommodate two bullock carts. The lanes of Chamkalan could just take three men walking abreast or two men riding stirrup to stirrup. They twisted suddenly and sharply at points where there might have been gates or massive wooden doors, and it was clear the community architect had designed for ambush.

In Jagtara, the drains ran along the sides of the brick-laid main street, the surface of which rose in a hump. In Chamkalan, the drain ran down the centre of the lane and was cut into now and again by smaller ones that emerged from the houses on either side. And the surface of the lane sloped down to the centre.

If Jagtara was now spreading out with little workshops and foundries and new farming enterprises like the fingers of an open hand, Chamkalan seemed at first glance to be still tightly clenched like a knotted fist. It stood starkly sentinel over the surrounding greenery and the two tallest terraces that reared up, with serrated walls like the battlements of a fortress, had been built by the great-great-grandfather of Balbir's grandfather.

The tractor veered past the temple and the *gurdwara*, both of which had been built long ago by the family, past the spreading tamarind tree and swivelling to the left between two crumbling brick structures came to a halt. Here the lane began but funnelled sharply and seemed to crash to a dead end against the plinth of a shop. But if you walked up, you found that the lane split like a stream round a boulder. If you turned to the left and walked single file along this tortuous alley, you would come to a perfunctory bazaar. If you turned right, you could walk comfortably, but avoiding stray dogs and the odd cow or buffalo and the hand pumps set at convenient intervals for the houses to share; you would then pass various doorways including that of the house of Balbir's grandfather.

There was not a person in these villages who did not know the old man in some way. He was a living legend. Even now, though Lok Raj was in his eighties, the legend was growing. His exploits spanned more than half a century and the shaping of his personality owed not a little to the fact that for twenty-five years from 1922, when his own father had been thrown by a horse and killed, to 1947 he had lived among the turbulent tribes of the extreme north, riding roughshod like a benevolent chieftain over the larger portion of his patrimony—twenty-two villages and many square miles of land in Montgomery District.

With the Partition of the subcontinent into India and Pakistan, he had lost all that property but not the manner of the kindly peasant warlord. His power had been basic without the frills and trappings of display or pomp. It was said that even now, despite his much diminished wealth and erratic health, his influence reached into a few hundred villages through the village councils or *panchayats*. This was influence that did not depend on the extent of his holdings but grew out of the respect that other peasants had for a man of their own sort who had controlled much and had done it well even in his twenties. He was innately a leader, and now that he was the patriarch of his vast joint-family and an elder of one of the martial Muhiyal clans and still one of the biggest landlords in the region, he was even more powerful perhaps than he had been in his youth. In a sense Lok Raj had successfully crossed over the bridge from the time of feudal authority to one of democratic values. His social strength was now based on the willing consent and respect of his peers. In most men's lives that period of transition is a gradual one covering a few decades if not an entire lifetime; for Lok Raj it had happened in a few nightmarish weeks. And the bridge he had had to cross was a very real one—the bridge over the river Ravi. In 1947, during Partition, that bridge had been choked with hordes of people murdering their way across in a shared cataclysmic transition. And below them the river had borne bodies as numerous as logs being floated to a sawmill.

By the seventies the Punjab, with its Green Revolution and three harvests per year, its smaller land holdings and diversification into industries, its large-scale migration and the money sent back by those earning abroad, its espousal of progressive methods of farming and the return of some prodigal sons, had fought free of the feudal mould but it had not lost its feuding spirit. A feud involved not just individuals but entire families. In agricultural Punjab the nuclear joint-family had not broken up but merely spread out. To the outside observer the links seemed tenuous for being underground but they were like telephone cables that could in a moment help to recall each member to its fold. Elsewhere in India too the joint-family continued to exercise its hold. That is why perhaps there was so much nepotism everywhere. But in other parts the family unit was content usually to keep its grip subtly on an area of business, politics, administration or the field of entertainment. A slight to a family could be avenged through the manipulation of commerce, the law, bureaucratic red-tape or star value. Reparation was possible through a form of barter. It was enough to get the better of an exchange. It was enough to return insult with humiliation. The standard was money and prestige. In Punjab the standard was blood.

Indian society is a jungle of familial vines. More correctly perhaps, it is a maze of hierarchical social structures. At the top of each of these intricate and interlinked pyramids are the elders. Even in the worst, most criminal families, age brings respect, though it may not necessarily bring respectability.

Traditionally it also confers an unshakeable confidence on the elder. The gerontocracy of India sits secure in its conservatism, often unaware and unashamed of its blind spots of ignorance. The preservation of the family and the regulated extension of it is a prime concern. Therefore a marriage is not a matter for two persons but for two families. Most marriages are arranged.

So it has come about that four thousand year-old values and viewpoints have been passed on unaltered. Over these, like a camouflage, is placed the verdigris of whatever civilization is currently dominant. This schizophrenic dichotomy is most pronounced naturally in the westernized urban élite of today. Thus: though the waters of the Ganga may be seen to be filthy and unhygienic they are also sacred, and eminent bacteriologists will sip them along with millions of less sophisticated pilgrims.

The real core of India has not merely survived but won over the centuries. More important, it has won over every conquerer—absorbing every thought, language and mode, accepting each new kind of sword but pledging allegiance to none—remaining itself always. It has passed over honours, distinctions, titles bestowed by rulers, native or foreign, and not bent the knee to the honoured or the honouring. It is this woebegone, bull-headed, recalcitrant core that has, deep down, kept India fighting.

This core, that traces itself back centuries through its very name and branches and bifurcations, accepted neither *satrapy*, nor *jagir*, nor *nawaby*, nor knighthood, nor republican benediction, nor even bribery by subtle democratic distinction. This core all over India knew itself and held to itself and kept studying more about itself in order to be sure. And it knew that, actually, because of its very unswervingness, it was the ruler not the ruled.

For all decisions of governance had to take into account this core that could not be moved except by its own will. This is what makes for the inner pride of India.

Later the Portuguese came and were rebuffed by it and called it *casta* because that was a notion they imported from their own land. And India took the word to herself and said she was caste-ridden. The Greeks and the Persians had come too and, because they could not pronounce the word Indus correctly but called it Hindus, they dubbed the people of the valley and beyond, the Hindoos. And India had taken the name to her peoples. The Moghuls came and said this was the land of the Hindus—Hindustan. And the British came and presumed 'Hindu' was a religion. And again India took that to herself. But the core remained what it was, unique and indivisible. And they dubbed it indecipherable.

In the name of all these—caste, country, religion—battles were and are fought, people died. But the core remained, spreading its tentacles as far as research could see. And further. It was not overlooked by the foreigner but its strength was underestimated. Yet two Indians from the same region meeting anywhere today will still try to establish how, through the core, they are linked. To overcome the possibility that they may not be, there is the tradition of adoptive blood relationships. Call a family friend 'uncle' and he becomes one; call a woman 'sister' and sex with her becomes incest.

The institution of the family in India goes beyond the nuclear joint-family with its forty or fifty members, often living under the same roof; it reaches out, embraces villages in kinship, shares a sense of ownership in the deepest friendship ('My house is yours' quite literally) and makes a relative of a relative's relative.

Generalizations are easily, but not always correctly, made about entire families. That is a family of crooks. That is an honest family. That family sucked up to the nawabs. That family depended on Raja—. That family served the British Raj. That is a family of reformers. That family fought the Moghuls/the Raja of —/the British. That family took part in the freedom struggle. That family went to jail. That family made its money by unfair means. That family betrayed the cause/the party/the people. That is a family of hangers-on. That is a family of industrialists/engineers/lawyers/soldiers. That is a professional family. And so on.

Balbir's was a farming family of the rambunctious, warring

kind that inhabits most areas of Punjab. It had its individuality, its own peculiar and particular characteristics and it had spread out too to other regions as most such families had done. But the head of the clan remained Balbir's grandfather Lok Raj, generally known as Babaji, the patriarch.

The emphasis on family spirit is so great that the best of the breed will follow like lemmings or a herd of wild horses over the cliff. And the generic language, Sanskrit, has more words to describe familial relationships than any other language in the world. There is a specific word to describe each of the following: elder uncle on the paternal side, younger paternal uncle, and each one's wife, paternal aunts, maternal aunts, their husbands, maternal uncles, and every in-law and spouse is delimited and defined precisely—and the yardstick is comparative age. Even grandparents are delineated semantically as maternal or paternal by the way they are addressed. And in an adoptive relationship too, as when a child calls a family friend 'uncle', all these factors are taken spontaneously into account and it is immediately worked out whether the adoptee is younger or older than the parent on whose side he is to become linked.

But there is no word for cousin! At that point the family springs shut around the children of uncles and aunts, locking them into its warmest embrace; they are termed directly as brothers and sisters. They are addressed so and usually treated as such. That is why Indians with scant knowledge of western terminology are being quite honest when they avow in official documents that someone is their brother or sister; they make no distinctions between cousins and kin born of the same parents for at that point the family system, like a canny spider, has drawn the thread back to the centre. The web is strengthened, reinforced.

If English-speaking Indians are pressed to make the distinction, most will try to amalgamate the dichotomous strains in their personality and perhaps admit, 'Yes, he is a *cousin* brother but what difference does that make? He is my brother.' To call someone a cousin is to set him apart from yourself. Europeans have never really tried to comprehend this. To call someone a cousin, even in English where the term exists and belongs, is somehow to level an insult at the nearest of kin. Cousin is a bad word. The phrase 'cousin brother' is now gaining reluctant currency but even that is to be avoided within earshot of the person to whom it refers.

So the family grows, making the distant near and closing upon its own extensions. It grows not in a linear way but in concentric circles like widening ripples in a pond, always turning round to greet its farther end, bigger each time but always in perfect relationship to the centre, the eldest elder, the patriarch.

In the agricultural communities of the north, a patriarch has great power and his will can hold sway over the life and death wishes of the clan.

Even as patriarchs go, Lok Raj was unique. He was half Caesar, half child. He could be iron-willed, loving, playful, boisterous, blunt. He was somehow not just a man but the embodiment of two villages at once. Both Jagtara and Chamkalan carried the impress of his personality. He seemed to be their very soul.

The old man was easily accessible to everyone but, in carrying a marriage proposal to him, the family's hierarchy had to be kept in view. It would not do to go straight to him ignoring his eldest son, that is Khushi Ram's elder brother.

So when they dismounted from the tractor, the two men did not hurry immediately up the lane but made enquiries from some villagers regarding the whereabouts of Pandit Gyan Chand. They were directed to the stable. This was a large, walled-in compound on the outskirts of the fields. It had a giant archway enclosed by an iron barred gate. Inside, there were old troughs of stone and some modern ones of wood. There were numerous stalls and hay lofts.

The stable might at one time have held fifty horses but now it was inhabited by one piebald mare, some magnificent bulls, buffaloes, calves and goats.

In the centre of the yard, rubbing down one of the mammoth bulls, was Gyan Chand. Sixty-four years old and bow-legged from his addiction to riding, Gyan Chand with his grey moustache and stiffly-cockaded Frontier turban seemed intimidating, but was indeed the most docile of the Chibber family. He had his back to the visitors and was calling out fond curses and endearments to the animal which snorted, shifted and pretended to butt.

A servant was mixing gram into the feed of the piebald mare who turned her neck to look at the intruders, put her ears forward then back, showed the whites of her eyes and whinnied.

Gyan Chand turned and saw them.

'Come, come, welcome!' he said in his high-pitched voice as

he moved towards them with a sideways rocking gait, wiping his face on the end of his turban.

They sipped cool sugarcane juice from metal bowls as they explained their mission to him.

'Good, good,' he nodded. And that was that. He had given his approval. Then he added, 'You'll be looking now for Father. He is sitting with the chess players on the verandah opposite the platform of the singers.'

He was referring to the platform reserved for performances by wandering bands of minstrels who came for occasional night-long concerts, plucking their stringed instruments and crying out ballads in gypsy-like tones about heroes of the north such as Guga Peer.

By giving them directions, Gyan Chand seemed to indicate that he was averse to going along with them. He avoided his father as much as he could. The old man had a habit of making upsetting statements.

But Gyan Chand saw that they were waiting for him to lead the way, so he sighed, 'All right, all right, I'll come too.'

As they strode up the lane they were greeted by a number of men and evaded delicately by various women who, lowering *dupattas* and veiling faces, stepped aside like careful turkeys.

Turning a corner they came upon a small gathering of men, most of them seated in a huddle, all intently watching the moves being made in their midst.

Suddenly the silence was broken by hooting and cheering and exclamations of surprise. The knot of chess players burst open like a budded flower. The game was over. The recipient of the compliments was a young Jat who grinned broadly from ear to ear. The target of the analysis and jeering was the tall, heavy-set, jowly man of eighty-four. This was Lok Raj.

Gyan Chand called to him. But he didn't hear, or wouldn't. Instead, he smiled slowly as though bemused by the impact of the unexpected endgame.

He leaned back, and covering the mouthpiece of the *hookah* that was being circulated he dragged deep, making it gurgle as loudly as the surrounding noise. He blew out the smoke, engulfing the spectators in a cloud that they began to fan away.

'That's one game over,' he said, 'and the match still to be decided.'

The spectators jeered, laughed or responded with a flourish of innuendo.

'Lok Raj,' a feebler contemporary with a nervous tic in his face and a palsied right hand cried, 'give over the match then. Some men live to play chess, others love to play it and yet others keep longing to learn. We are no longer as young as we used to be.'

Balbir's grandfather laughed and said, 'Speak for yourself, old man.'

Gyan Chand again made an attempt to draw him away.

'Father,' he said, 'someone is here to see you on very important business. The lost game can be avenged another day.'

'Lost game! What lost game?' Lok Raj roared. 'This youngster has managed to draw me to a stalemate, so they rejoice and he is content with that. But he is good. Yes, he's clever. I didn't see the stalemate coming. And I'm one piece up. May you not prove the son of an ass! Don't tell me any son of mine is fool enough to speak up before the village without first seeing how matters are on the cloth!'

The cloth he was referring to was the squared one on which chess or, to give it its original name, *shatranj* has been played here ever since it was first invented in this part of the world.

Gyan Chand was not only sensitive to the unpredictable rebukes of his father but he was also acutely aware that he was a ripe sixty-four and himself a man of some consequence, not to mention the fact that he was the father of the powerful and popular Satyavan who was now philandering somewhere in Europe along with that rascal Raskaan. Gyan Chand had a light complexion and blushed easily. He was embarrassed that he blushed now like an adolescent. The crowd guffawed. Gyan Chand turned to his brother and said quietly, bitterly, 'Let's go.'

Lok Raj bellowed over the din, 'And they tell me I am going blind! Here are sons with the sight of an owl in daylight. Lost game, indeed!'

But he hefted himself up, pressing down on a couple of unwary shoulders, and made his way carefully up the lane to the house. The children who had gathered about the chess players ran along with him, bumping into him and terrified by his shouts but not afraid of his towering stature for his hands were gentle with them. Most of them stopped at the entrance to the house and hung about the doorway but a couple sidled in behind him and one of them, a five-year-old who still kept a finger in his mouth, squirmed between the old man's legs when he had sat down, and tried to climb up on his knee.

V.P. Joshi had been so astounded by the character of the man that on coming into the house he had quite forgotten to take off his solar topee.

'So you want to marry Aadran to the Bank Manager's son,' Lok Raj said directly.

V.P. Joshi had prepared himself to wait for the conversation to present him with the proper cue for broaching the subject, but he was glad the old man had come straight to the point. He cleared his throat and said, 'Yes.'

'What does he do?'

V.P. Joshi cleared his throat again. Perhaps it was the smoke coming from the other end of the hall where the tea was being prepared. He coughed the irritation down and asked gravely, 'Who?'

'Who do you think? She's not marrying the Bank Manager. She's marrying his son, isn't she? Well, what does he do for a living? What does he earn? Where does he live? Is he educated? Is he crippled, deaf, tubercular, leprous, asthmatic, blind? Have you a photograph of him? What is he like?'

V.P. Joshi coughed furiously then said, 'I haven't got his photograph but I've brought his horoscope.'

'Lahh!' the old man laughed, 'What good is that? But you can be easy on that score. If we want to marry them and the horoscopes don't match, we can have new ones cast. I get them done all the time. After all, the stars and planets don't know what they should say till you tell them what you want. But I've heard that the boy has gone away. He is in England.'

'Yes, sir.'

'Have you met him? Do you know him personally?'

'No. That is to say, our Manager has been transferred here on promotion from the Chandigarh branch. He's been here a couple of years and in that time Harmesh has not returned. It's a good family. The Manager is known to be honest. And shrewd. He was an insurance man before and never let a claim get by without cutting it down.'

'To hell with the Manager!' the old man yelled and carefully extricated the little boy who was clambering about between his knees. 'I am not depositing my granddaughter in an account. I'm marrying her to some fellow no one has seen. Down in the village of Maina they're marrying off a girl called Gulnari to a photograph. The man is in Canada and such a miser that he won't even come back for his wedding—'

Gyan Chand interrupted despite his misgivings. 'It's not that he's a miser but the law there is getting so peculiar that if he comes back he may have difficulty getting in there again.'

'So they're marrying her to this photograph! Doing a complete wedding ceremony round it. I tell you there's something odd there. They're trying to get rid of her.'

Gyan Chand spoke up again. 'But the fellow can't be a miser. He's sent money for her to travel first class on the plane and he's paying for half her trousseau besides.'

'Can you only harp on one point like a parrot? All right, he's not a miser. He's a man without respect either here or in Canada. That is clear to me. But I tell you, no daughter of this house is going to marry a photograph or a god. She will marry a man we can all see and examine and approve. Is that clear?'

'In other words, Panditji, your answer is—'

'No. My answer is no.'

V.P. Joshi suddenly felt his hat tipping over his eyes. It gave him a bit of a start but then he realized that one of the children had knocked it accidentally from behind. He nudged the child away and thought that he wasn't so pleased after all to deal with such blunt men. He liked transactions to be concluded smoothly and open-endedly.

He accepted the cup of tea that was brought to him by someone; he didn't notice who. This was his umpteenth cup of tea for the day.

He said, 'I shall tell his father then that if the boy comes back and meets with your approval, you are agreeable.'

'Tell him what you like. I have said what I wanted to say.'

When V.P. Joshi had swallowed his tea like a bitter draught, the old man asked Gyan Chand to show the guest round the fields and the village. He was suddenly so polite that V.P. Joshi fell in with it and let himself be led away. In his wake went the little mob of excited children.

'Now,' said Lok Raj to Khushi Ram, 'I want to talk to you.'

'And I want to talk to you,' Khushi Ram said.

'You think I'm a fool.'

'No, old man, I don't.'

Khushi Ram was like that with his father. Patriarch or plough, he addressed them both with equal brusqueness and informality.

Now Lok Raj circled the subject as his eldest grandson Satyavan might have done.

He muttered, 'If you don't think I'm a fool, then why are you behaving as though foolishness were a tradition in the family?'

'I don't understand.'

'Last night you informed me that Balbir had forged a cheque in order to pay Tarsem. I told you to warn Tarsem immediately.'

'I did.'

The old man nodded, then blinking furiously as though clearing his sight or his thoughts, he said, 'But you did not take the money from Balbir.'

'I was going to.'

'But you delayed. You hesitated. You did not know how to tackle him unless it was to give him the thrashing of his life. I've told you not to hit him. You cannot tame an animal that way. Balbir is full of animal spirits, as well he should be. It shows daring and mettle. He's like a young leopard. He moves fast. You have to understand him and anticipate his moves. But you,' the old man shook his head, 'you cannot do anything without anger and beating. You don't know how else to talk to your son.'

'Old man, control your tongue!' Khushi Ram stood up and tapped his walking-stick a number of times on the floor.

'That is it!' said Lok Raj. 'Look at you even now, sending me signals with your stick. You hate that stick. You hate having a bad knee and limping about like a cripple. You're like a lamed animal that's irritable and wants to find easy prey. You're becoming a man-eater.'

'Old man, I haven't come here to be insulted. Human beings are not just animals—'

He was interrupted by Lok Raj's chuckle but he continued. '—the boy is going crooked. We have to straighten him out. You told me not to hit him ever again but I did, not one hour ago. Just once. Not the way he deserves it. Not the way I would have liked to. I controlled myself because you told me to. But . . . but you are an interfering old man! I know how to deal with him. I am the boy's father.'

'And I am yours!' said Lok Raj as he stood up to his full height. The chair fell behind him. 'You are ruining that boy. You have no idea how to handle him. Don't you dare disobey me again about hitting the poor lad. And don't dictate your wishes to me. You, who I have dandled on my knee! You, who couldn't make a horse dance until I showed you how!'

Khushi Ram said ironically out of the side of his mouth, 'Balbir says you are half-blind and the time of horses is going altogether.'

'So now the father learns to quote the son! Well may the time of horses go, but it will always be the time of men who know how to ride.'

Khushi Ram readjusted the turban on his head and sat down. He massaged his knee with one hand as he said, 'Balbir will destroy the honour of the family.'

Lok Raj studied his son—the tough skin, the strong hands, the brush moustache, the clan turban, the Muhyali turban with its proud cockade, its *turrah*. 'No,' he said, 'the honour of the family is safe as long as I uphold it, it will stay erect like the *turrah* of our turbans.'

Khushi Ram murmured, 'Old man, old man, these are probably the last days of the turban.'

To Khushi Ram's surprise, Lok Raj chuckled. 'It was only a way of saying it. When it has served its purpose it may go. But there will always be a way of saying it.'

The flexibility of the old man never ceased to amaze Khushi Ram. You might have expected him to be caught in the quagmire of his opinions but no, his mind moved lightly round you, outflanking you. Lok Raj was the sort of man who fixed his eyes on an objective and then exercised a number of options in manoeuvring towards it. He never really pushed against your strength, he would rather pull you on in the direction of your charge and catch you on the side. He benefitted by your excesses; he took advantage of your energy.

Now Khushi Ram decided to deliver the blow. He said, 'I struck the boy because when I asked for the money, he . . . told me it was stolen. He has lost it!'

He watched the old man's face, dreading the pain and anger that it was bound to show. But the old man smiled. 'At least he didn't have time to run away with it.'

'What?' It was Khushi Ram who began to be angry. 'You don't think he would have dared to go off with the—!'

'Put yourself in his place. He's forged for the money. He was prepared to go off with it anyway. But you blocked his escape through Tarsem. Given time he would have gone off with the money and found another passport racketeer. My point to you is, never give that boy time. You've got to be quicker. Give a young leopard a few seconds and he'll carry off your pet dog from beside you.'

Khushi Ram licked the edge of his moustache thoughtfully. 'Perhaps the boy is lying. Perhaps Tarsem disobeyed me and took the money after all.'

'No, he did not.'

'Then the boy has really lost it.'

'Balbir has lost it,' the old man said. 'But the family has not.'

Lok Raj walked to an *almira* in the wall, reached under his rough homespun *kurta* and brought out a key from the pocket in his vest. He unlocked the *almira*, took out a *ghee* tin and from it withdrew the bundle of notes. He flung the bundle on the divan.

Khushi Ram looked at it, then at Lok Raj.

The old man said, 'I took a precaution, in case you delayed getting the money from Balbir. I knew he couldn't walk around with it. He had to keep it somewhere. So, yesterday after hearing from you, I sent for two people—Jheera the *Afeemchi* and Parsini the sweeper woman. One was to keep an eye on Balbir at the well and the other at the house. He would not suspect either of them.'

'Neither did I, old man. And I saw both of them this morning.' Khushi Ram was grinning and nodding.

'I had a third person at the bus stop, ready to divert Balbir and bring him to me if all else failed. Fortunately, Parsini came through with the money. I suggest you don't tell Balbir yet. Let him suffer over it for a few days.'

Khushi Ram picked up the bundle of notes, undid the string and distributed the money into his pockets. A few grains of wheat that had become wedged between the notes fell out. He laughed as he said, 'Balbir didn't have a chance!'

'Sometimes I wonder if we shouldn't give him a chance. If he wants so much to go, why not let him?'

'No,' said Khushi Ram abruptly. 'I need him here. Someone has to be with me. At least one son.'

The old man nodded but said sarcastically, 'He is your crutch.'

Stung, Khushi Ram whirled on him. 'Old man, I appreciate what you've done but I will not take your taunts.'

'Beware,' said Lok Raj. 'Balbir is my blood after all. The more you thwart him the more dangerous he will become. You should not hem in a wild animal completely. If he has no other way to go, he will go for you.'

Khushi Ram was about to bluster a reply when he heard V.P. Joshi and Gyan Chand returning from their round.

He bent down and touched the old man's feet, though it was hard on his knee to do that. He did not say 'thank you'. That was understood.

The old man accompanied them as far as the verandah of the chess players and was welcomed back with loud camaraderie by his cronies.

Driving back, Khushi Ram reminded himself, 'Don't give the boy time. He's as quick as a leopard.'

3
∴

Favour for Favour

The bump on Balbir's forehead throbbed. It was blue even outside the patch of lint and plaster that held a spot of medicine over the gash. All that would heal whether he rested or not. He allowed his mother to cluck over him and dress the wound. Then he fled the house, promising her he would go to the well and rest.

They knew that he liked to be alone, away from his father. He preferred to sleep, even at night, in the shed by the well or out under the *peepal* tree. His mother kissed him on the cheek and let him go.

He went straight to Tarsem.

He said, 'I will get you some guns. And I will try and connect you to the pipeline. But I need a favour of you. Urgently.'

Tarsem spread his hands and leered, 'I am here to help.'

Balbir felt sick but he pressed on. 'Twenty thousand rupees. To be put back in my father's account in the bank at Jalandhar.'

Tarsem's face fell. Balbir waited.

Balbir could have told him everything and how he had questioned his mother and sister about the theft. He could have told him that, most of all, he suspected Aadran who had every motive for repairing the dent he had made in plans for her future. But he didn't say any of this. Partly, he wasn't sure Aadran was that concerned to ensure her marriage to a man she didn't know, though it certainly nagged her that she was twenty-six and a spinster. His mother might have done it. But she was a bad liar and he would have known. No, he needed time to track down the thief. Meanwhile, he wanted to get his father off his back. A kind of psychological tit for tat. If the money was back in the bank, his father could hardly belabour him for it. He didn't say any of this because, largely, he felt it was a family matter.

Tarsem said in astonishment, 'You had all that money this morning. Didn't you put it back?'

Balbir shook his head. 'Someone stole it from me.'

Tarsem whistled through the gap in his teeth. Then he asked, 'What guarantee do I have that you won't skip with the money?'

'You can have it put directly into the account. I'd be a fool to try and forge another cheque.'

Tarsem smiled and said, 'OK. We'll do that. Early tomorrow. The bank will be shut by the time anyone gets there today. Don't forget about tonight. We've got a meeting here ... partner.'

Balbir nodded and left. Now all he had to do was locate the family armoury in Chamkalan, not an easy job with Babaji around. But he'd do it. He knew it wasn't a big collection of weapons; Satyavan had been building it up slowly, only as a precaution against the increasingly volatile situation in Punjab.

Since 1961, the authorities had encouraged the population to be armed; this was evident from the generous policy with regard to the licensing of guns. Almost every land-owning farmer had weapons. Punjab was a border state. It was thought that an armed population could help to fight off an invader. But many of these weapons had fallen into the hands of terrorists and criminals. And now the situation within Punjab was what is termed a 'disturbed' one.

Licensed revolvers and guns were worn and displayed. On an average peaceful day in Punjab in any one area you might see at least three gun-toting men going about their chores. Swords were even more common. The tenth Guru, Gobind Singh, had made this a religious tenet at a time when sikhs and hindus were fighting the fanaticism of the Mughal Emperor Aurangzeb. But there were other weapons that were never displayed; these were kept for possible use in an emergency. It was these weapons that Tarsem and his men were intent on collecting and conveying to their clientele.

Big zamindars and their families had stocks that could arm entire bands of followers. This attitude was traditionally condoned. For centuries, zamindars had functioned as chieftains, supplying men and arms in time of crisis. Thus, standing armies used to be small but reinforcements were gathered in considerable numbers from the countryside.

With the advent of democracy, new laws had laid down ceilings on the amount of land an individual could own, but though the land was parcelled into smaller holdings distributed among family members, the law could do nothing about emotional allegiances. So the zamindar families that used their wits continued to be powerful. Now, instead of delivering battalions of armed men, they could deliver votes.

Satyavan, who was the politically active member of the family, could deliver votes, men, guns, passports, documents, the works. Plus, he could always rely on the family's vast legitimate holdings.

Though Tarsem was small fry trying to link up with and emulate the big fish, he didn't have the background. He was a Johnny-come-lately, a nouveau riche intendant. He had but three or four members to his gang. Satyavan was a popular figure, offspring of an established family. Tarsem was an operator. Satyavan was a director of various above board and underworld businesses.

And yet Satyavan had only one suit in his wardrobe. To do him justice, let us say he travelled light.

Punjab was booming with enterprise and rackets. Prosperity was on the increase and so was crime. It was becoming more and more unsafe to travel the roads at night especially if you were unarmed. A few urbanized women, who had access to such novelties carried pearl-handled Dillingers or Browning pistols in their handbags. Village women going in small groups to the evening or late night cinema shows in nearby cities were invariably escorted by a couple of men carrying some sort of weapon.

Along with other forms of crime, rape too was on the increase.

Indeed, that is the crime with which Uday Singh Kumhareya was eventually accused. But was it fact or only a stratagem on the part of his enemies? That we shall find out.

One thing is clear and certain from the beginning and that is that Uday Singh was not part of any racket. He had a genuine commitment, rightly or wrongly, to Bhindranwale's politics. The murders he did commit he did not think of as crimes but as political assassinations, as assignments fulfilled. He did not even know his victims. He had no bond with them. He did not feel guilty, though he did initially feel revulsion. And then there was only a sense of triumph.

It would have surprised nearly everyone in the village to know that Uday Singh, the Kumhareya, the potter's son, was leading such a double life. If you were of the village, depending on your point of view, you would have considered him a Jekyll and Hyde figure, a schizophrenic, or a scarlet pimpernel, a *chhupa rustam* or to put it in severely rustic Punjabi a *ghuaan*, a deep one. For instance, no one knew that during the time Kumhareya was away, supposedly visiting a relative in Jammu, he was in reality attending a training camp in guerrilla tactics. Which does not mean that Kumhareya had attained any great prowess for, after all, no one has yet become a competent commando in a mere fifteen days. The camp succeeded more with indoctrination than with physical training.

Nevertheless, compared with Uday Singh, Balbir was a mere dilettante, a mere featherweight to his heavyweight. They were not in the same category. They were not even in the same fight. They came together merely by virtue of circumstances, though within the ambit of those they exercised the choices that kept them together—at least some of the time.

This was one of those times. Just as Balbir was stepping out of Tarsem's courtyard he came across Uday Singh Kumhareya heading the other way in a desperate hurry, going to the village of Maina. Kumhareya had looked perfunctorily for Balbir and then, not finding him, had decided to proceed on his own. Balbir was a friend but not essential to him.

Kumhareya might have confided more easily in one of his terrorist comrades, for while this was a matter of the heart it was also one that hinged on the organization of those activities. But he was glad to meet Balbir. Glad, in this moment of need, to meet someone who would boost his sagging, love-damaged morale. Balbir was, in that sense, an extra-curricular friend. And he was titillated enough by the circumstances to be drawn along.

'Oy, Kumhareya! Where're you off to? What's the matter?'

Kumhareya hardly paused as he said in exasperation, 'Where have you been?' Then in anguish, 'They're marrying her to a photograph!'

'What? Who? What're you talking about?'

'I must go. She's waiting.'

'Hang on.'

'No.' As he moved on briskly, Balbir turned and fell into step. At this point he was more curious and amused than concerned. After all, you can't really be concerned about an affair of which you know next to nothing.

'Who's the girl?'

Kumhareya hesitated, slowed and said, 'Gulnari. Gulnari Kaur. The Ahluwalia girl. From Maina. Everyone knows they're marrying her off to a photograph. You'll hear of it anyway.'

'Don't be silly! Marrying her to a photograph. I've never heard of anything so ridiculous.'

'Of course you have.' Kumhareya said brusquely as he quickened his pace.

He was right. Balbir had. Many girls from India, especially from Punjab, were sent as spouses to bridegrooms-in-absentia. Thus, registered as wives, they could get into western countries through the loophole in immigration laws. Wives were naturally allowed to join their husbands. But sometimes the husband's citizenship status in the other country was not quite certain or firmly established; in that event, the girl went through a wedding ceremony with a photograph.

'They're doing it to get her away from me. They think we've been . . .' He couldn't bring himself to say it but his meaning was clear. He cursed and lengthened his stride. He was having difficulty walking fast. He wasn't in his cotton shorts or *tamba*. To that attire he was accustomed. He was wearing what he called his 'special clothes'; tight-fitting shiny trousers, a maroon turban, a terrycot shirt and squeaky new shoes.

Despite the gravity of the situation, Balbir couldn't help a little dig. 'If you haven't been . . . then what have you been doing together?'

Kumhareya stopped. His eyes blazed. 'Mother-fucker, is that all you can think about?' Then he sighed. 'But I can't blame you. That's what it seems like. That's what they all think.' Then he flared. 'But can't you see, she's an educated girl? I'm only a potter's son. She was helping me!'

Balbir tried a shot in the dark. 'Maybe they don't like that either.'

Kumhareya frowned. 'That's it. They don't like that either.' Then he looked sharply at Balbir. 'What do you know about it?'

Balbir shrugged. 'Nothing. Only guessing.'

Kumhareya had too many other things on his mind to let it snag on that. He nodded. And spat. Balbir wondered what he had been doing with Gulnari.

They walked on in silence, skirting the bazaar, avoiding the brick-laid main street. Past the old disused well. Past the cow-dunged mud houses, through the lane of the *harijans*, round by the stagnant pond and the butchers' stalls.

Balbir said, 'You don't mean to walk all the way to Maina, do you?'

Kumhareya said, 'No one's forcing you to come.' The thought

had occurred to him that it would be less conspicuous, better, advantageous, if he went there with Balbir. Balbir was from a well-known respected family. No one would suspect they were going to meet Gulnari Kaur together. These particular Ahluwalias were sikhs, they were cloth merchants and shopkeepers. They didn't want the status quo disturbed. In Kumhareya's own mind, he was a revolutionary under the banner of Bhindranwale. If the Ahluwalias didn't like Gulnari being mixed up in all that, their suspicions would be allayed when they saw him accompanied by a non-sikh. He patted Balbir on the shoulder, 'But you're welcome. As a matter of fact there's a friend of mine in Chamkalan with a mo'bike. I'm going to borrow it so we can ride to Maina.'

It struck Balbir that he had never seen Kumhareya on a motorcycle but he let it pass. The bump on his forehead was pulsating with pain. He lowered the upward swoop of his muffler over it. Covering his left eyebrow like that lent him a wicked, slanted look.

The action was noticed by Kumhareya. 'What's that swelling on your forehead? What happened? I thought you'd be out of our lives in one hour.'

Balbir groaned and said, 'Don't remind me.' Then he told him. About the forgery. About the loss of the money.

They were now beyond the little shops of the sweetmeat vendors, the cobblers and the vegetable sellers with their wares in baskets by the roadside. They were on the dusty road to Chamkalan; on either side of them, fields. To the right of them, in the rolling, glittering green, stippled with the yellow mustard flower, a peacock and a peahen danced, trampling all like a king and queen. While his tail burgeoned in a fan, she stepped daintily this way and that, pecking up little delicacies. Disturbed by the squeak of Kumhareya's shoes, the peacock uttered a raucous cry and went hop, skip and jump onto the flat roof of a pumphouse. Further out another pump had started up and coughed short whistles of smoke into the air. It was a glorious afternoon.

A tractor was approaching them at full throttle. It was Balbir's father bringing V.P. Joshi back from Chamkalan. Balbir cursed. If he had known they were going to be on this road, he would not have come.

His father slowed and braked. 'So you've recovered.' His hands were gripping the steering wheel hard and he was shouting over the roar of the engine. Balbir kept his eyes down.

'You've found out, have you? Well, don't argue with your grandfather. Just thank him.' With that and a nod to Kumhareya, he drove away leaving them choking in the dust.

Balbir coughed and muttered, 'What the hell was that?'

'He thought you were going to see your Babaji.'

Balbir shuddered. He had no intention of receiving a scolding from the old man. He was through with relatives. The old man had never really reprimanded him. But Balbir was terrified of the myth that surrounded the patriarch.

Kumhareya misunderstood his thoughtfulness and said, 'I'd rather you didn't see him now. It'll delay us. She's waiting. We've got to be quick. Perhaps you can see him on the way back from Maina.'

Balbir said carefully, 'I don't want to see him. You see him. Keep him busy. I want to look for something in the old house.'

'You can't make me an accomplice without telling me what you're up to.'

Balbir considered that. He felt the bump bobbing like a ball on his forehead. There was a copper taste in his mouth. He bent to vomit but nothing came. They moved on. He said, 'I'm going to look for some guns.'

Kumhareya murmured, 'Satyavan always wears a revolver, even under his *kurta* when he wears a *kurta*. And he keeps a rifle in his car when he travels. His driver is armed too.'

Balbir shook his head. 'Not those guns. Others.'

'Why? What do you need guns for?'

Balbir felt he had said enough. He kept quiet.

'You wait here,' Kumhareya said. 'I'll go and get the bike.'

They were outside the Chamkalan *gurdwara*. Balbir nodded and sat down on the verge of the road. He tried to dull into inconsequence the pain in his forehead. He lay back, his head cradled on a milestone, and studied the sky. The clouds were brilliant and moved like athletes in slow motion. A couple of crows hung and wafted, froze and flew away.

The loudspeaker of the *gurdwara* began to intone mellifluous stanzas from the sacred *Granth*.

Balbir arose. The scenery swam and rearranged itself like bits of bangles toppling into patterns in a bazaar-made kaleidoscope. He staggered. And went in to the *gurdwara*.

In the courtyard, four sikhs were in intense discussion with the venerable old head priest. They glanced at Balbir and continued. They were arguing about details of a small resting place for travellers which they intended to have constructed in the compound.

Balbir removed his shoes, covered his head properly with his inseparable muffler and stepped into the sanctum where, under a canopy, another priest was reading from the giant-sized *Guru Granth Sahib*. In accordance with custom, he prostrated himself before the holy book then sat down to listen. He felt the need for blessings in his predicament.

In front of the priest was the microphone that carried the hymns out to the village.

But Balbir found that he could neither listen nor pray. His mind was in dialogue with itself. Here I am, a hindu, worshipping at a sikh shrine as millions of other hindus do. This *gurdwara* was built by one of my ancestors. So was the village temple. Sikhs go to hindu temples too. Here, in the village, everyone goes even to the little shrine built long ago by someone in honour of Guga Peer. What is all this prayer about? Does it do God any good? Are we not praying to and for ourselves? Does it matter then where we pray or how?

He remembered the attitude of his grandfather and began to understand it a little. Babaji rarely went to places of worship unless he had some work there or in the vicinity. He would stride into temple, *gurdwara*, church or mosque, look around as though to ensure that God was at His job, nod and stride out again. Strange man. Balbir smiled.

Just then he felt Kumhareya touch him on the shoulder. He had been so absorbed he hadn't even heard the motorcycle outside.

In the courtyard the head priest offered them some sweet *prasad* which they popped into their mouths. He stared at Kumhareya then glanced at Balbir. As they were putting on their shoes, he said to Balbir, 'Your uncle has kindly offered to donate some bricks from one of his kilns. Please tell him we'll start building next week.'

Balbir nodded, Kumhareya was taking longer with his new shoes and their laces. The head priest took Balbir by the elbow and led him towards the motorcycle. It was almost a whisper as he asked, 'What are you doing with him?'

'Kumhareya?' Balbir was surprised. 'He works for us sometimes on the land.'

The head priest scratched at a point where his grey beard and blue turban met. He said, 'Be careful.'

Kumhareya came up, pushed the mo'bike off the stand and

began to kick the starting pedal. 'So?' he enquired looking at the head priest as though continuing a previous conversation.

The head priest shook his head and replied gently, 'We are men of peace.'

'Humph!' The engine thundered into life. Kumhareya gestured to Balbir to mount the pillion and said to the old priest, 'You have forgotten the sacrifices of the gurus.'

The head priest ran a hand over his flowing beard. 'Uday Singh, this beard is longer than the hair on your head.'

The muscle on Kumhareya's jaw jumped as he clenched his teeth, turned the motorcycle and roared out of the yard.

They raced towards Maina, passing houses emblazoned with legends that indicated they had been built by men who had returned from abroad with money: 'Jasjit Singh Canadian 1969', 'Gurdit Singh Inglandia 1982', 'Germany Ram 1978', 'Sukhbir Singh Kenya 1957', but soon Kumhareya turned off the road onto a track. The Yamaha 350 swivelled and teetered on the edge of potholes as it was braked and manoeuvered. Kumhareya was being discreet. He was approaching his destination by a circuitous route.

They turned off the track onto a path, which eventually dwindled to an overgrown trail. Their progress was screened by the enfolding phalanxes of sugarcane.

The lurching, jolting bounce and sway of the bike was playing havoc with Balbir's injury.

'I can't bear it,' Balbir shouted. 'My head is killing me.'

Kumhareya glanced at his wristwatch and said, 'It's not yet four o'clock. We're in time. We can walk from here. It's just round that field.'

Kumhareya switched off the engine and coasted to a stop. They dismounted and walked, trundling the bike along. They turned left and suddenly they were in a vast clearing, concealed from view by trees and the crop in the fields. And yet they were only a few minutes' walk from the village of Maina.

At the farther end of the clearing was a ruined farmyard and a gnarled old peepal tree. A wooden feeding trough, crippled in one leg, stood waiting for cattle that never came. A kingfisher swooped, alighted, waddled in it and took off again. From the ruin of the barn and cattleyard came the gurgle and coo of pigeons. And, to their right, from the depths of the well with its rusting Persian Wheel, the croaking of frogs. All around, the grass, the bushes, the untamed pumpkin vines clambering over the walls, resounded with the gentlest of insect sounds like the ticking of a wristwatch. There was everywhere the quietude of disuse.

'My uncle's,' Kumhareya said. 'He went with his family to Singapore.' Then he added apologetically, 'I'm supposed to look after it while they're away but it's so far from Jagtara. Anyway, I come once in a while. There's nothing that can be done with it till he sends some money. Sold everything before he left. Writes to me on his letterhead. He doesn't do pottery now. He calls it "ceramics". Must be rich. Go in there and lie down. That room is full of hay. Go and rest your head. I'll call you when I find them. Gulnari and her friend will be out there pretending to collect vegetables. The adjoining field belongs to the Ahluwalias. Take the bike with you. Prop it somewhere.'

Rockets seemed to be exploding in Balbir's head. Kumhareya placed the back of his hand against Balbir's neck.

'You've got fever, Balbir!'

Balbir began wheeling the motorcycle in. Kumhareya held the handlebar and said, 'Wish me luck.'

'Of course. Do you have a plan?'

Kumhareya shrugged. 'I can only ask her. She may not have the same feelings for me that I have for her. It ... it was a working relationship. She never encouraged any other conversation.'

Balbir was bewildered. 'I don't understand. What work did you have with her?'

Kumhareya sighed, ignored the question and said, 'They're starting preparations tomorrow for the wedding. She'll be married within a week.' Suddenly he took Balbir's face in his hands, gripping it so firmly that Balbir winced.

'No one would suspect you. Will you help?'

'With what?'

'In case she agrees to elope—'

'Elope?'

'What else? There's no other way.' Kumhareya turned and looked around as though literally searching for some avenue.

'When?'

'Now.'

'What!' Balbir almost relinquished hold on the motorcycle.

'There may not be another chance.'

Balbir took the motorcycle in and they both hefted it onto the stand.

'All I want you to do is take a message for me.'

'To whom?'

'Will you do it?'

'Naturally. No problem in that. I thought you wanted me to help you elope. I thought you wanted money or a place or something.'

'No, no. I have a place ready . . . for other purposes. It's safe. We can go there. Till we arrange to get away.'

'Are you sure you want to do this?'

Kumhareya smiled with one end of his mouth. 'You don't know me, Balbir. When I have to do something, I don't waver.'

'All right. Who do I take the message to?'

'Amar Singh. Got that?'

'Yes. Where?'

'Amritsar. The Golden Temple complex.'

'What?'

'He can be found in the third room on the first floor, just above the water taps. You turn right from the main entrance, go along the *parikrama* and climb up the steps. You know the Golden Temple complex, don't you?'

Balbir was stunned. He said, 'I've been there. But nowadays—'

Kumhareya nodded impatiently. 'The police are watching the place. But so what? Pilgrims and worshippers go in and out. You can go in.'

'But the place is crawling with . . . ' his voice trailed off as he began to realize something, '. . . terrorists, extremists.'

'Are you afraid?' Kumhareya looked hard at him. 'You're not a political person. You have nothing to worry about.'

'All those murders and bombings and—'

Kumhareya sighed, 'All political.'

'Those four hindus on the bus, and the six before that—'

Kumhareya's voice snapped like a whip. 'Strategy, tactics, that's all. You have nothing to worry about. Many sikhs have been killed too. Are you afraid of me?'

Balbir looked at him. He had wrestled Kumhareya to the ground many times. He punched him lightly on the shoulder, grinned and said, 'Why should I be scared of you?'

'Then you won't be scared of Amar Singh or the others.'

'I'm only—'

'Just go to Amar Singh, third room above the water taps. You're scared because you don't understand all this. That's why it frightens you. He'll explain. He's educated. He can tell it better than I can. You'll enjoy talking to him.'

'What do I say?'

'Just tell him I'm at Fat Aunty's place in Chak Deedar.'

'I'm doing this only for you.' Balbir sat down in the old hay that was still piled at the back of the barn.

'Don't sing me a song about it.' Kumhareya was about to step out when he turned and added, 'One more favour. Talk to Kulwanti, the other girl, keep her occupied when we go. She won't know we've gone. I'll make sure of that. But don't let her get alarmed too soon.'

'What about me? I don't want your Gulnari's relatives jumping on me!'

'Kulwanti has kept bigger secrets than that. Don't worry. I know her. She may not like Gulnari going away with me but she won't blab. She'll probably say that Gulnari took a walk on her own and disappeared. But people will know we've eloped because I'll be gone too.'

Balbir's head was spinning. 'I don't like all this.'

'You think I do? But that's the way the world is. It forces us to take action.'

It sounded like a well-rehearsed line that Kumhareya was used to quoting.

Balbir lay back in the hay and wished he wasn't there.

Kumhareya stepped out. He went towards a gap in the rear of the farmyard wall. There, moving across a dead tomato patch and a carpet of stubborn strangling vines, like one entering a secret cave in childhood, he went through the gap, with a thudding heart. He was entering the domain of his immediate hopes. Somewhere out there Gulnari had to be waiting. Unless they had prevented her from coming. Panic caught at his mind.

He scoured the area with his eyes. The acre was divided into *kanaals* of beetroot, ginger, potatoes, brinjals, green peas. He turned the other way and caught a whiff of boiling sugarcane juice in the air. A light breeze was rumpling the plants. Further out at one of the neighbouring farms they must be stirring out *gur* in a huge cauldron over a roaring fire.

He cupped his hands to his mouth and burbled the call of the woodthrush. Then he waited. And again repeated the call.

Suddenly, to his right, there was a welcome swish and brush as someone parted the foliage. But it wasn't Gulnari. It was Randhir Sian, a neighbouring Jat. It was his clothes that were smelling of *gur*. He had been at the task all morning.

'So!' chortled Randhir Sian. 'This is where you meet her! I knew her uncle was wrong. He thought you might even have been sneaking into their house at night. But I knew you had to be sneakier than that. You're lucky her father's an invalid and her mother's half crazy, otherwise they would have roasted you like a pig.'

'Go away, Randhira. This is none of your business.' Kumhareya scratched at his left armpit. Under his shirt, the short *kirpan*—the dagger—that he had strapped to his chest came into position, its scabbard tilting so that he could reach in quickly and grab the hilt.

Randhir Sian said, 'The honour of the village is my business. I heard that motorcycle and wondered. Then I guessed what was happening. Give up your games, Uday Singh. Playing at politics and involving a girl who has only half a family!'

'I didn't involve her. She was in this before I joined.'

Randhir Sian laughed and pulled at a pod of sweet peas. He opened the pod and flung the peas into his mouth. 'Amateurs!' he snorted. 'You could learn a few things from ordinary criminals. Imagine leaving your name on those papers her uncle found in her trunk! And what papers! Blow up the Bhakra Nangal, bomb people's houses, burn railway stations!'

'She was supposed to destroy those.'

Randhir Sian played with the steel bracelet, the *karda*, on his wrist. 'Her uncle can have you all arrested. Those papers are full of names.'

'It's for the faith.'

'Don't kid me. It's for power. *Sirf hukumat karan lai hai*! You can't frighten people into following you. As for you, it's just your way of trying to come up in the world, you bloody Kumhareya. You stay away from the Ahluwalia girl, understand? They're flying her off to Canada to get her out of all this.'

There was a clumping sound in the foliage near a rank of mulberry bushes. Randhir turned to look. It was a stray buffalo.

He turned back as he heard the swift movement of Kumhareya behind him and the squeak of the new shoes but it was too late. Kumhareya had the dagger in his hand. With his left elbow as a fulcrum at Randhir Sian's shoulder and the top of the wrist pressing up under Randhir Sian's chin, the jugular was bared and the tip of the blade was on it.

'Uday!' That was the only word Randhir Sian could manage before the knife sank in, down into his wind-pipe and gullet.

Uday Singh Kumhareya had practised this method but never used it before. Till now he had never been in a close encounter. Till now he had only used a firearm from the safe distance of the pillion on the motorcycle as it sped past their appointed quarry. He had sprayed bullets from a rapid-firing carbine but he had never stopped on the scene to examine his victim.

He was trembling on his feet as Randhira's body slumped, the blood spurting up and out in a bubbly froth onto the cuff of his left sleeve.

He looked around. Now he did not want the girls to appear just yet. He let the body drop backwards to the ground. Randhira's eyes were bulging, his mouth was open, and two green bits of peas were on his tongue, the blood was fountaining over the hilt of the knife. If he withdrew it there would be a mess everywhere. He let it be and, with another quick glance round, he bent down to pick up the body.

It felt heavier than when Randhira had been slumping against him. He put it down, took off Randhira's *saafa*, the cloth he tied as a turban. Randhira's knot of hair had a few strands of grey in it that glinted in the sunlight. He wound the *saafa* round Randhira's neck over the hilt of the dagger. No point in getting blood all over his own clothes. Now he put both arms under and heaved up the body. Staggering with it, he went sideways through the gap in the wall to the disused well. He put the body down on the rim. The sensible thing would be to weigh it down with a heavy stone.

That was when he heard the trilling bird call that would normally have responded to his signal. Gulnari was out there.

He shoved the body over the rim. It fell, hitting the rusty Persian Wheel, making it clatter and clang and then it struck the water with a loud noise, parting the green scummy surface, silencing the frogs.

He looked at his clothes. His shirt was drenched in sweat but only the left sleeve had blood on it at the cuff. If he washed it quickly, it might not leave too much of a stain. But for that, he'd have to lower a bucket into the well and get water. He considered tearing off the sleeve then reconsidered. He rolled it up so that the blood did not show. Then he rolled up the other sleeve to match.

He took out his handkerchief and wiped his hands. Putting the handkerchief back, he felt impelled for some reason to smell his hands. There was no scent to murder as far as he could make out but they reeked faintly of the sweet fragrance of *gur*.

Putting his hands to his mouth now, he gave the low burbling call of the woodthrush. In a second he heard the answering trill.

He moved away from the well and waited.

Gulnari appeared at the gap, smiling. The moment seemed to freeze as she prepared to cross over. In that instant he remembered another time when everything had seemed to stop suddenly. Years ago, Kumhareya along with his parents and two married sisters had gone to a photographer's dingy studio in Jalandhar. At the entrance there had been a placard in colour of a little American boy, his mother and a dressed-up chimpanzee drinking Coca-Cola—all of them grinning happily—and in the background was a funfair. There was a caption on the placard. Mustering up his smattering of schooling, Kumhareya had laboriously read the logo. It said, 'Snap it forever'. The old photographer had adjusted his lights, his tripod, draped a black cloth over his head and become the trunk of an elephant. The lights had dazed everyone. They had been immortalized pop-eyed and astounded in a photograph that was a faint brown and growing browner with age.

Now too the moment seemed to freeze but without a camera. Kumhareya felt this sight would stay with him forever—in vivid colour. Gulnari in her white *salwar* and azure *kameez* printed with blue flowers, clutching the improvised bag of her *dupatta* in which she had stored her alibi of vegetables picked along the way. Behind her was Kulwanti with the wicker basket, holding the hem of her pink *dupatta* to her mouth, giggling. She giggled too much, that girl. Kulwanti's face had a more classic structure, the slim, sharp features of a Mohenjodaro figurine. She plaited her hair in the same way, centuries old, preferred heavy earrings and had a blue dot tattooed on her forehead. The dot had four little streaks splashing out from the centre like the petals of a flower. But she was awkward and rather unsure of herself.

Gulnari was self-assured, light complexioned, brown-haired like her female ancestors who it was said had been inhabitants of Kulu and Kangra. She had a Gandhara nose, a dimple on her chin, a slightly plump figure and what Kumhareya thought of as a duck-like walk. With these last two traits she might not have won a beauty contest but she was ravishingly attractive. Her personality contributed to her attraction. She had a direct manner and a quick, agile mind. Her eyes were sometimes like dancing peacocks, sometimes tabby cat grey.

Now they seemed coldly grey though she was smiling.

'What was that noise?' she asked.

He said, 'Oh, a portion of the protective wall fell into the well.'

She accepted that. The rim was as jagged as broken teeth.

But by asking him she had reminded him of Randhira, of the body, of the danger of discovery. His forehead felt damp as he wiped it with his hand.

'Oy!' Gulnari said, shouldering Kumhareya jocularly, 'What's happened to you? I'm the one in difficulties.'

'Let's go in,' he muttered distractedly. 'I have a friend waiting there.'

'A friend!' she exclaimed. And they hung back.

'Don't worry. He's a good friend. Balbir. I work for them sometimes, on their land.'

Balbir was curled up on the hay, fast asleep. His muffler had come off. The plaster and bump showed.

Kumhareya whispered, 'He's got fever.'

'And it looks like someone knocked him on the forehead,' Kulwanti said in an awestruck voice.

Kumhareya bent down and shook Balbir by the shoulder.

'Don't do that!' Gulnari said. 'Let him sleep.'

But Balbir had sat up. His eyes were slightly bloodshot. Perhaps it was the way the girls were staring at his forehead or the way his hair coursed down and hung over his left eye that made him reach behind for his muffler and tie it on, but he was offended by the laugh it brought forth from Gulnari.

'What's the good of that?' she asked.

He allowed himself to be introduced, then said to Kumhareya, 'Be quick.'

The girls looked enquiringly at Kumhareya. To their bewilderment he said, 'Got any cucumbers among those vegetables?'

They shook their heads.

'I'm hungry,' he said. 'I'd love a few cucumbers and tomatoes.' He looked directly at Kulwanti.

She took the hint and nodded, 'I'll get some.'

'Carefully,' he called after her in a hushed tone.

As soon as she was out of earshot, he reached for Gulnari's hand and said, 'Come with me.'

She seemed startled and, with a frown, withdrew her hand. 'What do you mean?'

'They're marrying you off, aren't they? Sending you away to Canada.'

She said, 'I'm sorry about those papers. I shouldn't have kept them. I just thought that some day it would be interesting to look at them again as . . . a record of these times.'

'Never mind that now.' Kumhareya seemed to grind his teeth.

'What's happened can't be helped. What do you plan to do now?'

She said, 'I thought of . . . running away somehow, getting to the others in the Golden Temple and staying there among the pilgrims. That's why I sent you the message to come. So that you could help me get there. But I've been thinking about it. If I run away, everyone will start gunning for you and Jassa and the others. My uncle has the papers, all the names. He might even give them to the police.'

'He won't. He'd have to explain your part in all this. And he won't want them to arrest you.'

'I don't know. It's better not to push him. You know he doesn't really care for me all that much. We're a burden to him, my parents and I. He'd only be concerned about his family's name. In fact they think we've been lovers.'

She said it directly, straight from the shoulder like that. The odd thing was that it was Kumhareya who could not bring himself to say something like that. There was a sort of puritan, virginal, coy streak in *him*.

Now he looked somewhat aghast though he knew all about the allegation. He just couldn't think of such an act with her, at least it seemed he couldn't dream of such an act with her out of wedlock.

He said, 'You won't be able to get to Amritsar on your own. Every *tongawallah* and tempo-driver here knows who you are. You'd have to change transport a number of times. It takes three or four hours from here if all the connections are on time. They'll have you stopped at the gates by the police.'

'I could go in the way our squads come out, from roof to roof, terrace to terrace!'

He shook his head. 'Sometimes you have to walk high up on a ladder placed horizontally between two ledges. You couldn't do that. You have to have practice for that. And you've got to be able to do that in the dark, at night. No, you wouldn't get there on your own.'

'Perhaps I should just give up and go to Canada. I could help organize something there'.

'You mean, allow them to marry you to that . . . that beefmonger?' It was known that the family she was to marry into had a small canning factory in Canada. Malicious wags had put it about that they also canned beef. Beef is an abomination to both hindus and sikhs, though some sikh youths of the Bhindranwale faction had indulged, recently, in the killing of cows as part of a plan to arouse communal reaction from hindus. They had flung the severed heads and tails of cows into the vicinity of temples.

She shrugged, though it was an effort for her to be uncaring in the face of a tradition she had been brought up to follow. She said, 'We have to get over this cow worship. That's for hindus. Anyway, it's only gossip. They're only canners. They don't butcher or eat the stuff.'

He said ruefully, 'You don't care that they're marrying you off?'

'It's a good family. I would be married off some day. I might as well accept it and go there.'

Girls are brought up to marry by parental arrangement. She could not buck her entire conditioning. He was conditioned to that too but he hoped on his own behalf. He was in love with her.

He looked round and saw that Balbir had curled up in the hay. He assumed that Balbir was asleep. He went to the wall and removed some bricks.

Balbir heard the sound and opened his eyes but did not sit up.

Kumhareya reached into the opening and from the hollowed-out hiding place he withdrew an army-issue carbine. It was folded compactly. He pulled out a store of ammunition. He also brought out a bayonet which he put back. His right hand felt about in the cache as though checking the contents. Then he withdrew a revolver. He sifted about till he had cartridges for it. He thrust the loaded revolver inside his shirt, under his belt which he adjusted. He stuffed a handful of rounds into his trouser pocket. Then he replaced the carbine and other equipment.

Putting the last brick into place, he said, 'It's a good thing I am a bit of a mason. They might need me at the Golden Temple. They're making bunkers. The General is supervising.'

She thought he meant Jarnail Singh Bhindranwale. Jarnail is the Punjabi variant of General.

'Santji is supervising the construction himself?' There was awe in her voice.

He half-laughed. 'General Shabeg Singh. He's giving the boys training on the roof and they're erecting barricades in the streets and building bunkers inside.'

Major General Shabeg Singh was a guerrilla tactician who had been one of the Indian Army officers (he was then a colonel) sent incognito into East Pakistan to train the *Mukti Bahini*, the Liberation Army, of what was to become Bangladesh in 1971.

Shabeg Singh who in any case was a *mona* at the time, i.e. a sikh who had cut his hair, went behind enemy lines as Shabeg Khan. There he grew a beard, invariably wore a balaclava and, apart from cutting a dashing figure, did an excellent job in training the *Mukti Bahini* in guerrilla warfare. However his career in the army was not totally admirable. After he became Major General he was implicated in charges of corruption. He was due to face a court martial with the strong possibility that he would be given a dishonourable discharge. But he was allowed to retire, albeit under a cloud. Chagrined and disgruntled he took revenge by joining Bhindranwale and training his adherents. Shabeg Singh was in a sense the commander-in-chief of Bhindranwale's bands of terrorists.

Gulnari said, 'Perhaps I could appeal to him to get me there. You could go to him and say, "She wants to come here, help her and she'll take training and become a guerrilla herself." '

Kumhareya laughed, 'I trained for one week under him. He kept saying we lacked discipline, we were too impatient. There're all sorts there. It's hard to weld them together, like different metals. That's why we concentrate on small groups. He kept calling us platoons. We used to laugh. The old fellow still behaves as if he's in the army. Then he divided us into squads. That's easier. One day he joked and said, "At least you fellows won't spoil the whole show, you'll only give a few others away." '

She sat down on the hay. 'You haven't answered me. Couldn't he help me get there? He could issue orders.'

Kumhareya shook his head.

She hissed, 'What do you mean by that, oy? You think he doesn't want women to train just like the men?'

'Oh he does, he does. His own daughter is there.'

'Is she?'

He nodded. 'And she's already notched a few killings on her gun. There's a fellow there who sticks brass tacks into the wooden butt of his rifle. One for every life taken. He's made quite a pretty design of it. No, the General wouldn't be able to spare the number of men needed to get you there. He's got his own problems guarding the headquarters. That's what it has become, the headquarters. But I'll get you there by and by. Come with me. We'll go underground. You know the place I have ready.'

She nodded.

Suddenly a fear took hold of him. 'It wasn't mentioned in any of the documents, was it?'

She shook her head. 'And you didn't write it down anywhere, did you?' She shook her head again.

He sighed. 'This is one time I thank God I am not quite literate. I never have the urge to write things down. It's too dangerous.' He waited a moment, then said, 'Well?'

She picked up a handful of hay and seemed to be shredding it. 'It will look like we've eloped. They'll think they were right after all.'

He said very slowly, 'I am fond of you. Very fond of you. Perhaps you might one day . . .'

Despite the fever raging through him, Balbir almost felt her shudder as she sat there beside him. He hardly heard her whisper.

'No.'

Kumhareya said, 'Think about it for a few minutes. It might be best. And I'd get you to the Golden Temple eventually. In fact, I've already told Balbir to take a message to Amar Singh. He'll get through without any difficulty.'

Balbir had had his eyes shut for some time. Nor had he heard Kulwanti approach. He was hardly conscious of anything but the pain in his head now. It had been a very hard blow.

Kumhareya said, 'Why, Kulwanti! You've been a long time.'

Kulwanti replied from the doorway, 'I sat down in the light to peel the cucumbers for you. You can cut them into slices if you like. The vegetable knife is in the bottom of the basket.' She came in and put the basket down.

'Thank you,' Kumhareya said. Then, 'Hey, where're you going?'

'To the well to wash these tomatoes.'

'Wait! It's . . . it's dangerous . . . that well. You could fall in. The rim's caving in. Let me draw a bucket up for you. You stand back from the well. The last time someone looked down in there, he fell in.'

Kumhareya went out with Kulwanti.

Gulnari noticed that Balbir was curled up shivering on the straw. She wiped her hand on her *salwar* and eased the muffler back on his head. He tried to push her hand away but it had touched the bump and he winced.

'Let me see it,' she said and held his forehead firmly. 'Oh God, you're burning. No wonder you can't sit up.'

Her hand felt as cool as . . . as newly-prepared potter's clay! Despite his annoyance at being fussed over, he found it soothing. He closed his eyes; the hot tears of rising temperature were welling up. He resented her affectionate caress as she pushed back his hair. Yet he had to grant again that Kumhareya had made a sensible choice. She was efficiently kind.

Her bangles clinked against his ear and he had a vision of himself eating slivers of ice gathered in little stalactites from the freezer of his longed-for fridge. Her fingers had a faint smell of mint that mingled with the fragrance from her sleeve, of her body and the common talc called Himalaya Bouquet. He couldn't help inhaling deeply.

'Why do you sigh like that?' she asked. 'Are you in pain?'

He frowned and opened his eyes. She was just a silhouette against the light that seemed to be held in the frame of the door.

'You're crying!' she exclaimed.

'It's the fever,' he mumbled and turned away on his side.

She got up quietly and went out. He must have dozed for he awoke to the sound of munching and the crack and crunch of cucumber being bitten through. They were sitting near him and he could catch snatches of their whispered conversation. But the words trailed him into intermittent sleep and he would rouse himself only to dangle at the end of a new phrase and find that too slipping away as he receded into a fathomless cavern. The air seemed to grow chilly and he shivered.

'What did you say?' He heard Kumhareya's voice boom and ricochet.

He couldn't remember whether he had spoken. Kumhareya repeated the question.

'He said he's feeling cold,' Gulnari said.

'The bump has swollen like a bulb,' Kulwanti whispered, and he heard it like the rustle of tissue paper. Suddenly he saw himself wearing a crown of electric lights and sailing step for step through the air, proclaiming, 'Diwali is here! O what a festival!'

'Don't laugh like that,' Kumhareya said and patted him on his extra shoulder. It didn't seem to belong to him. It didn't feel the same. It was as if his entire body was an appendage and he had to assess the sensations it was recording.

'My shawl is at the bottom of the basket under the vegetables,' said Kulwanti.

He heard a scraping noise like rats scampering and a gust of air and the frayed edge of the shawl like a centipede moving across his face. He revolted against it and turned. But in that instant he felt warmer and relaxed.

Again, they seemed to be discussing something. Then someone sat down beside him and he felt a warm pad being placed on his forehead. The bump throbbed and sent out sensors of pain. He felt his body returning to him and moaned. The pad was removed and replaced again, warmer. With an effort that sent crinkles across his forehead, he opened his eyes for a few seconds. It was Kulwanti. She had made a pad of her *dupatta* and was warming it each time with her breath.

'Thank you,' he said but his voice sounded far away and between it and him was a growing heat. He feared the words had evaporated. He said it again. The phrase shot off like a cannonball, diminished to a marble speeding away and echoed minutely in a distant corridor. He must have repeated himself for Kulwanti's whisper rippled like streamers in the wind.

'All right, all right,' she said.

The three of them seemed very remote. He had to reach them, make contact. He heaved himself up from the ocean floor and suddenly he was supernatant and turning with an amazing buoyancy till his shoulder rested against Kulwanti's hip. The waves of nausea receded leaving him lying there like something heavy and solid on the bank of the Sutlej river. Kulwanti continued her ministrations.

Kumhareya's voice seemed to be referring to something. He heard him say, 'Balbir, don't forget the message.'

The voices of the girls lapped and overlapped in hushed tones. Balbir's attention focused on his shoulder which seemed to be drawing the last rays of the sun as through a magnifying glass. It was a pleasant sensation and he was sorry to lose it each time Kulwanti rocked back to blow on the pad before replacing it. It was her hip that was aflame. He hoped vaguely that she would not mind. He hoped that she would understand. He needed that warmth. He wanted to bathe in it, luxuriate in it.

He heard footsteps receding. Kulwanti's voice was close by, echoing as in a cave: 'Come back soon. We have to go home in half an hour.'

Balbir suddenly remembered the twenty thousand rupees and his appointment for later that evening with Tarsem. He hoped he would be well enough to go. He wanted to force energy and wakefulness back into himself.

He must have moved because Kulwanti said, 'Lie still. Try to sleep.'

He lay still and tried to sleep. The silence began to reverberate like a deep drum beat. He felt sure the walls were fluctuating, converging and regressing and forcing a pressure on his head. He could never sleep on his back anyway. He turned on his side, towards her, and found his arm, up to his elbow, resting on her thigh. He realized for the first time that her *salwar* was made of a kind of velveteen. Under it a slow conflagration seemed to glow and again he was aware of that igneous tingle. She shifted as though to make him comfortable but he shifted too so that the full weight of his arm absorbed heat not just from one thigh but both and the junction in between. He let himself breathe heavily and deep.

He couldn't remember what she looked like. He tried to conjure up her face. But though he could easily visualize Gulnari, Kulwanti's features refused to coalesce. He hadn't really noticed her. But still he knew she was warm and human and smelt of baking bread and ashes.

The intervals between the removing and replacing of the pad, which she still managed despite his averted face, seemed to have grown longer.

Suddenly she made a new movement that brought his hand fully into pressure against her for just a few seconds. With a thudding heart, his pain and fever almost forgotten, he caressed once with all his desire, brushing aside the folds of cloth and feeling the tuft of hair underneath. She leaned back and adjusted the flap of her *kameez* over his hand. But she didn't remove his hand. His being took joy in that.

Now each time she bent forward, he caressed her. And each time, his fingers were a little bolder. Pretending discomfort, he groaned and rearranged himself and raising his head off the muffler brought it down a little above her knee. Now his ear too became an instrument for gauging reaction, like a stethoscope. He could *hear* her trembling. He could hear each flick of muscle and the fluxion of blood and the anxious tremors of breath.

She did not remove his face from her lap but cradled it instead. The dabbing had given way to an involuntary stroking of his neck. He was ablaze with a fervour he could barely control.

He pushed his hand up, under her loose *kameez*, to her breasts. She wore no shift or brassiere. They hung there, free. They were larger than he had thought. Suddenly he caught himself thinking of Gulnari and wondering whether her breasts weren't smaller and surely the colour of milk with a dash of tea like they were given to drink as children wanting to be grown-ups. He was wrenched back to Kulwanti by his astonishment that her nipples were long and tapering thin like cloves. He hadn't imagined breasts would feel like this. He expected all young girls' breasts to be no bigger than teacups and taut, and he thought that the breasts of old women became pendulous and sagged because they had been fondled so much by their husbands. All nipples, he had imagined, were like buttons. Kulwanti's breasts were firm but big, curving upwards to nipples that were resilient.

She brought her hand up and placed it on his, over her *kameez*, as though to restrain him but as he rolled a nipple between his fingers, she sighed, caressed his hand and returned to stroking his neck. He felt he would burst and was exasperated that she did not take more initiative. He had never known any other gratification but masturbation and felt an instinctive resentment at her neglect of his need. Just then she froze as though in apprehension of the approach of some intruder. But it was only the flutter of pigeons in the cotes. And she leaned down and kissed him on his temple. He wanted to rise up, strip her and feed himself to her. He struggled up, propping himself on an elbow.

'No, no,' she said quite ridiculously. 'You must lie down. You must rest.'

'Later,' he said with decision. And his determination surprised him.

He pressed his hand to her strong, slim belly and probed down below the navel. She caught at his hand now as he thrust under the string of her *salwar*. But he pulled her onto the straw and his hand was halfway over her pubic fleece. It wasn't at all coarse and wiry like his own hair. And even as she tried to close her legs, his finger forged in to the moist upper portion of her gully. He felt a sense of hallelujah. This was it, for the first time in his life!

'What are you doing!' she gritted. 'You're hurting me!'

He relented and became more temperate and apologized with a kiss on her cheek. She was looking at him, her aquiline nose bisecting the dull light as clearly as the raised roof of a hut, and her eyes were sloe and shining. Her lips were finely cut, not full like Gulnari's. Her eyebrows arched and angled into a flourish like urdu calligraphy. He was struck by her perfect looks, not roused but awed by them, and had to remind himself of her body with his grasping hand so that he might continue—not as a lover now but as a plunderer roiling in to desecrate and sully.

His finger moved into the softness and it parted, enclosing on the tip. He persisted and it sank while, with his palm, he cuddled the fullness of her growth, compressing and rotating upon it despite the biting tension of the cord on his wrist and her writhing pincering legs; and suddenly it was all give and her thighs had opened wide and her eyes had a startled look and with her mouth quivering and dilating between smiling and anxiety and gasping and sighs she weaved her torso down on and around that digit.

He saw her, grown vast now and careering strangely like the earth itself heaving up to be tilled on a plough. Her mouth was the centre of a storm and it ravaged her face with all the forces of nature gone berserk. And yet her teeth sparkled like white clouds on a fuscous evening. He was amazed at what he had brought out in her and was numb with awe. She was now uncontrolled and uncontrollable. And she was in command. He felt as helpless as a dove in a hurricane. She was on the rampage, striding across his world and universe. Even the plait that lay across her bosom quivered like a chain and mace.

If he had forgotten the pain in his forehead, he could not overlook the agony of the string cutting across his wrist. That brought him back to the humdrum dimension of that hay-filled shed. He winced. She noticed it and for a fraction of a second was Kulwanti again.

He said simply, 'The string.'

She was almost shy then, and there was a little spasm at the corner of her lips and he was afraid she would lapse into giggles. That would have destroyed it for him completely. But she looked up at him, surveying his face like a conqueror might a new domain. There was that light in her eyes again. And he knew she was not responding to him but to some spirit in herself that needed triumph.

Even as she quickly undid the cord about her waist, her mouth changed shape and her lips drew back thinly in the way he had not liked before. If a sound had escaped her throat he might have known whether she laughed or snarled. She reached down and took his lips in hers, biting and sucking them. It was obvious that she had never kissed before. Nor had he. But he had heard that it was more a matter of the tongue. And he guessed it should be a gentler act than this.

Yet something in him was roused by the very fact of her ignorance. And as she started succumbing again to her own insistence with his hand, he realized that women did it too—this solitary, lonely exercise of the damned. He freed his hand, and as he moved it up to push back her *kameez* and bare her breasts he smelt on his fingers the aroma of ripe guava.

He was more confident now, and undid his trousers, lowering them just enough so that she might not see him to his embarrassment.

'They might come,' she said.

He made no answer but guided her hand to himself and made her clench. She seemed afraid now to let even her curiosity work. But she had demonstrated how her hesitation could be overcome.

He began to kiss and fondle her breasts tickling her nipples with his tongue, appraising their pliancy with his lips. This knowledge too was new to him that nipples could go erect.

One of her hands was on his back feeling the smooth boyish skin; the other was where he had disposed it, ineffective.

He caressed the contours of her hips and as he approached the rich pubescence, her hand shot off his back, impatient, and forced his fingers to it. He rose on his knees and would have settled on and plunged, had she not cried, 'No, no, not that, not that!'

He understood the edge of terror in her voice. He sat back on his knees to savour the safer delight that they yielded to each other. He could see her better like this, scrambling to the communion of his hand. And now that she could see him, stiff and beckoning, challenging her ignorance, she reached out, of her own volition, and smoothed and stroked and moved it and kissed it, wanting to know.

The two of them in that straw-filled, windowless room in the ruin, pulsating spasmodically to their own impulses, were sharing an act and a moment but not their thoughts.

She reached her culmination first, with a low wail which she could not suppress. Then she would have let him languish, allowing him only the grateful affection that diffused out of her, but he intrigued her with his strange intoxication, kneeling over her as though she should supplicate. She gave in to his wish then and watched with a detached wonder this looming monstrosity seem to leap and rear. This young man with a penis more urgent than his fever, this young man making her do this to this slippery object he had sprouted out of cloth and buttons, this young man who could make her laugh with his passion. But he might think she laughed at him! That would be intolerable to him. He would withdraw. And that was unbearable to her. He had only just entered her life.

She must make him understand some day that she laughed with passion. Her own nature embarrassed her. She wished she could hide it but it escaped in awkward giggles and she hated herself for it. She must make him understand her.

And why was he taking so long? All the women she had heard talking of it had said that the male animal is quicker, even to the touch. Was he disgusted with her, or thinking something else? He had become important to her, this not unhandsome, gawky young man. Was it bothering him that she might be a year or two or three older than him? Was that putting him off? She felt compelled to satisfy.

Pretending renewed desire, she grasped him harder and was more vigorous and raised herself once more to kiss when he showered and there were drops, like unguent cream, on her hands and face. She was torn between love for him and her urge to laughter.

He noticed that and the moment of his supreme generosity was shattered. As both, philanthropist and pillager, he had failed. He was a mere philanderer of his bounty, a laughing stock to her. He hated her. She was stupid. He was determined to despise her.

She giggled and said again, 'They might come,' and tidied herself and sat back reassured.

Gulnari would not have sniggered like that at such a sacred moment. And he hated himself for thinking of Gulnari at all. And had he welded himself now to this snickering, tittering, idiot girl? Would she hold him to some unspoken, unwitting promise? He wanted to be rid of all this. He wanted to be free.

'I'm going out to the well,' he said when he was ready. 'I want to wash and freshen up.'

'But you're ill!' she exclaimed.

'I'm better,' he muttered and started to walk out, but the fever was on him and he staggered.

She helped him lie down again and covered him with the shawl.

He tried to sleep but he was overcome by contrition, shame and remorse. He hadn't wanted to feel like that. But Kulwanti made him feel such a waste.

He didn't speak but gave himself up to his fever and for a while he could hear her chewing on a slice of cucumber.

He thought of the noise that buffaloes make when they eat.

And he tossed about and cursed inwardly and readjusted his thoughts. And hating himself for it, but knowing no one would know, he dreamed of Gulnari's soothing hand.

As cool as newly-prepared potter's clay.

In a minute she said, 'Why haven't they come back? He was just driving her to the road on the motorcycle. She was going to bring some medicine for your fever. They said they'd be back soon.'

He forced himself to sit up. Now it was he who wanted to giggle. She must have thought him stupid. He couldn't help it.

She asked in panic, 'Do you think they've run away?'

He giggled now and almost said that they had 'eloped'. Then he drew a deep breath and stood up. 'I must wash my face, clear my head.'

'Wait,' she said getting up and supporting him at the arm. 'I'll draw the water. You might fall in, the way you're staggering!'

He tied the muffler tight round his head. It seemed to hold in the pain. He said, 'I think they've . . . gone underground.'

She gasped. 'What'll I do now? What'll I say?'

'Nothing,' he shrugged. 'You don't know. Gulnari wandered off and that was it.'

She was looking at him, her eyes wide, her mouth open. 'I won't say you were here but if I need to get in touch with you—?'

'Send a message to Tarsem of Jagtara. He's my partner.'

She seemed to be absorbed in her thoughts as she dropped the bucket into the well. Then she began to tilt it for water. That's when she screamed.

The body was floating face up but for a moment even he thought it was Kumhareya.

He tried to calm her, kissing her, caressing her. She might have let herself get hysterical but she couldn't afford to. She went to a corner and was sick. He drew up some water for her, being careful to stand as much away as he could.

She shook her head. 'It's got blood in it.'

He let the water leak slowly out of the old bucket and went and half leaned against the lame wooden trough. He was collecting his thoughts and biding his time. An idea had occurred to him.

She said, 'I'll go. I won't say we were here. We weren't. We were only picking vegetables in the fields. Hai, my basket!' She ran in and brought it out. 'I'm going.' She seemed to hesitate. Then she blew him a kiss.

He smiled and said, 'I'll rumple that hay so that it doesn't look like we've been sitting there. I'll tidy up whatever I can.'

She nodded, smiled worriedly and stepped round towards the back, towards the gap in the wall, and was gone.

He went in, looked round, found an old sack, shook it free of dust and laid it ready on the ground. Then he removed the bricks over the cache in the wall. It was getting really dark inside. In order not to miss any later, he counted the bricks as he removed them. Fifteen in all.

Then he took out the carbine, the ammunition, the bayonet in its case, a .32 pistol, two hand grenades, some sticks that he couldn't identify in the gloom, some string-like things, some objects wrapped in cellophane, a piece of metal that looked like a pipe and a few tiddly odds and ends. He stuffed them all in the sack.

He replaced the bricks, counting carefully as he did so. All fifteen.

He went to the hay, shifted it and spread it.

Then he carried the sack with him out into the fields. He was glad it was getting dark. But still he didn't relish the thought of being discovered with a sack over his shoulder.

When he was on the track that led to the road, he walked till he was almost there, then under the last culvert, he shoved the sack.

He walked on feeling suddenly light. Nothing like a bit of fright, he thought, to clear your head of fever.

He hurried along the road till a *tonga* already loaded with passengers stopped and, after some brisk bargaining, took him on. The passengers without exception talked of the increasing incidents of terrorism in Punjab. They all wanted to be home before eight o'clock. For some reason that had become the Cinderella Hour after which it seemed extremists and robbers ruled the roads.

Sitting there in the *tonga*, with the nag clip-clopping between the creaking shafts and the passengers shielding their faces against the scything January wind, he listened to the muffled, muttered conversation about events that were rocking the countryside but he thought of Tarsem and the meeting to which he was going. He wondered how far he should be prepared to collaborate. Then suddenly he realized he was hungry and the remembered aroma of Tarsem's chicken curry seemed to sweep up into his nostrils. His stomach spoke. He smiled. At least there was that ahead of him.

He felt warm though he wore no sweater or jacket. The others in the tonga were swaddled in blankets or rough shawls that smelt of woodsmoke and farming. He knew he still had a bit of fever but he hoped the worst of it was over.

And he thought of Kulwanti's lust and his own, and a half-laugh broke from him even as he shook his head. The villager next to him stopped short in mid-conversation with the others, turned and said, 'It's no laughing matter. The body was lying there on the third floor. The Guru Ram Das Sarai is part of the Golden Temple. It's a sacred place. Imagine killing one of your own Nihangs! Terrible!'

Balbir sighed and nodded. And he thought of that other corpse, the one he had just seen floating in the well. He hadn't quite seen the hilt of the *kirpan* that had come free of the *saafa* wound over it at the neck. But he was sure the weapon would be traced to Kumhareya.

And his heart wept for the deeds of his friend.

Yet, engrossed as he was in his own thoughts, he could not help hearing the words being bandied about in the *tonga*. As the rattling horse-cart clattered on towards the falling sun, only a sliver of which was now visible, a sort of communion seemed to develop between the passengers. They were no longer strangers but a group related by the common cause of successfully accomplishing together this simple journey. They addressed each other without introduction, expressed concern for the other's comfort, shifted to grant another some additional space, and soon they were a unit with an intangible inner cohesion. They were not all literate, but like most Indian peasants they were educated in philosophic concepts and aware of political intricacies. They spoke loudly too, as most peasants do, so that it seemed the countryside reverberated with what they said.

'It's all the fault of these politicians,' declared a hoarse voice from the back interrupting itself to hawk and spit a fulsome gob over the side. 'They want smaller states based on language so that they can be petty dictators!'

'Aye, it's all at our cost. Now look at me, I can't read or write but they come and ask what script I prefer.' This statement from a bemused *beedi*-smoker was punctuated by a sharp drawing-in of smoke.

There was laughter.

The *tongawallah*, sitting on one of the shafts, made clicking sounds with his tongue, urging the animal on, and suggested, 'Punjabi. That's what you should have answered. We all live in Punjab and we all speak Punjabi.'

'Oh ho, you dumb fool!' said the *beedi*-smoker, encouraged by the audience reaction he had received. 'Of course we all speak

Punjabi. But that's not what they are interested in. They want to know how you write it.'

'I write it in Urdu,' the hoarse voice at the back affirmed while snorting at the phlegm in his nose.

'Then,' said the man next to Balbir giving Balbir a jocular nudge, 'they'll put you down as being a muslim.'

'I'd be a funny muslim,' said the hoarse voice, 'with a name like Roop Lal. But my wife writes Hindi and my children write Gurmukhi.'

'It just depends on what you've been taught,' shrugged the *tongawallah.*

'Aye, that's what I meant.' The hoarse voice coughed vigorously and added, 'The best Punjabi programmes are broadcast by Radio Pakistan and their Punjabi is written in Urdu, not Gurmukhi or Hindi. Anyway Gurmukhi is only four hundred years old.'

The lone woman in the group, certainly not less than seventy and with the courage of her years, spoke up: 'Roop Lal, they'll cut you in three pieces—one for the Koran, one for the Gita and one for the Granth Sahib.'

'That's it!' cried the *beedi*-smoker triumphantly. 'What they really want to know is what religion you follow!'

'So what did you answer when they asked you about the script?' The *tongawallah* cracked his whip, which was no more than a bit of hide tied to a stick.

The *beedi*-smoker sighed, flicked away the butt, and said, 'I have no script. And I am an atheist. Looks like I'll have to make a state of my own.'

The others exploded with laughter.

'That makes two of us,' said the man directly behind Balbir. 'I come from a sikh family but I'm a communist. The politicians are clever. They tempt us into selling our humanity for a little opium. They're turning us into addicts.'

'Opium?' the old woman was aghast. 'What opium?'

'Religion,' said the communist sagely. 'They dangle a bit of that in front of us. They're all fascists.'

'What's that?' asked the *tongawallah.*

'They say they'll divide us up by language but it's really religion and race they mean. Can you imagine what would happen to the USA if there were religious, racial, linguistic states? In one state Hebrew, in another Italian, then Greek, Puerto Rican, Spanish and so on. You wouldn't be able to shift jobs from one state to another. Your children's education would be a mess if you were transferred from one area to another.'

'All right, all right,' said the *tongawallah* clanging the footboard bell as they drew near a cyclist. 'They must have thought of all that. They're people who read and write. They can't be such fools.'

'They're not fools,' admitted the communist. 'They're just shortsighted, blinded by political greed.'

'Aye, that I can see,' agreed the *tongawallah*. 'Now look at me—I'm a sikh as plain as anyone can see, but all of us Punjabis are the same race, aren't we? We may be hindus, sikhs, muslims or christians, but we're all aryan.'

The cyclist pedalled up alongside and made a slightly breathless request. 'Mind if I tag along?'

'Hang on to the side then, *sardarji*,' nodded the *tongawallah*. 'You shouldn't be out cycling alone at this hour.'

'Got delayed repairing a thresher,' said the cyclist.

'Hey, hey,' called the hoarse voice. 'Why're you stopping?'

'To light the lamps,' said the *tongawallah*. 'It's getting dark.'

'Ach, forget it,' said the man next to Balbir. 'Don't stop. There's still enough light to see.'

'Aye, but it's to warn anyone on the road. I don't want to run over someone.'

'No one will be out walking,' said the old woman. 'And if anyone tries to stop you now, do run them over.'

The *tongawallah* sighed. 'Oh, all right. But really all this terrorism is bad for business. And I don't want a smaller Punjab. I'll have fewer passengers!'

Everyone laughed. Someone called him an idiot for reducing it to such absurdity.

The cyclist had recovered his breath. He said with a chuckle, 'With all due respect . . . I mean I do admire Bhindranwale for some things—'

'Like what?' asked the communist.

'Oh, I mean sticking to his beliefs and taking up guns against the government and all that.'

The man nearest him lit a new *beedi* and muttered over his cupped hands, 'He thinks even tea should be banned along with alcohol.'

'You may admire him,' said the *tongawallah*. 'But you're still afraid to be out alone in the dark because some young fellow may like to leave another body on the road.'

'Yes, yes,' said the cyclist. 'But you're not letting me finish.

Have you heard the latest one about the admirer who went to join him?'

'No,' admitted the *tongawallah*.

'Well, it must have been someone like me,' said the cyclist, giving a short laugh in anticipation of his joke. 'Anyway, this man goes to Bhindranwale and offers to join the terrorists. Bhindranwale nods and says, "All right, go to that bag there and pull out any one among the slips of paper inside." The man does so. On the slip of paper is a name and address. "Right," says Bhindranwale, "your first task is to go and kill that person within the next twenty-four hours." The man breaks into a sweat, trembles and finally confesses that he cannot kill someone in cold blood. Bhindranwale smiles and says, "Doesn't matter, don't give it another thought. Now just write *your* name and address on a piece of paper and drop it in the bag along with the others." '

The group of travellers roared with laughter.

Someone said, 'Bhindranwale put up some candidates for election. None of them won. It just shows why he's had to resort to terror tactics.'

A motorcycle could be heard approaching. The group went silent. The nag clopped on.

They all peered at the machine as it barrelled towards them. No, no rider on the pillion. No youth there with a sten gun. The passengers seemed to give one united sigh.

Balbir felt the tears start to his eyes. He didn't know whether it was the fever or whether he wept for Kumhareya and himself and the whole region. He was glad no one could see to ask. He was glad that it was suddenly dark and they were journeying deeper into darkness. There is no twilight in these parts. Night had struck the land as swiftly as a slap.

4

•••

A Connection in Europe

Five thousand miles away and five hours later the same sun was setting over a different land—West Germany. And the twilight held no terror for Raskaan.

So removed was he from thoughts of his younger brother Balbir that had someone told him a crisis was brewing for his family in faraway Punjab, he would have conjectured first that the news had to do with the health of the patriarch or one of the elders.

Even the fact that his cousin Satyavan had come to visit him in West Berlin aroused no suspicion or foreboding. After all, Satyavan travelled often, and those who loved him never asked why; he would not have answered that question plainly anyway.

Satyavan was obviously here on some errand of his own. He had said he was on a tour that would take him through Europe and England and on, perhaps, to Canada. It was not for Raskaan to probe. As a conscientious younger relative, Raskaan's duty was simply to see to the comfort and desires of Satyavan.

Standing on the pavement outside the smallest of his restaurants, he watched the golden disc descend the wedge of sky between two buildings. He rarely planned anything. His decisions usually came to him extempore. They came to him, he did not make them. In that sense, he was deeply religious and therefore outrageously generous at whim with his wealth, which too 'came' to him. Life was a lark, one long adventure through illusion. He had only to read nature's signals and be guided to fulfilment. He liked to think he was in harmony with the cosmos. That is what gave him inner peace and the consequent detachment from his material riches. He enjoyed them, used them, gave them away—and they multiplied. It amused him.

He delighted in being mischievous in the midst of the anxieties of the world. In childhood he had been as naughty as an imp and now he was as unpredictable as an errant genie. Smoothing down his neatly clipped beard, he chuckled. Altogether, he felt quite gleeful. What entertainment should he line up for Satyavan?

The sun dropped like a coin in a slot machine. That was it! A perfect evening for going to the Spielbank! The casino was as good a place as any to launch his dear cousin on the joys of Berlin's nightlife. He himself didn't care particularly for gambling. His thirty-four years of happenstance existence had proved him master of the incalculable intuitive risk. He invariably won. That is what made him so boringly successful a businessman. He now had six enterprises, all working more or less automatically with the minimum of bullying and badgering from him— always between three and six in the afternoon when he was just awake from the night before and girding up for the night to come.

No, casinos were like false teeth set in a perpetual smile. He made it a point never to make friends there. He knew all the regulars. Conditioned fanatics of the table who had bartered their souls and would now wager their bodies for the casual but timely gift of a few plastic chips from the winner's pile.

But he would go tonight for the sake of Satyavan. A feeling of genuine satisfaction rose in him. He had great respect and affection for his unfathomable cousin.

And yet he remembered that queasy feeling when, on arrival, Satyavan had indicated that they were due for a deep discussion. Raskaan did not like deep discussions, especially with relatives who were older than him. It would be a one-sided conversation anyway. You can't argue against the authority of age within the bond of family. You can play truant, you can avoid, evade, escape but you cannot disagree openly or refuse. In short, a discussion with a respected elder, no matter how small the gap in years, was a matter of listening to a clearly stated opinion and saying yes. It meant taking orders.

Raskaan, with his propensity for cutting straight to the heart of any affair, would rather that Satyavan had thought fit merely to command him. He resented wasting time on anything but pleasure.

As it was, during the last couple of years he had put all his resources at Satyavan's disposal and they had recently been deployed a few times in the most extraordinary way. It was clear that of late Satyavan had developed an extra dimension even to his convoluted business activities.

But, thank heavens—Raskaan sighed at the temporary deliverance from nerve-wrack and complexity—they had agreed to postpone all discussion till later. Today was for just getting together. The epicurean in Raskaan exulted. He wondered what, after the visit to the casino, he could do to make the visit a memorably pleasant one for his cousin.

Satyavan was at the house in Münchenstrasse, resting, perhaps having a leisurely bath or just watching a film on the video. He hoped Jackie the Alsatian was not being a nuisance. Satyavan was not used to friendly dogs. He only knew them as ferocious guards who were shut away during the day and released at night to attack anything that moved. He should have brought Jackie with him when he left the house on his rounds. Jackie could have been deposited with Renate. She needed to have the Alsatian around especially as she would be taking home the collections from the two restaurants and the shop.

Jackie. What a silly name for a dog, and a male at that! No resonance to it, no meaning, no significance. Altogether too western. But there it was, the superficiality of life in the west had seeped into him too. He did not waste time now in searching for depth and tone. He was becoming accustomed to running on without pause like the second hand on his wristwatch.

He had a terrible guilt about being here. And a terrible guilt about leaving Balbir there. Balbir, poor sop, a sacrifice on the altar of tradition! Times were changing but, in the process of change, they ground some slower beings underfoot. The juggernaut of progress rolls on unavoidably and regardless. Then he thought to remember it in the original way, the Indian way, the semantically generic way, and he said half-aloud to himself like a cook too much alone in the kitchen: 'Lord Jagganath's chariot rolls over all bodies that fall under it.'

'Hey, Ruskin!' somebody called, '*Guten Abend. Wie geht es Ihnen?*'

He winced at the way in which his Indian name had been westernized. Drawing his sweater down over his beer belly he turned slowly and saw against the cold grey haze that surrounded the cold grey buildings, the thin drug-stricken professor of Mass Communications, Eckhardt Stiltz.

'Eckhardt,' he said, 'if you call me that again, I will murder you.'

'Ach, but you *are* the new Ruskin. I tell everybody that. You have introduced a whole new set of aesthetics into our lives, no?'

'No. I don't even know what that word means. I have only entertained you with idle talk so that you would patronize my tea shop and bring a horde of students with you.'

Eckhardt laughed and tugged at his salt-and-pepper goatee. Digging into his red velvet jacket he produced a small cellophane packet. 'Real Indian *bhang*,' he said. 'You should stock some in your Spice Bazaar.' He pronounced it bah-saar. 'Expensive. You could make another million.'

Raskaan Chibber shook his head. 'God has given me enough.'

'Even clichés you make good use of!' exclaimed Eckhardt, in his enthusiasm lapsing into an inverted sentence structure that he often corrected in those of his students who attempted Mass Communication in English. The professor had now wheezed into a whine of giggles. Raskaan had a brief vision of an asthmatic mosquito. When Eckhardt realized that Raskaan was not joking, that he really believed in God and His great generosity, and that he might with equal conviction mouth other eastern platitudes such as 'My house is small but my heart is big' or 'Life is a play of illusion', the colour rose to his pallid cheeks and he sobered but, like a badly-tuned engine that continues its revolutions after the ignition is turned off, a crackle of chromatic wheezing rattled from his chest.

Eckhardt hated Raskaan.

And Raskaan knew it.

In the tea shop known as Chai Khana, meaning both 'a place for tea' and 'tea and food', Raskaan waited perversely till Eckhardt had ordered. The rough-tough waiters, all hauled in from Punjab, were schooled to present the bill to the patron who ordered. Raskaan was the proprietor. If he ordered, it would be contrary to eastern hospitality to charge anyone who sat with him at table.

The tables were long slabs of wood, thick, rough-hewn, sturdy. Not planks. Slabs. There were no chairs, only benches. And the tables and benches sat out on the pavement like a mad version of a French café. Pedestrians had to step off onto the road. The sheer illegality of this encroachment in a society so used to administering itself to the law, whatever that may be, good or bad, for laws can be bad too, was startling. The debonair effrontery of it drew attention to its individuality almost as if it were a naturally-growing garden in Switzerland. It was like a trumpet call to the spirit pining for freedom from restraint.

Eckhardt could not resist it.

Eckhardt was served a tray of tea. He stirred the *bhang* into the pot. And sipped from a cup. And was stoned out into exhilaration in a few minutes. He gorged on: *kebabs, rumali roti, saag, chhole*, the works. The food was excellent, original, true, perfect—even without the intoxication. It's just that Eckhardt ate much more than he could have otherwise. His gut had expanded. His heart had grown. His house was small but his heart was big.

'I love you, Ruskin,' he said, lying through the *bhang* and the food and the childhood that had warped him.

Raskaan looked at his watch. He was later than he intended by half an hour. But no matter. He had not specified a definite moment to Satyavan. It was only that he had told himself that it was time to go home, collect Satyavan and wander into the Spielbank. The night was not even young, it was adolescent. He could wait. So could Satyavan. When the dark greyed to the maturity of dawn he would add a special treat to it for Satyavan. He made his promises only to himself. He was no politician. Satyavan would screw the whore of his choice in Berlin. That was a promise to the ideal he carried of Satyavan. Life is a play of illusion. You have to understand the illusion.

'I love you, Ruskin,' muttered Eckhardt, 'because you once said that the muscularity of European sculpture shocked you. You said it was a glorification of brutality. Michaelangelo's *Pietà* is different but only just because the theme is humane. Otherwise we have cast our prejudices into the statues we venerate. The east deals in concepts, the west in fears.'

Raskaan nodded at one of the waiters. It was time for whisky rather than tea but—what to do?—here was Eckhardt, all said and done, a paying, crowd-bringing customer farting on. The tea shop served no *hard* drinks, unlike the restaurant he owned and unlike the retailers of the brewery he controlled. So the waiter brought him his special tea. In a glass. Tea flavoured with *masala* grass and cloves and cardamom.

'Now that's what I mean, Ruskin,' sighed Eckhardt. 'You get your tea in a glass and I have it in a cup. Why?'

'In my village,' said Raskaan scratching his thick, black, trimmed beard, 'we drink tea in glasses.'

Without asking permission, Eckhardt took up the glass of tea and sipped it. 'Ach, delicious!'

'Flavoured with spices.'

'Different.'

After a while, Eckhardt added, 'But you . . . ' he lapsed into low German, 'screwed my wife.'

'Your ex-wife.'

Eckhardt waved in response to greetings from a group of young people who were settling down at the other end of the table. Their voices were lively, enthusiastic. He said in a dull monotone, 'You have played with my life.'

Raskaan shook his head. Then with deliberate cruelty, he savoured the crass rhyme, 'I have played with your wife but not with your life. There were others before me. She's a nympho.'

Raskaan rose to leave. Eckhardt pointed to the glass of tea. 'You haven't finished that.'

'You drank from it. There's a word in India for which you have no equivalent. *Jootha*. It means the tea is spoiled. Unhygienic.'

'So I'm an untouchable,' muttered Eckhardt mockingly.

'That's neither clever nor true.'

Eckhardt snorted, 'You Indians!'

'Just for that,' said Raskaan, 'I will screw her again.'

'*Schweinehund!*' Eckhardt spoke softly with a slight note of alarm. Then, careless of the waiter who had come up to adjust the bench Raskaan had pushed back, he added with heavy irony, 'My wife you can have but not the tea I have touched!'

The shaven-headed waiter with the rolled-up sleeves and bulging biceps smiled and wiped his hands on his short apron. He turned to Raskaan and spoke in Punjabi. 'Brother, will you be coming back later? The accounts—'

'Renate will see to those. She'll come about midnight.'

'We're running short of ginger, turmeric, garlic . . . '

'Well, send someone to the Spice Bazaar. You don't have to consult me on every little thing.'

'I just thought—'

'Don't waste my time.'

'Yes, brother.'

Raskaan went in for a quick survey. A few hippies stood at the counter, eating. The two stand-up tables jutting out of the wall were also occupied. A girl was looking for space where she might tack up another hand-scrawled advertisement. There were notes and posters everywhere. 'Stick it on a lampshade,' Raskaan joked. 'Someone is sure to see the light.' She smiled and nodded, '*Danke.*'

There was not much else to the Chai Khana, except for the kitchen and the toilet. The kitchen was so small that part of the cooking was actually done right behind the counter. It gave the place the authentic feel of a North Indian *dhaba* or roadside eatery. *Pakoras* were sizzling in pure *ghee* in a huge frying pan. A delicious aroma hung in the air. And through it wove the lilt of a popular Hindi film song snapping out of a cassette-player.

In the kitchen, the cook clad only in vest and shorts was busy slapping thick village-style *rotis* on a giant hot plate. The cook squinted through the smoke of the coal fire and shouted over the clatter of aluminium plates being washed by another man at the sink, 'We've got no *tandoori* chicken left. These Germans eat early. Not yet seven thirty and the night's stock is over. Of course, we had a large order from that students' party. *Naans*, chicken, curd, *daal*, even salad. Had it delivered in the van.'

'Good,' said Raskaan. 'Send to the big restaurant for more chicken.

'Everyone's busy. If you would just—'

'Sister-screwer, I said send for it!'

'Yes, brother. But—'

'Telephone them. They'll rush it over. You bastards don't think for yourselves, that's your ball-up! If we say we serve *tandoori* chicken, it's got to be here. Understand?'

The cook nodded and spun round to fill an order brought by a waiter. Outside, the benches and tables were all occupied. People stood on the pavement, chomping and munching as though at a buffet.

As Raskaan stepped out he overheard with pleasure a bead-bedecked young man telling an elderly couple who seemed to be his parents on a visit from the country, 'This is the cheapest, cleanest, best eating place in Berlin.'

'It certainly is informal,' said the podgy old lady casting a nervous glance about her.

Three motorcyclists roared up drowning all conversation. They parked at the kerb. Six helmeted, leather-jacketed figures dismounted. Their precision and uniformity made them seem dangerous but in fact they were just three couples who felt safer looking alike.

'*Gruss Gott!*' shouted the big Bavarian who was obviously the pace-setter of the group.

'*Alles gut*,' said Raskaan. 'Where have you been, Wilhelm?'

'Trying to become a farmer like your father-in-law, Rasky. Growing grapes along the Rhine. Then I thought I must take a holiday in wicked Berlin and here we are! I see your pavement parties continue.'

'*Ja, Ja*, I am building a tradition here.' A number of people laughed.

'Good,' nodded the Bavarian as though granting some sort of permission. Then he asked in a whisper, 'But your friend lost the election, *nein*? These others will take away your licence for using the pavement.'

'I made a small donation last week. Five thousand marks. If they behave well with me, I shall make another donation.'

Wilhelm guffawed and slapped Raskaan on the shoulder. 'You are a miracle man!' Then he raised the Plexiglass visor of his helmet and said, 'But what is this? You are no longer looking the same. Where is your long black hair down to the shoulder, your beard coming to your chest?'

'I got tired of being mistaken for a hippie.'

'But no! You were the café messiah, no? Now you look like a filthy rich Arab!' He turned to his group and widened his eyes. They laughed.

Raskaan did not flinch. He said calmly, 'You see that Rolls Royce there, parked between my vans?'

'*Ja-ah*?' Willhelm was puzzled.

'It has a little bar in it and other refinements, like special mahogany panelling, a telephone, slumberette seats and a few custom-made frivolities. In the days when I cooked and hawked *samosas* from a tray strapped to my neck, I dreamed of sitting in a limousine like that.'

'And now you own it?' Wilhelm was incredulous and impressed.

'There are only two such cars in the world.'

'*Wunderbar!*' sighed the girl, nestling against Wilhelm.

'I own both of them,' said Raskaan. 'The other one is in my garage at home.'

After a moment Wilhelm said, 'It is too much, no?'

'Yes,' said Raskaan simply.

'Ah, you are clever always!' Wilhelm's eyes narrowed and he poked a finger in Raskaan's ribs. 'Why did you buy the second Rolls?'

'Shall I tell you the truth?'

'Of course.'

The dome-headed waiter came up and indicated that there was now a place for the group to sit. Raskaan held Wilhelm back as the others moved to the table.

'It is for you to drive.'

'For me?'

Raskaan scratched in his beard and removed what seemed to be a speck of goo. 'That Ingrid's little daughter,' he muttered. 'Always kissing me on the beard after blowing bubble gum.'

'You are still a funny fellow,' said Wilhelm, taking off his helmet and unzipping his jacket. 'But the Rolls . . .? Oh no, how can it be for me to drive? I have been away in the Rhineland. You did not even telephone.'

'I thought of you. Or someone like you. You can take your friends on a long trip. The bar in the Rolls will be stocked. It has a fridge. I will give you the money for petrol and expenses. You will enjoy travelling through Turkey, Iran, Afghanistan, Pakistan, Nepal . . . '

'Ach, I would love to visit Kathmandu.'

'You will.'

'I cannot believe it.'

'Then come to me at home tomorrow. Late breakfast. Eleven o'clock. I will give you the keys of the car, money, a map, whatever you require.'

'But—'

'Wilhelm, farming has dulled you.' Raskaan clapped him on his elbows. 'You used to be quick to seize an opportunity.'

'Ja, ja, of course, but—'

'My card. I am no longer in the old flat. That is for my bachelor employees. I remember you used to play table tennis—'

'My favourite game, ping pong.'

'I have a table at home. Or billiards if you prefer. Bring your friends.'

Driving home, Raskaan thought, 'Eighteen years and now I can do it to them!' He looked in the rear-view mirror, then readjusted it and examined his own reflection in quick glimpses. Bushy eyebrows so neat they might have been shaved into place. Goggle eyes. Gargoyle eyes. And pouches. Little pouches. Slightly darker than the rest of the olive brown face. The imprint of a restless mind in a body that seemed always at rest, always relaxed. Shining mischievous eyes. Still naughty in a youthful face. 'But I *am* young,' he reminded himself.

Suddenly, he changed his mind about going home directly. Instead, he turned down Rutgerstrasse, towards the big restaurant. Wouldn't harm to check that all was well.

He pressed a button. The window slid down electronically. It was very cold outside. The draught made him want to pee. He pulled up. Went to a bush. Peed. Cleared his throat, spat. Funny how urinating always made him want to spit.

He sneezed. Damn! It was the change in temperature. The heating system in the car was incubating weakness in him. He must turn it off.

He blew his nose loudly between his fingers, flicked them clean, then wiped them on his handkerchief. He couldn't get used to carrying his snot around with him in a piece of cloth.

He climbed into the car, lit a cigarette, turned off the heating and rang his house. There was no response. What the hell! He tapped out another number on the buttons. This time he got through to the telephone which had an extension in the guest-bathroom.

A tentative voice said uncertainly, 'Hello?'

'Elder brother, it's me!'

There were a few scraping, struggling noises. The receiver was being fumbled with. Then Satyavan's healthy rustic baritone said in a strained way, 'Why?'

Raskaan was astounded. 'What do you mean, why? Elder brother, it's me, Raskaan. Where are you?'

'At your house, of course. Didn't *you* telephone?'

'Yes, yes. But are you in the bedroom or the bathroom?'

'In the bathroom.'

'Are you all right? I'm sorry if I disturbed you. Having a bath, are you?'

'Can't.'

'What do you mean, can't? I told Renate to see that you had clean towels and soap before she left the house. She said she'd run the hot water for you. She was going to fill the tub.'

'She did. But I can't bath using a soap-dish.'

'What on earth do you mean?'

'There's no mug here, Raskaan. How do I pour the water over myself?'

'For heaven's sake, elder brother, get into the tub and lie down.'

'What? In my own dirty water?'

'That's how people bath here.'

'Ugh!'

Suddenly there ws a muffled crash. The line was not dead. Despite the cold Raskaan began to perspire with anxiety as he yelled into the mouthpiece. 'Elder brother, what was that? Are you—? I'm coming. Just don't panic.'

The receiver clattered as it was retrieved from the floor. Satyavan said, 'I fell. The commode is too small and slippery.'

'Small? Slippery?'

'It's not safe squatting on the rim. You feel like a bird perching on two telegraph wires. I hate this kind of commode. Why don't you have one with sensible foot-rests?'

'That's the French style, brother. We'll have one installed tomorrow. But now you've got to *sit* on the rim, not squat up on it.'

'Raskaan, you're trying to tell me I should let my bottom come in contact with the germs of other filthy bottoms, not to mention penises and assorted urine?'

Raskaan laughed. The exchange was really a joke between them. Satyavan was not as ignorant of European ways as he made himself out to be. He had been to the west many times, to arrange for guns, to ensure that Raskaan's Spice Bazaar was well-supplied, to visit relatives abroad, and he travelled often to urban cosmopolitan areas of India. This was just his method of reminding Raskaan of his rural North Indian origins: it was his way of retaining a sentimental grip on his cousin.

'But what I find most repulsive is having to shake hands with people over a deal,' said Satyavan. 'People here don't even wash their hands thoroughly after going to the toilet. For that matter they don't even wash their bottoms. They just wipe them with paper and then go through the day sweating brown stains on their underwear.'

'Brother, brother!' laughed Raskaan. 'You know as well as I do that Europe has a different civilization, a different culture—'

'Barbaric!' grunted Satyavan. 'Sheer barbarity allied to technology.'

'But you like the technology. You come here because of it.'

'And for you,' said Satyavan quickly. For a split second he had worried that Raskaan, in referring to technology, might mention guns or explosive devices. Much could slip out in jest; and they had agreed never to talk of such things over the phone.

But Raskaan was sharper than that. 'You also come for the beefsteak,' he said.

'And the lobster and snails and frog legs,' Satyavan agreed. 'I enjoy a change of food now and again.'

'And a change of women.' Raskaan almost shouted in glee. 'You're a pretty smooth operator for the country yokel you make yourself out to be. And a rather rotten *brahmin* who has fun on both sides of the black water—a *pandit* without a prayer!'

Satyavan burst into a coarse bubbling laugh. 'OK, king,' he said using a customary form of Punjabi address. 'Come on over and let's go.'

This waving of peasantness like a flag, common to most Punjabis even within India as a means of distinguishing themselves from others, was compounded in their case by the snobbery of *brahminism*. To be a *brahmin* was to belong to the most élite, most distinguished, ancient blood line in the world. Education and personal merit may have laid the foundation for it thousands of years ago but now seemed of no essential consideration. It was a genealogical club to which membership could be had only by birth.

To be Punjabi was to be tough and resilient, to be *brahmin* was to be naturally bright and able; and to be Muhiyal *brahmin* meant that you were descended from a small cluster of seven clans, renowned warrior-scholars of Central Asian Aryan stock, who carried in their veins a rich history of relentless daring and conquest. In the past the Muhiyals had ruled parts of Arabia, Afghanistan and Persia; as allies of Genghis Khan they had surged across the steppes and stormed Europe, incidentally introducing the stirrup and horse as instruments of war.

Of course, some other *brahmins* had other things to say of the Muhiyals: the Muhiyals had debased themselves by taking up the plough and the sword, they enjoyed wielding power, they had stooped to becoming mere kings. *Brahmins* were traditionally superior to kings.

'Well, king,' said Satyavan when his cousin reached the house, 'Now that we're alone for a while, I might as well tell you straight. There's trouble brewing at home.'

Raskaan tied and manoeuvred a floppy velveteen bow tie into place. He had changed quickly into an expensive brown suit which he had casually purchased the previous week in Sweden. The deep chocolate of the bow tie matched the lapels and cuffs of the coat. It was a new style, slightly outrageous. Satyavan would never have considered wearing such an outfit. He was rather handsome compared with Raskaan but he was more conservative in his tastes. He preferred to conform and be lost in a crowd. He would never have looked twice at that suit if it had been draped on a hanger but he had to admit that Raskaan wore it with a panache bordering on genius.

'You mean the Khalistan movement?' Raskaan asked. He had been dismayed and worried by the actions of the separatists in Punjab. They were trying to drive a wedge between the sikhs and the hindus. There had been a couple of cowardly, nauseating incidents. Both times a bus had been hijacked by a small band of demented extremists. The first time they had shot, in cold blood, six defenceless hindus and the second time four. The massacre of these innocents had provoked no retaliation, no upheaval. The stupid strategy had been frustrated. The fabric of unity seemed stronger than the nipping of a few rabid puppies.

'We'd better be prepared of course. We're increasing our own family's stock of guns, improving it. But, hopefully, sikhs and hindus will never fight each other. They're blood brothers. No one wants another partition. Punjab has been divided and reduced twice already, first by Pakistan, then by Haryana. Khalistan is like cutting off your nose to spite your face. No, I don't worry on that score. Indira Gandhi is clever. The extremists are few and in factions and badly led. Leave it to the *panditani* and her police. They'll mop up the fools in a few encounters as they did the Naxalites in Bengal and the secessionists in Nagaland. They can't function without a strong base among the common people and they don't have that.' Satyavan brushed his hair forward. He never used a comb. His hairstyle was unique and resembled the tonsure of a monk. The shining black strands lay in a short even fringe circling his forehead. From a distance it looked as though he were wearing a woollen cap or balaclava. He sighed, 'No, the problem is smaller, local and therefore more immediate. But if we don't nip it in the bud, it could get us embroiled with the extremists.'

Raskaan picked a couple of hairs off his cousin's coat. In passing he noticed that the blue pinstripe was fading. It needed drycleaning. The centre button stretched the fabric over the stomach. Satyavan was putting on weight. And there was a touch of grey at his temples. He must be—what?—forty-five?

Raskaan made a mental note that he would present Satyavan with a new suit. First thing next morning. Blue. The colour would show off Satyavan's light complexion and ruddy cheeks. 'Elder brother, it's not a political problem, is it? I thought you'd won your election?'

'I'm here celebrating, aren't I?' Satyavan's laugh had a gurgle to it. 'All my men are in place. We control ninety-eight villages.'

Raskaan thumped him on the shoulder. 'Well done!'

Satyavan went pale and twisted his body away, bending slightly. He stifled an involuntary curse.

Raskaan realized at once what it was. 'I'm sorry, elder brother. I had no idea it still hurts.'

'That mother-fucker wound! Each time it begins to heal, I screw it up. Tore it open again last week, wrestling.'

'At your age, elder brother, you shouldn't be—'

The affection went out of Satyavan's eyes for a split second. With a swift sweep of his foot and a reverse thrust of his arm, he unbalanced Raskaan who started to fall backwards but was caught by Satyavan before he hit the marble-tiled floor.

'Younger brother,' said Satyavan, 'the day you can catch me unguarded and throw me, I'll take your advice.'

He held Raskaan like a lover about to kiss his mistress in a ballet. There was deliberate humiliation in the mock-romantic graceful attitude. Then he gurgled with friendly laughter, his eyes narrowing at the corners. Raskaan began to laugh too. There was something faintly mongoloid in both their features when they laughed.

With a bark Jackie the Alsatian intervened, interposing his snout in Satyavan's crotch, sniffing in some mysterious doggy way to make sure that no ill will was intended.

'Now that bit of me injured would be disastrous!' said Satyavan, making light of a serious fear. Nor did he like dogs. He was careful of his own guard dog in the sprawling ancestral establishment he supervised in the village. He was watchful at any moment to kick the hound in the ribs and destroy him for infidelity.

Raskaan regained his feet and, while Satyavan was renewing a Machiavellian truce with Jackie, looked in his wallet: not enough there to support an evening at the Spielbank. He would have to stop off on the way there and take some money from Renate. Ten thousand marks should be all right.

'What happened to the fellow who shot you in the shoulder?' he asked. 'I hope you didn't give up searching for him.'

'He was killed last month, squealing like a pig in the fields. He had come back to see his father. The old fellow is dying of old age anyway. I have a feeling he will be bitten by a snake or something. He always sits too long in the same place reading the newspaper. Takes him half the day. The poison flows from him. Corrupted communism. Used to be a card-carrying party member but there was a scandal about his handling of funds. Actually he now wants control of the steel works, the carpenters, all cottage industry and the booze joints. He's trying to set up a sort of protection racket with ideological jargon. Everyone resents it. To obtain his leadership they'd have to pay him a regular subscription. He'd reap a fortune. Greedy bugger. His son was an alcoholic. Wanted free booze everyday. Didn't get it. So he took to talking against me: why did I own so many of the booze joints in the surrounding villages, etcetera. He couldn't get up the initiative to own even one. No one was stopping him. I could have shut him up with a bottle a day but it wasn't worth the price. We stopped his credit. A few days later, crazily drunk on that rotten Tarsem's booze, he took a pot shot at me, bungled it and ran. We didn't even chase him. It might have been a ploy to get me out in the darkness of the fields. We just waited. Kept a watch on his father's house. Last month we got him.' The eyes slanted again with amusement. 'Actually, the police got him. Flipped like a fish on a line when the bullet hit him, wriggling for air. The first shot hit his gullet. I was there, with a few others. Just in case they missed. The sub-inspector was strongly recommended for promotion. He's now an inspector. Good man.'

Raskaan said, 'It sounds utterly horrendous.'

'It was. But now it's over. There's peace again in the village.'

'Shall we go? I've got to stop by at the restaurant and also drop Jackie off at the Spice Bazaar.'

'Fine. By the way, I saw you eyeing my suit. Sorry it's the only one. Haven't worn it since I was here last. You know how it is at home, we don't bother with such things.'

Still the same old observant henchman of the patriarch, thought Raskaan. He doesn't miss a glance. No wonder the old man plays his hand through him. He's the most dependable, well-trained grandson of us all.

In the car, with the dog huffing like a steam-engine in the back, he said, 'What about the theft of your car? It was an attempt to belittle you, wasn't it?'

Satyavan gurgled. The instrument lights of the dial made a jigsaw puzzle of his face. 'That right-winger, Hari, was trying to show I couldn't take care of law and order. He's lost every election since his mother's dugs dried. Anyway, I take it easy with him. He's a distant relative after all.'

'Oh oh, there's a motorcycle cop. Better strap on your safety belt. It's the law here. They're very strict about that.'

'Good.' Satyavan fiddled for the catch. 'Whoever sits here is thin. I've got to loosen the whole contraption.'

Raskaan chuckled. 'You're quite astute, brother. It's always a woman who sits there. And it isn't Renate. She has her own car to drive.'

'You've given away more than I guessed.' Satyavan's gurgle expanded as though a stream had become a river.

'You eventually got your Fiat back, didn't you?'

'Naturally. Took eighteen men down to Kutch, five of them plain-clothes policemen. We didn't have to trace it. One of the gang who had stolen it was indebted to me for small favours. He wrote me a letter . . . two letters. I didn't believe the first because he hadn't signed his name. The second time he still didn't sign but he indicated who he was. There was a small, stagey shoot-out when we got there. Killed two men, picked up the car, plus fifty thousand rupees and a rifle with ammunition. The leader of the gang died in jail. The others are still there. The fellow who wrote to me collected part of the fifty thousand, a good part, as a reward. They'd fallen out, you see.'

'What about Hari? He's the one who set those dacoits after your car—'

'Actually their plan was to kill me. They'd positioned themselves on both sides of the lane. But, as luck would have it, I didn't step out that night. I cancelled the trip to Chandigarh. Mother was ill. I couldn't leave her. It saved my life. They settled for taking the car.'

'But what about Hari?' Raskaan repeated the question, not without some impatience. He was always irked by Satyavan's habit of avoiding a direct answer. Satyavan talked in order to give himself time to think. He stalked a subject, pouncing on it like prey only when he had ramified the surrounding area. He was known to be one of the most careful, and successful, fighters in the feud-riven hinterland of Punjab. He talked the way he fought, making sure of every step.

He said, 'Well, that friend of mine among the dacoits came to see me a few days ago. Amazing how quickly a man can spend reward money when he's not used to having any. He seemed to want to kill Hari. Indignation. Honour. The old vengeance bit for involving him in a gang of dacoits or whatever. I knew what he was after—more money, blood money. But I said, no, you go to Hari and beg his forgiveness for your anger. And take this money and get out of the area before someone gets you.'

They both laughed.

As Raskaan parked outside the big restaurant, he said, 'You haven't yet told me what the problem is. It must be something quite close to you.'

'To us,' nodded Satyavan.

'Then a quick drink here will help to bring it out.'

They went in, leaving Jackie to wait in the car.

5
❖❖❖

Getting it Out

The restaurant had a makeshift elegance. It was big and roomy compared with the Chai Khana. The decor relied on tastefully-selected Indian handicrafts. *Batik*, tie-and-dye, *pichwai*. Wood carvings from Kashmir. Gentle illumination over every table from long, cloth-shaded, Orissa-style suspended lights. 'They remind me of elephant phalluses,' Satyavan said. It had all changed since he was last here. Renate had taken charge of the interior decoration which had earlier consisted of cheap, flashy gewgaws, mainly plastic and chrome, and unconcealed electrical wiring. Now the subtle lighting supplemented by candles burning demurely on each table gave the whole place a rubescent atmosphere. Stepping in from the dull dark street you felt you had entered the warmth of a womb.

'The heart of a pomegranate, that's what it is,' said Satyavan. 'Please compliment Renate for me.'

'Do it yourself, elder brother. We'll be going to her as soon as you've finished your Scotch and unburdened your worry.'

But Satyavan refused to take the opening. Whatever was bothering him was not easy to talk about. He muttered, 'You should have called this place The Treasure House. It seems to be lit by the glint of jewels.'

Raskaan smiled. 'Aladdin's Cave, perhaps. Look at my forty ruffians.'

It was an apt description. The waiters, all bustle and bonhomie, as they moved from table to pantry, joked cavalierly with the subdued and somewhat intimidated clientele. Bottles of wine were plonked down as though the corks would be opened by teeth and the contents drunk in swigs. There was no concession to uniform, unless the preponderance of rolled-up sleeves and open top-buttons displaying hairy chests was considered de rigueur. Meanwhile, the ladies and gentlemen, dressed for a special evening out, gave indication by their flushed appearance and watchful manner that this was indeed a treat and they would willingly pay an exorbitant bill for it. The food came piping hot, trailing aromas and flavours. A woman turned from the endearments of her escort, the diamonds glittering in her necklace, distracted by the outsize balloon-like *kulcha* that someone at a neighbouring table had been served. People looked up from their menus helplessly—it was as good or better than going to a French restaurant and not knowing a word of culinary French. They pointed shamelessly to dishes spread before other patrons, breaking tenets learned in childhood: 'Never point at people in public, darling!' 'You must not stare!' 'Don't ask silly questions!' 'Stop sniffing the air—you're not an animal!' 'You must never comment on the eating habits of other people!' 'If you don't know which piece of cutlery to start with, wait for Mama or Papa.' They ordered by gesture and ended eating with their fingers.

As diners entered, they were politely helped out of overcoats and fur coats which were then dumped unceremoniously over the backs of their chairs. The clatter of fierce endeavour in the kitchen rode on the back of a mellifluous urdu *ghazal* and even managed mercifully to drown a screechy female voice that threaded through a tintinnabulation that might have been contrived of pots and pans. The place reeked of someone else's nostalgia and therefore was fantastic, surreal, enchanting.

'But why,' asked a tall man stepping precisely to their table, 'have you named your restaurants Chai Khana and Mai Khana? It is so confusing! My girl is not here. She must have gone to the other place.'

'*Mein Herr,*' said Raskaan nonchalantly, 'if she can make such a mistake, then you would do well to mistake another woman for your own. Help yourself.' This with an extravagant gesture that covered the restaurant. 'And carry on.'

'Impossible!' The man seemed about to explode. Then the tension travelled downwards and escaped in a click of the heels. 'I am Schliemacher. If she should come, please tell her I waited fift-ee-ee-en minutes and have gone. I am indeed sorry to have reserved a table and kept it when others are waiting to sit down and eat. It is deeply embarrassing. Once again, I apologize.'

'No need, Herr Schliemacher. Please join us. One of my men will telephone the Chai Khana to enquire.'

'*Danke, aber das geht nicht!* Always, always, she is making us late. I have tickets for the theatre and the *Schauspielhaus* is miles away. We can neither eat nor go there. The evening is spoilt, finished, *ist ruiniert, hin*!'

'A true Prussian does not easily surrender hope,' said Raskaan with such flair that it sounded like a proverb.

The man's face cracked open in a smile. 'How do you know I am Prussian?'

'Ah, you ask a jeweller how he knows a jewel.'

Schliemacher sat down with neat precision.

'My elder brother,' said Raskaan.

'Your real brother?' Schliemacher raised his eyebrows, bringing piercing blue eyes out of their caves. 'I only ask because my Indian friends tell me that a cousin is also treated as a brother in India.'

'Real brother,' said Raskaan to save further explanation. Then with Schliemacher's help he rapidly put together a message to be relayed to the Chai Khana. 'Herr Schliemacher is waiting for Fraülein von Brauer at the Mai Khana, the other Indian restaurant.'

While a waiter made the call, Raskaan explained to Schliemacher that Mai Khana signified a tavern or a place where drink and food may be obtained.

'But why the rhyme—Chai Khana, Mai Khana?'

Raskaan shrugged.

Satyavan said, 'Maybe he is a poet. You see, his mother named him after a famous poet who wrote in a dialect called Brij Bhasha. That Raskaan was a muslim but he wrote the most exquisite verses on the hindu god, Krishna. Some say he was a convert to hinduism. Others say he used the pen name Raskaan, meaning one who has an ear for the essence, but his real name was Rais Khan, which is a muslim name meaning a noble person.'

'Well, our Herr Raskaan,' said Schliemacher attempting a joke, 'is both. He has an ear for the essence and is a noble person.' He went off into a high-pitched, staccato, whinnying laugh.

The waiter returned to say that there was no Fraülein von Brauer at the Chai Khana.

Schliemacher pursed his lips like the top of an orange and nodded. When the waiter had gone he accepted a Scotch-on-the-rocks and petulantly showed them a couple of nude photographs of the missing Fraülein.

'Your profession? You are a photographer?' asked Raskaan.

'No, no, my hobby. She is beautiful, *nein*?'

They admired the breasts, the figure, the pose, the lighting. 'But maybe she is angry with me,' Schliemacher said. 'Yesterday, I burnt her here on her thigh with a cigarette. She is naughty, naughty. She bite me, I burn her.'

Schliemacher's second drink came automatically. He was sitting with Raskaan and his elder brother whom each one of the waiters had greeted dutifully. An empty glass would be an affront to the host's generosity.

Schliemacher's chin twitched as he drained his glass, leaned forward and murmured, for some reason in French, '*Avec votre permission.*' He held the photographs in the flame of the candle. They curled and burned quickly. He let the remains fall meticulously into an ashtray.

Satyavan covered his own glass with a hand as a waiter came up. He cleared his throat and said to Schliemacher, 'How can you destroy what you love?'

'My wife would not understand. I return to Vienna tomorrow.'

He tried to pay for the drinks, but was not allowed to do so. He was about to get up when he saw that his glass was full. He swallowed the contents. For a moment he looked as if he had downed sandpaper. His accent slurred slightly as he stood up. 'Chentlemen, *mit dis* I must leave you that Europe is again in danger of paying for the foolishness of war. In my opinion, the Americans and the Russians must stock their Cruise missiles on artificial islands in the ocean not on land where people are endangered by retaliation. We are living on the brink. No one understands. But here in Berlin, where you have the Checkpoint Charlie under your nose, you can feel the tension. The cold war has divided families here but after a real war with nuclear missiles there will be no families left. It is not too late to allow love to enter our thinking. Love, which you chentlemen of the east know is the only grace in our lives. Mahatma Gandhi was a great man, a great man. "How will you meet the atom bomb?" he was asked. He answered, "With a prayer!" That was the answer.'

Raskaan signalled discreetly to a waiter who came and stood behind Schliemacher's chair and whispered politely, 'Goodnight, sir.'

Schliemacher leaned forward and tapped the top of the table with a finger. 'But you are yourselves making the atomic explosions in India!'

Satyavan murmured, 'Implosions.'

'What?'

'Implosions not explosions. Implosions for peaceful purposes. Nuclear energy for development.'

'Ha! Words. But you have the atomic capability. You have the bomb. Why?'

Satyavan sighed and said, 'Perhaps because, after all, it was a bullet that killed Mahatma Gandhi.'

For a few seconds Schliemacher nodded his head slowly. Then he straightened up, clicked his heels, gave a half-bow, '*Wiedersehn*,' and was gone.

Satyavan pushed back his chair. 'Come on, king, let's move. What I have to tell you can wait till later tonight.'

'Oh no,' said Raskaan rising. 'I'm curious and worried. You tell me in the car.'

But before they could leave, Raskaan was requested by a waiter to soothe an irate lady. He followed the waiter.

A family of three children and a rotund, balding husband sat grimly silent as the lady, in a sequined Dior sheathe, held up a piece of meat on a fork. '*Was ist das?*'

'I should think it's obvious, madam, that it is a piece of meat.' Raskaan smiled benignly.

'But I am a vegetarian!' She almost screamed. A ripple of curiosity stirred the neighbouring tables to attention.

Raskaan berated the waiter. Then assured her that such a mistake would never recur.

'It has touched my lips,' she cried. 'And I had taken a vow in the name of Krishnamurti.' She ran a hand over her mouth so that part of her lipstick came away.

'Krishnamurti is a fine philosopher. I have attended some of his lectures myself.'

'Then you know what disgust I feel!' she persisted. Somewhere, somehow she had to punish him or someone for this baulking of her will and intention.

'No need for disgust, madam.'

'What do you mean? No need for disgust. I feel sick.'

'Look at it philosophically, as perhaps a great guru might. All life is interrelated. We all know that even flowers, vegetables and grass scream when they are cut. Life animates the universe, the cosmos, everything.'

'Yes, yes,' she nodded.

'The least a sensitive person can do is become vegetarian.'

'Ah so. You are a vegetarian too?'

'I'm afraid I'm not among the sensitive, and one bit of

knowledge bothers me—that, after all, meat is only grass in another form.'

'In a way perhaps, but—'

'When meat touches my lips I say it is only one form of life converted into another that is supporting mine.'

'Of course, but—'

'Now look at your children, madam. Growing up healthy and strong without the need of meat. As tall as giraffes, as wise as elephants, as magnificent as horses. All vegetarian animals.' The woman glowed. Raskaan lowered his voice so that a couple at the adjoining table craned slightly to hear. 'But you know, madam, a cousin of mine once had occasion to discuss this subject with no less a person than Mary Lutyens, the famous biographer of Krishnamurti, and you know what she said?'

The lady shook her head. The family were intrigued.

'She is a vegetarian herself, mind you, this daughter of the great Lutyens who built New Delhi. She said, with sadness and regret, "But do you notice that in the animal kingdom the vegetarians are all eaten by the non-vegetarians?" ' Raskaan paused dramatically. Then said with wonderment, 'The royal lion, the mighty tiger, the swift cheetah.' Again he waited but now he was beaming at the children. 'What lovely children you have, madam!'

'Thank you.' It was no more than a whisper. Her face was creased in uncertainty.

He bowed and left them thinking but pacified.

'No one can say you don't work hard,' said Satyavan to him as the Manager of the restaurant saw them to the door.

When they went up to the parked Rolls, they received a shock. Jackie was giving a low, almost inaudible snarl. His jaws were firmly round the neck of a man sitting in the driving seat. The man was rigid with fear. No noise escaped him but his eyes bulged.

Raskaan opened the door but made no move to free the man. He switched on the roof light, examined the grizzled visage, the pleading green eyes rheumy with cold, the battered felt hat that had fallen and lay propped against the steering wheel and the man's belly.

He turned to Satyavan. 'I had Jackie trained for defence against hijack. It was Renate's suggestion. She often has to carry large sums home in the van. Banks don't stay open at night. We have no choice. Of course she carries a pistol in her handbag but . . . a dog in the back is sometimes better. See how he has been taught to grip the neck, not the wrist or the collar? Terrible. These Germans are so efficient and thorough. I wouldn't have thought of it but the trainer . . . ex-Gestapo, I'm sure.'

'Stop joking and relieve him,' said Satyavan. 'He might have a heart attack.'

'Not Schneider,' said Raskaan lapsing into Punjabi. 'Schneider is the world's most impervious human being. Nothing soaks into him but the strongest alcohol, the hardest stick and the longest prick. He's been at this game for years. Third time he's tried to steal. Twice it was the solid gold emblem on the bonnet. Now he thought he'd take the car itself. Schneider is also the unluckiest man in the world. If you fixed a casino table for him, he'd choose that moment to play Russian roulette.'

He freed Schneider, who shot off with a rolling, bobbing gait. A few yards down the street, Schneider stopped under a lamppost, rubbed his neck, looked at his hand to reassure himself that the dog had not drawn blood, then he spat on the ground and, shaking a fist, shouted, 'Bloody Indian! Cocky *Gastarbeiter*! Death to all *Gastarbeiter*!'

Jackie barked.

Raskaan reached into the car. Seeing the movement, Schneider turned to flee but he stopped when Raskaan called out, 'Hey, you forgot your hat! Here.'

Raskaan had the green felt hat in his hand. Now he drew a currency note from his pocket and stuck it in the hatband. Then he sent the hat spinning through the air to Schneider who suddenly stretched himself straight, caught it and collapsed again into his accustomed posture.

Schneider drooled as he examined the note and slipped it carefully into his pocket. Putting on his hat, he muttered, 'Scum of the earth. Parasites. *Gastarbeiter*.' Now he raised his voice. 'But your money won't save you, Raskaan. I've known you when we shared the same Salvation Army dormitory. I've seen your tricks—those shoes of the maharaja, that ticketless tour on the trains, the horse-carriage for weddings. I know how you've done it. You're a con man and you'll end up where you began— bankrupt. You can't pay me to like you. I'm not one of your whores. I'll take your money and drink to your destruction.'

He ranted on as the Rolls pulled away from the kerb.

In the car, Satyavan said, 'It has to do with Balbir.'

Raskaan's foot left the accelerator. For a second he thought he had stopped breathing. If anything had happened to his young brother, Balbir, he would not only not forgive the man who had done it, he would never be able to forgive himself. Raskaan had years ago abandoned everything to escape abroad: he was semi-literate, half-schooled, but he had educated himself in the ways of the world and had graduated to wealth, which he now dispensed generously to those he had left hostage to the old traditions and customs of the village. Balbir was prisoner while Raskaan was free, at least that is how Balbir looked at it. And Raskaan made every effort to persuade Balbir to remain prisoner. He told him of the hardships he had faced, the education he had foregone; of course, he meant it. He could be nothing but sincere with his own brother. And yet it bothered him to think that it might not be the whole truth.

So Balbir had stayed, and gone to an excellent school and a fine university. Raskaan had made sure that Balbir 'received only the best, from the best, among the best.' With that phrase, which he thought of as appropriately Lincolnesque without parody, he had steered the family to granting Balbir what he regretted not having himself. The family could afford it, they were still rich land-owners but they were also peasants, they did not have an awareness of the need for a good education; Raskaan had countered that with all the weight of his worldly success.

Now, instead of being grateful and staying put in the village, Balbir wanted to get away. It was an old refrain and nobody listened to it much. But each time Balbir was thwarted, he created problems. It was as if his mind was so volatile that he needed to apply it in peculiar ways.

There had been the escapade phase when Balbir had run away from school and then from the village. There had been the ideological phase when he had declared himself a Naxalite and hidden other juvenile delinquents in the family fields. There had been the idealistic phase when he had wanted to shift from college to an agricultural university so that he could help improve the ancestral environment. And most recently, they had seen the start of what seemed to be outright rebellion against the patriarch. This was worse than criminal; it was callous disdain of all that was dear to the family.

'What now?' Raskaan's voice had a note of exasperation. It was partly annoyance with himself. He knew that he too had not behaved particularly considerately in the early stages of his own break towards liberty. The family had seen that as a dash towards licence. But his gamble had paid off. His early mistakes were condoned. He was a success, a contributor of substantial sums to the family fund, he visited India often, he participated in the family's concerns, he had reinstated himself magnificently. That place within the structure of insular antiquated values had cost him a few obvious lies. Everyone knew they were lies. For instance, it was obvious that in order to stay on and work legally in West Germany he had married a German national—Renate. Yet he denied it to the family, speaking of her as his secretary. Nevertheless, whenever they visited the village, they were given one room and no one questioned his intimacy with his secretary. She was spoken of as his friend. So there were other lies; the web of illusion served reality.

At the same time, Raskaan, being ten years older than Balbir, was expected to behave like a surrogate father; their father, Khushi Ram, had too much else to do, what with the land and the cattle and the farming. Furthermore, there was no real communication between Balbir and Khushi Ram. Khushi Ram was like a leftover from another century.

'Don't worry,' said Satyavan, 'I think we can handle it easily enough. I just thought I'd better alert you—in case Balbir or Tarsem gets in touch with you.'

'Tarsem? You mean, Balbir has got himself mixed up with Tarsem and his gang?'

Satyavan nodded. 'You know Tarsem's methods. Every person who goes to him for help ends up a fish on his hook.'

Raskaan stopped at a traffic light. He offered Satyavan a cigarette.

'Never smoked yet.'

Raskaan nodded and lit one himself. 'How is Balbir involved? Tarsem has many rackets going—cement on the black market, passports, guns, opium.'

'Balbir is trying to get fake papers. He wants to migrate. Tarsem will accept payment in either cash or kind.'

'What do you mean kind?'

The light had turned green; horns blared behind them. Raskaan lowered his glass and, sticking his head out, yelled in German. 'Impatient buggers! Can't you give a man some time?' He sighed, 'These Huns.' Then he added, 'But they don't mean any harm . . . I think.' Just for fun, he put the car into reverse and let it go back a bit. There were loud imprecations and exclamations. Raskaan laughed and drove forward. He had never got over his childlike yen for mischief.

Satyavan said, 'Balbir actually came and asked me for four revolvers or one LMG.'

Raskaan braked so hard that the car behind screeched to avoid a collision. Raskaan ignored the man who stared and drove away shaking his head.

'What does he want a Light Machine Gun for?'

'He wouldn't tell me but, of course, I checked around and found out. It was for Tarsem. As payment. You see, Balbir has no money. We've made sure of that. Tarsem has his own setup for gun-running but he can't easily lay hands on sophisticated modern weapons. He knows we have the resources.'

'But Tarsem—'

'He's one of the gun-runners for the extremists.'

'What!' The Rolls slowed but glided along.

Satyavan nodded. 'He's only concerned with the money. He couldn't care one way or the other about Khalistan. He's really on the look out for weapons with a high rate of fire. He's got orders for LMGs, MMGs, AK47s, Kalishnikovs, RPGs—'

'RPG? What's that?'

Satyavan's gurgle sounded sardonic. 'You don't even know what that is, and you know your light weapons. It just goes to show the kind of firepower they are after. An RPG is a rocket-propelling gun. They also want anti-tank guns. Mortars. They'd go for an anti-aircraft gun if it could be brought in piecemeal.'

'Good heavens! What are they preparing for—war?'

'At minimum, they hope to provoke a civil war. Karnail Singh is my man in the Tarsem setup. He won't live long if it gets out that he's mouthing on Tarsem.'

'I remember him. Karnailleya the trucker. How did he get into this? He's a sensible fellow.'

'They hired his trucks. He doesn't mind a bit of smuggling once in a while. But when he found that his trucks were carrying crates of explosives and arms, he became nervous. He loves India. He doesn't want to be instrumental in breaking it up. Also, the whole thing was getting too deep for him. He can't fathom who is behind it all. It could be just big money, big arms dealers. It could be Pakistan or the CIA. It could even be China.'

'Bloody hell!'

'Karnailleya is a brave man but he doesn't want to go to the police. He doesn't trust the police.'

'What does that mean?'

'He thinks there are some active supporters of the extremists within the police force. In fact he knows it because—'

The car telephone buzzed. Raskaan spoke into the mouth-piece. 'Ja?'

'You've got Jackie with you?' It was Renate, speaking in German.

'Oh damn! I forgot all about dropping off the dog and collecting some money from the Spice Bazaar. Sorry, darling, could you send someone in the van? I was so deep in conversation with elder brother that—'

'I know,' said the metallic voice over the phone, 'you were probably driving straight to the Spielbank.'

'You're right as always, sweetheart.'

'OK, you park outside the Spielbank and I'll send the van to you.'

'Have you counted the collection for the day?'

'Ja.'

'Can you spare ten thousand?'

'Ten thou—!'

'Elder brother isn't here everyday.'

'Of course.'

'She's a pet,' said Raskaan in Punjabi as he replaced the receiver.

Satyavan said carefully, 'She's just right for you.' What he meant was that he thought her a good wife.

Raskaan shrugged. 'It's a good arrangement.'

Again the lie. Satyavan wondered why he needed to do that. As they drew up outside the casino, the doorman stepped forward with an open umbrella in his hand. It had begun to drizzle.

'No, thank you, Gunter,' said Raskaan in German. 'We'll wait here awhile.'

The doorman saluted and withdrew.

Raskaan switched on some music. His taste was atrocious. A syrupy *ghazal* sprang from the cassette-player.

He said, 'I worry a great deal about all of you in Punjab. There's more and more terrorism.'

Satyavan continued looking at the glittering lights under the awning of the casino and the chandeliers in the plush lobby. He told himself he was going to enjoy himself. A man can't live in constant tension—he would snap. He owed it to the impending crisis to relax now; being refreshed was part of the preparation for action.

'The trouble is,' muttered Satyavan, 'they're bringing religion into politics and guns into religion. The extremists are terroriz-ing the average sikh. The moderates are losing their grip on the situation. The vast majority is being intimidated by small cliques who've entered some *gurdwaras* as pilgrims, as worshippers, and then by a show of sophisticated arms frightened the others into silence or submission.'

'It's unbelievable!'

'But it's happening. Tarsem's last consignment of rifles and rapid-firing carbines went into the Golden Temple.'

'The Golden Temple—in Amritsar?'

'There is only one like it in the world. Karnail Singh swears his man drove straight up to the main doorway. The stuff was unloaded and carried in.'

'That's ridiculous! Surely, the place has been under police observation ever since the Deputy Inspector General of Police was shot to death inside the temple?'

Satyavan said, 'Of course.' Then he heaved a deep sigh. 'There are about seven hundred people living inside the Golden Temple complex. Some genuine pilgrims, some terrorists, some politicians, a few priests, also some thugs, *goondas*, wanted criminals and smugglers.'

Raskaan couldn't help a sneer as he muttered sarcastically. 'God may not discriminate among his motley creatures but surely the law does. Why don't the police go in and clean up the place?'

Satyavan burbled into a chilling laugh in the dim light. 'Who would dare go in against such modern weapons? The terrorists have not only shot policemen and specific officers but wiped out entire families one by one systematically.'

'So the guns go in and the murderers come out as they please?'

'Not quite. There is a modicum of restraint.'

'But you said the last consignment was driven right up to the—'

Satyavan smiled. 'All those people have to be fed. Bags of wheat, rice, provisions, have to go in. Furthermore, hundreds of visitors eat daily at the *langar*. It is perhaps the biggest free feeding centre in the world. The truck was carrying foodstuff and the guns were inside some of those bags.'

'I don't like it.'

'Nor do many sikhs. But they're intimidated, scared to speak out. The brave ones who do are mercilessly gunned down. The Golden Temple is becoming a hideout of assassins and smugglers.'

Raskaan sighed. Then laughed and said, 'Maybe we should

go in too. After all, depending on your point of view, we might also fit that description.'

Satyavan's low laugh was like the gentle rumbling of a *hookah*. After a moment he said carefully, 'There's another matter, the one I really want to discuss with you. Perhaps you've guessed what it is. After all, I've been using your sources in Europe these last two years. You must've realized—'

'Brother, if you tell me to realize something, I will. If you don't, I won't.'

Satyavan burst out laughing. But he sobered quickly. 'Look, king, we all know there's a whole international network behind the troubles in Punjab. The only way to defeat it is to pool all our strengths and put everything at the disposal of . . . I think we shouldn't talk about it now. Not in the car. Not in there either. Later, tomorrow perhaps, we could go out for a walk in some park and have our chat.'

Raskaan was incredulous. 'You mean, with all your other activities and concerns, you've gone and got yourself involved in helping the Indian intelli—'

'We'll talk tomorrow,' said Satyavan sharply. 'It's more dangerous than you know. I didn't want to startle you, that's all. I'm using many of your links, your connections. I just thought it fair to give you some inkling, prepare you for our discussion. Now, let's drop the subject.'

'Yes, brother,' said Raskaan.

Jackie sat up in the back seat and gave a couple of high-pitched, welcoming barks.

'He recognizes the sound of the van.'

Sure enough, the little van rattled round the corner and drew up alongside.

Jackie's tail thumped the upholstery. Renate was driving the van herself. Now Jackie was whining to be let out.

'OK, OK,' chuckled Raskaan. 'I know whose company you prefer.'

He opened the door for the dog. Jackie sniffed at the rear wheel of the van, watered it and got in on the front seat beside Renate.

Renate pushed back her wire-rimmed spectacles. Her eyes were innocent, wide, refracted bigger by the thick lenses. She was dressed in jeans and a grocer's overalls. She handed Raskaan a brown envelope and smiled at Satyavan. 'Have a good time,' she said in English.

Satyavan nodded, grinned, 'Thank you . . . ' then added, '. . .

sister.' He knew it sounded awkward. He couldn't openly call her sister-in-law because of the continuing lie. And yet he wanted to compliment her by accepting her as a relative. The highest compliment was to make someone part of the family.

She blushed, pushed the floor-shift gear into first and the van rattled away just as the doorman stepped up again with the umbrella.

Raskaan said in German, 'Gunter, this is my elder brother.'

Gunter went round to the other side, sheltered Satyavan across and returned for Raskaan. He handed the keys of the car to the doorman. 'Take it down to the basement garage.'

Going up in the lift, Raskaan said, 'Elder brother, here's five thousand marks to start with. If you run out just let me know, my credit is good here.'

Satyavan hesitated, then said, 'Put it on my account. You shouldn't pay for my vices.'

Raskaan laughed. 'The best presents are always luxuries. A gift of essentials is always resented.'

'No wonder you're such a cafeteria prophet here. You turn everything into a saying. Anyway, you're younger than I am. It is I who should pay for the evening.'

'Elder brother, this is my adopted country. You are my guest here.'

The man at the desk welcomed Raskaan, glanced at Satyavan's passport, checked the name against a list, gave him a *Tageskarte* and waved them in.

Raskaan said, 'They've got a small blacklist. It's embarrassing to be on it but not dangerous. This place is government-run. But in England and America, many of the casinos are mafia-controlled. Video cameras watch you from the moment you enter. If you're a big player, they wine and dine you as much as you like. They'll foot the bill for your parties, fly you to other casinos, offer you free gambling cruises on luxury liners. But if you cheat on them, they'll go for you by the short and curlies. A few of us are gold card holders.'

He looked in his wallet, sifted between various credit cards and pulled out one with a thin strip of gold at the base. 'They say you can count the gold card holders of the world on the fingers of your hands: mainly Arab sheikhs, assorted millionaires. No one expects an Indian to have one. I keep being mistaken for a left-over maharaja or an Arab sultan. For all their practicality, westerners are incurable romantics. But we have at least one other cousin who is a gold card holder.'

Satyavan said, 'The bar is deserted.'

'It's still early. Later the winners will celebrate and the losers will be there hoping to be offered a drink. Blackjack, poker, roulette.' He pointed to various tables, all thronged by avid players. It was like a beehive. The buzz and murmur were punctuated by the sharp call of croupiers and the clatter of dice and the rake of the stick as it separated or gathered plastic chips on the baize. The place was ablaze with activity.

'Roulette,' said Satyavan. 'We'll begin there. You must tell me what to do. You're the veteran in this sort of thing.'

'Watch how the table is going first.'

But Satyavan was impatient. The moment some of his money had been changed for chips, he plunked a few down on a couple of numbers. He lost. And lost again. And again.

Raskaan wandered about and returned. Then he covered the table by halves, the chips straddling the dividing lines and he placed a biggish pile on a colour—red. He won on a number and he won on the red.

The croupier looked at him, smiled, exchanged a greeting.

Raskaan usually waited till the others' chips were down before placing his bets, sometimes in the very nick of the croupier's closing call.

'Elder brother,' he muttered, 'you notice I always hedge my bet with a colour. That's a fifty-fifty alternative, a safe one. It may be dull but it's sure. Then I ravage the numbers.'

Suddenly there was a subdued roar of approval from the men and women round the oblong table. Number nine which carried a substantial pile had come in. The observer in his high chair looked at Raskaan and nodded. The croupier's fingers worked deftly as he counted out a minor bonanza of multi-coloured chips and swung the lot into position then used the stick to push it all to Raskaan.

Raskaan slid a small pile back to the croupier. A big winning entitled the croupier to a traditional tip.

Now the players cunningly waited for Raskaan to place his bets. In this temple of chance and in the uncertainty of luck it was best to follow the one on whom Goddess Fortune smiled. They were all biding their time, watching the tubby easterner who was now calmly pocketing his dues.

Speaking Punjabi, Raskaan murmured, 'In Reno, they give you metal chips for low denominations. As you go up the scale, you get plastic and finally wood. There is a sound psychological reason for that. After a while you're playing with fifty dollar chips and thinking of them as just so much wood.'

He let two spins of the wheel go by, disappointing those who were waiting for him. Then he played. He covered the cloth.

There were a number of pay-outs. A number of hands reached for their winnings. Before Raskaan could collect his, a stubby-fingered hand swept up the small mound and moved away. He was a tall man with a broad back dressed in a blue serge suit. They couldn't see his face, only the back of his head. His wavy ginger-blonde hair betrayed nothing as he joined the crowd at the adjoining table.

'Hey,' whispered Satyavan, 'that was your winning, younger brother.'

'I thought so too.'

'I'm sure of it. I saw you cover number sixteen.'

'Hm. I'll tell the croupier and submit it to the observer.'

'Let me catch that thief.'

Before Raskaan could prevent him, Satyavan had thumped the big man on his shoulder. He turned round, his blue eyes uncomprehending, the chips still in his hand. The man seemed not to understand English. He answered with peculiar choking, gagging sounds.

Satyavan, by ferocity and sign language, communicated his meaning. The man shrugged. Satyavan pulled him back to the table where Raskaan had explained the accusation to the croupier and the observer. They nodded and spoke to the man. The man made himself out to be deaf and dumb. Perhaps he was. They left the chips with him. He wandered off. From now on, he would be watched by other staff of the casino.

Play recommenced. After a while, Raskaan's objection was sustained; he was given chips in compensation for those that had been swiped. Perhaps there was a hidden video camera some-where and they had run through a replay of that game.

Satyavan lost the five thousand marks he had started with, distributing the amount over the various tables. Raskaan lost a few times but, overall, emerged with a profit of twenty-eight thousand marks. 'Let's have a drink,' he said.

Over the whisky, he muttered, 'Now that woman there, the old one with the dragon brooch and the flat shoes—she's playing with her pension, poor thing. It's a habit. I despise it. She's going to end up begging. That young man there with the shaved neck, he's a student with a greedy girlfriend. I know them. That old man there in the wheelchair—'

'He really looks half-dead. His suit is even more worn than mine.'

'Uhhuh,' Raskaan nodded. 'But he's a multi-millionaire. And a miser. He plays to try out systems that he buys. They think he's a sucker for the right song. But he's clever. Even that young woman near him will get nothing beyond her salary; she's his nurse. That fellow on the barstool is waiting to be paid. Now he's drinking to keep his hopes up. But the old man has never yet coughed up for a system that does not work absolutely. There's no such thing. The young man will get a night's drinks and the contempt of the old man and perhaps a condolence kiss from the nurse.'

Satyavan said, 'I lost it all. Nearly twenty thousand rupees worth of Deutsche Mark.'

'No, elder brother. We've come out on top.'

'You have.'

'Together, we have.'

Raskaan brought out a fistful of plastic counters and shoved them into Satyavan's pocket. 'A few more rounds, then we go.'

The establishment they went to later was elegant and intimate. Soft music, smooth service, subdued lighting. Tables laid for dinner. A couple at one table, a group of four at another. It looked like an expensive late-night restaurant.

They selected a table. The big Turk behind the bar sent them a bottle of champagne in a bucket of ice. The head waiter came to take their order.

'*Nein, nein,*' said Raskaan, 'we cannot order till we have asked the ladies.'

'You are expecting them, sir?'

'Indeed.'

'I am sure they will be here shortly.' The waiter placed a matchbox-sized object on the table. 'If you would be so good as to press the button when the ladies you are expecting arrive . . .' He bowed and withdrew.

Satyavan looked at the buzzer.

'It's wireless,' said Raskaan. 'It sets off a beep in the waiter's breast-pocket. He then shows the women to our table. It's quite ingenious. Saves them having to pay the police or get a licence. Furthermore, some quite respectable women come here for an evening's lark. The management doesn't object. They just add a percentage to the bill for dinner. And, of course, they serve a very expensive meal.'

'Where do you take the women?'

'Wherever they suggest. Sometimes to their flats or to a hotel. For very special clients, the management permits the use of a rest room at the back. But they prefer not to. It's risky, in case of a raid. Also, they like to think that each woman is free to push off after a good meal. It can happen. Sometimes, a woman gives a customer the brush-off.' Then he added quickly, 'That can't happen to us. The management is indebted to me. But theoretically it's just a place that offers company. It doesn't promise a screw. You've got to work for that.'

'Younger brother, you know I don't screw.'

'What!' Raskaan nearly choked on the champagne he was sipping.

Satyavan didn't know how to explain. Raskaan wouldn't hear any excuse. He said, 'You mean, every time so far that I've shoved you into a room with a woman, you've sat and had a chat?'

'Or slept.'

'Good God!'

The women were coming in now, at short intervals. They were nearly all slender. Only one had a jaded appearance. They were without exception smartly dressed.

'I love female company,' said Satyavan. 'But I don't screw.'

'For company's sake then, elder brother, tell me when to buzz.'

'If that will please you.'

'It will.'

The women were sailing in from an inner room and moving across to what might have been a cloakroom.

Just then the front door opened and a middle-aged blonde entered, looked around, studied the various tables, adjusted her sight to the dim light and, removing her wrap, went to the bar and ordered a Martini.

'She's not a regular,' said Raskaan. 'Probably a disappointed housewife. Or a divorcee without a lover. Shall I buzz?'

Satyavan emptied his champagne glass. 'She looks motherly.'

'I like motherly women, don't you?'

Satyavan was silent.

'Look at those podgy arms, that soft face, those baby lips. She'd be a comforting fuck.' He looked at Satyavan and chuckled. 'Maybe your trouble is that—'

Satyavan glared, his voice dropping to a hiss, 'I do have a mother.'

'Oh boy!' Raskaan drew back involuntarily.

'I'm sorry,' said Satyavan, 'I'm just tense with ... with the situation at home.'

Raskaan nodded understandingly.

Now, from the inner room, a petite, slant-eyed woman came trippingly in.

Raskaan nudged Satyavan. 'Look at that beauty. Not more than nineteen. What do you think she is? Korean? More probably Thai.'

'She could be Burmese.'

'I've never had a Chinese. Do you think she's Chinese?'

Raskaan pressed the button. The corresponding beep was inaudible where they sat but the waiter moved quickly to the young woman and ushered her to the table. She bowed and gave them a smile and to their 'Good evening' responded with a deferential, nasal 'Excuse preese, you spik Ingrish. My Ingrish not so good, *non*?'

'I speak German,' said Raskaan, 'but we'll speak English for my brother here. Do sit down.'

'*Hai*!' she giggled and sat down.

'Sweet,' whispered Raskaan.

'I am Japanese. And you are,' she settled herself as though she were at a tea party, 'Arab, *non*?'

'No,' said Raskaan. 'Indian.'

'Aa-ah!' she moved her head up and down. Then she giggled and said, 'Kamasutra.'

Both of them burst out laughing. She seemed bewildered. 'Excuse preese, I make mistake?'

'No, no, you make good joke,' said Satyavan.

Just then the outer door opened and a slim, slightly top-heavy redhead came in. She was smoking a cigarette in a holder and was obviously tipsy.

Raskaan paused in the act of pouring champagne into the Japanese girl's glass. 'Wah!' he said softly, appraising the newcomer. At the two other tables that were occupied, conversation had stopped. In the dimness Raskaan was aware that the couple in the corner had disengaged; the man had withdrawn his hand from inside his companion's blouse.

Raskaan looked at Satyavan and said, '*Kya cheese hai*! I've seen her somewhere.'

The woman was looking about her uncertainly. The head waiter went up, politely shaking hands with himself.

The woman said in a husky, almost tear-filled voice, 'Can I get some food here? It's not too late?'

The head waiter seemed a little startled but he appeared to have recognized her. 'But, of course, Fraulein von Brauer.'

The lady dropped her car keys. The waiter picked them up. 'She is the actress, you know. Ingrid von Brauer.' The little Japanese was thrilled. 'I have seen all her movies, preese.'

'I haven't,' said Satyavan. 'I've never seen a German film. And yet I feel I've seen her before.'

Helpfully, the Japanese girl said, 'Maybe her photograph. She is in all the magazines.'

Raskaan snapped his fingers. 'That's it! We've seen her photograph, elder brother. Earlier this evening. She's the Prussian's girlfriend. You remember that man—Schliemacher.'

'Of course!' said Satyavan.

Raskaan pressed the buzzer and exclaimed, 'Now I'm sure, God, You are on my side after all!'

Satyavan laughed.

The head waiter looked as if a pin had been stuck into him. He turned and glanced at Raskaan and shrugged. Raskaan waved, beckoning him to bring her to the table. But she was already moving to an unoccupied one. The waiter was out of his depth.

Raskaan rose and went across in his best hotelier manner. In German, he intoned, 'Compliments of the management, madam, but they tell me that all the tables are either reserved or closed for the night.'

'Oh.' She was nearer to tears than ever before.

'But it so happens, madam, that we have kept a place for you with us. We were expecting you.'

'Expecting me? How so? I have never been here before. I did not know I was coming here.'

'Ah, but I knew. You see I have—how do you say it in German—mystic vision?'

'Ja, ja. But I do not believe you. You are a funny man.'

'So I will make you laugh. You need to laugh. Otherwise you will drown in your tears.' She sighed but was not to be taken in. She turned as though to leave. Raskaan said, 'Is the burn on your thigh hurting you much?'

She stopped. And turned slowly to face Raskaan. She sounded almost frightened. 'How do you know?'

But Raskaan had a faraway look. He seemed to be drawing ideas out of some mystical lucky dip. 'It was not an accident. No. It was deliberate. You were burned by a thin, soft object. Not a rod, not a flame, yes, I have it—it was a cigarette!'

'Amazing!' she gasped in her hushed, husky voice.

'Fraulein Ingrid von Brauer, I have never seen your films, but I know more about you than most people.'

Suddenly she gritted out bitterly, 'I would like to die.'

'No,' said Raskaan firmly. 'You will not die for a long time yet.'

'You think so?' she was anxious.

'I know that to be so,' he said. And with his hand on her arm, he guided her to the table. 'Come, I will tell you more.'

Fifteen minutes later he had her laughing.

That night Raskaan made love to both women in the actress's flat.

Satyavan slept in a spare room, tossing about and worrying about events that were shaping five thousand miles away in the north of India, in Punjab. Most particularly and immediately he was naturally worried about Balbir.

6

♦♦♦

Smugglers and Searchers

In Punjab, some others were worrying about Balbir but for entirely different reasons.

He was due to arrive any minute for the meeting at Tarsem's *chabara*.

'I don't like it,' said Karnail Singh the trucker, playing with the waxed ends of his moustache. 'You shouldn't involve the boy. The Chibber family is powerful. You wouldn't be able to step within forty miles of here if anything went wrong.'

'Nothing will go wrong.' Tarsem poured himself another 'Patiala peg' of country liquor. 'You know that American fellow from the Anandpur Sahib *gurdwara* said we should tap our own resources. Well, Balbir is a potential resource.'

'That American fellow Bob is a CIA agent.'

'Don't be silly. CIA agents don't make themselves obvious. All those *whiteys*, families and all, dressing like sikhs and living off the free food and lodging. They're just hippies. Bob is only interested in drugs.'

'He may be using us.' Karnail Singh tattooed thoughtfully on the butt of the .32 repeater rifle in his lap.

'Of course he's using us! For cocaine, heroin, ganja and opium. Small, safe quantities from Nepal and Pakistan.'

'He's never told us what he does with the stuff.'

'You're too suspicious. It's obvious. He's a middleman. His hippie chain retails some of it in Goa. He's got links with the locals there. Remember that midget with muscles and piercing eyes? You know who I mean, the fellow with wavy hair and the thin moustache—?'

'Shiv Kumar.'

Tarsem made a derisive sound with his blubbery lips. 'Stupid of him to choose a name like that. I could tell he was an Indian Christian, a Goan. Anyway, he came the first time we delivered. He'd come to check the stuff was genuine. Probably a little gangster from Calangute Beach. I think most of the stuff is smuggled out by sea from Goa. The land routes are blocked. The Iran-Iraq war is on. Afghanistan is in Russian hands. Turkey is severe with its penalties. So India is the only route out and Bombay's bigtime types control the coastal traffic. No, Bob is only a peddler in smack. A CIA man would've helped us with guns, especially in this situation.'

Karnail Singh sighed and adjusted the strip of black cloth that was holding his beard neatly in place tight about his face. He used a special *fixo* and was a bit of a dandy. He had an appointment with a woman for later that night. He was estranged from his wife though they still lived together. His domestic life was complicated. For equally complex reasons he needed to build himself a secret fund, though legally he was a prosperous man and owned seven trucks. Nevertheless, he was wary. He had much to lose. 'I'm not so sure,' he said. 'It may just suit the Americans now to keep a low profile.'

'That's politics,' said Tarsem, popping half a boiled egg into his mouth and pushing the plate towards Karnail Singh. 'And we are not in politics. We're in business, that's all. Bob can't help us. The Pakistani drop-men can't deliver enough without risk. We've got to find an alternative. Look at all those weapons that get to the dacoits in Chambal. We've got to latch on to that operation and divert some to our clients. They're desperate enough to have raided the armoury in Ferozepur for a few sten guns. Balbir thinks we only want some guns from the family stock. None of us wants to tangle with the old fellow in Chamkalan. He would blow our whole thing through the roof. What we want are the channels that are open to Raskaan and Satyavan.'

'I know, I know. We've been over this. But you know the saying—never shit on your own doorstep.'

Tarsem sneered. 'Don't tell me you're scared of the Chibbers.'

'I'm not scared of the Chibbers or all the Muhiyals put together.'

'Then maybe you have a soft spot for them.'

Karnail Singh was about to say something, then thought better of it and popped a slice of egg into his mouth.

There was a shout from the courtyard below. 'Tarsem! O Tarsemaa!' It was a precaution. No one who knew Tarsem's ways came up without calling out. Tarsem could be in a delicate discussion and might resent the intrusion.

'Come on up, Hazara!' Tarsem shouted back. Then said to Karnail Singh who was pouring himself a tot of whisky (he was finicky about the quality of Tarsem's country liquor), 'Listen to me, Karnail. I want you to send that boy Balbir on your truck the next time we collect a drop near the Pakistan border. I want the boy to feel important, part of the outfit.'

Karnail Singh stared at him, then nodded, 'I'll take him myself. I'll go too.'

Tarsem frowned but now his attention was diverted to the habitual checking of the sound of footsteps on the stairs. Yes, only one pair of feet.

Hazara pushed open the door and stopped on the threshold without removing the shawl from about his turban and the lower half of his face.

'All well?' Tarsem asked.

Hazara did not answer. Then he glanced at Karnail Singh and muttered '*Sat Sri Akal, ji.*' Karnail Singh returned the greeting.

Tarsem said, 'Bring yourself a glass from the cupboard.'

Hazara and Karnail were in two different branches of Tarsem's activities but both knew something about the other's work. Tarsem's group was small and could not afford to be rigidly compartmentalized. He didn't yet have the resources or the size of organization for that sort of strict division. Hazara worked in the passport trade, on illegal emigration. He was, as he said of himself, a travel agent.

'The best *tharrah!*' he rasped in the sneering tone that was usual with him. Lowering his shawl to reveal an unkempt straggly beard he sniffed at Tarsem's liquor.

'There's orange, cashew, walnut and almond in it.' Tarsem's pride in his concoction was unmistakeable. 'It's my very special one.'

Hazara swigged from the bottle, felt the searing, spreading surprise of it and nodded. He poured out half a glass and cocked an eye at Karnail. 'Didn't see your car so I wasn't expecting to find you here.'

'It's parked in the next lane. The driver's looking after it.'

'Always sensible!' There was a hint of mockery in Hazara's voice. And envy. 'I thought for a moment they'd withdrawn your curfew pass and you couldn't get here.'

'No,' said Karnail twirling his waxed moustache. 'Five of my trucks have curfew passes. We carry essential goods.'

'It's a helluva thing!' Hazara was suddenly angry. 'No motor traffic allowed on the roads after eight o'clock. What are people to do? Go back to the age of mule carts and horse-drawn *tongas* and—?'

'How did you get here?' Tarsem made the question concerned and sympathetic.

'On a bicycle.'

'All the way from Phillaur? So you've brought the cable. All well?' This was the second time Tarsem was asking for reassuring news.

Hazara cursed and said, 'No. They've been stopped at Heathrow. It's the batch sent by Banta Singh. He went all the way to Delhi to see them off. The British High Commission may have changed something in its style of Entry Permits. There may be some new indication we've overlooked.'

'That's the Delhi man's fault then. We'll take it up with him.'

'But these five who're being sent back from Heathrow— they'll be after Banta's blood. Four of them sold all their land to go.'

'We told them it was risky.'

'But we guaranteed that our side would be perfect.'

Tarsem considered the dot of snot he had picked from his nose, then flicked it out of the window and muttered, 'As soon as Banta gets back to you, tell him to go underground for a while. We can't return that much money. Give me some better news. What about the two that went to Canada?'

'They're in.'

Tarsem gave his leering smile and his head bobbed as he continued nodding. 'Has your Naples trick worked?'

'Aye,' Hazara grinned and added in his thoroughly rustic mode. 'We could reap a good harvest that way. They go overland to Sweden, get employed and, after a year, move into Germany. If they're caught, they ask for political asylum as refugees from the persecution of the Indian government.'

'Are they all sikhs?' Karnail Singh broke into the exchange for the first time. It wasn't really his area of action but he thought it only polite to participate. And, of course, he was curious.

Hazara's face took on a look of shrewdness as he shook his head. 'Two of them are not but their papers call them Singh. Norway is well-inclined to our refugees. So is Germany but it's getting crowded. Canada is the best but it's too far from there. The trouble is really that each of these men has a particular country he prefers. They won't just take what we offer. I mean we could give them an easy choice in the Middle East and Africa but no, they want some land of their dreams.'

There was the sound of feet on the stairs. Conversation stopped.

Karnail Singh undid the safety catch on his rifle and quietly worked the bolt back and forward again into place. Tarsem reassured himself with his foot that his own gun was lying there ready beside the chair. He shifted slightly to be sure that he could reach down without being obstructed by the wall. Hazara Singh placed his right leg on his knee and, under his shawl, rested his hand on the hilt of the knife strapped to his calf.

It was Balbir who entered.

'Son of a mother!' Tarsem said. 'Haven't you been taught to call out before coming in?'

Balbir was bewildered. For some reason his arrival seemed to be a cause for laughter. He said lamely, 'You asked me to come, so I thought I would.'

'How did you get out of the house at this time?'

'I slept at the well. And anyway, I haven't been home since this morning. They don't watch over me like that.'

'Then have a drink. Get a glass from there.'

Balbir liked that. Not that he could drink. But to be asked to join in so casually was a kind of compliment. He felt honoured.

They watched him as he self-consciously wiped the dust off with his fingers.

'Don't worry,' Tarsem said. 'Alcohol kills all germs.'

'The progeny of pandits, after all, has got to be clean,' Hazara said and they laughed.

He was reaching for the bottle of *hooch* when Karnail Singh restrained him with a gentle touch on the arm. 'Not that, son, I suggest you have the whisky. It's easier on the gut.'

'Oh, go on,' said Hazara, 'have the real stinger. That's Tarsem's special Scorpion brand. You're a Muhiyal, a Chibber, not one of these delicate *topiwallahs*. If you drink only whisky you'll end up a *babuji*.'

Balbir fell for the flattery. He uncorked the bottle of Scorpion. The contents looked like thin linseed oil.

Karnail Singh murmured, 'Don't say I didn't warn you.'

Somehow Balbir resented his concern and was glad when Hazara Singh retorted. 'Sardar Karnail Singh, you'll refine him into a teat-sucker. Look what a milksop you made of that tough truck-driver's boy.'

It was a nasty crack. Balbir didn't know what it was all about but he saw Karnail Singh's eyes flash as he stood up. Slinging the rifle over his shoulder by the strap, Karnail Singh went down into the yard to pee.

'That wasn't fair,' said Tarsem. 'You've hurt him.'

Hazara shrugged. 'He's mollycoddled that boy into his wife's arms. Everyone knows it. He might as well face it. He was cruel to his wife because she was barren. He wanted a son. So he adopted this greedy truck-driver's sixth child.'

'Hardly a child,' Tarsem leered. 'He was fourteen then.'

'And twenty now. And his wife's doing the jig-jig with him. Poor Karnailleya's out in the cold with a mistress. If I was him, I'd kill them both, wife and stepson.'

Balbir coughed and the tears blotted out his vision for a moment as a bomb seemed to explode in his head. He felt he had swallowed molten steel.

'Ah,' muttered Tarsem appreciatively, 'the first sting of the Scorpion.'

Balbir smiled and tried to speak but his voice seemed to have been abrased out of existence.

'Stage two,' said Tarsem. 'Now take a piece of boiled egg and drench it with another swallow.'

Balbir did. The second dose snaked after the first but now it sat more comfortably in the furrow that seemed to have been cut for it.

'I have another kind,' said Tarsem, 'but I save that for real occasions. It's called Thorny Lightning.'

'Who's that man?' Balbir asked. His voice sounded deeper. He cleared his throat and added, 'The one who just went down.'

'Karnail Singh. Don't you know him? I thought he knew your family. Anyway, he'll be taking you with him next week.'

'He's not from the village.'

'Oh no, he's from Ludhiana. He's got some trucks plying between Delhi and Kashmir. He's agreed to take you along when he goes himself.'

Balbir was assimilating this when Karnail Singh called up from below. 'Oy Tarsem! Shall I bring up the *sigri*? Its blazing beautifully.'

'Aye, do that,' Tarsem responded.

Balbir glanced out of the window. Karnail Singh was gingerly carrying up the brazier.

Tarsem produced the large utensil full of chicken curry and slid back the cover. 'Every kind of meat is best when it has had time to soak in its juice and absorb the flavour of the spices.'

Next, he placed on the table a plate of salad; sliced tomato, cucumber and radish, all sprinkled liberally with salt and pepper. Then a mountain of *chappaties* dripping with *ghee*.

Balbir wondered when Tarsem ever went home to his wife and two little children. This was his office in a manner of speaking but he seemed completely self-sufficient here. His wife was a strict vegetarian, lean and sepulchral, given to speaking in a staccato low monotone full of complaint at his neglect. She was taller than him, dressed drably like a pious social-worker and moved wraith-like through the bazaar on her domestic errands. Her hair was prematurely grey. She seemed older than him by years; at any rate she referred to him with a sort of affectionate regret as though he were only an over-bloated scamp. It was plain that there was something between them that could pass for love. Tarsem was, in his absent way, kind to her and generous. She saved all the money for the children. Those who had seen husband and wife together—which was a rarity—said that Tarsem never retaliated when she chided him with her quick, efficient enumeration of his faults. He allowed himself to be wrapped in the winding-sheet of argument like a body being prepared for burning. People in the village said that he did actually have some corners of guilt in his conscience. And young men, when they discussed the couple, wondered how they made love, for they were certain that, if he mounted her, she would snap in two.

To Balbir's surprise he noticed that Hazara was now drawing something out from the region of his underwear. It was a folded sheet of paper which he held out to Tarsem. 'Here's the cable.'

Tarsem laughed. 'It's not necessary to be that careful, Hazareya. After all, everyone in the post office can read it if they want to. But it'll mean nothing to them.'

'You never know,' said Hazara mysteriously popping the last piece of egg into his mouth. 'Remember those two French fellows, Aubin and Riendeau?'

Karnail Singh had come in and put the brazier down by the table. Tarsem hefted the chicken curry on to warm. 'What French fellows?' Tarsem always had difficulty remembering foreign names and faces.

Karnail wiped his hands on a long bandana that he drew from his pocket. 'He means the Golden Goose.'

'What Golden Goose?'

Karnail sighed. 'That's what the Customs men called that fellow Aubin. He had the heroin packed in condoms and shoved up his rectum. They stripped him and made him go to the loo and they watched as he moved his bowels and the stuffed balls of heroin dropped out. Each egg he laid was worth thousands of dollars. The Bombay customs nicknamed him the Golden Goose.'

'Ah yes,' Tarsem murmured, half intent on checking the curry. 'That was another Goa connection. Probably by the grace of Bob. But those men weren't French, they were Canadian. Anyway, what was the point of that, Hazara?'

'They got caught because the Intelligence people read their telegrams.'

Tarsem guffawed. 'Don't be simple, Hazareya. There was a tip off. Ask Bob. He'll know about it. Their telegrams between Goa and Bombay were meaningless, like ours. Things like "Baby arrived, five pounds, mama OK"; "Happy Birthday"; "Uncle died. Come soon." That's the beauty of the system. We don't use ciphers and all that crap. We send greetings or condolence telegrams. And if something goes wrong we know there's a squealer somewhere. Then we take it from there. Now look at this—"Regret failure in exam. Returning to study harder." Now who could break that to read "Five men returning from Heathrow Airport because they were not allowed into England"? '

Balbir took a small sip of Scorpion and mumbled, 'I wish you'd send me to Germany, Tarsem.'

'I will. I will. But it's not easy. You can see that. You don't want to go as a tourist. That you can do anyway, though they're making even that difficult. You want to go so you can stay on a few years. Now that takes a lot of effort on our part. We've got to pay a lot of people, for the papers and so on. You don't have the money. On top of that we're lending you twenty thousand that's going straight into your father's account in the morning. That means you've got to get up forty thousand before you can begin planning your future abroad. Now here we are, giving you a chance to make quick money so you can get on with what you want. And all you do is sit here and moan like a child about going to Germany.'

'Easy, easy.' It was Karnail Singh. 'The boy's only saying that he's got no heart for this sort of business. We shouldn't push him.'

'Look here, Karnailleya. I'm sick to my testicles of your qualms. You're all making money on the basis of my ideas. Am I also supposed to collect your tears like pearls? What do you think I'm running—a charity outfit? Let's get one thing straight. If Balbir doesn't have the money, he's got to get us guns. Cash or kind, that's fair, isn't it? And I'm going one better than that. If he can't get us either, then he works with us, learns the ropes, puts us in touch with Satyavan's pipeline, collects his commission, pays for papers and passage, and we get him to Germany.'

'Sweden is better,' Hazara muttered snidely. 'Vast open spaces. Small population. And the girls there will lap up a young fellow like you.'

Balbir blushed and lied. 'I'm ... I'm not that interested in girls.'

'Germany's too crowded for you,' Hazara persisted. 'It's crowded by one big mob called Raskaan.'

Karnail Singh winced and scratched under his starched collar. 'Lahh! Raskaan is his brother!'

'But he doesn't want him there,' said Tarsem. He swung the pan of chicken curry onto the table. 'Anyway, we'll send him wherever he wishes to go. We're being really decent. Any other villager and we wouldn't care. But our Balbir has the benefit of three choices—money, guns, pipeline.'

Balbir choked down the 'thank you' rising in his throat and said, 'I agreed this morning to get you some guns.'

Tarsem nodded in his continuous toy-like manner as though he had a coil-spring in his neck. 'Understand this clearly, Balbir. We don't want to steal guns, especially not guns that your family might have. We're not thieves, we're ... businessmen. We'll buy guns and sell them at a profit to clients who are desperate for them. Don't fool around with your grandfather and his stock. We don't want the village lynching us just so you can get to Germany.'

Balbir allowed a grinning Hazara to pour him another sting of Scorpion. The aroma of chicken curry hung like festive decorations in the room. But he was dismayed by Tarsem's words; he had hoped he could simply raid his grandfather's stock of weapons and get away with it. These were sensible men, professionals, not one-shot amateurs.

He nodded. 'I understand.' Then he took a deep breath and asked, 'How much would you pay for a carbine—the rapid-fire, folding kind?'

'Fifteen thousand.'

Balbir played with the rim of his glass. It began to make a musical sound. Without being able to look up, he plunged on. 'It's worth much more.'

Tarsem did his toy nod, 'If it's bought on the market with a licence. But you can't buy those carbines. They're strictly for the Defence Forces. So whoever sells a carbine is selling a risk. Look at us—none of us carries that kind of weapon though we've dealt in them. We don't want to be too noticeable. I'm no different from any farmer with this double-barrelled gun. Karnailleya is like any trucker with his rifle. But we'll buy carbines, LMGs, anything.'

Balbir said, 'I've got a carbine, a pistol, some grenades and other little stuff you might like.'

In the silence that followed what was obviously a surprise to them, he could hear the violin sound his finger was producing from the glass.

Tarsem finally asked, 'Ammunition to go with the carbine and pistol?'

Balbir nodded. 'Some. And a bayonet.'

'We'll have to look at the stuff.'

'Will you give me twenty thousand for the lot?'

'We might. Depending.'

'So my debt to you would be repaid?'

'Right.' Tarsem sounded reluctant. But there it was. What could he do? The boy, he had to admit, was clever. These bloody pandit brains!

Then to his relief, Balbir continued, 'And I would have to work only for my passage?'

'That's it.'

'Fine. How much do I get?'

'For what?'

'Going with Karnail Singh and delivering your goods.'

'It depends on the consignment, how big it is.'

Karnail Singh said quietly, 'The look-out man is paid a hundred rupees per gun we carry. That's because he's got to be a sharp-shooter. If it's a big load, we take two or three look-outs. They're gunmen really. You'd come as a . . . trainee. We'd pay you somewhat less for just tagging along.'

Balbir had the uneasy feeling that Karnail Singh was actually trying to discourage him. He was distracted by the thought. He said suddenly, 'I'm hungry.'

'Help yourself!' Tarsem was at once the solicitous host. 'Dip into the pot. We don't bother with plates. Saves washing up.' Then he added with a laugh, 'Breaks caste. We're modern in this outfit.'

They all laughed. The tension dissipated.

The *chappati* was tender and soggy, tearing apart as easily as wet blotting paper. Not at all like the thick *rotis* Balbir was used to in the village. The meat was soft and sailed in on the curry, redolent with flavours that redoubled appetite. You had to stop yourself from eating.

Tarsem watched with growing approval, then nodding his nod and rubbing his hands together joined in.

'How many guns will there be on the next trip?' Balbir prepared to do some quick calculation.

'Not more than ten,' Karnail said. He was the only one who ate with his mouth shut.

'Is that all?'

'Exactly,' Tarsem belched and reached for the Scorpion. 'That's why we need the pipeline. The border is risky. There's the army, the Border Security Force and so on.'

Karnail explained with great gentleness, 'We have to hide each batch. There are checkposts to cross. We have to carry legitimate cargo.'

'Now if we had the pipeline,' Tarsem looked at each one in turn, pausing for effect, 'if we had the pipeline, we'd bring in big consignments from safe areas like—' he shrugged. ' . . . Lucknow, Gwalior, Indore. We'd be driving up from the heart of India with much less danger. We could carry crates of explosives, gunpowder, grenades, guns.'

'The fact is,' Karnail added smiling at Balbir, 'we've carried in large quantities of country-made pistols and cartridges from the Lucknow area but they're no good. They're crude, unreliable. They fall apart. They could blow up in your face.'

'They're just junk to these clients. And quite rightly too.' Tarsem's eyes were wide with ethical affirmation. 'General Shabeg vets every batch himself. You can't pull a fast one on him. Sure, he's got his own sources and a few friends or followers in the army but what does that get him? One rifle here, a carbine there. Most of his real gun-running contacts were in Bangladesh and that's too far away. Also, those weapons are going to the rebels in the north-east. He's even asked for stuff that's left lying around after the Indo-Pak wars and skirmishes. Now that sort of scavenging job is for . . . ' he laughed in a suggestive manner ' . . . little piddlers. We need the big pipeline.'

'Elder brother Satyavan is away in Europe.'

'So what? He'll be back. You work on him.' Tarsem glanced at the telephone in the corner. 'I'd tell you to start by making a lightning call to him but that would give the game away. The Intelligence boys and the CBI listen in to every trunk-call, especially from Punjab. I could tell you to go to Phillaur or Ludhiana and phone from a post office but I won't. They'd pick you up like a tadpole in a tin. What I can suggest is this—when you know you can hook Satyavan, call him wherever he is and ask him to fly back. He'll come. Then hook him. The faster you do that, the better. And I promise you, we'll have you out of the country the day after we deliver the first big consignment.'

Balbir got up, went to the sink and washed his hands and mouth. It sounded easy but the thought of tackling Satyavan daunted him. His mind searched for means of getting together the money. 'Couldn't I be a commission agent in the passport trade? Everyone knows me. They'd trust me if I said I could help them migrate. I'd pass them on to you.'

'Sure,' said Hazara. 'Lots of people want to go somewhere. But very few have twenty thousand to spare.'

Balbir bit his lower lip. The cap fitted him.

'Anyway,' Hazara continued, 'if you find some genuine customers, you'll get five hundred rupees per person—when we see their cash. And don't bring us any idiots who want to go to Khalistan. It doesn't exist. What I mean is, we don't ferry extremists to Pakistan. It's too much bother. There's enough good trade the other way.'

Tarsem had been sucking at his teeth to remove a shred of meat which he now spat out. 'Hazara is right. That part of the business can do without the Intelligence types jumping on its back.' He sniggered and added, 'In fact it's better for us to keep all these extremists in Punjab. It takes the heat off us. The police have their hands full.'

Karnail Singh had washed and was now standing in front of the mirror, reaching above his turban to untie the strip of cloth—the *thatha*—over his beard. But for his uneven teeth he looked quite dashing. He said, 'So, Balbir, I'll have you collected from here at eleven o'clock in the morning on the sixteenth of January. Today is the tenth. That means six days from now, Monday.'

'In the daytime?'

'Obviously. All that night-time stuff is for the movies and criminal gangs. We'll be carrying regular cargo.' His reflection in the mirror winked. 'Vegetables for the troops. And we'll probably bring back a few carpets and rugs from Kashmir.'

He looked at his watch, sighed, picked up his rifle and muttered the casual Punjabi farewell, 'All right, then.'

At the door, he turned round, shook his turban into place with a jerk of the head and smiling at Balbir asked, 'You can shoot, can't you?'

Balbir wanted to lie but was afraid he wouldn't be able to carry it off. He kept quiet. Karnail Singh looked at the others then back at Balbir. His smile was steady like a torch that has been forgetfully left on. 'If you don't know how to shoot, how is it that you have a carbine?'

At that moment, Balbir hated Karnail Singh.

Tarsem came to his rescue. 'As long as he assures us that it isn't swiped from the family stock, that's OK. A carbine is a carbine.'

Balbir had recovered enough by now to say, 'A friend gave it to me.'

'And the grenades? And the pistol?' Karnail Singh seemed unable to stop smiling.

Balbir nodded.

But Tarsem was content with his own line of reasoning. 'If he had dipped into the old man's arsenal he'd be offering us much more than one carbine and a pistol. Now, Balbir, you bring me this stuff you have tomorrow. We'll send it in directly. Small loads are easy to distribute and deliver. We've got some of our own "pilgrims" going in. As for learning to shoot—Karnail is there to teach you. Right, Karnail?'

Karnail reduced the intensity of his smile, nodded, glanced again at his watch, waved and went down the stairs.

Tarsem said, 'Have another slug of Scorpion. You look like you need it. Then make out the receipt.'

'Receipt?'

'For the twenty thousand we're putting into your father's account. It's just a precaution, between ourselves.'

'But I'm giving you the carbine and pistol and—'

'Aye. When you bring me those, we'll tear up the receipt together.'

'Surely you can trust me till tomorrow afternoon!'

'Nowadays,' Hazara purred sarcastically from the corner, 'you couldn't trust your mother to deliver your father's baby ... '

' ... on time.' Tarsem completed the statement. It was one they obviously bandied about often.

That night, in the shed by the well, Balbir slept fitfully. Was it the tail-end of the fever, the excessive alcohol in his veins, the day's events or the dread of tasks to be done? He had night-mares.

But the next day, refreshed and congratulating himself on his new-found ability to wheel and deal, he set off in a borrowed Austin 10 to recover the sack from under the culvert. The rickety car was practically a village heirloom. It was used by all and sundry, and was now considered the community car. Balbir had learnt to drive in it. It went to weddings, feasts, fairs; if it broke down, whoever was in it at the time had it repaired. There were, of course, other cars in the village: modern Ambassadors and Fiats and even a Buick. But this car was the village mascot, everyone felt he owned it.

So it was natural, when he was returning with the sack safely in the boot, to find himself being flagged down by various villagers trudging towards Jagtara. The car was an established feature in the free transport system.

The two old women among the four people he picked up first commented on the nicely warming winter sunshine, then re-marked that the village of Maina was in turmoil—a girl had been kidnapped. The Ahluwalias were assembling for action. There was going to be trouble.

Balbir dropped off his passengers then drove to Tarsem's yard and delivered the sack. They carried it upstairs and, after bolting the door, examined the contents. A used but excellent carbine, nearly two hundred rounds of ammunition, a .32 pistol with twenty cartridges, two grenades, five sticks of dynamite, a cylindrical object that was part of the machinery of a flour mill but which Tarsem explained was now used as a centre-piece for home-made bombs, a number of fuses, four sophisticated delayed-action timers wrapped in cellophane and a silencer for the pistol.

'Good,' Tarsem nodded and bestowed on Balbir a double-handed-grip handshake.

Balbir had not the heart to bargain for more. He knew he was selling cheap but at least it cleared his debt. He took the receipt and, using Tarsem's box of matches, burned it.

Tarsem grinned. 'Monday, eleven o'clock. Take a sweater and jacket. You'll have to spend a night out on the job. It'll be colder where you're going.'

Balbir felt a sense of exhilaration. Whatever he earned this way would be his own. No one would know of it.

When he went home to change and carry away a small bundle of clothes, his mother said, 'Son, don't be angry with your father.

He didn't mean to hit you. He just lost control. You're right to try and stay out of his way for a couple of days. He'll soon be over it.'

Balbir said, 'I'll take the food to the men today but from tomorrow someone else will come for it.'

'Billu,' she tried to hug him but he grimaced and turned sideways. 'Billu, you mustn't cause us pain. That bank forgery—'

'I don't want to discuss it.'

'Your brother Raskaan is doing so much for us but it can't make up for his absence.'

'What has that to do with me?'

She wiped her hands on the end of her *saree*, pushed back a strand of hair and reached into her blouse and brought out an airmail letter. She couldn't help her joy. 'This came from him today.'

He wanted to rebuff her, hurt her, scotch her happiness, but curiosity got the better of him. He resented the letter that she had kept so close to her heart.

He glanced at it. 'It's not written by him. It's written by Renate.'

'She's his secretary.'

'Hmph!'

'He's signed it. Read it. It's from him. He's sending two bank drafts.'

He scowled and went through the letter, his being churning over every line of it. 'So he's sending one and a half *lakhs* for your pet project—a rest house for travellers in the holy city of Hardwar.'

'And ninety thousand for your cousin's eye hospital. When your grandfather's cataract is ready for operating, we'll take him there.'

'Why can't he write his letters himself?'

'He's busy.' Then he heard that touch of regret. 'He was never fond of writing. It's a chore for him. He didn't have your kind of education.'

Suddenly he couldn't stop himself. He thrust the letter roughly into her hands. 'All these donations for good causes. These bribes! But he can't buy me.'

His mother was startled but equal to it. Raskaan was her son as much as Balbir. She would always rise to the defence of both. Her eyes snipped at him like a pair of scissors, her angular face shaking from side to side as though on a stalk. 'Oh ho ho, such grand airs you give yourself! And you know you'd be the first to run if he called you.'

'Not from now on!'

He stomped out of the house with a strange feeling of relief. He wanted to sunder them from himself, cut all ties, be independent, be free of responsibility for their emotions, be rid of the enslavement of gratitude.

At the well, he ate with the men.

Someone said, 'Kumhareya's been missing since yesterday. The Ahluwalias of Maina say he's abducted their girl. They came to Jagtara and threatened his father this morning. The old fellow's so distressed he's smashed all the pots he made last week.'

'They'll kill him,' said another.

'They'll kill his father?' Balbir asked.

'And his mother, of course—if they don't find that Kumhareya. They've got to revenge themselves somehow.'

'These potters!' said the first man. 'They're getting beyond themselves.'

'Aye,' agreed the other. 'Imagine, running off with a girl who was about to be married—and a higher caste girl at that! I never liked that fellow. He always behaved as though he were hiding something.'

They were talking of him as if he were dead. Indeed, as far as they were concerned, he had been tried, convicted and condemned. The carrying out of the sentence was a mere formality. If Uday Singh escaped, the next of kin were there to take the rap. This was the essence of the feuding spirit. No one interfered, everyone acquiesced. Those who did not actively help to see justice done stood aside and watched discreetly or approvingly.

'What I can't understand,' the tone of the farmhand was a little accusing, even jealous, 'is how you let him get so close to you, Balbiraa. I mean, wrestling together is all right. But sitting together, yakking and joking.'

Balbir said, 'I'm sitting here, eating with *you*, aren't I?'

'Aye, but that's different. . . ' His voice trailed off into grudging silence. He knew he had been chastised, put in his place. Balbir had used the whip of traditional prejudice to scourge him. In the old days, the higher castes did not deign to eat with persons of low caste. To dine together was to reach across the barrier of social status.

Balbir pulled a string-bed out by the peepal tree and lay down. He wasn't inclined to bestir himself too much today. He needed rest.

But two thoughts buzzed in his mind like relentless wasps.

How did the money vanish from the storage bin? And when was he going to deliver Kumhareya's message?

If he wasn't feeling so enervated he would have tackled his mother and Aadran about the money this morning; and in the afternoon he would have gone to Amritsar. But so much had happened so quickly that what he wanted most now, especially in the aftermath of the fever, was to relax.

His mind drifted to Kulwanti and the sheer abandon of that experience. He knew he would be tempted to repeat it sometime, somehow. He allowed himself to luxuriate in the memory of those moments but the face that rose over the remembrance, swelling like a distant film star's giant visage on a billboard, was Gulnari's.

He slept. And dreamed.

It was a good thing he slept, for that night a disturbing complication arose that he had not foreseen.

In the village of Chamkalan, just before the curfew hour, about ten Ahluwalia *sardars* had driven in from Maina and scoured the narrow lanes of the bazaar side of the village till they located the shabby dwelling of Jasbir Singh, also commonly known as Jassa. It had not taken them long to discover that Jassa was the owner of the motorcycle which Kumhareya had been seen riding. Jassa also figured on the list of names found among the papers discovered in Gulnari's trunk. Jassa was obviously a terrorist colleague of Kumhareya's. The Ahluwalias, searching for the 'abducted' girl, naturally assumed that Jassa was an accomplice. They decided to grill him.

Jassa was not an easy person to tackle. He was a tough, hardened jailbird with a criminal record that pre-dated his indulgence in political extremism. He had many personal reasons too for feeling disgruntled with life. People said that his own father had died in despair over him. His widowed mother received nothing from him but abuse, and depended largely on charity and her own ability at knitting. They had two large, grimy, smoke-blackened rooms. In one, there were tethered a buffalo and calf; on the wall were a few pegs, used by Jassa for hanging his clothes. He had moved his string bed into this room rather than share the other room with his mother who was constantly begging him to reform himself.

Into this dank, fly-ridden atmosphere stinking of buffalo urine—but warm as a cattle-shed—the Ahluwalia *sardars* had stepped. Some of them were armed and they were prepared to do Jassa physical injury should it be necessary, but to the curious villagers who naturally thronged the doorway it was clear that the merchants, used to considerably better surroundings, were unhappy at being in such an atmosphere.

Jassa himself seemed bewildered. He was wearing a tatty pair of striped cotton pyjamas and took his own time as he covered his muscular torso with a rather soiled *kurta*. After a while, in answer to their questions, he grunted that his motorcycle had been stolen. When they asked whether he had reported that to the police, he snorted, 'Huh! The police!'

Pressed to be specific about how it was stolen, he turned on his trembling old mother who had joined her entreaties to their threats and snarled, 'Aye, you bitch! You've let me down again. You're to blame. I wasn't even here. And out of the goodness of your stupid heart you let him take my bike away. If he had asked to walk off with your buffalo you would have said no, but since it was just my bike you let him— '

'Hai, son!' the woman addressed him but looked about her for support as though she had never been able to face him alone. Perhaps that was one of the aspects of her character he resented, that she was always seeking reassurance from the rest of the world for her disagreements with him. She looked briefly at him and continued, 'The potter boy is your friend. He is often here.' She searched the faces about her. 'At all hours of night and day, he would he here. They would sometimes go away together, Jassa and he. How was I to know . . .?'

Jassa muttered, 'Bitch!' Then glancing at the leader among the *sardars*, he said, 'Let me tie my turban and I'll come with you. I'll kill that Kumhareya myself.'

But as he reached inside a tin trunk, one of the Ahluwalia *sardars* stamped the lid shut on Jassa's hand. He cursed their mothers into oblivion and put his injured fingers to his mouth. They pushed him aside and shoved a rifle at his ribs. They looked more afraid than he. Looking inside the trunk, they saw that he had been reaching for a revolver.

'I thought you were up to something!' exclaimed the *sardar* who had stamped down the lid of the trunk. 'Your turban is hanging there on a peg. Lucky for us I saw that!'

Despite this quickness of wit, they were unused to dealing with men like Jassa. They were traders, merchants, shopkeepers, more accustomed to bargaining than threatening or using physical force. It took them time to get through to the taciturn Jassa, so much time that it seemed natural to let him go to the lavatory an hour later. They were genteel enough to let him shut the door. He merely pulled apart the rusted old iron bars that formed a grill in the toilet window. If they heard a grunt or two, they were not suspicious.

Ten minutes later there was pandemonium when they discovered that Jassa had escaped. It was well after the hour of curfew. The noise brought the police. More time was lost in explanations. They couldn't set out after him in their cars for vehicular traffic was forbidden on the roads at night. They assumed he had run into the fields and would make his way as far as possible from the area.

News of all this was brought to Balbir that same night by the opium addict known as Jheera the *Afeemchi.*

'Balbir, Balbir!' he gasped. 'If you know where that Kumhareya is, you must warn him. And be prepared yourself. Though they would not dare implicate you, they'll want to question you.'

'What are you talking about?'

Balbir held open the door of his room in the shed while Jheera, blowing on his fingers and shivering in his wretched blanket, stumbled in.

'Balbir. O Balbiraa!' Jheera moaned, shaking with his own visions and prognostications.

'Are you high?' Balbir asked.

'Do I look high?' he replied rhetorically.

'All right. Go on.'

'Oh Balbir, I'm frightened for that foolish fellow Kumhareya.'

'So are we all.'

'I'm also frightened for you.'

'Why me?'

'They'll want to know why you were on the pillion of the motorcycle! You were seen with Kumhareya heading towards Maina. And the next thing that happened was the girl was missing. Kumhareya killed a man. They found the body in a well. Aieeya!'

'Have they informed the police?'

'Hai, hai! What shall we do?'

Balbir took hold of Jheera by the shoulders and shook him. His own fear made him impatient. He repeated his question. 'Have they told the police about it?'

Jheera wagged his head, 'But they will. They don't want the Ahluwalia name ruined. They want to get the girl back as soon as they can. The girl's due to be married. If they registered a police case no one would marry her—'

'Jheera, wherever Kumhareya is, he is out of their reach.'

'Oh no. He was stupid to use a motorcycle from Chamkalan. They were in Chamkalan, talking to the man who owns the motorcycle. I had gone there to pay my respects to your grandfather. Coming out through the bazaar . . . ' Jheera hesitated, his eyelids flickered as he explained awkwardly, 'I usually go through the bazaar . . . to buy myself a small present . . . That's when I heard this commotion. About ten Ahluwalia *sardars* had cornered that Jat, Jasbir Singh. He's a *goonda*.'

Jheera's eyes searched Balbir's for comprehension but Balbir only seemed puzzled.

Jheera grimaced impatiently. 'You know who I mean—Jasbir Singh, everyone calls him Jassa. The fellow whose father died last year.'

Balbir shook his head. 'I don't know him.'

'Your grandfather does. He felt sorry enough for the swine's mother to give her a knitting machine. Her son could have sold his motorcycle and bought her that, but no! Your Babaji had to do it. Some of her stuff now gets exported to Russia.'

Balbir couldn't remember who Jheera was referring to. He had never bothered much about his grandfather's feudal, patriarchal philanthropy or about the complexities of existence in the villages which he despised anyway, but he did begin to recall that he had heard either Gulnari or Kumhareya mentioning an accomplice named Jassa. He reached for his clothes and began to get ready. It was sharp of the Ahluwalias to begin the search by tracing the owner of the motorcycle.

'Anyway,' he snapped, controlling a rising panic, 'what did this Jassa tell them?'

'Nothing. Then they let him go to the toilet. And he escaped!'

Balbir felt under the bed for his shoes. 'So they'll come to question me next.'

'Aye. First thing tomorrow morning. Oh Balbiraa, I was so frightened when they said you had been seen with Kumhareya. Did you really go towards Maina with him on the motorcycle?' Jheera was wringing his hands.

'All right, all right. I went for a joy-ride, that's all. How did I know what Kumhareya was up to?'

'Thank God, Balbiraa! Thank God. At first I wanted to rush to your grandfather, then I thought I should come and alert you.'

'Are you sure Jassa said absolutely nothing?'

Jheera nodded. Then he sucked in his cheeks so that they almost met. 'What surprised everyone was how upset Jassa got.

He said he would kill Kumhareya himself. This was the only clean holy thing in his life and he was not going to let Kumhareya spoil it with abducting a girl. That was very frightening.'

'When he escaped, did the Ahluwalias go after him?'

'Couldn't.' Jheera's eyes were like points of light. 'There was so much noise and shouting, the police turned up. There's a picket just outside the village. The chief constable thought they were all extremists or whatever. That got the girl's uncle in a flap. He started shouting that he was a respectable shopkeeper and they couldn't treat every *sardar* like a sneaky terrorist. That was a good point because the chief constable was also a *sardar*.'

'Fine. So they're all there till dawn.'

'They'll set off at first light. O Balbiraa, why did you get mixed up in all this?'

'Stop moaning like an old woman. I'm not mixed up in anything.'

Jheera's haggard face elongated a little more with anxiety. 'Where're you off to now? Your grandfather will kill me if anything happens to you. I only came to tell you to be prepared.'

'How did you get here?'

'How do you think? I ran. It's the little present I bought for myself that did it. Three miles like a staggering athlete. That opium can help. Only I'm thirsty and hungry. I could drink a gallon of water.'

Balbir looked at Jheera's earringed face with its hollows and horrors, and he felt like clasping him to his bosom. He said, 'Thank you, Jheera. You spend the night here, understand? You sleep cosy in my bed. I'm going to find Kumhareya. Don't ask me how, I won't tell you. There's water in that pot and food in that meat safe.'

'Do you . . . do you want some of this?' Jheera opened a small paper packet.

Balbir smiled and shook his head, 'I'm not going to run. It's too many miles to cover. I'm going to ride.'

'A bicycle? This'll help with that too.'

'No, thank you. There's no bicycle here, Jheera.'

'Then?' Jheera frowned and scratched at the bristling hair on his head.

'Younger Uncle Gopal Chunder's farm is next door.' This enigmatic reference to his father's cousin's possessions didn't enlighten Jheera whose frown only deepened.

'Aye, that is so.' But a question hung in his voice.

'He breeds good animals. Among the best in Punjab.'

'Yes, yes?' Jheera was like a child, hanging on every word.

'When he buys a mare, it's bound to be fast and sturdy.'

'God! You're not thinking of riding that mare? She broke the shafts when they tried to hitch her to a *tonga*.'

'That's because she doesn't like *tongas*. She's a riding mare. She lets Chachaji ride.'

'But only him!' Jheera cried in a fervour of trepidation.

'I have to ride her tonight.'

'But you've never ridden in your life!'

That was true. It gave Balbir pause. Then he shrugged. 'I'll have to learn now.'

'You're mad.'

Jheera trailed him, mumbling, 'You're out of your mind. You're mad!' Balbir led the way across the fields to a vast outline of black in the grey night. This was the huge animal shed of his father's cousin.

Jheera dipped into his pocket. 'I have two pieces of *gur* here. Sometimes when I give myself a present I get the urge to follow it up with something sweet.' He held up the two lumps of unrefined sugar. 'Horses love *gur*.'

Balbir ignored him but was glad of his moral support. He had never really ridden anything more obstreperous than a bicycle but he took heart from the thought that his father and grandfather had been—what he often scoffed at—tireless riders in their day. He was not unaware of the irony that the Disturbed Areas Act had by its necessary restrictions propelled him to understanding the ambience of the turbulent times his father, grandfather and forefathers had known.

When he entered the enormous cattle shed, slipping in through the partly opened doors, he felt he was not only stepping forward in the act of helping Kumhareya but back in time to a link he could not have guessed existed between him and his forefathers.

The first animal Balbir and Jheera encountered was a Jersey stud bull. This animal, on loan from the Agricultural University of Ludhiana, took immediate cognizance of their surreptitious entry. He blew through his nostrils like a pair of bellows and tugged at the rope despite the ring that went through his nose. He moved back then charged forward at his trough; he raised such a commotion that the two cows tethered nearby mooed and manoeuvered agitatedly. Their udders swung with the weight of their famous eighteen litres of milk.

It was always a pleasure to enter such a cattle-shed; during the day the livestock munched contentedly at the troughs outside and, at night, their combined body heat made the shed the warmest place in all Jagtara. That perhaps was why Gopal Chunder's three dogs too curled up just inside the door. They raised no alarm now but greeted Balbir with much tail-wagging, slavering and leaps of delight. They followed the two intruders about curiously, avoiding the kicking legs and butting horns. The mare was in a stall by herself at the end of the shed. She scrambled up with her ears forward and unafraid.

Balbir tried to pat her but the movement of his hand was too sudden and she retreated with a very vigorous stomping of hooves. She was not tied but barricaded in. Balbir tried again, but she merely yawned and shook her neck and sent shivers of wakefulness rippling down her back. Then she stood, alert and still, shining splendidly black in the faint light of the dimmed lantern hanging from the beam above them. Behind her a square of moonlit sky could be seen in the ventilator and it threw a soft, caressing patch of visibility on the straw.

Balbir nudged Jheera and took a lump of *gur* from him. He held it out invitingly on his palm. Her nostrils wrinkled and flared. She came forward carefully and Balbir felt her warm breath on his hand as she nibbled up the unrefined sugar. He ran a hand down her neck and talked to her soothingly.

Jheera took the coiled rope off the peg and gave it to him. He slipped it round her neck. She seemed unconcerned now as though she were among old friends.

'I hope she's as easy to ride,' Balbir whispered, then saw that Jheera had unhooked the lantern and was searching the adjoining stall. 'What are you doing?'

'Looking for the reins and the saddle.'

'There they are, on that wooden rack.'

Younger Uncle Gopal Chunder did everything as perfectly as possible for the few animals he owned. He was perhaps the only farmer in all of Punjab to have a proper stand and shelf for every appurtenance of his livestock. Balbir could just imagine how he must have stood over the carpentering of every square inch of that rack for saddle and tack. And his toolroom was not just a jumble of pitchfork, rake, spade, pickaxe and the motley of muddled farming but, as neat as the window display of a shop, there was space, place and peg to suit the shape and contour of every object. Balbir admired his younger uncle's particularity and precision, and hoped he would be forgiven the borrowing of the mare. He hoped, in fact, that his younger uncle would never come to know. The mare should be back in her stall by dawn.

Jheera carried the gear and Balbir led the mare out quietly into the night.

When they were well away from the shed and standing in the soft earth of a field, Balbir broke off a piece from the second lump of *gur* and let the mare gobble up the sweet. Then, while Jheera held the rope, he forced the bit between her teeth.

She skittered back, glistening in the wash of brilliant moonlight, with her mane flouncing on her neck and the forelock dancing on her forehead. She was a beautiful animal and awesome as they looked up at her head pulling back against the reins. Balbir reached up to the white dagger-like patch on her forehead, the Mark of Good Fortune was what the villagers called it, and caressed and coaxed her till he had the cavesson buckled.

Then Jheera somehow flung the saddle cloth on her back. But she would not take the saddle. She kicked and heaved and broke free from Balbir.

Luckily Jheera grabbed the rope; he hung on while she sprang away to the end of it and reared. And then they saw something they had never seen or heard mentioned before—a capriole. She rose straight up in the air, horizontal, with her forelegs tucked under and her hindlegs stretched straight like a leaping gazelle. For a moment she seemed to snag like a giant medallion among the stars. Then she came down, cantered round with her mane flowing and fanning and her neck held in taut as the curve of a sickle.

'Surely,' Jheera the Dreamer said, 'she is descended from Uchchraisravas, the King of the Horses. Did you see the way she jumped as though she would fly to the house of Ashwini?'

The sense of wonder was not lost on Balbir but the implication of the mythological reference was. He knew, of course, as any village boy did, that the King of the Horses had been swirled out of the ocean when the gods had churned it for nectar and he knew that Ashwini was one of the traditional lunar mansions, but the ramifications of such things were not real to him. They were profoundly true for Jheera. Jheera believed in the exactitude of every phrase of lore he had ever heard. He believed that Nataraj danced not as a representation of cosmic flux but might appear any moment, coagulate and noctilucent on the horizon. He believed that Kali might be seen exactly as she was depicted, and that Brahma, Vishnu and Shiva could be identified not by philosophic concepts but by their appearance in the anachronistic dress to which they were partial. His night was peopled by gods and demons and his days passed without blasphemy—but both with the help of opium.

'Get away,' Balbir said. 'You and your imaginings! Remember the witch?' And he laughed.

Jheera remembered and was abashed. That was the night some village boys had decided to play a joke on him. They had lured him out into the fields and suddenly they had come upon a shape walking hunched up like an old woman in the distance. He hadn't known it was Balbir all hooded and bent in a shawl. He hadn't realized it was Balbir walking forward with sandals tied backwards on his feet. One of the boys had shone a torch on the ground and said, 'Look at her footprints, her feet are back to front.' Jheera had not needed anyone to tell him that only witches were capable of that anatopism. Just then the witch had turned round and come towards him. Her face was as hideous as any mask that dangled vacantly in the bazaar but her red tongue stuck out and waggled while she cackled and pointing to Jheera cried, 'I want you!' Jheera had abandoned all and run and had not stopped till he was home. But that night she had appeared at his window and had laughed in a chorus of many voices. It was only when Jheera had screamed and brought everyone in the house running to his side that Balbir had flung off the mask and the other boys had revealed themselves as conspirators.

Jheera bit his tongue to stop himself from saying any more though it did seem to him that the mare had a fluency of movement that was almost celestial. Perhaps some spirit took hold of her at night. Perhaps she would carry Balbir away into the skies. But Balbir had been warned. Now Jheera would say nothing. He drew in the rope till the mare was neighing close to his ear, then he caught the reins.

Balbir had picked up the saddle and now he placed it on her back over the cloth and reaching under fearlessly pulled up the girthband and tightened it. He tied the red martingale sash into place then lowered the stirrups on either side. Jheera held on to the rope while Balbir brought the reins back over her ears and, catching the pummel, put his left foot in the stirrup. But as he raised himself up clumsily with all the slow motion of a cyclist, the mare bucked and lunged; he found himself caught and hopping alongside on one leg and holding on to the saddle for dear life.

Jheera instinctively grabbed both reins tight under the bit and the mare was captive at the mouth. She opened her jaws and her lower lip quivered away from her gums but she was restrained. Balbir extricated himself and with the thought bludgeoning his mind that this was too much delay, he gestured for the mare to be led to the edge of the field where the embankment of the track would give him the advantage of height. There, he took hold of the reins again and lowered himself gently into the saddle. The mare stood still and the only indication of tension was a little flick of the tail. Balbir held on to the saddle with one hand and dared not help Jheera as he grappled with the knot in the rope.

When the rope was off, Balbir said, 'Put it back in the shed.'

Jheera nodded and watched with bated breath as Balbir tugged lightly at the right rein. The mare wheeled slowly and moved into the centre of the field. There she stood and danced a little tattoo as though kneading dough with her hooves.

'Be careful!' Jheera called, but no sooner had he done so than the mare reared up as though the sound were a whip that had lashed at her hind-quarters.

Balbir gripped with his knees and pressed in with his legs, held on with both hands to a tuft of mane, gritted his teeth and tried to recall all that his father and grandfather had ever said about horses. But the first thing was, he knew, to hang on and stay in the saddle and subdue her to his will. Fortunately, she had not reared high—the martingale held her down. Now she bucked, kicking up her hindlegs and lowering her head. Balbir almost went over. But all the stories of horsemanship that he had ever heard were now quick lessons to him. Someone could keep an old silver rupee coin held tight to the saddle-flap with the ball of the knee—Balbir kept his knees glued to the mare and he stayed in the saddle.

Suddenly, even before she brought her head up, she shied and went sideways with a shrill neigh of terror. Sikander, Sikander, Alexander the Great with the great horse that went crazy when he saw his own shadow flung down by the sun. The bright moon threw dark blobs and patches everywhere and the mist was full of ghouls. Balbir took a rein in each hand and pulled her head in and talked as though to a child. She twiddled her ears like thumbs, first back then forward then back then forward again. She stood like a squeezed-in spring.

Balbir was almost deafened by the pounding of his own heart. He dared not vary the position of a limb. He was atop a volatile chemical that, at the slightest disturbance, might explode. He was astride a creature of muscle that he could not control. Fear flashed through his being with all the urgency of a wayward electric charge.

Someone—was it his grandfather?—had said that that man is master of his horse who is master of himself. He waited.

Jheera, with his mouth agape and eyes wide and the rope clenched in one fist, worried and wondered what Balbir was doing. He could see the mare exhaling fiercely into the mist. He could see her champing at the bit. He was afraid she might float up again and vanish towards the moon. Really, he had never seen anything like that leaping up in all his life!

Balbir was praying. He was astonished at himself. Not that he was a sceptic or an agnostic, nor had he ever worked out a personal philosophy; he was just surprised that his mind retained so accurately a formula prayer in Sanskrit the meaning of which he didn't even understand. He knew it was prayer for wisdom but the details of it were hazy. And it was absurd, he thought, that he should be praying for enlightenment when all he wanted was to be able to ride this mare safely to Chak Deedar and back.

All at once a sickening estimation of his cowardice overcame him. His recurring plunges into bravado—the wrestling with Kumhareya, the insistence on forming links with Tarsem, the seduction of Kulwanti, even the attempt to rebel against the authority of his father by fleeing abroad—seemed motivated by a desire to prove a courage he did not have. And now this tackling of the unbroken mare.

Had Balbir not been as stubborn or as determined as he was, he might have dismounted then and there. But he felt again that if he did not possess courage, he would force himself to beget it by pretending it. So he relaxed and prepared to fight the mare no matter what it cost him.

She was twitching and trembling under him now as though every atom and molecule in her were in opposition to itself. The nip in the air did nothing to calm her. She was anxious to let herself go. There seemed more energy in her than she could contain. Balbir eased forward the reins. She did not move. She wished to counterpose every action of his, to resist. He felt his fear returning, but bravely he touched her flank with his heel. She pawed the earth and put her head down. He yanked her head up. Suddenly she shot forward almost unseating him but he hadn't forgotten the trick of the knees and he was carried with her, his hair flying in the wind like a ridiculous little flag. The muffler had fallen somewhere long before.

Now she bucked, reared and went bounding and prancing over the field as skittish as an outsize lamb. She tried every ruse of twist and turn and executed a medley of curvet and caper and frisk. He stayed firm.

Jheera wanted to sing out and shout encouragement to him but, and that was the strange part of it, he felt he would interfere. A form of communication seemed to be building between man and animal and it was still delicate and, yes, he felt he would intrude. But he told himself he didn't want to add to the noise. As it was, the mare's hooves were thudding into the tilled field. He was glad the earth was soft and deadened the sound. He could hear Balbir talking to her, calling her Rano, the affectionate form for Rani or Queen. So Balbir was master of a capricious, unpredictable queen! He felt a surge of pride in the daring of his young master Balbir and also a pang of envy.

Balbir now guided Rano towards Jheera. She came at a comfortable gallop and he pulled her short, sure enough of himself now to stand in the stirrups. Balbir was showing off. And so was she! She stood there mincing elegantly like one impatient to be off.

Balbir said, 'Right then, see you in the morning!'

Jheera nodded and smiled and waved. Balbir swivelled Rano round smartly with her haunches going down and she made a little whirring, furry noise with her mouth and there was a delicious click and clank from the joints of the iron bit as she eased her neck under the reins. And they were away in a fine canter with a spraying of dirt as though they were in shallow water.

Jheera watched as they climbed the embankment and trotted along the track, behind a clump of trees to the turning on to the main road. Then they emerged going at a breakneck gallop full tilt with a clatter of hooves on the hard dry surface under the dust. In the moonlight the glistening black silhouette streaked like an arrow. But Balbir's outline had lost its grace. It had a wild, haphazard, abandoned look.

Jheera's heart skipped a beat.

It was clear that Rano was bolting with Balbir.

Over the canal the mist gathered as blinding as a bridegroom's veil of flowers. Balbir knew every pothole and turning in the road. He had to reach the village of Chak Deedar and there, at this hour, find the home of a woman known as Fat Aunty. Ridiculous! The thought of going so far without being sure of his destination! He had cycled this way many times. The problem was the riding.

As the mare rose up over a culvert and the furious rhythm of the hoofbeats changed in tone, he realized that he was being guided more by sound than by sight and a new terror took hold of him. He had adjusted to the idea that she was bolting and he could not in a moment stem the panic that seized her. He had to let her exhaust herself and, fortunately, she was racing along the road he wanted to go. There was no traffic. Once or twice he thought he saw the silhouettes of men, perhaps a police patrol, but the mare thundered on. Perhaps they thought he was a mounted policeman. No one challenged him. Everyone had their own fears.

He had ten miles of almost straight travelling in which to let her have her head. To try and jump off at this speed would have been suicidal. Staying in the saddle was not difficult; she was not trying to throw him now, she was running from the demons in her head. But, and this was the danger, if she veered even slightly, they would tumble ten feet off the road down a slope of bramble and boulder and stone. He had to rely on her instinct of self-preservation. He listened too for the dulling of her hoof-beats which would mean they were on the soft margin of the road; that would give him a split second in which to change her course. She was most responsive now to the reins as long as he let her career on in a forward direction.

She clove on like a meteor parting the mist a few feet before her with the force of her rush and her breath and the heat of her body. Despite the cold, Balbir was perspiring. Then quite suddenly, due to some quirk of wind and weather, a quarter of a mile before the village of Nahar Nagar, the mist lifted and the road unwound like a silver turban in the moonlight.

Balbir gave a whoop and cry of elation and the mare, with a start as though spurs had been dug into her sides, shot forward crashing into the realm of her utmost. Balbir yelled, screamed and shouted like a madman. It was a blood-curdling triumph. And he laughed as much as to say, 'Do your worst and I shall treat it as the best.' The mare flew over the ground, paddling the air with her legs.

'*Aii shabashe*! Bravo! Well done!' he cried as the wind sang past his ears. And he reached forward and petted her sweaty neck and called her 'Rano'.

The village of Nahar Nagar was a modern one, sleeping on either side of a tarred road towards which Balbir was now riding. Five hundred yards from the junction, Balbir pulled on the reins and cajoled the mare. She slowed.

He was riding now, really riding, as she eased into a trot and he brought her down to a walk. And he felt no fear now and did not reach at all for the horn of the saddle. He sighed and sat back and felt like a king. He knew that he was capable of riding Rano.

But there were other fears. Fears of being stopped and victimized by either side, terrorists or police. He had turned left at the junction and would now have to continue on the tarred road for a mile before branching off again on to dusty tracks winding and splitting through small villages.

Somehow on the tarred road he felt more vulnerable. These were the accustomed arteries of terrorist action. Rarely did the extremists move to remote villages, unless their squads lived in the vicinity. The terrorists sought publicity. Indiscriminate killing in distant unknown hamlets might easily be overlooked. They preferred to come out into urbanized areas, cause quick havoc and get away. In crowded towns and cities, they could mingle, merge, escape; in small villages, they would be noticed, isolated, caught by the inhabitants or trapped in the maze of lanes and pathways.

A bus came roaring towards him, its headlights obliterating both darkness and vision. The mare trembled. He kept her firmly to the side of the road. The bus was obviously late returning to its depot. It stormed past, buffeting him with a wave of air. He saw that apart from the driver and conductor there was no one in it.

From behind him another vehicle approached, a smaller one, a jeep. It came slowly, warily, its dull lights resurrecting the scenery. The mare almost broke into a gallop but he held her in. In the process he managed to glance at his watch. 10.45.

The jeep drew up. Someone shone a torch at his face. He saw uniforms. Policemen.

Balbir took courage. He shouted, 'Get away! You're frightening the mare.'

The men laughed. A voice called out, 'Idiot! Are you out on a picnic at this time?'

'Going home,' said Balbir.

'Then get on with it!' One of the men slapped the side of the jeep.

The mare shied and catapulted forward, her hooves firing like crackers on the road. He struggled to hold her in. She slipped, swerved, turned sideways, quivering, while the jeep made an arc to avoid her.

'Come to the Police Fort at Phillaur if you want to learn to ride!' one of the men called from the back as the others laughed and the jeep accelerated away.

'Bastards!' Balbir hissed but he was glad they were on the road. It made him feel a little easier.

He had never known a time when the entire population was under such siege to terrorism.

The moonlight hit the mist making it seem as tangible as spun sugar. He felt he could eat it like candy floss. His eyes adjusted to the gloom and glimmer around him. He found the bullock-cart track he was looking for and he eased the mare off the road. He moved more quickly now, trotting up a cloud of dust and keeping ahead of it.

He went through three villages and noticed only two lights on. No one dared step out to see who was riding by.

The landscape was transfigured by the night into a surreal blend of the familiar unknown. He couldn't be sure of his landmarks. But his mind scoured the map it had contrived. He had been to Chak Deedar before, to collect chaff and bran for poultry feed. The place was a hive of small illegal flour mills. It was a poor village, a village of the lower castes and *harijans*, the so-called untouchables.

Yes, if Jagtara was old and Chamkalan ancient, the village of Chak Deedar was primitive. Yet it did not pre-date the other two. It was primitive in the sense that most villages in other parts of India are primitive. It could have come into being a hundred years ago or just a decade before and it might just as easily be abandoned altogether tomorrow. It was more transitory than the old and ancient villages of Punjab. It consisted of mud huts.

He remembered that a haphazard mud wall encircled the settlement, like the broken rim of a wheel. Wherever it was interrupted you came upon little squares with outdoor troughs for cattle. Shacks and shanties leaned against the inside of the wall and on the outside were rubbish heaps that, during the day, were snouted by snuffling pigs and investigated by crows and tenanted by flies. The village was less protected, less secure and poorer. But all around were signs of the new prosperity which his rural upbringing had automatically assessed. The fields were green and gold, there were stacks of hay, and the unlicensed flour mills had popped their illegal advertisement proudly into the air. He had seen the men going robustly about their work in their underwear and had noticed that the children were all clothed and the women smiled if they knew you weren't a government inspector. Transistor radios had played in relay, and commercial jingles and strange city accents had sprung out in announcements that had somehow dissipated easily amid the warbling magpies and the guttural thrushes, the whirring sparrows and the sudden swift blue kingfisher.

Now in the silence of the night, as he walked the mare along the periphery of the village, the complex of directions he had visualized became etched and dramatized with pictures of the reality like a work of medieval cartography or a child's book of geography.

Where should he begin to look for that unknown entity, Fat Aunty? He stopped and wondered. In the stillness he could hear the mare breathing heavily, and now as he rested a hand on her neck he became aware that she was wet with sweat.

There was a light somewhere in the innards of the village. The huts were built so low that from the saddle he could scan a large part of the area. As he straightened his back, craning his neck to look, the mare moved forward slowly, one hoof striking a tin can that clattered and resettled in the rubbish. A dog barked.

He decided to find his way to the house with the light. He could hear the hooves squelching in the mud. The village seemed to have no paving or drains. A second dog joined in the barking. A moment later from another direction, a befuddled cock crowed.

He heard a movement behind him and thought it was perhaps a dog and then he heard an unmistakeable click. He stopped. He would have been delighted to find someone awake at this hour but an uncanny feeling warned him that he was being stalked.

'Anyone there?' he called. There was an ominous silence. He tried again, 'I'm just looking for my friend. Can you help me?'

'I don't believe it!' said Kumhareya stepping out of the shadows. 'It's you. On a horse. Alone! I thought it was the police.'

'Phew!' Balbir dismounted and almost collapsed. His legs were buckling under him. 'I didn't know how I was going to find Fat Aunty's place. Lucky you were out here.'

'No such thing. I came out to see who was sniffing around.' Kumhareya gently returned the hammer of the revolver into position and reset the safety catch. 'Are you really alone?'

'Of course.' Balbir found himself resenting the undercurrent of suspicion. 'What did you think, I would lead the Ahluwalias to you?'

Kumhareya's right shoulder twitched in a half shrug. 'The world is full of deception. We can't take chances.'

They were talking in whispers. Balbir's voice broke as he said, 'I could hit you for thinking that of me.'

Kumhareya gestured with his head. 'Follow me.' He didn't have his turban on. The small knot of long hair on his head was tied with a white handkerchief that bobbed like a buoy in the moonlight as he led the way through an alley and into a cattle-yard that had one cow and its calf tethered to a stake by a trough. 'Wait here. I'll light the lamp. We'll talk inside.'

Balbir ran the edge of his hand along Rano's neck. The lather came off like shaving foam. 'She's thirsty.'

Kumhareya pointed to a circular cement tank. Balbir nodded, led Rano to it and watched as she pushed the scum away with up-and-down movements of her mouth and began to suck at the water.

There was no spare rope that he could see. He needed to tie Rano before she finished drinking. The reins were too short to reach the stakes in the ground. He saw a length of cloth, a turban or a cotton *saree*, strung out to dry in the yard. He quickly unhitched it from its moorings and with it tethered the mare. He thought to himself, a turban has many uses, no wonder previous generations considered it essential. It keeps the head warm, protects it like a helmet and you can use the end-flap as a handkerchief, a mask, tear it for a bandage or use the whole length as a rope!

He felt a touch on his shoulder and spun round. 'Damn it, Kumhareya! I wish you'd keep your squeaky shoes on. At least I'd know you were creeping about.'

Kumhareya smiled and beckoned him towards the door. A clay lamp burned inside, its illumination casting elastic shadows.

A finger to his lips, Kumhareya said, 'Talk softly. Everyone's asleep.'

Balbir glanced round the mud-and-wattle room. Three shapes lay under ragged quilts on beds that were joined together and between two of the shapes he saw the face of a baby. On the other side of the room were two string-beds placed at right angles to each other. The bedclothes of one were rumpled, the quilt flung aside. In the other was Gulnari, fast asleep with her mouth slightly open. Dishevelled as she was, she still looked beautiful.

For some unfathomed reason Balbir was aware of a surge of relief; Kumhareya and Gulnari were not sleeping together. Yet. Yet? What was it to him?

Kumhareya patted the space beside him on the vacant bed. They sat down.

One of the figures on the other side of the room stirred and turned over and then began to sit up. The face was dark, and puffy with sleep. 'Who's that?' The voice was worried, female and throaty.

'It's all right.' Kumhareya whispered. 'A friend of mine.'

'Oh. Do you want me to make some tea?'

'No. Don't get up.'

She lay back obediently and turned over with a sigh, no doubt relieved that there was no demand on traditional hospitality, and soon they heard the intermittent purr of her snoring.

'That's Fat Aunty,' Kumhareya murmured. 'Now tell me.'

'The Ahluwalias have got to your man in Chamkalan.'

'Jassa?'

Balbir nodded. 'Where's his motorcycle? I didn't see it outside.'

Kumhareya snorted softly. 'Can you imagine coming here on a phut-phutty announcing our arrival to everybody? We ditched it a mile from here, in a sugarcane field.'

'You'd better get it and get out of here. Fast.'

Kumhareya shook his head. 'Impossible at night. We'd be challenged a hundred times before we got to Amritsar. The main road is clogged with pickets and barriers made of drums round which you have to manoeuvre. It's been like that since the bloody Asiad.'

He was referring to the Asian Games that had been held two years before in 1982 in Delhi. The Akali Dal had threatened to disrupt them in order to draw the world's attention to their demands. Mrs Indira Gandhi, the Prime Minister, had retaliated with strict security measures that prevented demonstrators from travelling freely or reaching Delhi. There were frequent check points along the main arteries and all sikhs were searched for weapons. In the neighbouring states the checking was even more rigorous. As matters turned out, these measures offended the sensibilities of many law-abiding sikhs who felt they were being treated like potential criminals. Retired senior officers of the Armed Forces who happened to be sikhs, and sometimes were also nationally known and respected war heroes more accustomed to being saluted than searched, were in particular distressed. They began to feel that discriminatory orders had been passed. Later, Bhindranwale shrewdly tapped this feeling and invited retired sikh officers to a meeting. More than 150 attended; they included Lt Generals, Maj. Generals, Brigadiers, Colonels and Majors. A few of them eventually actively assisted and advised Bhindranwale in military tactics. In fact, as subsequent events were clearly to prove, Mrs Gandhi had never intended an iota of bias against the general body of sikhs; she was, if anything, enamoured of their renown as a brave, martial, loyal community. But India's politics thrive on communal innuendo and the creation of a slight out of an oversight.

Nevertheless, Kumhareya was right. He could not have evaded detection at night, especially on a motorbike.

Balbir glanced at Gulnari's sleeping outline and muttered, 'You'll never get through with her during the day. Every villager will be able to say which way you went. But you could make a dash for it before they can catch you.'

'No need of it,' said Kumhareya ruminatively running his tongue over his teeth.

'What? But the merchants will be gunning for—'

Kumhareya glared at him. 'You should have delivered my message, that's all. Only Amar Singh and his boys can arrange for us to get through.'

'But Jassa may break down and tell them where—'

'He can't. He doesn't know.'

'He doesn't know?'

Kumhareya grinned. 'You are a fool, riding here at night on a needless errand, fighting your own fears.'

'And bringing you courage.'

'What's that?'

'Never mind.'

'Ah, another of your smart cleverisms. You should meet Amar Singh. He'll put you in his pocket. Maybe we should make a sikh of you.'

Balbir smiled, 'I'm not even a good hindu, I'd be a very poor sikh.'

Kumhareya was teasing now. 'Either a sikh for Khalistan or get out.'

Balbir made a sideways movement with his head. 'Don't be silly.'

'You'll see. It'll come to that. I didn't believe it till I saw the light.'

'And what if I were a sikh who didn't agree with your politics or Khalistan?'

Kumhareya's eyes developed a faraway look. After a pause, he sighed, 'But you're not political.'

'No,' Balbir admitted. 'But I'm a human being.'

'It's just politics,' said Kumhareya, 'When we're on top, we'll be kind to everyone. You'll see.'

'But you're not under anyone. It's everybody's country. You're a citizen just like me.'

'Hmph.'

'You only go along with these extremist types because you want to be important. You want to be part of some movement. You want to do things secretly, to be trusted, valued—'

'Yes, I like being given special assignments. I like being part of a group.'

'You should have gone to a good school. You would have joined the Boy Scouts.'

Kumhareya's lip trembled. 'Don't make fun of me! We're not playing games.'

'They're using frustrated young men like you. They only want to rule.'

The words were an echo of Randhir Singh's scoffery near the Old Ruin as he ate green peas. 'It's for power. *Sirf hukumat karan lai hai!*'

Kumhareya's eyes dilated. 'Shut up!' He said it so sharply that Gulnari awoke.

She sat up in a sudden flutter as of pigeons' wings. 'You? What are you doing—?'

'It's all right,' Kumhareya said firmly. 'Nothing to worry about.'

Balbir had never seen Kumhareya in this role of master, leader, protector. He was actually commanding. 'Go back to sleep.'

But she was Gulnari, with a mind of her own, and questions. 'Did you ... did you get to the Golden Temple?'

'Tomorrow,' Balbir nodded. 'I'll go there and give them your message.'

She was completely oblivious of how attractive she looked as she twisted there in bed rummaging under her pillow. 'Here! Will you post this for me?'

'What's that?' Kumhareya asked suspiciously.

'A letter to Kulwanti. Thanking her. Begging her forgiveness. Nothing specific. Just to say goodbye.'

'What's the point of that?'

'I've also said we're going on the train to Delhi. If he posts it near Ludhiana railway station or at Amritsar, they'll really think we've gone out of the area.'

Kumhareya thought about it and his face brightened. 'That's not a bad idea. They'll stop looking for us around here. So that's what you were writing this evening!'

She nodded, 'But I didn't know who we could trust to post it. I was going to ask Fat Aunty in the morning. Now you can post it.' She actually winked.

Balbir smiled. There was nothing delicate and coy about her. She was strong. And didn't let her brains rust. She had quietly worked out this red herring that he was to lay across the trail. No wonder she had enjoyed conniving with the terrorists in their activities. But why had she joined them? He had no time now to think that out.

He stood up and nodded, 'All right then.'

She said, 'All right.' Licking the envelope shut, she handed it to him.

Outside, Kumhareya cursed. 'You bastard, you've tied your horse with my turban. It'll smell all day.'

'The horse or the turban?' Balbir joked.

'*Hut oy*! Get away with you!'

Untying the mare, Balbir said, 'You'll have to help me. Hold her at the mouth. I'll get up on the edge of the tank and mount that way. She's skittish.'

Kumhareya took hold of the bit. He frowned and pursed his mouth. In the sprinkle of moonlight, his face took on the vacant configuration of a skull. 'You'll be able to face the Ahluwalias, won't you?' Then he added slowly. 'You're the only one who knows.'

'They won't tamper with me.'

'You mean, you're not just a potter boy.'

Balbir started to protest then said, 'They wouldn't dream that you had confided in me.'

'I had no choice.'

'Nonsense. You could have told that man Jassa.'

Kumhareya shook his head. The handherchief over the ball of hair flapped at its corners. 'He wouldn't have understood.'

Balbir turned and peered into the skull to decipher its expression. 'But he lent you his motorcycle.'

'I would've lied to borrow it. As it happened, he wasn't there and I took it anyway. Just told his mother and wheeled it out. Started it by joining the ignition wires. He had taken the key with him.' The skull grinned. 'We've been taught to start cars and motorcycles without the key. Actually I broke the wheel lock. It doesn't matter. I'll explain it to him when I see him next. We'll get married in the Golden Temple.'

Balbir nodded, turned to the tank, put one foot on it and stopped.

Kumhareya waited. Then he said, 'What is it? I know you've been trying to ask me something or say something. What is it?'

'Kumhareya . . . '

'Uday Singh. I've got a name.'

'Uday . . . did you really kill a man, that farmhand in the well?'

There was only a slight pause. 'He had a name too. Randhir Sian.'

The chill night air seemed to be corkscrewing into Balbir's belly making him nauseous. 'Why? I mean, why did you have to kill him? Didn't it . . . frighten you?'

'No.'

Balbir had his back to him, wanted to look at him but couldn't. He felt short of breath, as though he were suddenly claustrophobic.

Kumhareya's voice was a controlled hiss. 'He was against our cause. He mocked it. He was a sikh and yet he mocked it. We don't want to have to fight for people like him. We can do without—'

'You're lying, Kumhareya.' Balbir was surprised that he spoke up at all. It was the sick feeling in his stomach churning out of him. 'He must have stood in your way somehow.'

'That too. Fate brought him there to meet his death. You know what they say—you can run from it everywhere and then when you rush to a safe place you find Death sitting there and Death says, "Ah welcome, child, I knew you would come to me at the right time." He came to the Old Ruin. He was spying on us.'

Balbir was frightened of what he now wanted to ask. He forced himself to look at Kumhareya and he hoped his anguished twitching cheeks were not visible in the dark. 'Have you . . . have you killed before? Ever?'

Kumhareya laughed. 'On assignment.'

Something caught at Balbir's heart and he sat down on the

edge of the tank. The mare rubbed her nose on his chest.

He had never realized that a terrorist could be someone he knew. People who killed beyond the level of the emotional personal scale were not expected to have faces. They were horrifying unknown quantums in newspaper reports. They were aberrations of social rationality, clusters of group insanity. They formed the black hole in the universe of social perception. Where did they come from? Where did they go? They were only explanations. They were a gorging violence that swallowed. After the explosions, the sabotage, the murders of innocent men, women, children, there was only the unbolstered knowledge that something had happened, wiping a slate clean; life had been erased, rendered extinct. Not extinguished as in a *crime passionel* or vendetta by the likeness of a vengeful hand that, unmindful of the hurt to itself, squeezes out a flame, but extincted by a suddenness beyond the build-up of passion, a polar region that comes and goes in a second, a whiff of cold breath. The targets of terrorism are so many, often so unsuspecting, the motivation receding to the infinitesimal point of distant publicity, that the mind sees only numbers, statistics, and a pyramid of blank corpses piled for cremation or mass burial. Terrorism is a cold act without a shiver.

Balbir wondered how Kumhareya was capable of it. How could he find satisfaction in the creation of unhistoried, unsung bodies?

'How could you do it?' he cried in an anguish that made him whisper rather than shout.

Kumhareya's answer rocked Balbir for it was almost as if he had followed the sequence of Balbir's tortured thoughts. He said, 'It is the only way out of our impotence in this situation.'

'What situation?' Balbir swallowed to keep back his sense of desolation.

'Amar Singh will explain that. I can't.'

And then Balbir realized that Kumhareya had not indeed read his mind, he had only been quoting a mentor who had been put such questions before. The answer had been a glib stopper that clamped down on emotion.

Those guns and grenades that Balbir had taken were indicators of Kumhareya's involvement but somehow he had assumed that the cache was like the one maintained by his grandfather, a store against an unforeseen eventuality. He had not allowed himself to think that this farmhand, this labourer, this son of a potter, this friend, actually used those weapons on order.

'I am a soldier,' said Kumhareya. 'I do what I have to do.'

'No. Soldiers fight wars. You fight against peace. You attack unarmed, unprepared people.'

Kumhareya shrugged with one shoulder. 'That's not my fault. Nobody stops them from being armed and prepared. We are.'

'But don't you see, they don't want to do that!'

Kumhareya gave his peculiar shrug again. 'That's not my concern. We know what we want. You'd better go now.'

Balbir nodded, sighed and stood up.

Kumhareya said, 'Don't betray me.'

Balbir looked up at the sky. The mist was clearing. A few stars were visible. He sighed again. 'I should. But I won't because you say you are in love with this girl and want to marry her—'

'I'm risking my life for it.'

'What's your life when you've taken others?'

'Don't be clever with me.' There was a hard edge to the voice. His lips had drawn thin over his teeth.

Balbir ignored the threatening tone. 'We won't want you back in the village.'

Kumhareya seemed to be thinking. 'You're nobody to tell me that. But I won't return because I can't. After this.'

'I even regret that I'm going to help supply arms to people like you.'

'What's that?' Kumhareya had drawn closer.

'I might as well tell you. I have to tell someone. The thought of it is killing me.'

'You can trust me.'

Balbir snorted. 'The way things are, yes.'

'You were saying about arms for us?'

'Tarsem is in the business. I'm joining him.'

'So that's why you were coming out of his *chabara* that day! I was surprised, but then I thought it may have to do with getting a passport and papers. I had too many other things on my mind to—'

'But only for a short time. It's for the money. Quick money. So I can get away from all this.'

'It's blood money,' said Kumhareya with what seemed a sneer.

Balbir was caught unawares. 'I thought you would approve!'

'I do. But not of your reason for doing it.'

'Would you rather I didn't do it?' Balbir asked eagerly.

'No, no. We need the guns, you need the money. But . . . it would be better if you really felt like helping us.'

'How can I feel that when you are—?' Balbir's indignation

was on the rise but Kumhareya cut him off.

'That's the trouble with you hindus. You won't join us. You have no love for the cause.'

'There's no love left in me for anything. I hate myself.'

The bitterness touched some responsive chord in Kumhareya. He embraced Balbir. 'Thank you for coming all this way for me. Goodbye.'

The cold metal of the revolver that Kumhareya kept tucked under his belt repelled Balbir. He withdrew and tried to turn the revulsion into a joke. 'You're quite a little politician, you bastard. And you're illiterate and crass like most of them. But you almost fooled me just now. I couldn't join your movement even if I wanted to. Even if I were an extremist in some ways—'

'Some of your Naxalite friends are with us.'

Balbir laughed. 'That was something else.'

Kumhareya didn't know what he meant but gave his shrug and said, 'They're helping us.'

'But your movement is only for sikhs. Extremist Khalistani sikhs.'

'Still, you could sympathize.'

Balbir swung into the saddle. 'I don't.'

Kumhareya laughed. 'You're just a fool, a stupid hindu.'

'You mean if I were a sikh and disagreed with you—?'

'I'd be only too happy to put a bullet into you.' Kumhareya wasn't laughing.

Neither was Balbir. He touched a heel to the mare's flank. She moved eagerly towards home.

He rode back, thinking. He hardly needed to guide the mare. She was anxious to be back in the warmth of her stable.

It was darker now. The vastness above was speckled with stars. Even stars die and are born. Man is dwarfed by the questions that surround him.

What impels you to value life, to fight for it? And why do you condemn some who take it and not others? If some men jumped out of the night suddenly, blocking the road? Who knows why? A mistake. A mistaken identity. Murderers. Terrorists. Murderous fools. Last month, on this road, an old man and his wife were stabbed to death for saying a stupid thing. The couple had only five rupees on them but the old man said to the robbers, 'You won't get away with this, I recognize you.' And he was stabbed and the old woman's throat was slit. But he was found breathing next morning and told the story and died. If a murderer jumped out now? Ride down on him with the mare at full gallop. If there were too many? Swing down the incline and through the fields. Even if they were in a car they couldn't follow. Good to be riding a young mare. But why do you fight for life if there is life after death?

There was that soldier who came back years ago to the village and people asked him how the war had been going on the border and they wanted to know the brave deeds he had done and he looked at them, without his turban on and his hair unknotted and down to his waist and his eyes staring through everything, and said, 'Do you know who I am? I am a killer. I kill for a living.' And they locked him up.

He told the truth but they locked him up. What made him suddenly dangerous? Perhaps it was that he had ceased to distinguish. He didn't know friend from foe. He was prepared to kill anyone but he thought everyone was his friend. And he confided his self-reproach to everyone. For a simple villager he must have thought a great deal. He wasn't even schooled but he educated himself. You don't need words to think, only to explain.

But you can't think like a saint and be a soldier. You've got to understand that by the light of the world it's right to kill some men sometimes and wrong to kill others at other times. You've got to decide, this is friend, this is foe. Or it's decided for you and you fight. Sometimes you have to fight to stop injustice and oppression and to defend yourself. A soldier is for defence. You have to defend because, after all is said and done, you don't really know what happens. The whole world fights for life as if this were the only life despite all the religious beliefs about afterlife. So, in fact, the whole world disbelieves. It hopes but, in fact, it disbelieves.

All this would be resolved if only you knew what happens. Till then it seems the world only knows that it's wrong to start a fight but right to fight back. But is it really right to fight back? Should you not find an alternative, some system that side-steps conflict? There was the non-violence of Mahatma Gandhi. And that of Martin Luther King. The same as that of Jesus Christ. The way of the unyielding martyr. The cause grows. The legend grows. And the individual life goes. You cannot really disarm the assassin till you disarm him of his fear. He is afraid of you, afraid to let you live, afraid of your potential even if it is non-violent. The answer lies beyond just non-violence.

He was still thoughtful as he led the mare quietly into her

stable. He petted the dogs in passing and, having unsaddled her, put her back in the stall.

'Thank you, Rano,' he whispered in her direction as he stole out of the vast shed. Then he walked towards his family well with an unintended swagger and quivering calf muscles that he was sure would ache the next day. He glanced up at the sky. Still two hours to dawn.

Before he knocked on the door and ousted Jheera the Opium-eater from his bed, he took out the envelope Gulnari had asked him to post and looked at it. She had slightly masculine handwriting slanting to the right. Kulwanti's address leapt at him in a whiplash of lust but to his bewilderment what he was conscious of most was the smell on the flap that Gulnari had licked shut. It was the fragrance of mint.

7
...

Foreign Hands and Indian Tricks

The time-bound call came through at exactly midnight Indian Standard Time. Karnail Singh's mistress spoke while he listened in on an extension with the mouthpiece covered and coached her in her replies. She had arranged the call at his request to a number in West Berlin. She had no way of knowing that she had asked to be connected to one of the many restaurants on the Kurfürstendamm or that it was seven in the evening there and the person-to-person call being answered by Mr Teohar Singh was in fact being taken by Satyavan.

'Mr Singh!' the jolly, cherub-faced bartender had yodelled. 'Your call.'

But Mr T. Singh was already on his way to the telephone and the other gentleman—another Mr Singh no doubt—had ambled up to the counter and slipped him another 50 DM note together with a fluent phrase of thanks in German. The only thing the bartender could remember later was the rather exorbitant tip for what he assumed was an incoming local call.

Karnail Singh's mistress remembered a little more. She was sure she had congratulated Mr Teohar Singh on his brother's new job delivering milk from the dairy which he was to begin doing next Monday; there had also been talk of cans, cows, bulls and bags of feed, all rather mundane, and then Mr Teohar Singh had given a number that was to be rung in Copenhagen, Denmark, two days later at a specific time. Karnail Singh had noted the number but he must have called it from some other telephone.

The men who had grilled her weeks later were determined, adamant and displayed every promise of being ruthless. She had actually picked out her child's exercise book and shown them the half-torn blank page which Karnail Singh had used. He had also used the child's pencil. Her interrogators were delighted. By employing a certain amount of basic skill in detection on the subsequent page, they discovered that Karnail had written Copenhagen 117587. When they checked with their colleagues abroad they were chagrined to learn that it was another restaurant, the Rio Bravo on the Vester Voldgade, and a couple of waiters there did dig up the memory of an olive-skinned gentleman who had received not one but four calls. No, he was clean shaven. No, no turban. He could have been Turkish, Sicilian, Greek, Indian, Pakistani, Arab . . . They hadn't quite forgotten him because they had made—'You know how it is, we amuse ourselves in passing,'—comments and conjectures about the couple. Couple? Yes, there was this skinny, leathery, trinket-laden lady, about fiftyish, with him. They sat close. At first they seemed to be lovers though he was younger. 'Oedipus' we called him, then we, well, he could have been her gigolo so we said 'Valentino' but then there were all these calls and his generosity . . . we thought he was an eccentric sheikh or maharaja. Eccentric? Well, dating an ageing woman when he could afford better and wearing an old suit, deep blue, when he obviously had money to throw around.

And so, through one clue or another, the trail led to restaurants and message-taking agencies, in Gothenburg, Stockholm, London, New York, Washington, Toronto and Montreal. Sometimes there were indications that the telephone callers had accents other than Eastern ones: Polish, Russian, Central or Southern European. But the scent petered out in each eatery. It was as if a giant spider had walked across the map with its legs resting briefly in specific but haphazardly chosen establishments.

On the morning of the 12 January 1984, in the well-appointed kitchen of the house on Münchenstrasse in Berlin, Satyavan warmed his hands round a mug of coffee. Raskaan sat over his *masala* tea savouring its vapours as Renate cleared the breakfast things and prepared to take Jackie the Alsatian for his morning walk.

'Don't bother with the dog,' said Raskaan, 'I'll take him for a ramble. Elder brother and I could do with a little exercise.'

She raised her eyebrows behind her wire-rimmed spectacles, then smiled and gave a quick nod. Raskaan the late riser was making many exceptions in honour of his cousin. She was a quiet person not given to probing the mysteries of the eastern mind. She loved its mystery and left it at that. To Satyavan, she

had not said more than, '*Guten morgen. Hast du gut geschlafen?*'
and before she could remind herself and rephrase it in English,
Raskaan had corrected her affectionately. 'He's my elder
brother. You shouldn't say *du* to him. *Sie* is how you should
address him.' Then even as she murmured '*Entschuldigen Sie
bitte,*' he turned to Satyavan, 'She wants to know if you slept
well.'

Satyavan gurgled goodhumouredly. 'How could I not in such
a cosy atmosphere?'

'*Danke,*' she said and remarked to herself that Satyavan's eyes
went mongoloid when he smiled.

'God, elder brother,' sighed Raskaan, 'I miss India, particularly our village. You know she's studying Indian architecture.
She's taken slides of the houses in Jagtara and Chamkalan—
excellent photographer, by the way. You should see them. Old
men smoking *hookahs* in elaborately engraved doorways, *sardars* lolling near fretted archways. You'd think every peasant
was living in a palace. And the children playing games in
courtyards and fields, games that need only stones and bits of
string. I once counted forty-eight games. We're an inventive
people and how rich we are in creating beauty! When you
contrast slides of modern European houses with the old village
ones of Punjab, you feel like flying home. Such attention to
detail, such—'

'OK, café messiah,' chuckled Satyavan. 'Let's go.'

They drove to some woods and let Jackie out. As they strolled
away from the Rolls, Raskaan said, 'Now, elder brother, what's
the latest?'

'Balbir is in with Tarsem. He is to accompany Karnail on the
next delivery. Just a few cans, I mean guns.'

'Oh God!'

'Nothing to worry about. Karnail is there.'

'But it could be dangerous.'

'Bound to be. But he's let himself in for it.'

'Shall I fly back?'

'No, not yet. He might pick up some useful info. That'll be
helpful. Let him get into place.'

'But . . . but you can't use my younger brother like that!'

'He's my brother too,' said the cousin.

'Aye, but you can't drag the whole family in with you!'

'We're fighting a bigger thing than a little racketeer. It's not
just local business and local politics. We've got to do whatever
we can.'

Raskaan kicked a stone, scratched in his beard and tucked his hands into his pockets. 'It's unnerving. Why should you think my car might be bugged? Why do we have to come out to talk?'

Satyavan grinned. 'In India I wouldn't give it too much thought but here we're in a region of high technology and we don't know the extent of the conspiracy.'

'Is there a conspiracy?'

Satyavan nodded. 'But we don't yet know how deep it goes.'

'Pakistan?'

'It could be even deeper than that. The pro-Khalistan groups are not scrupulous about the means they employ.'

'In fact, they may be being used!' exclaimed Raskaan.

'Exactly. For instance, can you be sure that that man Schneider—?'

'You mean that bum?'

'The dog caught him but was he trying to steal the car or was he up to something else?'

'Well now . . . '

'You see what I mean? We have to watch out for more than the police, more than Interpol, more than agencies that frown on certain . . . um . . . business activities. We all know that business is like a cloth hanging on a line, one side sunny and one side shady. We accept that. The law sometimes shines on one aspect and sometimes frowns on it. It just depends on the regulations, the policies, the licensing restrictions, the import-export allocations. All that changes, can be changed. You might be dealing in spices, textiles, guns, engineering big contracts, getting a cut, or you might be an industrialist producing more than your quota. You're legitimate but there's an area of added initiative that you keep underground, a kind of buffer—'

'It's like hedging your bets,' Raskaan interrupted impatiently. As usual, Satyavan was circling the subject, looking for a way in. Raskaan picked up a stick and threw it for Jackie. 'I appreciate all that, elder brother. But you promised me the last time you were here that you'd tell me why we have to risk all our international contacts, a whole network of business associates—'

Now it was Satyavan who interrupted. 'That's not accurate. Let's be blunt about it. All our legitimate businesses are not at risk. We are only involving our underground contacts, and they are used to risk anyway. I've also agreed to make a string of pick-ups from their agents. They need an unmarked courier.'

'But why do it?'

Satyavan gurgled and spread his fingers as though releasing an invisible ball. 'Because we were asked to help.'

'Why can't they gather their own intelligence?' Raskaan complained. 'They're rocking our boat.'

'That's simple too,' said Satyavan in his QED manner. 'They're gathering what they can but India is a developing country. It hasn't yet got the infrastructure for these kind of activities. Of course, there's the CBI, RAW and IB but they need every bee that can gather honey for them. We've got a whole hive that can be of service.'

'So,' said Raskaan a trifle sarcastically, 'this Inspector Dutt appealed to your patriotism and you melted.'

'Something like that.'

'You must have worked some deal.'

'Let's say that since Mr Dutt is at present posted to Punjab as a police inspector we worked out certain parameters of cooperation that would be mutually beneficial. We agreed that in this case international intelligence gathering and international business gathering could go hand in hand.'

Raskaan laughed. They were by the edge of a small lake. Jackie was carrying the retrieved stick in his mouth. Taking it Raskaan threw it a hundred yards into the water. Jackie barked with delight and sprang off to swim.

At the farther shore were a labrador and terrier frisking about around their owners. There were very few people. It wasn't a holiday.

Satyavan shivered. 'The water must be freezing.'

'Oh, dogs don't mind it.' Then he frowned at Satyavan. 'You're sure you don't want me to come with you to Copenhagen? You don't know some of these people you have to meet.' Then he added, 'We could also have fun.'

'That's what I'm afraid of.'

They both laughed. An old couple going by hand in hand smiled at them.

'Is there any way I can help?' Raskaan was waiting for Jackie to shake himself free of water and return with the stick.

'Yes. Mainly, use your own initiative. For instance, you said that Bavarian fellow who came yesterday has something to do with the Red Brigade.'

'Wilhelm is a crypto. Ideology is just a prop to him. He wouldn't agree with that, of course. He vows he's as committed as the rest. We get on well. To him I'm from a poor exploited country getting my own back on the capitalist west. In his eyes that makes me a sleeping revolutionary dreaming of poetic justice. He rather likes me for that. But actually he just loves action, secrecy, adventure. He's agreed to go on a jaunt with the Rolls all the way to Nepal.'

'Good.' Satyavan held Raskaan by the shoulders and pursed his lips. 'That's the business side of it. Is there going to be any . . . uh . . . contraband in the car?'

'No.'

'Excellent. So he needn't worry about extra searches and detours.'

'His lot are going to enjoy themselves boozing and bribing their way to Kathmandu. He doesn't mind going through wars and bombs and rebelling tribesmen. After that I've got plans for the car.'

'OK that's your end of it. My end is this. Get them to dawdle through Lahore and—hell, I might as well get straight to it. I want your Wilhelm to check out three places in Pakistan where Punjabi extremists from India are being trained in guerrilla tactics.'

'Name them.'

'Kasur which is just across the Sutlej, fifteen miles from Ferozepur in India. Sheikhupura which is near Lahore. And Aminabad which adjoins the Gurdaspur district in India. We want to know who is running these training camps and how. Also whether Pakistani commandos are being coached there in how to pass off as sikhs and infiltrate India.'

Jackie was leaping about, whining. Raskaan threw the stick again.

'Do you think there's American involvement, CIA involvement?'

Satyavan searched in his pocket, drew out a few cloves, offered them to Raskaan then bit on one. He breathed out, over the tingling sensation in his mouth. 'We must distinguish between the American people and the CIA. They don't always know or approve of what their agency is up to.'

Raskaan shouted, 'Come on, Jackie! Let's move on.' As they sauntered through a grove, he said, 'It stands to reason, elder brother. Pakistan is a wedge. They can twist it either way and try to break the Russian hold on Afghanistan and the other way split up India to gain a foothold there.'

'Quite. They've got about a hundred camps in Western Pakistan, in Baluchistan, to tease the Russians with. We're wondering what they've got on Pakistan's eastern side.'

'Did you pick up anything from America last time?'

Satyavan nodded. 'But when I passed it on to Dutt he laughed. He said that the IB had much more than that and RAW was studying far more explosive material.'

'All right, so fill me in.'

'Briefly and quickly.'

'Briefly and quickly,' Raskaan agreed. 'And thanks.'

Satyavan flinched and recoiled. He stared at Raskaan then sulked. 'Fuck off!'

'Why're you annoyed?' Raskaan was bemused.

'You can't be serious if you thank me for something you have a right to demand of me. Your western politeness sometimes makes me uneasy. It's as if you were practising diplomacy.'

'Come, come, elder brother. You're not upset with me, you're upset by what you're going to tell me.'

'Yes, you bastard, you're on the nail again. Bloody reformed hippie. Café messiah!'

Raskaan laughed. 'All right, unload it then.'

Satyavan gritted his teeth and muttered, 'You know that, in 1971, ten million refugees swarmed into India fleeing the genocide in East Pakistan. Indira Gandhi had to send the Indian Army into East Pakistan to liberate Bangladesh.'

'Three cheers!'

'OK, well and good, agreed. The USA could do nothing about it. The Seventh Fleet twiddled their propellers in the Bay of Bengal. Nixon cursed. Kissinger fumed. Around that time, Pakistan's intelligence set-up worked out a plan of revenge. They wanted to do the same thing to India and also teach Indira Gandhi a lesson.'

'Huh! Pakistan is too busy surviving its military dictatorship and internal tensions to risk another confrontation with India.'

'Right. That's what we thought and that's probably a correct reading. Pakistan is even smaller than before. It can't possibly go the hog alone. So where does it leave us?'

'You tell me.' Raskaan stopped and watched Jackie chase a squirrel.

'Anyway, you can't blame them for having a plan. There isn't a country that isn't peeping over the garden wall to see what fruit it can pluck from its neighbour. On the face of it, their plan would have seemed impossible to execute. The objective: split sikh from hindu, create smaller, more amenable little border nations out of India. They decided to give sympathy and financial support to a small lunatic fringe. The bait was dropped by way of an ad in the New York Times. The ad appeared as early as October 1971 and suggested a separate sikh homeland. It alleged that the sikhs were being oppressed in India. At that time it must have seemed absurd. I mean, the sikhs have always been looked up to in India as a special cadre. Especially in the context of the fact that Pakistan's General Niazi surrendered to a sikh, General Jagjit Singh Aurora, it must have seemed ridiculous even to the information department of the Pakistan mission in Washington which paid five thousand dollars for the ad.'

'Good God!'

'But there you have it. The bait drew fish. An Akali radical and one time finance minister of Punjab, Dr Jagjit Singh Chauhan, appeared in Washington and visited Pakistan twice at their expense. Through the same mission he met a high-up official in the American government. From then on his contacts in Washington grew. He began to set up so-called Khalistan consulates abroad. Suddenly he had over a million dollars to play with and such consulates came up in New York, Houston, San Jose, Detroit, Montreal, Toronto and Winnipeg. We've now collected tabs on a few others who were cultivated lovingly by Pakistan's intelligence officials. One of them, Dhillon, was befriended in 1975, and in 1979 he went to Pakistan at that government's expense and met President Zia-ul-Huq. The next year he led a ten member delegation and met the military dictator, General Zia, twice. Then in 1981, he visited India and spouted the sikh nation theory. He has since been prohibited from entering India. Both he and Chauhan maintain close links with the Pakistan missions in Washington and London. Fortunately Indian Intelligence is able to monitor these. As for us, dear brother, our part in this is to use what contacts we have in PIA, the Pakistan airline, and obtain the dope on all those pro-Khalistanis who have been issued free tickets.'

'That's not difficult. We've got a couple of business links there and a lot of bummers and boozing chums.'

'Develop more. Just get the lists—for business reasons, of course.'

'Of course. In fact I can depute Jehangir and Ahmed to do that in London.'

'Throw in a woman for good measure.' Satyavan rumbled. 'They probably have your sort of appetites.'

'Oh, Ahmed is quite capable of recruiting suitable help. And in the US, there's that lollipop, Niloufer.'

'Anyway you handle it.'

'Fine. How far back do you want to go?'

'Obviously till 1971 and keep the mill running through the present.'

'Done. Do we spend our own money on this?'

'It's our donation to the cause. We'll reap a harvest in actuals.'

'You bastard!' Raskaan shook his head and laughed. 'But it's going to cost us a packet.'

'Right, king, that's two jobs for you. Keep in touch the usual business way. Don't forget Wilhelm's instructions. But don't give yourself away. Better use the gun-running ploy or any business tactic.'

'Will do.'

'And from now on look under every bed you screw on for that little microphone. Better still, be like me, don't screw.'

They roared with laughter and walked on.

That afternoon Satyavan flew to Copenhagen for a dinner engagement with a lady whom he addressed as Miss Clausen. She called him Mr Gordon, though he had expected to be called Mr Govardhan. Much to his discomfiture she held hands with him again and again. But each time she passed on bits of folded paper. Nuzzling into his neck, she whispered, 'Now caress my hand under the table and take the ring off. It is for you.' It was a cheap silver Tibetan ring with a rectangular compartment for keeping sacred charms. He knew it contained a square of microfilm. His mind exulted but his heart shuddered at playing this embarrassing, compromising love-scene, especially in public. He still saw himself with village eyes.

Later having parted company with her, he drifted towards the Tivoli gardens and found to his consternation that the place had closed for the night. The guard at the gate pointed to his watch and indicated that it was after midnight. Satyavan was sure he had an appointment with a group of persons for 1 a.m. in the Jazzhus Slukefter.

Now he really regretted that Raskaan was not with him to indulge his flair for languages. Danish was completely beyond Satyavan. He made an attempt at sign language, dancing and playing an unseen trumpet.

'Ah!' the guard's eyes widened, his mouth opened as though for a dentist. *'Natdiskotek?'*

Satyavan nodded, not quite sure whether he was being bailed out of his dilemma.

The guard pointed to midnight on his watch and grumbled

'*Efter midnat indgang Bernstorffsgade.*' He spun his finger in the air.

'Taxi?' Satyavan enquired.

The guard shrugged and gargled out a stream of incomprehensibility that seemed to indicate that it was up to Satyavan to make that decision.

Satyavan nodded affirmatively. 'Taxi. Taxi.'

The guard called a cab and retailed instructions.

The Jazzhus *Natdiskotek* was just round the corner and packed when he got there. As his eyes adjusted to the candle-lit gloom of the cellar an American voice called out over the throb of the bass and the ripple of syncopating piano. 'Hi there, Mr Monsoon! Join us, won'tchya? We got a crazy beat goin' and an empty chair.'

He threaded his way past a few tables and sat down with the three afficionados of jazz. 'Yes,' he said, 'I'm Man Singh.'

'Mr Monsoon,' said the black American, 'we caint tell you how pleased we are that you got here with that English language noospiper under yer arm. We aint seen a one for days. Muh keds is worn out searchin' the streets.'

'Name your poison,' muttered the long-haired white man sitting opposite. He had a ginger beard trimmed in imitation of Jesus Christ.

Satyavan ordered a glass of the house wine.

The third man spoke with a felted accent that softened all 'd's and 't's. It wasn't a lisp. It was a Brooklyn-Italian accent. 'This thown agives me the woiks,' he confided. 'But here's awishin' your sightseein' alla success.' He raised his glass and drank.

'Man!' exclaimed the black. 'The third world caint take any more shit.' He was nodding at the music and beating time with the rolled up newspaper. A few minutes passed as Satyavan settled into his surroundings. Then he smiled at his companions. 'Nice noisy place.'

'OK, OK, OK,' muttered the man from Brooklyn as though conceding some demand. 'The boss is not apleased that you went over his head to Don Gugliano. But he says it don't matter. We're not looking for a markets that afar. He respecks your motive. We got their request but we don't supply. The pipeline is yours. Exclusive. He's doin' you a favour. You gotta respeck that.' He saw Satyavan glance at the others. 'Don't aworry. They's my cover.' He laughed. 'Couldn't come here with a bunch of Sicilianos or Danes, could I? This here's my vacation in Europe. So I've lugged the music for you. It's on tape.'

Satyavan said, 'I was in a hurry last time, that's all. I knew about their request. I was worried your people would make an offer. So I went straight to Mr Gugliano. There wasn't time for the usual—'

'Ya. But there's a kissing ladder you gotta respeck. The whole thing woiks on respeck.' He sighed. 'Anyway, we honour our commitments. You got the market, it's yours.'

'Compensation?'

'Nope. And for ayou we passed the word, understand? But not everyone is like us, get it?'

'Bonnano—'

'Don Bonnano's retired. He's enjoyin' his old age. But we talked to the right boys. Noo Yoik's closed. We even passed the word to Chicago and down state. But we can't aguarantee your ahold beyond our lines a supply. There's aplenty of old army stuff floatin' about. They junked a lotta AK47s.'

'I understand.'

The music stopped. There was applause. A pause. It began again.

'There's some fine singin' on that tape. But we stay away from that kinda thing. The boss said to tell you we got enough of our own parlour-tics, we don't mess with others. We was doin' you a favour this time.'

'I appreciate that. What about Canada?'

The man took the felt hat off his lap and placed it on the table. He dug into his coat pocket, took out a packet of Camels and tapped one out. Jesus leaned forward with a Ronson and lit it for him.

'Man, you got a hat there! Some hat!' the black picked it up and admired it.

'Eye-talian,' said the man from Brooklyn proudly. 'Feel the linin'. It's like feathers.'

Satyavan became aware that something was being transferred by the black from a pocket inside the felt hat to the folded newspaper. He said again, 'About Canada?'

'Yup. About Canada. You know what happened when Don Bonnano tried to finance a cheese factory there? They made a hero of him—they shoved him inna the can. But there was no way he had violated any law. So they put him on the next plane out, Napoleon cognac, cigars and all.'

'But now?'

'We're a little way in, not enough.'

'Who's running the line?'

'Ain't one to speak of.'

'Another drink?' Jesus suggested as the waiter came up. Satyavan shook his head. They ordered. The waiter hovered long enough to write it in his pad and whirred away.

Satyavan rose to go. 'Give my regards to the family.'

'Sure. But if you're in the US, stay clear athem till this parlour-tics blows over. That's why they sent me. You may be hot there. This is election year in the US. The Reagan administration could get tough with us. We gotta play it cool all round.'

'Right.' Satyavan collected the newpaper, gripping hard to make sure the cassette didn't fall out.

'Take care,' said the black.

'See ya,' said the man from Brooklyn.

'OK,' said Jesus scanning the exit and the clientele with a professional eye. He scratched under his jacket, near the armpit, where the shoulder strap of the holster itched him. 'I'll tail ya till ya get a cab.'

As Satyavan walked out followed by the languorous Jesus, he thought: how organizations change with the times! Some years ago you could have spotted one of the mob a mile off—dapper clothes, tie-pins, gold rings, slouch hat, overcoat. In the heydey of Migliano, Costello, Bonnano, Magadino, there were only men of Sicilian descent who traced their allegiances through ancestral links with feuding groups in the rugged hills of southern Palmas but now they were no longer tight-knit 'families', they were extended business empires employing all sorts and their protection rackets covered—what they abhorred before—white slavery and trafficking in drugs. Satyavan had never really known these men though he had on occasion met them to work out certain lines of supply. But he did know this: though he was only forty-five, he preferred dealing with the older men. They were somehow more eastern in their thinking with their emphasis on principle, honour, the patriarchal structure and vengeance. He smiled as he remembered how he was often characterized in the village as 'the best henchman of the patriarch'. But then he also recalled the youthful Balbir's words: 'It's all so stupidly egotistical—this feudal hierarchy, this violent feuding, this childish pride. It's medieval!' And he frowned.

But that was why he had gone straight to old Don Gugliano. During the Second World War the Don had put his resources at the disposal of his country and in his own way helped the Allies in Europe. He could understand that archaic word patriotism. And yet Satyavan had not ventured there only with an emotional appeal. That would have been silly. He had gone with his economic arguments neatly shaped: guns and goods to the underworld of Bombay, to dacoits in Central India and to criminal gangs everywhere was a lucrative business and comparatively safe, but to supply a breakaway movement was to lose out in the long-term for the sake of one tempting splurge. If the movement succeeded the market would be reduced; in any case, a vast in-flow of weapons would nullify the careful liaison built up with crime-fighting agencies since Intelligence organizations would be drawn to the scene. If the insurgency was heavily armed and became a threat to the police, the army was bound to be called in, and with the army would come Military Intelligence. That would play hell with the sources of the weapons. If the army was called in there would be a complete clampdown on the state and a sudden end to all such trade. The market would be lost, perhaps for decades.

Gugliano had agreed that restraint and refusal were part of keeping a market alive but he had remarked wryly that those who wanted weapons badly enough would acquire them somehow, even collecting them one at a time like stamps. But, yes, a big set-up flooding the market would drown it, leading to its closure.

Satyavan had said that he was aware a couple of powerful families in Delhi were scouting for links and meanwhile providing assistance to small-time runners across the borders of Punjab. A few thousand small arms had already trickled in. Don Gugliano had pointed out with a smile that if they were small-time they wouldn't last long without proper protection. But that's your market, he had said, I can only tell you what the little Dutch boy did when he saw a trickle in the dyke. He put his finger in and plugged it.

The cassette that Satyavan had received was for his ears alone. It had been obtained through his sources, and these sources were jealous of activity that impinged on their own so they had gone to the trouble of collecting a little data for Satyavan. The material would not hold up in court; it was a recording of a conversation, obviously conducted under some duress, and one person was, as the professional underworld put it, 'singing'.

In his hotel room, Satyavan fished out his Sony Walkman, plugged in the earphones and listened to a few startling revelations. Some extremist sikhs abroad and at least 'one sikh guy with muscle in India' had accomplished a liaison with crooks in Europe. At Posselt in northern Belgium they had engineered a robbery that fetched them about thirty million francs. With a large portion of this money they had acquired a sophisticated mobile printing press that could be dismantled and transported easily. The press had many uses but its main function was to enable a couple of expert counterfeiters to produce phoney money, especially one-hundred-dollar bills. This counterfeit currency was then 'passed' by a number of persons, including some extremist sikhs. The 'clean' money then obtained was used for financing the smuggling of heroin. From the considerable profits of this operation, weapons were being bought for the terrorists in Punjab. The 'singer' confessed that he didn't know much about the guns that were being bought but he thought they might be routed through a gang in Italy and Turkey. But he knew definitely that the press was in a place called Hasselt and a large part of the phoney money was passed through the Netherlands, especially since Amsterdam was the European centre for drug-trafficking.

The man was obviously an addict himself for though there were no sounds of blows or physical ill-treatment he seemed to be begging and whining. Eventually it became clear that he was asking for 'a shot'. The grilling was an all-purpose one with no specific emphasis on the Indian connection. Names were named, places mentioned, even financial details were elaborated. The 'singer' became even more fluent, almost flying into panegyric, as he spoke of the Zeydyke in Amsterdam. He spoke of it with affection as the heroin and criminal district, centrally located near the main railway station. He talked of a friend who had been 'busted' forty-eight times for offences. He mentioned acquaintances among the immigrant communities that had settled there. Some names were Chinese, some Surinamese, some Dutch, some German, a few French and a few American or British. The Zeydyke seemed to be a welter of nationalities and activities.

As Satyavan listened fascinated, his mind conjured up the ambience of those dimly-lit streets, the scruffy gangs of muggers and maudlin burnt-out cases haunting the shadows. He visualized the understaffed, outnumbered police rarely if at all checking this crazy area after 11 p.m. He saw the casual tourist wandering innocently into this hell-hole stippled with risky cafés and bars. And then he smiled, for the 'singer' suddenly related a sad experience that had given him a shock at a time when he was desperate for just a couple of hundred guilders to buy a day's supply of, the man moaned, anything, anything, even methadone. Three of them had set upon an Easterner who seemed to be snooping around as he walked towards the railway station. It was nearly midnight. They grabbed him and started to strangle and rob him. To their astonishment the victim laughed and went into a blur of precise movements that broke collarbones and noses and had them calling for reinforcements. The rest of the gang came, one with a rod, another with a stiletto. But in the flurry that followed, the intended victim left four men unconscious. They had taken him for a diamond merchant or businessman; he was probably a commando or a martial artist. Such were the hazards of the 'singer's' life on the Zeydyke!

Sometimes it seemed the man was begging not for his life or for heroin but for sympathy. He said his mother was a 'heroinwhore'. 'She was a resistance fighter during the war, helped many jews, fooled the Nazis, but who cares? Now she works the men for heroin for us both.'

One of the two interrogators on the tape muttered something about how the 'singer' had done well by becoming a 'pusher' for this new set-up. The answer was a whine of protest. 'What are a few thousand guilders when the dealers are making a quarter million each evening?' There followed a spate of statistics and percentages that ended with a subtle attempt at vituperation against 'these foreigners who are cutting in on the market to get themselves some guns.' He was trying to ingratiate himself with his questioners, to get more money and perhaps a new job that would fetch him a cut both ways. The tape ended with an abrupt 'OK', from one of his captors.

After a moment's silence, a new voice said hoarsely but clearly. 'No copies to be made. Erase and drop for your own safety. Repeat. Erase and drop.' There was a snap and then the hiss of the remaining portion of tape.

Satyavan listened again to specific points in the material, then erased it and during the morning accomplished the 'drop'. It was a marked cassette. They would expect it back as an indication that the favour had been acknowledged honourably.

Then as a precaution he bought another blank cassette, unobtrusively recorded some women nattering in a café and left the cassette in mid-playback in the recorder. The recorder itself went into the depths of his suitcase which he locked carefully.

To himself Satyavan mumbled, 'Their strength is their weakness.' That paradox was a favourite admonition of the patriarch. 'Strike the enemy where he feels most secure—because he will least expect it there.' So what was the strength of this rival racket? The drugs, the guns, the money? After mulling it over, he decided it was the counterfeit money. On that foundation the structure rested. He had somehow to dislodge a corner-stone, pull down the pillars of support. He would have to depute someone to 'finger' a key 'passer' who would be caught red-handed by the police. He knew just the person he could trust to set it up. But he had other details to attend to before that.

Next stop Sweden, first Stockholm then Gothenburg. In the bitter cold, Satyavan denied himself the luxury of discussing matters comfortably before roaring log fires. In both cities, shivering in his overcoat and balaclava and rubbing and slapping his gloved hands together, he outlined details of Operation Backup. 'When the squeeze is on,' he said, 'terrorists and sympathizers will make for Scandinavia. They'll do the obvious thing. You've got to be ready to take it from there.'

'Shades of Libya and Israel!' exclaimed the gentleman with whom Satyavan was stomping the frozen ground of Gothenburg. 'Do you think it will come to that?'

'I'm not here to give opinions,' said Satyavan exhaling jets and plumes of breath. 'I'm only telling you what has to be done if the worst happens. The ball is in their court. It's up to them. There's only one condition I must lay on you—no innocent person must be hurt. Make sure your network of information is utterly reliable. Then be precise, accurate and discreet. We don't want attention or international incidents.'

In London, New York, Washington, Toronto and Montreal, Satyavan ran a gamut of contacts. They included sikhs, hindus, christians, muslims, jews, not to mention agnostics and atheists; some of them were naturalized citizens, expatriates or natives of the countries he visited. One fact emerged clearly: the vast majority of sikhs everywhere were horrified by the statements and actions of the pro-Khalistanis who were only a small vociferous group. Satyavan felt reassured. Nevertheless he emphasized to his agents the need actively to encourage the splitting and splintering of the movement.

A couple of times Satyavan had the feeling he was being followed and not at all stealthily. Once a lean, blonde, droopy-eyed gentleman with a camera hanging by a shoulder strap entered an airlines office and stood about watching the endorsement on his ticket. The man smiled as though waiting his turn but then came out soon after Satyavan and tried to strike up a friendship. Another time, Satyavan stepped out of a shop and was accosted by a helpless-looking Asian of indeterminate nationality—bald, bespectacled, in a brown suit and grey overcoat, scanning a map of the city. 'Excuse me,' simpered the Asian nervously. 'I seem to have lost my way. Could you help me?' He said he was from Uganda, an international refugee from the days of Idi Amin. He invited Satyavan to join him in a coffee. He tried to tag along as a fellow tourist. For a while Satyavan enjoyed being as rude to him as he pleased, marvelling at the man's determination to string along. Then, on the third try, he lost him, not in a crowd or a busy thoroughfare but in the dark of a cinema when they were being ushered to their seats.

Twice during his travels, the hotel rooms he occupied were burgled. He lost a little money, a few traveller's cheques and the sheaf of unrelated clippings and papers he had deliberately stuffed in his suitcase. He also lost the recorder and all cassettes. The real material had either been delivered to specific points en route or had simply been mailed to a poste restante address for safekeeping. He knew that the pro-Khalistanis had no intelligence network to speak of and that these 'burglaries' bore the stamp of an accomplished, cool-headed organization. It made him consider how the world's affairs were really being controlled more and more by an international fraternity of assorted Intelligence agencies. Sometimes they played games with each other; sometimes the stakes were so high that they gambled with their lives. But usually they played with the lives of others.

These were men and women familiar with the naked machinery behind the smooth façade of power. At first they took pride in the potential of a particular machine with which they were associated; they had an allegiance to it. But as the organization employed more and more mechanics, became more impersonal, cynicism set in; cynicism that was sometimes sublimated into a 'pure' love of machines. Then the mechanics were open to enticement and some of them transferred their loyalties from one organization to another like specialists do in other fields. Words connoting ethics and emotion lost their meaning; they had themselves fabricated, contrived and created too many traitors, betrayers, martyrs, heroes, nations and governments to feel more than a passing pang for a childhood illusion. Of course there were exceptions; but if cynicism took note of exceptions it would soon revert to idealism.

Satyavan was an amateur helping out with his expertise as a businessman-racketeer so he easily retained his sense of allegiance. But he was also aware of the professional side of it so he retained his sense of humour. After the first burglary, he couldn't resist a small practical joke.

Going into a bookshop he bought the first suitable tome he saw. It happened to be an edition of Charles Darwin's *On the Origin of Species*. Back in his room, he resorted to one of the most common tricks in the trade. He hollowed out a square hiding place in the central pages of the book. Then he fell back on another cliché—a cryptogram. He worked out a simple cipher based on numerals corresponding to the alphabet. He knew they would decode it within minutes.

And he gave his deep gurgling laugh as he thought of the analytical minds of the upper echelons inhabiting that rarefied atmosphere of agents, double agents, treble agents, spies, moles, information and disinformation. And he wrote his communication down and folded it neatly into the niche. Then he placed the volume under the clothes in his suitcase.

The coded message tucked into Darwin's book read: 'You bastards, a booby-trap is wasted on you since this again makes a monkey out of you!'

After the next visit from the 'shadows' a few days later, there was no other. They had got the message.

While Satyavan was threading his way through Europe and the US on the track of men who celebrated distant tragedies with champagne and provoked far off violence from the safety of foreign countries, matters were growing deadly serious in Punjab.

Even in Southall and Birmingham urbane discussions about the intricacies of the pattern of bloodshed were possible because the murders did not reach home there except as emotional resonances. Many pro-Khalistanis abroad talked brashly of heroics but very few dared indulge in them; they had too much to lose. They had migrated to alien lands not because Khalistan lay there but because the comforts and luxuries of the economically advanced countries beckoned them. They had arrived like their fellow-Indians and other hope-filled migrants from the Third World, not unaware that racial discrimination abroad might reduce them socially to second-class citizens but they were prepared—as a man once mistakenly advised Mahatma Gandhi in South Africa—to 'pocket the insult along with the money'. They had not all made good but they had certainly made better. They had jobs, houses, social security, a modicum of wealth, access to sophisticated entertainment, and they had their immediate families with them or, in some cases, a substitute wife and family. Most such men were hardly likely to abandon all that they had built up in order to enter the embroglio personally. They had fled the discomforts of a struggling economy in a country once fabled as the land of silks and spices, the very wealth of which had drawn colonial invaders to rob it of its riches; they were certainly not going to return to those discomforts now compounded by turmoil. Worse, if Punjab were indeed to be divided again to make room for a new nation, Khalistan, they were hardly likely to return then either. They would remain where they were comfortable.

So even the small group of pro-Khalistanis abroad had really only a tiny hard core of self-seeking politicians and true religious fanatics who dreamed of a separate fundamentalist state. How minuscule their number was is indicated by the fact that, though they busily issued threats against distant adversaries, when events came to such a boil that their own individual lives were threatened they sought the help, in England, of Scotland Yard and dog squads and, elsewhere, of local law-enforcement agencies. Though they fostered violence by their *braggadocio* they had neither the men nor the means to protect themselves when the violence seemed likely to boomerang. Yet, to give it its due, it was an active, catalytic hard core.

Its utterances, though disapproved of by the sikh intelligentsia, were not rebutted by most of these intellectuals out of sheer personal fear. It was just champagne abroad but blood in Punjab. From the sanctity of the Golden Temple, Bhindranwale spoke to the rhythm of unexpected bombings and stray terrorist gunfire in the countryside. The silence of the five high priests of the Akal Takht was deafening; there were daily expectations that they at least, being holy men, would condemn the murders, but no condemnation came.

You might ask why these provocations did not quickly start the massive conflagration that they were intended to spark. After all the Punjabi psyche is conditioned to react violently to all outrage. Was it just that India is so politicized that the average citizen could see through the antics of the politicians? Was it not also that the Punjabi more than anyone else in the world is familiar with the dread calamity that was waiting in the wings for a cue?

The ancestors of Satyavan, Raskaan and Balbir had taken that visage to Europe in the unforgotten savagery of Ghengis Khan. But in the twentieth century, twice in less than twenty-five years, Punjabis had unveiled that face on the Indian subcontinent.

Once at the time of partition and then when the Pakistani Punjabis went wild in Bangladesh.

Which is not to imply that other regions are without blemish in this regard; it is merely to point out that Punjabis possess a legacy of violence that is actually treasured though it is kept stoppered like a genie in the bottle. Violence *is* forbidden but it is not always frowned upon. The corollary is that most Punjabis are romantics when it comes to notions of honour and dignity; the need to affirm these with ferocity is communicated by osmosis if not by deliberate teaching. When a Punjabi wishes to do good, he can be totally self-sacrificing; when he wishes to do damage, he can be terrible. He will often martyr himself unhesitatingly in order to avenge what he thinks is a wrong. As a popular folk-song has it: *Doh din jeena par jeena taord dey naal*. Live two days but live with flair.

Yet, when you think back on Partition and consider the horrors and havoc wreaked by the generation of that time, you would think that that generation would soon after be denied the privilege of authority that it exercised. When you look beyond the horrible politics and the economic motivations that spurred on the communalists, when you remember that here, in Punjab, muslim was friend of hindu and sikh and shared a conglomerate culture, when you think that in the daily tussle with nature farmer was farmer and yet these ordinary law-abiding men rose in a fury of murder and arson and rape and totted up, in two months, a toll of massacre exceeding the entire casuality list of the Second World War, you can then begin to comprehend a little bit of the insanity that takes hold when a man is conditioned to react violently to all outrage. During the Partition then, a whole province of people went outlaw—rioting in blood-thirsty mobs, tracking down individual foes, butchering caravans of families, razing entire villages, slaughtering by the train-load—and when it was all over, they settled down to law and order again. But even in that time when the circumcized were being butchered on one side and the uncircumcized on the other, no family rose against another that had adopted a member of the other as brother or relative; communal enmity sank in the embrace of the family; often at grave risk, the hunted were hidden and sheltered and helped to escape. It became a matter of honour; honour worked both ways.

Now among Punjabi hindus and sikhs the ties were even stronger, closer, and often literally bonds of immediate blood kinship. If the extremists had their way they would turn father against son and brother against brother. There would be murders within the family.

But the family is the strongest, most unassailable unit in Punjab.

8

An Ant's Eye View

In the village of Jagtara, Balbir woke early after the night of the long ride. His calf muscles and thighs felt knotted, sore and stiff as he bathed and changed. He automatically switched on the little transistor radio by his bed. The news it brought was not uncommon: there had been another killing by terrorists in Amritsar the day before.

He couldn't find the muffler which he usually wound about his head so he took care to stuff a large handkerchief in his pocket. He would need it to cover his head as a sign of respect when entering the Golden Temple.

Then he waited for the Ahluwalias who were bound to come and question him about the absconding Kumhareya.

But it was to be a morning of surprises. The Ahluwalias did not come. Instead they took the wiser course of going to his grandfather and enlisting his support. There were sensible reasons for this: not only might the patriarch have resented any intimidation of his grandson but he could more successfully and quickly bring pressure on the boy and squeeze the truth out of him. Balbir was known to be stubborn, withdrawn, secretive and—well, not a bad sort but a wayward kind, loose not like a girl might be called loose but rather free and easy with his social sympathies and favours—he had even been mixed up for a while with Naxalites. Everyone, including the Ahluwalias, knew that; and it had then caused a certain amount of consternation among the established families of the region. It had seemed an anomaly that Balbir who came from one of the richest houses of the area should espouse the cause of Communist Marxist-Leninist youths. He had even run off to Bihar for a while in order perhaps to probe the origins of his anguish and affiliations. It had taken months to dissuade Balbir of active association. All sorts of arguments had been tried: means must be in consonance with the ends, the poor policemen being attacked were only hired servants of authority, the youths he was encouraging were merely the frustrated unemployed, the philosophy may be Maoist but the alignment was unabashedly pro-Chinese. This last carried the implication that it was antinational, for China was just beyond the northern border and there had been a war over the demarcation of the boundary. But Balbir had replied that it was a hangover from Imperialist times when the British had whimsically drawn the McMahon Line. There had been detailed discussions about Aksai Chin, Tibet and how Nehru had died disillusioned at the deceit of Chou-en-lai. A small dent had been made in Balbir's adamance when another tack was tried—that China was encouraging a movement for the breakaway of Nagaland from India. But still Balbir had said there must be some injustice there. Then three developments occurred that halted his participation. China welcomed Nixon's visit and forged closer ties with the capitalist US: this sudden turnaround startled Balbir and jogged his concept of a scrupulous champion of the downtrodden; newspapers carried reports that China was actually financing some of the Naxalites. Whether this was true or not it shook his sense of self-reliance and independence. Finally, there was his own discovery that not all Naxalites were young revolutionaries. In Punjab there were older types among them who were merely big landowners using the movement to settle their blood feuds. But perhaps the emotional factor that caused a curdling in Balbir was that the youths he met personally were nearly all of urban origin who had no notion of whether it was time for the *kharif* or the *rabi* crop. They had no agricultural background, often they were not even from Punjab and their attempts at the language and apeing local dress seemed like a patronizing mockery. Some smoked *beedis* and wore *tambas* and swore but it didn't bridge the gap. They were only a little less alien to him than the American Peace Corps. He wished revolutionary movements would start from the grass roots up. But in India all attempts at change seemed to come from above or from outside. So while he kept his sympathies, he cooled his ardour. And his frustration with himself grew. And his desire to rebel increased. And feeling hemmed in, he longed to get away, to fly out of himself.

Perhaps the most surprising aspect of that morning was how the news reached him that the Ahluwalias were consulting his grandfather.

The herald was Tarsem who roared up on his old 650cc Norton Dominator. But the actual messenger was Kulwanti, biting her nails and waiting in Tarsem's *chabara*.

The farmhands scattered as Tarsem swept round in a tight circle, one foot trailing. He stopped, revved, heeled into first gear and yelled, 'Get on!'

'But I've just sent for my breakfast. And I'm expecting some people.'

'Don't argue. Climb on. I'll drop you back in fifteen minutes.'

With an involuntary groan, Balbir swung a cramped leg over the pillion. They thundered away, the edges of Tarsem's white pyjamas fluttering like agitated prayer flags and his shirt billowing so that he looked bigger, more grotesque.

'Never do this again!' Tarsem shouted out of the side of his mouth. 'What'll people think? I've never allowed women in my *chabara*. I've got a wife and family. Go to Jalandhar and Ludhiana if you want to do this sort of thing. But not in the village. Fooling with women is dangerous, more dangerous than gun-running.'

Balbir laughed. 'What're you talking about?'

A spray of saliva accompanied Tarsem's reply. 'That Arora girl from Maina. The hindu shopkeeper's daughter, the one who used to hang about with the Ahluwalia girl.'

'You mean Kulwanti?' Balbir wished the motorcycle were going the other way.

'That's her name,' Tarsem nodded. He slowed for a moment, looked over his shoulder and leered, 'You been fucking her?'

Balbir said, 'Stop the bike. I want to get off. I don't want to see her.'

Tarsem accelerated. 'You donkey's prick, she's there with her younger brother right now. I believe in proper alibis. I'm not going to have people thinking she came to see me. Why, they'll ask. Why? Her friend's run off with a bloody potter and you've probably got the koochie-koochie going with this one. No, you'll see her. Why the shit did you have to make me a go-between?'

'I didn't—'

'You did. She says you asked her to make contact through me.'

'We're partners, you and I.'

'Not in this. You do your own mucking about, Billu, or they'll string me up as your partner.'

'But Tarsem—'

They were about to turn into the streets of the village. Tarsem stopped and turned part way to face him. 'Listen, you prick, whatever you do, never antagonize the people of your area. They're your support, your base, your protection. Upset them with stuff like fucking their daughters or wives and they'll hand your head on a platter to the cops.'

'You don't know enough to accuse me of—'

'OK, OK, I'm just saying, whatever you've been up to, do it in your own time, in some other place, at your own risk. Don't involve me. Now you tell that bitch never to come to my *chabara* again.' He was about to drive on when he added, 'I'll drop you at the door and come back in ten minutes. Ten minutes. Make sure she pushes off. I don't want to see either of you there when I get back.'

The motorcycle grumbled through the streets to the *chabara*. As Balbir got off, Tarsem made a point of greeting various passers by of his acquaintance. Then he sped away.

In the courtyard was a boy of about twelve absorbed in a game with a length of cane which he had picked up. He was pushing the stick ahead of him as he moved so that it bent and stuttered along the ground. From his mouth came the purr and drone of an engine, 'Brrrrrrr . . . brrrrmmmm.'

'That's a super motorcar you have there, driver sahib,' said Balbir.

The boy stared at him. His eyes appeared more luminous for being rimmed with antimony.

Balbir looked around. She was obviously up in the room. He swiftly climbed the steps. Behind him he could hear the boy brrmm-brrmming on with his interrupted play.

She stood up and rushed to embrace him. He extricated himself and saw that she was crying. She looked thinner, drawn and miserable.

He couldn't prevent himself from sounding brusque and annoyed. 'You shouldn't have come here. Don't do this again.'

'They . . . caught Jassa last night. But he managed to get away from them.'

'I know.'

She seemed surprised. Then said in a rush, 'Instead of leaving the area, he came to Maina.'

Now he was startled. 'Jassa came to Maina, to their own village! They'd never have expected that!'

'He came to see me.' Her voice broke and she drew a long hiccupping breath.

'What the hell did he do that for?'

Suddenly she began to cry and went off at a tangent. 'I had nothing to do with their . . . their crimes! I didn't know they were . . . extremists. I was just helping Gulnari. I really thought she was having an affair with Uday. I . . . I envied her. It was a kind of freedom, wasn't it, to have a lover? When you're so watched and stopped, you . . . you want to do something on your own. I just thought they liked being together. I passed on messages. I thought they were love letters. But I should have guessed. Uday can't read or write properly. I should have realized. But I thought love . . . conquers everything.' She stopped, sobbed, looked at him hopefully and asked, 'Doesn't it?'

He felt sickened. He snapped, 'This is not the time to talk about love and all that. Why did Jassa come to see you in the middle of the night?' A thought struck him. His eyes narrowed. The animal in him made him grab her by the shoulders. He knew he had no right; worse, he had no interest in her beyond the passing. And yet he gritted out the words, 'Was he your lover . . . too?'

To his chagrin, she giggled her denial. 'No. You are my only . . . one.' Then she added with distaste, 'He's so ugly . . . so coarse, so uncouth.' She spoke with the bias of her education.

He wanted to slap her because he wanted to slap himself for having demeaned himself enough to ask such a question. If she had not giggled, if she had answered equivocally, she would have hooked him on anger and inner argument. But he only felt nauseated by her sentimental tone. He turned away and said, 'Hurry up with what you have to say. The Ahluwalias are probably at the well now looking for me.'

She shook her head. 'They've gone to your grandfather.'

'To Babaji?'

She nodded. 'Jassa told me they were planning to do that. That's why Jassa came to me. He wanted to know how you were involved. He was annoyed and upset. Very disturbed. In the past, he had seen Uday tap at my window to pass on messages. I have a room to myself. The window is barred but it looks out on the street. You see, Uday could never meet Gulnari directly. Her uncle's house is at the back of a shop and the whole family sleeps upstairs. So Uday used to fix their meetings through me. Last night at about one o'clock I heard the same rat-a-tat-tat signal on my window. I thought it was Uday, perhaps even Gulnari. But . . . it was Jassa!'

He said as calmly as he could. 'What did you tell him . . . about me?'

'You will forgive me, won't you?' She grasped nervously about her for the end of her *dupatta*, then took the handkerchief he held out and wiped her face and blew her nose and burst into fresh tears. 'He wanted to know if you had been at the Old Ruin with us. That's all I admitted. I didn't think it mattered. Jassa is one of their group after all. Then he asked if Uday had taken a lot of guns and things from the Old Ruin. I said I didn't think so. I had not seen him carrying anything. Then he asked if you had stayed behind after I left. I couldn't deny that. I had to say yes. There was no harm in that. Then he told me that he had just been to the Old Ruin to arm himself but all the stuff was missing! Oh Balbir, I didn't know they had guns hidden in the Ruin. That's why Jassa really came to me. He was looking for the guns.'

Balbir stood still. Then he shrugged. 'So what? The Ahluwalias could have found them and taken them.'

'No,' she said. 'He knew they hadn't. When they questioned him, they kept asking if Uday had a gun and if so where he kept it. They wanted to know if Uday was armed or could arm himself. They wanted to know how dangerous he might be if they cornered him. They obviously hadn't found the guns.'

Balbir's hands felt like ice. He cleared his throat and said, 'So Jassa also might come looking for me!' He shook his head and sighed. 'God! Have I got myself into a—!'

She interrupted with a sob which she stifled in his handkerchief. 'He said Uday was a traitor if he had trusted you more than one of his own comrades. Uday had also broken their code of behaviour, and Gulnari had betrayed the cause by being careless. He was so furious, it frightened me. He . . . '

She was simpering and blowing into his handkerchief.

He said quietly, 'You'd better go. And don't come here again.'

She was about to protest when they heard her little brother driving his make-believe car up the steps. 'Brrrrrrrmmm. . . '

'Forgive me,' she whispered. 'Oh please forgive me. I didn't realize Jassa would feel . . . cheated. Yes, that's what he said— he had been cheated by people he trusted.'

She thrust the handkerchief into his hands. Then looked at him worriedly, 'You didn't take their guns, did you?'

He said, 'Ah here's your brother.'

She hesitated, turned to her brother as he changed gear at the threshold with a tremendous vocal accompaniment and pushed him out with the command, 'Go on down. I'm coming. We'll go and get your shoes.'

As the boy steered his imaginary vehicle out and down, she put her arms round Balbir quickly and hugged him. He gave her an impatient, understanding pat on the back and guided her gently to the door.

He waited till he heard them leave the courtyard. The handkerchief felt soggy as he stuffed it into his pocket. A few minutes later, Tarsem came and drove him back to the well.

Not everyone in Punjab was worrying all the time about extremists and their actions. At least one person was worrying that morning about the condition of his mare which he had found in a lather. The farmer Gopal Chunder saw that the saddle on the rack was out of place and the cloth was wet with sweat. He wondered what had happened during the night. Then someone found Balbir's muffler in the field and he saw the marks of the hooves and the way they led out along the track and towards the road. He was aghast that anyone should have dared to venture into his shed at night. He was disappointed at his dogs and angry with the man who had slept through it all, shuttered and bolted and barred and snug in the hutch beside the tool room. He was, most of all, surprised that anyone could have ridden the mare. Glowering under the dark patches of discoloration that had recently begun to afflict his face and, holding the side of his *tamba* in one hand and the incriminating muffler in the other, he went off grimly to see Pandit Khushi Ram and complain about Balbir.

Khushi Ram listened to his cousin and saw that he was so agitated that he would not even sit. He saw that Gopal Chunder was aggrieved and at the same time astonished that the mare had been ridden by a young man as callow as Balbir.

Gopal Chunder said, 'It may be, Brother, that he let the mare escape riderless and then led her back when she had stopped to eat some grass.'

'This is wrong! Wrong!' Khushi Ram exploded and called for Balbir. As he stood up and reached for his walking stick he thought it was strange that Gopal Chunder should be so short when everyone else in the family was tall, and yet he was a good farmer and bred, in his own way, some of the finest livestock. He called for Balbir again.

Meanwhile, Gopal Chunder said, 'Don't be too hard on the boy. It shows spirit that he tried such a thing.'

'It was foolish of him!' Khushi Ram replied. He had no intention of being lenient. The man who brought Balbir his breakfast said, 'Your father is calling for you.'

'My father? You mean my grandfather?'

'No, no. Your father Pandit Khushi Ram has asked you to come home.'

Balbir chewed through his *makki di rotti* and *saron da saag*, gulped down the glass of milk and feeling ready to take on the whole world except his father, went to the house.

'Where were you last night?' Khushi Ram asked.

'In bed,' he replied with a look of bewilderment.

'Then how does your muffler come to be found in Gopal Chunder's field?'

'I . . . I lost it many days ago.'

'But it was found only this morning.'

Balbir shrugged and said, 'What can I do about that?'

That was a mistake.

'Impertinence!' Khushi Ram shouted going livid in the face and striking Balbir once across the shoulder with the cane.

'Papaji, what have I done?' Balbir cried.

'Done? Done? You ask me that! You scum of the family! You blackguard! There was a time when people who stole horses had their hands cut off and their foreheads branded. Now you're lucky to get off with a whipping.' He swung again and Balbir cringed against the blows and retreated as they became more relentless till he was in a corner and sheltered by the obstructing walls.

'Brother!' Gopal Chunder shouted catching the arm that flailed the cane. 'He may not have done it. We may be mistaken.'

'You *are* mistaken,' Balbir cried, clutching at a straw. 'I lent my muffler to . . . Jheera the *Afeemchi* and he must have done what you say.'

His father glared at him for a second and Balbir's face must have betrayed him for his father seemed to recoil internally at some unendurable deduction. The sun-toughened features spilled awry. The mouth pulled to one side, the lower lip curled almost in a snarl, the eyes misted with humiliation, the voice quivered with rage.

'Have I fathered a coward?' he screamed. 'A coward so afraid to take punishment that he will sacrifice the skin of an innocent man. You think that poor sop could have ridden such a volatile mare? No, Balbir, I know you. You have the rashness, he doesn't. You are brash, he isn't. You think you're clever but he has more sense than you. I know you, Billua. I'm not one of those fathers who blame others for the mischief of his son. It's you who are capable of leading the fool astray. He is like a lamb. He'd follow the family anywhere. You have the blood of a young lion. Behave like one. Be bold. Admit what you have done, Billua. Don't be afraid.'

There was a quality of pain and pleading in the rage. Balbir was drawn by the flattery and ashamed to have hurt his father. He knew he loved him. And he wanted to be brave. There was a stinging sensation in his shoulder where the cane had first struck and he didn't want to be beaten any more. But his father was begging in some obscure way for him not to defeat himself. He understood that. And the fear that he might, almost made him cry. The blows didn't matter. Physical threats only made him more stubborn. But his voice broke as he spoke for he anticipated what was in store for him.

He said, 'All right, Papaji, I did it.'

His father gave a sigh of relief and turned to Gopal Chunder. 'You see, he did do it.'

Then he swung the cane low catching Balbir behind the knees. With a groan, Balbir went down on the floor.

'Get up!' his father said and Balbir rose, supporting himself against the chair and holding on to its back when he was standing and hoping he wouldn't run behind it when the blows began again.

But Gopal Chunder now interposed himself.

'Brother, for my sake, don't. It must have been bad enough for him being thrown by the mare.'

'I wasn't,' Balbir said. He was now prepared to go the whole hog, admit every bit of the truth about the riding and take every ounce of punishment.

Gopal Chunder looked at him, amazed at the ingratitude he seemed to detect in the words. He was, after all, trying to save Balbir.

'You weren't?' he frowned and blew out his cheeks in the manner that was habitual with him.

'No. She gave me a bit of trouble and then she was all right.'

'And then what did you do?' Gopal Chunder seemed intrigued as much at the behaviour of the mare as at the audacity of Balbir.

'I rode her almost to Phillaur and back.'

'In the fog and the cold and never having ridden a horse before?' Gopal Chunder laughed hollowly and turned to Khushi Ram. 'Your son is a liar.'

Khushi Ram seemed disconcerted.

'I'm telling the truth,' Balbir said.

'We'll soon find out,' Khushi Ram muttered, and moving Gopal Chunder aside gently, he said to Balbir, 'Take off your trousers.'

Balbir was perplexed and then shy. He looked at the open outer door and the two villagers standing there as casually as though they were a part of the air and atmosphere. He hesitated.

'Go on,' Khushi Ram said. 'Everyone has a prick and bum and these fellows have seen more mating of bulls and buffaloes than you'll ever do in your life.'

Balbir went red in the face. His father had that kind of tongue. The years that Balbir had spent in school and university had taught him that fathers ought not to talk like that. He undid the belt and lowered his trousers, careful to leave the shirt-ends hanging decently before and behind.

'Look there, Gopal Chunder. Do you see that?' Khushi Ram said almost with pride and he pointed with the end of his cane at Balbir's calves and thighs. They were still bruised and pink from the friction of the previous night's riding and there were two bald patches on each leg where the sparse hair had come off.

Gopal Chunder stared. Then swallowed and said, 'Fine. Come along any evening. Give her another work-out. And, yes, I'll tell you how to ride so it doesn't leave marks on your legs. Rub some *ghee* on them now, otherwise they'll hurt.'

He turned to go and stopped at the door and said to Khushi Ram, 'It takes something to ride that mare without getting thrown. If he was a better rider and there weren't any marks, I wouldn't have believed him. But he has willpower, that boy. He must have just clung on.'

'He's got some of the worst things of the old fellow in him,' Khushi Ram said. 'He has no sense of danger and that's a weakness. In my childhood, when the old fellow was young, I saw him slip, saddle and all, to the flank and the horse stopped and turned and bit him as he struggled. But he didn't get off. The girth band had broken and the saddle fell off but he stayed like that cursing, and clambered up and, ignoring the blood and the pain, he rode off. An hour later he was back with his right sleeve all red and drenched where an inch of muscle had been nipped away but he was quiet and so was the horse. He had been to a doctor and had had his wound stitched. That entire night he swore about the ruination of his shirt and the next morning he tore off the sleeve and tied it to the chain that dangled under the bit. Every day he rode the horse like that till the animal seemed sick of the smell of human blood in his nostrils and shied each time the sleeve was brought near him. But the horse never nipped anyone again. The old fellow was more concerned about curing the horse than keeping his arm in a sling, and the stitches had to be done twice again.'

'Well,' Gopal Chunder said, 'the mare belongs to the family. Balbir has only to ask. But he must ask.'

'Quite,' Khushi Ram agreed and fondled the neck of the cane.

Gopal Chunder stared at Balbir and blew out his cheeks. Balbir fidgeted and shifted on his feet and felt that he was being called upon to speak.

He said, 'I'm sorry to have upset you, Younger Uncle. But if I had asked just like that out of the blue you would not, for my own sake, have let me ride Rano.'

'Rano!' Gopal Chunder repeated, saying the name for the first time and weighing it in his mind. He puffed up his cheeks again but there was a flicker at the corners like a smile. He said, 'Right then, that's what we'll call her. Rano. And don't be afraid now to ask.'

When he had gone, Khushi Ram sighed, 'Balbir, there is something to be said for being lawful. The world would be in chaos if there was no sense of right and wrong.'

In Chamkalan, Balbir's grandfather was saying almost the same thing about him to Gulnari's uncle. 'The trouble with Balbir is that his sense of right and wrong often conflicts with the law.' Then he screwed up his eyes and added, 'But so does yours. And who is here among us who does not at some time feel that man must demonstrate his supremacy over the law?'

Gulnari's uncle, a genial, bluff *sardar* who had great respect for Lok Raj, snorted with impatience. They had been at this discussion for more than an hour. He and two other elder Ahluwalias had batted the matter about and Lok Raj had twice said he would think of a way to help them trace the missing girl, and here he was rambling on about his grandson and the law. Nevertheless, out of continuing respect, he said, 'How so?'

Lok Raj dragged on his *hookah* and murmured through a coil of smoke, 'You were going to marry the girl to a photograph, which . . .' he coughed, '. . . may or may not have been strictly legal.'

They protested almost immediately and together.

Lok Raj nodded sagely.

'Yes, she could have gone through the ceremony once again with the bridegroom when she got to Canada. But to return to the point at issue. This young fellow Uday the potter ran off with her—'

'Abducted her. Forcibly carried her away.'

'Ah. If that were so, the law would be with you. But it appears she had been meeting him, perhaps encouraging him—'

'No! We've told you we found this literature in her trunk. Also a small tape–recorder and some cassettes of speeches by Sant Jarnail Singh Bhindranwale. It is obvious she had allowed herself to drift into some political group. She is impressionable, young—'

'We once had a similar problem with Balbir.' The old man chuckled. 'For a while he was a Naxalite.'

'So you understand.'

'Absolutely.'

'Furthermore,' Gulnari's uncle shifted uncomfortably, glanced at the others and taking a deep breath, went on, 'you know the girl's unfortunate circumstances. Her mother is . . . well, not quite insane but let us say unable to cope with ordinary life. It may have had some effect on Gulnari. And, of course, you know my brother is an invalid but I have been and am like a father to her.' He said this last with a look at the others in the manner of a challenge.

They murmured and nodded.

'Now,' said Lok Raj joining his palms together before his lips in an attitude of thought, 'this man Jassa was involved too.'

'A bad sort,' said one of the Ahluwalias.

'We should have shot him,' said the other.

'We will,' agreed Gulnari's uncle.

'You realise, of course,' Lok Raj pointed out, 'that Balbir could hardly be involved in Bhindranwale's politics.'

'Of course,' they murmured.

'It would be ridiculous if he was,' admitted Gulnari's uncle. 'The movement is only meant for extremist sikhs. I would be surprised if Balbir was linked in any way with that. It's . . . it's impossible! That's why we feel he may know nothing at all. On the other hand it seems he spent a lot of time with this potter. They were friends. He might have helped him.'

'That's possible,' agreed Lok Raj, 'in which case he may not talk anyway. I know my grandson. He does not respond to blows, beatings, threats. He's very *tiheet*.' The Punjabi word meant more than stubborn, more than self-willed, more than obstinate.

'What do you propose?' asked one of the older men stroking his beautiful cascade of beard.

'There are three avenues open to us.' Lok Raj paused as the tumblers in which tea had been served were cleared.

The men fidgeted and waited. Lok Raj scratched under his cockaded turban, belched, muttered '*Bismillah!*'—he had never shaken off the Islamic influence of pre-Partition days, he was too old to change his style, he had spent his youth in what was now Pakistan, his speech sparkled with Urdu decorations—then he removed the turban, placed it beside him on the quilted string-bed and, running a hand over his bald head fringed with grey, said, 'We can try to persuade him with affection. But that will take time. We can fool him with a ruse. But we have to think of one. We can have him watched. And that seems the best course at the moment.'

Just then the telephone rang. Lok Raj turned and blinked at the instrument. It sat trilling impatiently by the old radio—a Phillips with a green eye that glowed when it was switched on. That radio was his. That he loved. But the other devices were intruders. He had never adjusted to having three telephones in the house, courtesy of the requirements of Satyavan. He treated their summons as some people did letters and telegrams, wondering first who it could be and why. But he said nothing. The world hammered at his door through these installations. It didn't seem to appreciate that he had retreated to the ancestral womb. After the holocaust of Partition, sorrowing for all that had been lost, he had retired to Chamkalan. Yes, he had retired. But there was the world with its demands, its telephones, televisions, video-recorders, tape-recorders, transistors, calculators, telex machines, computers—all thrusting new responsibilities at him despite his withdrawal.

Someone picked up the receiver, listened and said, 'It's Pandit Khushi Ram from Jagtara.'

Though he reached for it gingerly, he grasped the handset firmly like a man determined to prevent a fish from wriggling away. 'Aye?'

'Old man,' said the metallic, metamorphosed voice of his son. 'I don't know what to do about Balbir. I couldn't stop myself. Forgive me. I beat him. Not severely. Lightly on the soft parts of the body. Because at least he admitted he stole Gopal Chunder's mare last night.'

'Stole her and sold her?'

'No, old man. He rode her and put her back in her stall thinking no one would know.'

Lok Raj ran his tongue over his toothless gums, wiped the left eye which was going hazy and muttered, 'Then he didn't steal. He borrowed.'

'But without permission. Old man, he's worse than you ever were. At least you never went against your own family's—'

'Khushiya, don't tell me what I was or was not. I had done a lot before you were born and much when you were a toddler. But I never beat you for the things you did.'

'You wouldn't have dared, old man. I would've left you to rot alone among the tribesmen of the—'

'Don't start another of your foolish arguments. Just tell me, which way did he ride?'

There was a pause. Khushi Ram had obviously misunderstood the question. In his agitation over the misdeeds of his son, he couldn't imagine that the old man was interested in the direction in which Balbir had ridden; he thought he was being asked about the manner in which Balbir rode. It was a feasible mistake to make. The old man had in his time been an authority on horses. He could tell by a glance which was a hack for long-distance travel and which a good hunter for running down the marauding wild boar. He could separate those that could jump from those that were swift. He could assess by feeling the shanks and watching the hooves, the ones that went over mountains and those that were best for the plains. You couldn't get past the old fellow with theoretical bluster either. He knew all the sayings of the sage Nakula about the horse, he had the discernment of the Rishi Parashara; he had read in his youth the best Urdu works on the subject. He could quote from the Farasnama of Muhammad Abdullah, the writings of Hashimi, the Zinat ul Khayl and the Farasnama-e-Rangeen. No, he wasn't an easy man to answer when it came to horses or swords.

Finally, Khushi Ram allowed himself to conjecture carefully. 'Judging by the red marks on his legs and how they had got shaved, I would say he didn't really enjoy the experience. He must have gripped her round the belly with no sense of stirrups, rhythm or balance. Probably just managed to stay in the saddle.' Then he added, a trifle proudly, 'After all, it was his first time.'

The old man noted the embellishment of emotion and laughed. 'You should have encouraged him before. It might have given him a sensible interest.'

'But—'

'Never mind. Where was he so anxious to go last night that he risked his neck on that mare? She's a little whirlwind.'

'Ah,' Khushi Ram said. 'Let me think now. What did he say?'

Lok Raj covered the mouthpiece and smiled at the Ahluwalias, his eyes sinking into slits. He chuckled, 'Brothers, I think
we would do well to watch Balbir. He was out last night on
horseback.' While they absorbed the significance of that, he
growled gently into the mechanism, 'Go on, son.'

'I think he said he rode "almost to Phillaur". Aye, those were
his words.'

'Good. And, son?'

'Yes?'

'Don't restrain him. Encourage him to take the mare for a ride
whenever he likes.'

'Gopal Chunder has told him that. No one helps Gopal
exercise the animal. He's glad someone else can ride her.'

'Excellent. He's more sensible than you.'

'Old man!'

'No arguments. No time now for all that. Let him ride the
mare night or day.'

'I don't know what you're up to but I will if you say so.'

'I do say so.'

'And, Father, there's one other thing.'

Lok Raj kept his ear to the instrument but reached for his
hookah and took a deeply satisfied drag. 'I'm listening.'

'V.P. Joshi phoned from Jalandhar.'

'You mean, the marriage-monger?'

'Aye. He said twenty thousand rupees has been put back in my
account—'

'What?' Lok Raj almost choked on the smoke as he tried to
speak. 'Did you—?'

'No. The money you returned to me is with me.'

The old man began to curse. The tempo became furious and
fast. It was like a steam engine chugging out and suddenly
releasing a vast exhaust of hot vapour. His swearing accelerated
and dissolved in laughter. 'That Balbir!' he expostulated. 'He's
cleverer than both of us put together.'

'Where could he get so much money? He must be involved in
something!'

'Aye, surely.'

'I'll flog the—'

'No, you won't.' Lok Raj suddenly roared, 'If you touch that
grandson of mine once more with that stick, I'll—God willing
my right hand stays able—behead you!'

Such things had happened before in the family's memory and
history. The Chibbers were not famous for mollycoddling each

other. There was also the renowned ancestor Parashuram who killed his mother and set off to avenge the death of his father at the hands of a dilettante warrior-king; his rage was so unremitting that he did not stop till he had sunk his battle-axe in the neck of every warrior-king through the length and breadth of India; having completed his vendetta, he wiped his axe and, like the Roman Cincinnatus, returned to the plough. 'The rage of Parashuram' had become a dread colloquialism in India.

Khushi Ram's voice when it next came over the phone was subdued but sarcastic. 'Very well, Father. He's your beloved grandson. You tell me what to do. But we've got to be quick.'

'There are a lot of impatient men here too,' chuckled Lok Raj with a glance about the room. 'But nothing is achieved by running about like headless chickens. Plan carefully and then be quick in execution. We are doing that.' He seemed to be talking as much to the Ahluwalias as to his son. They readjusted themselves in their chairs and tried to sit back.

'But you said yourself,' Khushi Ram couldn't restrain a note of petulance, 'that he's like a young leopard.'

'Aye, that he is. Remember what we used to do in the hills when we wanted to trap one?'

'Old man, that's too long ago, too faraway and—'

'Bait him with his own kill.'

'What was that? Wear your dentures, old man. I can hardly understand you.'

Lok Raj leaned towards the gleaming brass spitoon, cleared his throat and spat. 'I said bait him with his own kill. Now is the time to do it.'

'You're talking in riddles.'

'The money you have is his, right? Your twenty thousand is back in the bank.'

'I suppose that's one way of looking at it.'

'It's the only way. That twenty thousand you have—'

'It's a lot of money!' Khushi Ram protested. 'I hadn't seen twenty thousand till I set up my own house!'

'Don't be greedy. It's the leopard's kill. If you eat the lamb yourself you can't use it to get the leopard. Now listen to me. Let it be known among the family that we found some money in the storage bin. We want to return it to the rightful owner. Whoever can prove it is his, or hers, will get it. He'll come to claim it. We'll catch him on that. He'll have to explain how he came by it. *Inshallah*!'

'Aye, God willing indeed,' murmured Khushi Ram, then he

added tentatively. 'And, Father, V.P. Joshi says that they've cabled the Bank Manager's son to return so we can meet him and, hopefully, go ahead with Aadran's wedding.'

'That's more like it. We'll decide when the lad is here. Good.' Lok Raj replaced the receiver as though it were a baby being lowered into its cradle. To his visitors he muttered, 'These telephones! They interrupt whatever you're doing. But I'm glad he called. What he says has a bearing on our plans. I'm sorry I took so long.'

'Not at all,' smiled one of the men courteously. 'No need to apologize. Let's get on.'

Briskly now, Lok Raj outlined the scheme he had in mind. 'My grandson Balbir rode towards Phillaur. I suspect he went to meet this potter wherever he is hiding. Obviously he knows. Otherwise why would he undertake such a stupid journey in the dead of night?'

'Panditji, are you trying to tell us that Balbir did have a hand in the abduction of our daughter?' This from Gulnari's uncle and in some anger.

'The facts are these, I think. Balbir knows where the potter is but we cannot say whether he shares any of the blame for this escapade.'

'It's more than an escapade, Panditji, it's—'

Lok Raj held up his hand. 'If he was party to it, I regret it. I will deal with him. He is my grandson. But one thing is clear: the girl is with the potter, she is not with Balbir. First, we want the girl back safe—'

'And the potter dead,' said one of the men.

'Dev Singhji,' said Lok Raj addressing Gulnari's uncle, 'you know how much all this pains me but we must proceed with caution. Randhira's body is, from what you tell me, still rotting in that well. Sooner or later the police will enter the case.'

'The later the better. And the sooner we find Gulnari the better for everybody.'

Lok Raj nodded, 'Indeed. Now my suggestion is this. It's too cold at night for anyone to stay in the fields keeping an eye on Balbir's movements. There are two houses at the corner of the dirt track leading to the well where Balbir spends the nights. I shall arrange for those houses to accommodate a couple of your men. Also, on the road to Phillaur, we should station a few men, perhaps in a house near the first major junction. At least it narrows down our area of search.'

Dev Singh stood up, paced the room and said, 'I would rather you called your grandson here. We could force him to talk.'

'He is not amenable to force.'

'Panditji!' One of the other men gritted his teeth and stood up too. 'You are just trying to protect your grandson!'

To everyone's surprise Lok Raj admitted it. 'Naturally. Surely you don't blame me for that. Just as you want Gulnari safely out of the clutches of that potter, I want my grandson safely out of any entanglement in this affair. We have a similar aim. I sympathize wholeheartedly with you.'

'But our matter is urgent while yours can—'

'I assure you, you will succeed faster with the method I have proposed than by alerting Balbir with threats or force. After all, you tried threats on Jassa.'

There was an awkward pause. Then Dev Singh muttered regretfully, 'He escaped, that's all.'

Lok Raj put on his turban. 'You traced the motorcycle to him. You say his name is on the list you have. There are other names on that list I suppose. Have you spoken to them?'

There was another short silence.

Lok Raj now rose and reached for his grey *achkan* which was hanging on a peg. Putting on the long coat, he continued, 'I assume Balbir's name is not on the list.'

'It is a political list,' said Dev Singh softly. His lower lip was twitching. He hated the bewildering and rather dramatic responsibilities thrust on him by the thoughtlessness of his niece. He would much rather have been at his shop worrying about sales than unravelling the eccentric involvements of his brother's daughter. He had wasted half his life on that part of the family. O God, he thought, why have you made me your victim?

Lok Raj was now slowly buttoning his coat. 'That's one more reason why you can't go to the police—Gulnari's peculiar politics.' Dev Singh seemed about to object. Lok Raj made an impatient gesture. 'We must be frank with each other, Devji. We will fight this together. But we must lay the facts clearly before each other. You see, you have already gained this from me that Balbir went out towards Phillaur last night. I needn't have told you if I wasn't interested in cooperating with you.'

'We appreciate that,' nodded the oldest member of the group.

'Now,' said Lok Raj, 'would you like to give me that list or will you follow it up?'

'We will,' sighed Dev Singh.

'I understand how you feel. We are peace-loving men.'

'We can't avoid the tests that God decides to set us,' murmured Dev Singh.

They shook hands warmly, clasping with both hands in the Indian manner. It was as though a pact had been made. Then they followed Lok Raj out to see to the arrangements of the watch. Only once by a deep involuntary sigh did Lok Raj betray how much it hurt him to treat his grandson like a potential enemy. But he was a beloved enemy.

Meanwhile, Balbir had hopped on a bus and set off on the first stage of his three-hour journey to Amritsar. The moment he arrived there he realized that the ambience of the city had somehow changed. The tension was tangible. People on the street looked askance at anyone riding past on a motorcycle. When cars carrying youths slowed down, they cast an anxious glance at it and quickly noted where they could run for cover. Drivers and conductors of long-distance buses looked grim as they set off from the stand. Passengers eyed their neighbours and assessed those who boarded—but how do you recognize terrorists? Do you look for masks and guns? But all the necessary devices may be folded and packed in those little attaché cases. Those men in shawls, for instance, or those two with blankets wrapped round them, might they not be carrying collapsible sten guns under their wraps? That sour-faced youth, is he reaching into a basket for a grenade or a fruit? When the buses crossed the border of Punjab and entered the state of Haryana, the anxiety swung the other way; there had been episodes of retaliation against unsuspecting sikh travellers for the acts of terrorism against hindus in Punjab.

Amritsar's Lawrence Road, the hub of the élite's social and commercial activity, was nearly deserted. But this was the smart area where the restaurants and cafés were always bubbling and bustling with glitter and merriment, where crowds of happy ravenous customers began with *seekh kebabs* and waded through elaborate menus. These were the variegated shops patronized by coveys of women tittering and bargaining for the tempting inessentials that make life seem a little more civilized. Even late at night, this road was the great promenade and provider. Now, during broad daylight, only a few spectral figures moved wanly through it on their errands. No one wanted to find himself sitting beside a bomb in a restaurant; no one wanted to dawdle in shops or be caught in a crowd of who knows what. The life blood had drained out of this artery. Only the wind and the elements remained normal on this road and adjoining streets. Where were all the lovely preening, strutting peacock people gone?

Balbir hurried on. This was so different from the villages, where everyone went about their daily chores and continued their normal intercourse. A premonition clutched at him as he fled from the ghosts of the city. Things were going to get worse, much worse.

Balbir felt he was an ant crossing a vast canvas being painted by a brush that may daub or destroy him. He might leave a little trail where he crossed or a blob where his corpse mingled with the scene to be noticed later only by an academic with a magnifying glass. He might vary his course as he became aware of the strokes around him but he was intent only on his journey.

A bicycle bell made him jump. The cyclist veered, wobbled, shouted, 'Even on an empty street must you walk into trouble?'

A face-reader, a fate-reader, thought Balbir wryly as he stepped on to the pavement. Then he wished he had asked the prophet on the velocipede for directions. He had wandered off Lawrence Road and meandered so absentmindedly and so quickly that he wasn't quite sure where he was.

A little ahead of him an ageing *sardar* with a comfortable stomach was sitting on a stool beside a large barrow piled with second-hand clothes for sale. He was having lunch out of a stainless steel container, observed and catered to by a little sikh boy.

The man responded to Balbir's questions desultorily and then said in the same monotonous tone as he chewed his food: 'That's where I used to park my barrow, outside the Golden Temple. But now the place is crawling with criminals. Not safe any more. They shoot in the streets and there's police hanging about. You don't want to get caught in a crossfire. Business is finished. What're you going for? Prayers? Well, make an offering for me too. The closer you are to the temple the sooner you go home in the evening. No one's coming into the city anymore, except those who're going out on political marches and demonstrations. And they don't want to buy things. The village people are staying away. You from a village? Aye, I can tell from the look in your eyes. This used to be a fine city. It's like a war camp now. The lady has let it get out of hand.'

He meant Indira Gandhi, the Prime Minister, and referred to her as *bibi* or 'the lady'.

Balbir, remembering Gulnari's letter, asked for the nearest postbox and moved on.

As he approached the area surrounding the Golden Temple complex he noticed some police pickets and CRPF personnel. But on entering the network of lanes he became aware of an absence of uniformed persons among the people on the streets; there were more persons about here and most of the men had beards and dark blue turbans. Nearly all of them were wearing crossbelts with swords or *kirpans*, a few were carrying guns. He had the feeling he was being watched from various windows and balconies. Though many of the houses were two or three storeys high, they were built cheek by jowl as in the villages of Punjab. Glancing up he saw some youths carrying sten guns stepping from one terrace to another. That was when he noticed the sandbags on some terraces. At first his mind did not register them as part of a fortification process. He thought they were sacks of grain or potatoes. His rural conditioning could only make him think of them as stores of agricultural produce. He was marvelling at the effort required to carry them up so high when he saw the sunlight glint on a gun barrel pointing down at the street.

Yet from many of the houses came the sounds of domestic activity—cooking, squabbling, radios, children's voices—but invariably there was also someone looking down anxiously to see what was happening. There was a sense of imminence. In the small restaurants, a few customers sat, discussing or eating with great deliberation. No smiles, no jollity. The general mood was subdued; not intense but glum as though everyone had tired of frowning.

To his left now was Hotel Temple View, to his right the cycle stand—it held very few cycles. In front of him the main entrance to the complex with its domed clocktower. A few minutes to three. He shouldn't dally too long if he wished to be back in the village before dark.

Taking out his handkerchief he tied a knot at each of its corners to convert it into a cap. It still felt wet with Kulwanti's tears.

Slipping on his improvised headgear and removing his shoes he went up a few steps and then down a tier of others to the *parikrama*, the marbled walk that circumambulated the large rectangular tank, in the centre of which stood a vision more beautiful than any that had ever arisen out of water—the Harmandar Sahib, the Golden Temple. It took his breath away. He had seen it many times before. Indeed, a huge colour photograph of it, taken with a fish-eye lens, hung in Satyavan's drawing room. He was familiar with every aspect of its façade and its history. He could have made a model of it in his dreams and its every aspect would have matched the reality. He knew how Maharaja Ranjit Singh had gifted the gold leaf that now glittered in the sun which was moving on its westward journey, to his right, over the Akal Takht, the Throne of Truth. From the direction of the Akal Takht, devotees passed under the archway of the Gate of Benediction—the Darshani Deori—along a railinged walk that led over the water to the sanctum sanctorum.

He knew how and when the tank had been built and first filled with water; he stood there thinking, 'This is the Pool of Nectar, the Amrit Sarovar, from which the city derives its name, Amritsar.'

And there to his right stood the shady spreading tree which too had its history. To his left, across the vast complex, stood other buildings including the *langar* where food was cooked and served to pilgrims. Yes, just three hundred and fifty years ago when the Emperor Akbar made a gift of this area for the building of the temple, he came himself and shared the same food and ate it sitting among ordinary pilgrims, a great emperor because he was a great man.

That led Balbir to thinking of the men around him at that moment. Apart from the devotees, including women and children, nearly all of whom were strolling in clusters towards the walkway of the Golden Temple, there were at strategic points bearded, blue-turbanned men armed with carbines and rifles. Some stood, some squatted, some sat cross-legged on the floor. Everyone was barefoot, of course. From the temple itself came the gentle sound of hymns being sung.

The marble felt cool underfoot but when he stepped out of the shelter of the covered verandah on to the unsheltered *parikrama* he found it hot and blistering. He heard a clacking metallic sound and saw that the steel bracelet of a man sitting in the shade to his left had struck the weapon he had pulled closer to himself. The man was staring at him. The weapon was a Light Machine Gun.

Balbir suddenly spoke to him—whether out of fright or to disarm his suspicion, he wasn't sure. 'Could you tell me where I can find a toilet?'

The man took his time answering. He didn't take his eyes off Balbir. He seemed to be removing some particle from his mouth with the tip of his tongue. He flicked it out and said, 'Just here.' He had nodded to the left with his head.

'Thanks.'

The man was again working at his teeth with his tongue. It reminded Balbir that he hadn't had lunch. He felt hungry but there was no help for that. He crossed in front of the man and went in.

It was a urinal with a row of pissoirs screened off from the door by an iron partition. It had clean white tiles. There was no graffiti here.

When he emerged from the toilet, he nodded towards the man and said, 'OK.'

'OK,' said the man, scratching at a hairy wrist. But he had raised his eyebrows in an interrogative, bemused manner.

Nothing like communication, thought Balbir, to break an icy barrier.

He walked to the right now, to the corner with the drinking water taps, stepped back into the sheltered area, over a grilled manhole and to the steps leading up to the first floor. But here he was stopped by a youth with a turban that was askew. He had wisps of long hair straggling out at the nape of the neck. From under his shawl the youth produced a rapid-firing carbine. 'You a journalist or what?' The voice was heavy and nasal with cold.

Balbir shook his head. 'I've come to meet Amar Singh.'

'Why?'

Balbir kept quiet.

The youth wrinkled his nose and sniffed loudly with a grimace, but he kept his hands on his gun. 'Amar Singh, eh?' Then he called up the narrow passage of steps, 'Oy!'

That brought down a bushy-bearded, scowling young man. He was wearing a warm sleeveless jacket over a long grimy white *kurta* and tight grey flannel pyjamas. He had a carbine slung over his back. His thick eyebrows were set in an expression of distrust and superiority, his mouth curved down at one corner in permanent distaste. Balbir thought, a curd-face if ever I saw one!

The youth with the cold said, 'Not a journalist. Santji said there would be three. One more to come. This fellow has come for Amar Singh.'

Curd-face said nothing. His expression didn't change either. He frisked Balbir.

Sniffles sucked at his nose again and addressed Balbir. 'You came from the *langar* side. Been mixing with the Babbar Khalsa?'

Balbir shook his head.

'Know Bibi Amarjit Kaur?'

Balbir made a guttural 'huk' sound in his throat, a Punjabi way of indicating negative.

'Longowal?'

'I'm not political.'

'You're not a sikh either. Are you a cropped sikh? Show me your wrists. Huh. No bracelet?'

'I used to wear one sometimes. Just like that. Many hindus do.'

'You're hindu then. But you're sure you're not a lapsed sikh, a failed sikh, a cropped one, a *mona*? We know the Babbars are trying to get Santji. If we find you're one of them or up to something . . . ' He lost the rest of it in a sniffle.

Balbir was astounded. While all this was going on, people were moving behind him towards the Akal Takht or back towards the exit. He could hear families talking softly and then going silent till they had passed. He caught an old man's eye. In his expression he read consternation, perturbation, but the old man lowered his gaze and straggled out of vision. Balbir realized that he could be shot here as easily as blinking an eye and no one would muster the courage to say they had seen anything.

Sniffles prodded him with the snout of the gun. 'You could have come on behalf of the *Nirankaris*. You could be one of them disguised.'

'Look,' said Balbir, 'I've come to deliver a message to Amar Singh. You don't want me to do that, I'll go away.'

Curd-face felt Balbir's improvized cap. Small weapons had been carried successfully under turbans and other headgear.

Sniffles took one hand off his gun to run his forearm quickly against his dripping nose. 'Who is the message from?'

'Kumhareya.'

'Who?'

'Uday Singh.'

'Of?'

'Jagtara.'

'Why did he send you and not—?'

'Jassa was caught.'

'The police?'

'No. Some others. There's other trouble. Girl trouble.'

Sniffles and Curd-face exchanged a loaded glance. Sniffles exclaimed disbelievingly. 'Girl trouble! Hunh! Jassa is not the sort to—!'

'It's Uday.'

'He could have sent one of the others.'

'I'm a friend.'

'A hindu friend?'

'That's right.'

Sniffles took a deep breath, cleared his nose with another, not snort but snert, and nodded, 'All right. But we'll dump your carcass in the streets if you look like trying any stunt.'

Curd-face gestured upwards. As Balbir started to mount the steps, Sniffles called out, 'Did you look for Amar Singh on the *langar* side?'

'No.'

'Why not? We used to stay there till last month.'

'Kumhareya told me to come here directly.'

'Did he tell you about our little ... disagreement with the Babbars?'

'I told you I'm not political. I'm not interested in your politics.'

'And you're not a Jat. You could be a hindu Jat. Maybe from Punjab, maybe from Haryana.' Sniffles was fiddling with his carbine.

'No. I'm a Punjabi, a pandit, a Muhiyal, a Chibber.'

'So you think you can order everyone around?'

'I didn't say that.'

'That's how you spoke.' Sniffles caressed something on the weapon. 'Indira Gandhi is a panditani. You know that.'

'Yes.'

'Santji says we should kill the pandits.'

After a moment, Balbir said, 'Can I go and see Amar Singh?'

Just then a grey-haired man with a toothbrush moustache and a handkerchief draped casually on his head stopped by the bottom of the steps. He extended an identity card. Sniffles said politely, 'Ah, a journalist. We're expecting you. Go on to the Akal Takht. Santji is there. Ask at the entrance. They'll guide you.'

The journalist thanked him and walked on.

Curd-face spoke for the first time to Balbir. 'All right, go on up. I'm right behind you.'

They stepped out on the first floor terrace. For a moment Balbir thought that some sort of celebration was in progress. It was like a long and broad verandah decked with bunting. Then he realized that the fluttering, flapping, colourful banners were lengths of turban cloth hanging out to dry. The predominant colour was deep blue, the hue favoured by both Akalis and Nihangs. Further away a few older men were sitting out on string-beds, chatting in the sun. Some of them seemed to have their families with them. A little boy of about twelve stood playing warrior, dressed like a Nihang.

Nearer, the small, dingy, rather dark rooms seemed to hold only young men. It was like a barracks.

But from another part of the L-shaped terrace he heard hushed female voices. He turned and saw some sad-looking teenaged girls in *salwar-kameez* sitting in a circle, sewing. Everywhere, there were young men with guns.

Curd-face mumbled something to one of the sentinels. He came back and nodded. Curd-face unslung his carbine and nudged Balbir into the third room.

Kumhareya had indeed understated. Amar Singh was not only likeable, he was startlingly handsome in a gentle, un-affected way. He wore his deep blue turban coiled tight and burgeoning out at the top like a dumpy cone. It was tied in the manner of Bhindranwale. There were two other men in the room but there was no need to ask who was Amar Singh; he seemed to be the cynosure of their eyes. They were all sitting on a cheap rug. A small array of armament lay in the centre. Amar Singh had obviously dismantled a weapon for their benefit and was now putting together the pieces. He looked up at Balbir, smiled and continued with what he was doing. When he had finished, he patted the place beside him. Balbir sat down.

Curd-face remained standing and alert.

Amar Singh said to the two in front of him: 'Now you do it, slowly, carefully, one at a time.'

As one of them reached out to begin the task, he turned to Balbir, 'Yes?' He might have been a young executive in an office putting down the telephone receiver and diverting his attention to some new project.

Balbir couldn't help returning the smile. 'I've come from Kumhareya.' He corrected himself. 'From Uday of Jagtara.'

'I see,' Amar Singh nodded encouragingly. Balbir had stopped, not quite sure how he should explain it all.

He said in a burst now. 'You see, he ran off with Gulnari Kaur, the Ahluwalia girl from Maina. Her people are gunning for him naturally and he told me to—'

Amar Singh's smile had frozen. The click of the weapon being assembled had stopped. Everyone in the room was staring at him.

Amar Singh said, 'Just give me the message. You can't come here bringing rumours—'

'It's not a rumour. I was with him. I saw him again last night. I'm his . . . his friend. He also works on our land sometimes as casual labour.'

'All these rumours about abductions and rape and drunken misbehaviour! All lies. They're spread by our enemies.' The colour had rushed to Amar Singh's cheeks. 'Last year the newspapers reported that an old sikh from England had brought his newly-married daughter and son-in-law to the Golden Temple for blessings. While walking about the complex, it seems his daughter was dragged away at gun-point by some so-called extremists. Neither he nor the bridegroom could do anything. The girl was missing for more than two hours. During that time she was gang-raped. The father went to the priests and complained but, according to the papers, the priests confessed they could do nothing about it and suggested the time-honoured solution: that since the girl was now soiled for life, the father should kill her. Do you believe that?'

Even taken by storm as he was by Amar Singh's speech, Balbir was impressed with the fluency of his manner, the almost oratorical, rhetorical flourish. He said: 'I did hear about that—'

'And what did you think?'

Balbir murmured, 'Well, there are so many young men here with guns . . . and not everyone is a saint.'

'Exactly.' Amar Singh seemed satisfied. He inhaled deeply and said, 'There are all kinds of people here. Let's admit it, there's riff raff too. Smugglers, criminals who we have to deal with because the government has pushed us into this situation, gun-runners, men who can get us explosives and bombs; we also have to mix with petty scoundrels who know the borders and cross them for other purposes. Just this morning I was talking to some rogues who operate out of Nepal. This kind of people will be dealt with sternly once we are in power. You can only have contempt for them. They are morally weak. They live to indulge their passions. They drink.' Amar Singh looked at Balbir as though he had protested, 'Yes, they do! I can take you to their quarters and you will see stacks of bottles emptied during their carousing. But none of them dares bother us. Oh yes, they're here just to make money. We'll give them that. But they're not our people. They're not our responsibility. We can't be blamed for their actions. So, you see, not everyone here is an "extremist". If someone else has done something you must take it up with them.'

Balbir nodded dumbly.

Amar Singh smiled, 'That is why we are trying to do without such scum bit by bit. We are even trying to . . .' Now he hesitated but his youthful missionary zeal got the better of him, ' . . . to manufacture some of the things we need. Anyway, I don't want to bore you with our troubles. I just want you to go back with a better impression of us. I want you to understand that we're fighting for a cause, and we're fighting because the Congress government won't listen to us. When someone won't listen, what do you do? You make a noise that cannot be ignored. That is what we are doing. But we are not lechers and criminals. We are not adventurers and madmen. If someone among us misbehaves, we punish him. People will make rumours out of anything simply in order to discredit us. They've been saying that our boys have terrorized the neighbourhood, that they don't pay for the food they eat in restaurants, that they have dragged away young girls from nearby houses. Go and inquire. See how many families complain. And you'll find it's all lies. Let me put it like this: many girls have come and joined us out of conviction. You can see them here. They are free to come and go. But nobody will be allowed to drag them out by force.'

Amar Singh paused and examined the weapon that had been assembled. 'Good. Now take it apart again and let him do it. Then time yourselves to see how fast you can do it.' He pulled his holster round so that the revolver rested in his lap, then he smiled at Curd-face. 'Some sugarcane juice for our visitor.' Curd-face went out reluctantly. Amar Singh sighed, 'I talk too much.'

'Not at all,' said Balbir politely . 'It's good of you to waste your time on me.'

'It's good of you to have come. We appreciate that. But you see how it is. We are cooped up here. Caged. It's becoming like a zoo.' He laughed. 'Yes, like a zoo. And caged animals make more noise than in the wild. They talk more, they discuss, they chatter because they are deprived of so many normal activities. Oh yes, I know I talk too much and sometimes I repeat myself. Now give me the message.'

'Uday is at Fat Aunty's place in Chak Deedar.'

'All right. You said Gulnari Kaur has gone underground too?'

For some reason Balbir found himself breathless. He nodded to avoid speaking.

Curd-face came in. He had slung his carbine over his back again. In one hand he carried a bucket, in the other five wide-rimmed bowls of brass. Setting the bucket down, he scooped up some sugarcane juice in each bowl and handed them round. While he was doing this a few shots resounded outside.

Balbir looked up wide-eyed from his bowl but Amar Singh kept his to his lips and sipped. A rifle-toting sikh in shirt and trousers came in, glanced at Balbir and spoke for a while into Amar Singh's ear. As he left, he seemed to scrutinize Balbir again.

Balbir assumed the conversation had some relevance to the shots they had just heard but Amar Singh looked at him with pleasure. 'You've been recognized by one of our boys.'

'Oh?'

'I'm told you once helped some . . . er . . . Naxalites. You're a communist, then?'

Balbir wanted to say: no, I don't know what I am. I'm just dissatisfied and distressed by so many casual injustices. At one time I looked for avenues of redress; now I am disillusioned— not with the ideologies, but with the fact that man will misuse every means to gull others into giving him power.

Amar Singh smiled at his silence and said, 'We have many ex-Naxalites here. They've realized that sikhism is the best form of communism. We are more than comrades here, we are really one. You are educated. You read English too. You know what Eric Hoffer has written? Communists move easily to another ideology. Hitler knew that too. It's the liberals and those with doubts who are hard to win over. You see, that is why our movement has very few capitalist sikhs. Santji scoffs at them and calls them 'whisky sikhs'. True sikhism is against caste distinctions, against differences of high and low. But these old sikhs who are against us still talk in terms of caste. They call this a Jat movement though the Jats of the villages haven't yet joined in. We were less than two hundred when we started. But the whisky sikhs want it to be led by the higher castes—Ramgarhias, Aroras, Khatris, even bania sikhs. But we don't talk intellectual rubbish, we talk with our guns. Santji says that when the holy war really erupts, all these whisky sikhs will run. They come here from all over the world and say: 'But, Santji, twenty percent of the sikhs live outside Punjab. We'll be butchered if you start a communal blood bath.' And you know what Santji answers? He says: "Every movement must be prepared to make sacrifices. You are our sacrifices." Who asked them to go away? Why did they desert their brethren? Ah, you should hear Santji. Of course, the communists are against Santji too because they are against all religion. They're atheists! That's their only mental block. They only have to get over that. Once they're over that, like these boys who were Naxalites, they easily join us. They don't shy away from violence and guns.'

Balbir glanced discreetly at his watch. It was not that he was appalled by Amar Singh's sometimes contradictory rigmarole. He could see that Amar Singh was sincere and genuinely trying to widen the base of his fanaticism. He sympathized with Amar Singh's valiant effort even though he saw that the ideas didn't mesh. It was just that he had to get back to Jagtara before dark, safely.

Amar Singh noticed and misunderstood.

'Yes,' his face was suddenly radiant, 'it's time for Santji's discussion. You can come along. Have you ever seen him? No? He's magnificent. Carries a silver arrow in his hand like pictures of the Tenth Guru. Our enemies mock and say he's pretending to be a guru but it's only to remind people of those teachings.' He added bitterly, 'They malign him. But if you have an open mind, you'll love him. Wait here. I'll just go and check with him.' He threw a significant look at Curd-face who became more alert. To the two noviciates he said sharply, 'Come on, come on, improve that timing.'

He had just got up when a sixteen-year-old boy ran in jubilantly. 'Amrik has given me permission! I'll go with the others. I'm strong enough to use a crowbar on the canal. He's agreed!'

'Fine, fine. Come with me and tell me all about it.' Amar Singh went out arm in arm with the boy when he stopped and said, 'The man who recognized you says you're a Chibber, a Muhiyal.' Balbir hardly had time to nod before he added, 'I'm so pleased you've come. It's a kind of . . . fulfilment. Don't look so surprised. Surely you know that one of Guru Gobind Singh's most trusted ministers was a Chibber. Dewan Dharam Chand Chibber graced the court of the Tenth Guru. And now another Chibber, one of his descendants obviously, comes centuries later to the court of our Santji. Think about it. Just think about it.'

On that euphoric, heraldic note, Amar Singh left.

Balbir let it sink in. Slowly. He had no idea what Amar Singh meant but he did know that Guru Nanak had said that, though ways of worship may vary, the whole human race is one. He decided that another half an hour wouldn't matter too much. He shifted from his cross-legged position; his legs had cramped and were still painful from the ride. Rearranging himself he glanced out over the golden dome of the temple and realized with a start that on the south terrace opposite there were sandbags and gun emplacements. A couple of masons were laying bricks to build bunkers. There were armed men there too and one of them was cleaning a Light Machine Gun.

Curd-face sat down on a string-bed. The two students of weaponry began to argue about the adjustment of a mechanism.

A slim, delicate, ageing man with a flowing white beard came in surprisingly briskly. 'Where's Amar?'

Everyone sprang up. Balbir followed suit slowly. He wanted to be deferential but he didn't intend being shot by Curd-face for making any sudden movements.

'He's gone to Santji,' Curd-face actually grinned briefly but then reverted to a scowl, 'to ask if he can bring this hindu to the discussion.'

'I'm sure he can,' the frail gentleman said in a quick, clipped manner. 'Santji welcomes those who want to hear him. I've just sent three hindus from Tarn Taran to him. They want to ask him a favour.' He scratched at the wrinkles near the corner of his eye with one finger. The crow-feet became more pronounced as he turned to Balbir. 'Do you want to ask him something, son?'

'No, sir.'

'You just want to see him, eh?' a faraway look came into his eyes as he murmured, 'Tohra says he's a *badshah*, an emperor. I say he is a deeply spiritual man. He'll redeem us all. He's our only hope.' Then he smiled, rubbed his hands together as though to warm them and gestured at the handiwork of the noviciates. 'That's not the way to fit the magazine. It'll jam. Here, give it to me.'

He adjusted it with a snap, slapped it on the side as a man might a pet animal and flung a command at Curd-face. 'Tell Amar we've got to check in some stuff tonight. I want him to report to me at twenty one hundred—' He interrupted himself and winked at the solemn, uncomprehending Curd-face. 'I'm getting old and muddled. Even going the sixteen kilometres to my house in Khiala is getting bothersome. I'll stay here tonight. We'll yet teach them a lesson, what? Tell him to report to me at nine o'clock.'

Curd-face caught the manner and though he didn't salute, he gave a brisk nod.

Balbir's curiosity overcame him. 'Sir, are you . . . ?'

'General Shabeg Singh,' the old gentleman said, then added with a little twitch, 'Retired.'

'Curd-face made a movement as though to intervene. Maj.

Gen. Shabeg Singh (Retd) waved him back. He looked at Balbir. 'What is it, son?'

'I . . . I'm going to be bringing you some guns.'

Shabeg Singh's eyes dilated. 'Are you from Pakistan?'

'No, sir.'

'Not army?'

'No, sir. I'm with Tarsem.'

'Who?'

'Tarsem and Karnail Singh.'

'Ah, yes. Next week, isn't it? Make them good ones. I examine each one. You know that?'

'Aye.'

'You're a village lad. But educated. Obviously. Good.' At the door, he had a second thought. 'You one of those Naxalites?'

Balbir somehow felt embarrassed. It was all too complicated to explain so briskly. He looked down at his feet and mumbled, 'People thought I was one.'

Shabeg Singh scratched again at the corner of his eye and, without a word, left.

Balbir sank down on to the rug as the others resumed their activity. Amar Singh had suggested that he should keep an 'open mind', the General had asked if he was 'one of those Naxalites'. It took him back to the time he had gone to Bihar to visit a college friend whose father was posted there. He had wrested permission for the holiday with great difficulty; it turned out to be, not a vacation, but a shocking revelatory trip.

For a while he had left the land of dynamic action and instant redress and been plummetted into an abyss of accepted suffering and distress. Whereas Punjab was known for its feuding and bloodlust, Bihar was notorious for its apathy in the face of rank injustice and exploitation. Whereas Punjab toiled as vigorously as it fought, Bihar idled as hopelessly as it resigned itself to its fate. The very meekness of the poor rickshaw-men who outbid each other to starvation fares at Patna station horrified Balbir. In Punjab, a tongawallah would tell you to stuff it up your arse if you bargained below a reasonable rate; here the men pleaded for employment at any cost. And, among farmers, very few actually owned the land they tilled.

Balbir wished he could goad the people to action. Casting about for some means he came upon the Naxalites.

The Naxalites derived their appellation from the village of Naxalbari in Bengal where an agitation for land reform had been channelled into violent action. The Naxalites were, generally, educated boys and girls who fanned out into the country-side in order to spark off armed land-grab movements; they obtained their weapons from whatever source possible and resorted mainly to snatching guns from armed constables and shooting them dead. Since the police represented the established order, they were among the chief targets of the attacks.

On returning to Punjab, Balbir established contact with local Naxalites and hid and fed a number of them but his involvement never went beyond being a sympathizer, and that too ceased when disillusionment set in. He could not subscribe to cold-blooded murder as a creed for progress.

Yes, he had 'kept an open mind' but no, he was not really 'one of those Naxalites'.

Amar Singh entered sweeping a shawl over his shoulder. 'Come. He'll see you!' To the others, he said, 'Practise, practise! You've only got till tomorrow.'

Curd-face followed Balbir out. It was as though he had been deputed this task permanently.

Descending the steps Balbir tried to catch the words of the *kirtan*, the hymns being sung in the temple when all at once there was an uproar that drowned every other sound. Loud-speakers erupted with political slogans and battle cries. Coming through the complex from the eastern side were hundreds of men wearing saffron bands on their turbans. Pilgrims moved aside and watched.

Amar Singh said, 'They're volunteers. They're going to the Akal Takht. A priest will make them take a vow to lay down their lives if necessary. Then they'll go out and court arrest. It's part of the Akali Dal's holy war. Sometimes Santji addresses them. But today,' Amar Singh seemed to smile at some esoteric joke, 'the great dictator, Longowal, will talk to them.'

They were joined by two other gunmen. Amar Singh took Balbir affectionately by the elbow and led him towards the eastern end. He murmured, 'Santji is there on the terrace of the *langar* having a chat with some people. He likes going there, though he now stays in the Akal Takht building.'

'He sleeps in the Akal Takht?' Balbir was a little surprised.

'In a different room each night. Safer that way.'

On the terrace above the community kitchen, Sant Jarnail Singh Bhindranwale sat, guarded by men with sten guns and rifles. Four Light Machine Guns were set on the terrace covering all approaches.

Among the group of sikhs sitting before him were three

hindus, noticeable by the handkerchiefs on two heads and a turban over the clean-shaven face of the third. There was also a non-sikh photographer wearing a cloth hat.

Bhindranwale was driving a point home. 'That is why I say the injustice done to sikhs must be avenged. Now people say I am anti-hindu. That is not true. What I did say was that if the police do not return my minibus or if they burn it, five thousand hindus will be killed. This hindu government only understands that kind of answer. See what happened when six hindus were dragged out of a bus and shot. Just six hindus killed and the government declared President's rule in the state! What about all those so-called terrorists shot by the police in encounters? Who will speak for them? Now here we have some hindus sitting among us.' He turned his Rasputin-like visage and grinned displaying two prominent misaligned teeth.

The chest-length black beard swung back revealing the cross-belt of his sword and the bandolier of cartridges for the heavy Luger pistol at his hip. 'One of these hindus wants me to give him a note recommending him for a headmaster's job. The authorities have ignored his qualifications.' He snickered into his beard. 'They are better than mine.'

There was a ripple of soft laughter.

Bhindranwale looked up at the bespectacled, bookish *sardar* behind him—his secretary—who was taking down points, and said, 'We will give them a note to take back and I am sure he will be made headmaster. Those who are keeping him back will not dare to victimize him. Because? We stand by our word. Let the world see that if hindus come to me I help them but if they don't . . .'

The photographer now moved to another angle for a close-up of Bhindranwale, who giggled almost shyly, reddened and murmured into his beard, 'Be quick.'

A couple of clicks later the photographer shifted to another vantage and adjusted his lens.

'Enough,' said Bhindranwale curtly. The armed men stif-fened. The photographer backed away, nodded and sat down.

An old *sardar* with his hands reverently clasped before him asked a question. 'Santji, the Ninth Guru allowed himself to be beheaded by Aurangzeb. Hindu priests used to look after our *gurdwaras*. Maharaja Ranjit Singh gifted the Kohinoor diamond to a hindu shrine. Hindus and sikhs have fought battles side by side. And yet you say that we must now treat hindus as our enemies!'

'They will swallow us!' said Bhindranwale sharply. His voice rose. 'So many of our young men have shaved their beards and shorn their hair. A sikh must retain his identity otherwise he becomes another hindu who also worships at *gurdwaras*. There is no other difference between us but we must insist on the difference. Yes, we have fought for the hindus. You are right when you point out all that we have done. Our gurus have given their lives and those of their sons to stand by the hindus. But now we must fight for ourselves. Is it not an insult that, after a few planes have been hijacked by those sympathetic to our cause, the security men of the hindu government search in our turbans for hidden weapons? And what are they teaching our children in their schools? That Mahatma Gandhi was the father of the nation! That creaking old man with a walking stick! No, the men we call fathers should be men with weapons. We will not be fooled by talk of love and non-violence. We must face facts. It is time to hate and be violent. They don't listen to anything else. The lady doesn't listen. She should come here and see me if she wants peace. But does she come?' He adjusted himself and continued. 'They call me communal but do they arrest the hindu fanatics in the Arya Samaj and the RSS? Are they not communal?' He gave a little grin and lowered his voice. 'Now you have seen some of the Akali Dal leaders going meekly to attend talks with the government. And what do they bring back?' He showed his hands empty. 'Let them waste their time talking. I say we are slaves and want liberation at any cost. Arm yourselves and prepare for a war and wait for orders. Let every sikh boy keep two hundred grenades with him. Let every youth be armed with a revolver and a motorcycle. With our motorcycle groups we will take revenge. I have said this before and will go on saying it—I don't think that sikhs can either live in or with India.'

Balbir touched Amar Singh on the shoulder and began to get up.

Amar Singh whispered, 'You can talk to him now, ask him anything—'

Balbir whispered back, 'He's answered everything I wanted to ask him. I must go. I have to get back. About Uday—'

'I've already issued orders.' He smiled noting Balbir's surprise. 'I did that when I went out of the room.' He gestured with his head, 'Isn't he wonderful?'

Balbir rose and joined a couple of others who were leaving. Curd-face stayed back; he obviously felt his mission was over.

Going down, Balbir was startled to hear a good-looking, grey-eyed young sikh in front of him talking to his companion, not in Punjabi but in Urdu. Overtaking them he glanced at the fair-complexioned young man. His brown beard was recently grown and the hair by his ears and neck still bore signs of a barber's touch. But he was obviously letting it grow.

On an impulse he spoke to the man in Punjabi, once again repeating a ploy he had used earlier. 'Excuse me, are there any toilets in this building?' Plus, he really did need to go.

'Of course,' the man answered in Urdu. 'Right next to the Khalistan office, room thirty-two.'

Balbir decided to ask a blunt question, hoping his rustic manner would carry it off without offence. 'You don't speak Punjabi?'

He had phrased it like a statement.

The man looked at his companion then decided to be equally direct. They were in safe territory. 'No,' he admitted. 'I don't know Punjabi but I can understand it. I'm from Sind.'

'But that's in Pakistan!'

'That's right.'

'Your people . . . they came here before Partition.'

'No,' said the man with an amused look. 'I came over the border—oh, about eight months ago—brought a little gift for Santji.' There was a hint of self-importance. Then he added, 'Santji persuaded me to stay on and help in . . . the fortifications.'

He was waiting for Balbir's next question, ready to draw Balbir on perhaps and then—who knows what?—grab him, shoot him, sound the alarm and have him held as a nosey character. Balbir lowered his gaze and walked on casually.

'Down that corridor,' said the man, pointing.

Balbir nodded, 'Thanks,' and walked along the rather smelly hallway.

In the bathroom were three armed youths of the Babbar Khalsa in various stages of relief and repair.

'So,' muttered one of them sans introduction, 'you've been listening to the milk-drinking vegetarian talking about violence! Impressed? What kind of sikh is that? Vegetarian, huh! Six of us made two hundred of them quit this place.'

'Come on,' said another to him, 'don't bother him. He's a visitor.'

'Probably a journalist,' said the third.

'Oh, Santji loves his photo in the papers. Did you take photos?'

Balbir concentrated on affairs of the bladder, then said simply, 'I'm only a visitor.'

The first youth said, 'Why did Amar Singh escort you here? You must be special.'

Balbir kept quiet.

One of them muttered, 'He's probably a stooge of Santji's from the Intelligence Bureau.'

They laughed.

The first youth said, 'Did you touch his feet? He loves that. Makes him think he's attained as much respect as the gurus.'

Another remarked, 'But he won't let untouchables near him. He's so conscious of caste. To call someone Singh is not enough. He's got to know their last name, their caste name. He's a bad sikh.'

Balbir buttoned up and stepped out. They sauntered after him but didn't involve him any further in their comments.

The sun was lower on the horizon behind the Akal Takht. Balbir walked towards it and then turned briefly into the Harmandir Sahib, the main shrine, to pay homage to the great gurus of the past whose sayings lay embalmed in the Guru Granth Sahib, the sacred book. The verses from it that were being sung at that moment were in praise of Rama and Krishna, two so-called hindu gods. Participating in the prayers were two men whom Balbir recognized as high priests. The thin, fatherly, hesitant, bespectacled Kirpal Singh and the shorter, quick-eyed, younger Sahib Singh. They were the foremost among the five high priests who had jointly issued the edict against the heresy of the Nirankari sikhs. Out of an atmosphere of peace had been generated the momentum for a spate of killings.

But now the killings had gone beyond murder-inspiring differences in religious observance; the high priesst of the other sect had been despatched and a vast number of his followers decimated, now control had moved to other hands, political hands, and killings had become the method of building power structures within the factions inhabiting the Golden Temple.

It suited Balbir—in haste now to get to the bus stop—to leave by the eastern exit. In the street behind the building housing the political offices, he was engulfed by an overpowering stench. Holding his hand to his nose, he wondered whether it was garbage or dead rats. Then he saw a small group of policemen prodding at something. Pausing by them he discovered that they had had to take 'permission' from the Temple authorities to enter this territory. They didn't really need to investigate the origin of the smell. This was the fifth body in a few weeks that they had been asked to fish out of the manhole. It was of a sikh youth who had been beaten and tortured to death, then stuffed in a sack and shoved down the sewer. One more soul sent on a spiritual journey beyond temporal power, beyond suspicion of being a betrayer, beyond identification.

The hands of the police were tied politically: they could not enter the Golden Temple complex to investigate or arrest. But they could be depended upon to respond promptly to a call to come and clean up the stink and mess.

9
•••

The Saints go Marching Out

The police came that night to Jagtara too. To pick up a body. The body of Jassa Singh alias Jasbir Singh, till lately the terrorist colleague of Kumhareya and the owner of the motorcycle on which the couple had fled.

It was not quite clear who had shot him.

The police were aware that Jassa had been unpopular for many reasons: he had been jailed a few times for physical violence, he bullied and neglected his widowed mother, he had been the bane of his father's existence, he ran up huge debts and did not clear them, he intimidated local shopkeepers and lived on a sort of wanton credit that he extracted; he had even annoyed Lok Raj by spitting on a knitting-machine that the respected village elder had gifted to his mother in order to enable her to earn her living. Jassa had treated the gift as an insult since it seemed to reflect on his ability to support his mother. Jassa was generally considered a malefactor and malcontent.

Apparently he had stepped in the way of a 12 bore slug that had been fired, as forensic deductions later proved, from the proximity of one of the houses adjoining the path leading to the fields and well of Pandit Khushi Ram. In the shed by that well, Balbir slept through the commotion. He was tired after his exertions of the day.

But when he heard next morning of the sudden demise of Jassa, whom he had never met but whose motorcycle he knew for he had sat on its pillion with Uday Singh Kumhareya at the controls, he was certain, as only one other person, Kulwanti was, that this rum character Jassa had been coming to him for a private midnight chat.

It was possible one of the Ahluwalia men had fired the shot, no doubt surprised and taken unawares by the sudden appearance of the man who had thwarted them the night before; it could have been the result of an impulsive reaction. On the other hand, it could have been a deliberate act executed by one of Lok Raj's men; for, after all, if he had arranged for some of the Ahluwalias to keep a watch on Balbir, the old man had obviously also stationed some of his own men to keep a watch on the Ahluwalias. He wouldn't have wanted any harm to come to his grandson. The pact was that Balbir was to be watched and followed, not hurt. Jassa walked into a snare not really intended for him. He was a bonus.

It was generally felt that Jassa had invited death. A lot of people were gunning for him and someone had managed to shoot him, that was all that mattered; the villagers were therefore not very forthcoming with the police.

But for the police too there was a bonus. Busy as they were, they probed the affair and learnt from their own pickets and the bereaved mother that the Ahluwalias had raised a furore at Jassa's house the previous night. Pressing on, they learnt from the Ahluwalias of the 'abduction' of Gulnari, the unreported corpse of Randhir Sian and—this really was a feather in the investigating officer's cap and a step towards promotion—the list of local extremists. From then on the case moved into top gear. Those on the list were rounded up for questioning. Solving the murder of Jassa became a trifling and not particularly important detail in view of the terrorist dimension that had opened up. The police now joined the hunt for Uday Singh Kumhareya and Gulnari.

Balbir was cross-examined in passing but not intimidated. There was no proof that he knew more than any other villager about the doings of Kumhareya. The police concentrated on Kumhareya's parents and those who were listed as his comrades-in-arms.

Alone, Balbir heaved many sighs of relief. He was no longer worried that Jassa might come stalking up the path to his door. The knowledge that the police were on the case also had a restraining effect on him: he curbed his desire to venture again to Chak Deedar and visit his friend Kumhareya. His curiosity to see how the potter boy and Gulnari were getting on was otherwise irrepressible. What had happened to them? Had they moved, been removed, what?

But though he restrained himself, it does not mean he became subdued or inactive; oh no, his energy was like a tide that, dammed in one direction, only flows more forcefully in others. He set about learning to ride the mare, he assisted with a few farming chores, he tried to think of ways to claim the twenty thousand as his own and, as planned, he went the following Monday on the gun-running mission. With Karnail Singh and three others he set off in a truck to collect and deliver a consignment to the Golden Temple.

During this enterprise he grew to resent Karnail Singh even more; the man was so solicitous of Balbir's welfare that he kept Balbir sitting in the driver's cabin all through. At the spot near the border, the other men picked up the rifles and carbines from the appointed 'drop' and brought them to the truck. These were shoved under the legitimate cargo. Then they stopped like other truckers at a *dhaba* or roadside eatery for their evening meal. From here on, Karnail Singh's chief lieutenant paid out a string of bribes to various interested parties en route. Sometimes there was whispered bargaining and a quick consultation with Karnail but invariably it was a hardly noticeable procedure. Balbir fretted; he didn't even have a revolver under his warm clothes. Most enervating of all was the fact that, for most of the night, they slept. During the time they were parked, two of the more experienced men stuffed the weapons into bags of grain and, deftly, with needle and twine, sewed the mouths shut again. In the early hours of the morning they joined other truckers who had stopped at a stream and washed up and drove on as part of a convoy of vehicles carrying produce to market. The delivery was made in broad daylight to the kitchen-side of the Golden Temple complex.

Two weeks rolled by. Balbir had no news of Kumhareya and Gulnari. But, early on, the Ahluwalias thought they did. Gulnari's letter addressed to Kulwanti, posted by Balbir in Amritsar, arrived and was intercepted by Kulwanti's father and handed over to the Ahluwalias. They were dismayed to think that Gulnari and her lover had managed to get away to Delhi. The letter was passed on to the police who, while doubting the purport of it, nevertheless automatically issued the necessary orders to their counterparts in Delhi. The search spread to Delhi.

Meanwhile, Tarsem had not sat idle either. While he was cooking Balbir in the pot and hoping to fry Satyavan too, he rustled up a quick snack with other ingredients. He was hungry for a larger share in the booming weapons market. He made a hurried trip to Bombay and persuaded the large travel organization for which his group worked on commission that it was time to diversify, to use their resources in Pakistan and elsewhere for the purpose of obtaining and smuggling in guns. They were not averse to the idea. Though they were a big organization, they were not stodgy, only bureaucratic. Tarsem hated their impersonal methods. Though they were known as Travel and Trade, or TAT for short, they were so gargantuan that they referred to their business not as one of 'sending people abroad' but in terms of 'manpower export'. They talked like accountants and thought like computers; it made Tarsem sick and he was often humbled to think that they considered him too as just another statistic in their pyramid of figures. He had no real loyalty to TAT, only an awareness that now he might use it as it had used him, to increase his profits.

But Tarsem being Tarsem allowed himself to display an expansive sense of triumph when the deal went through. One evening in the presence of some of his men including Karnail and Balbir he chortled, 'Those days are gone, boys, when I had to dig into slums and mud huts for enterprising men with valid passports who would cross the border and carry in a few weapons. Now we're under a modern management. It works like a machine. We just do our bit and collect a fat commission.' He paused long enough to let his gaze linger on Balbir. 'Of course, this is not yet that big rake-off, that big jackpot we're all looking for. We've got to keep working at that. But as a step forward, it will do.' Then he made a lewd joke. Going to the cheap calendar on the wall he pointed at the picture of a busty female and pretended to pinch the breasts. 'See that? This tit is for me and that is a tit for TAT. Now *I'm* telling them what to do. We're that close!'

He guffawed and the rest joined in. But Karnail Singh smoothed down his beard and murmured, 'I thought they were annoyed with you over that Heathrow episode. Banta Singh is still in hiding, isn't he?'

'Oh that! That's on the travel side. This is another department. TAT is like an octopus with many tentacles; one limb may feel the pinch and swipe at you but the others respond with love.' Tarsem was positively exultant.

Karnail adjusted his *phiphti*—the band of coloured cloth that shows in a triangle on the forehead at the front of the turban. He seemed to be concentrating on that as he said, 'TAT is already into opium and drugs. You can't take the credit for—'

Tarsem shook his head and clicked his tongue. Then raising

his eyebrows, he whispered, 'Guns. Good guns. Modern guns.'

Balbir hadn't said a word. He was foxed. Later, Karnail explained it to him. Tarsem was inching towards the big time.

Soon they made four more runs, once to Jammu, twice to Ferozepur and finally to Gurdaspur—each time to the vicinity of the border. Though Karnail hinted that the frequency of the trips and the quantity of merchandise had increased, Balbir was unimpressed. He had slipped easily into the trade. Even the danger of it seemed routine. He was the sort who thrived on crises, and there had been only one minor crisis so far when they were chased by a mobile patrol.

But during these trips Balbir developed a feeling of respect for Karnail. He handled difficulties with the cool of a veteran and the aplomb of a daredevil. Yet it bothered him that Karnail often revealed an ambivalent attitude to the work they were engaged in. He didn't betray this in the presence of the others but he let Balbir see glimpses of it when they were alone.

Balbir was not prepared to take on psychological complications. He was afraid of becoming demoralized himself. As it was he had to shut out all thought of what these weapons were being used for in order to continue in the trade.

Try as he might to avoid reading newspapers and listening to the news, details of the growing terrorism sprang at him from the mouths of casual acquaintances:

A bomb had exploded in the Chitra Cinema in Amritsar injuring at least twelve persons.

A bank had been looted.

The Municipal Commissioner had been robbed at pistol point.

Buses were blown up or burnt.

Another bomb in another cinema, this time in Nawan Shahr, had exploded killing three and injuring many.

Hand grenades were being thrown at security force personnel.

A number of railway stations were sabotaged, telegraph wires cut; at other places, unsuspecting victims were shot dead.

A correspondent of the Indian Express was stabbed in the thigh in the Golden Temple complex.

Amritsar's TV station was damaged by a hand grenade.

Nirankari sikhs were being killed. Dissenting politicians were being shot at.

A gun battle erupted between extremists firing from the Golden Temple and CRPF personnel. Three persons were killed.

Yet despite the spate of incidents, Balbir knew that there were only a few hundred extremists altogether; they were certainly busy trying to provoke a population of millions.

And then came that horrible evening when Balbir thought the world would surely end. The day and date became etched in his mind for not only did they mark his fifth trip to the border but also a crucial turning point in his relationship with the gun-runners. Tuesday 21 February 1984. He remembered it was a Tuesday because his mother, suspecting some illegality in his absences from the village, said to him when he went home to collect an extra sweater, 'Son, are you off again? You shouldn't travel on a Tuesday. It's unlucky. It . . . it could be dangerous.'

She dared not say more. Her younger son had changed in the last couple of months. He had grown sour and abrupt and somewhat cynical. He no longer argued with her or smiled at her fears. When he wanted to disobey her, he no longer cajoled and wheedled and mocked, he merely ignored her with a grim look and a twist of the mouth.

Now with a set face he strode out and only a slight twitch of a nostril indicated his old mockery of her typical hindu superstitions. Tuesdays come every week and if the world stood still on this recurring holy day, nothing would get done. He had a job to do, his own job, his secret job that fetched him a secret earning all his very own. The hindu sabbath could go and suck eggs.

But the day stayed in his mind, as did the date because Karnail Singh said, 'It's a stroke of luck that we're going to the Gurdaspur border today. It's the district I come from. And the 21st happens to be my brother's birthday. We'll stop at his village and have a cup of tea with him.'

The emphasis in that remark was on tea. Karnail Singh was underlining the rule he enforced on such trips: 'No liquor, no drunkenness. Wherever we stop we must merge with the surroundings and be totally unmemorable. All personal weapons must be stashed under a rug in the cab of the truck, which will be locked. We don't want the villagers to think we are desperadoes.' He was a strict taskmaster.

For the same reason Karnail Singh would not let the truck be driven up to his brother's house but suggested that they park near the market square. Then while the men ambled about and sat down before a tea-shop—the space outside was furnished with a couple of string-beds—Karnail went off to fetch his brother. Balbir conjectured that perhaps the man was a cousin and not a real brother for no one in the bazaar greeted Karnail with familiarity. Obviously Kahnuwan was not his ancestral village.

It was nearly 6.45 pm when Karnail returned with a slightly younger, clean-shaven, turbanless man in tow. The man was wearing a striped blanket wrapped like a shawl over his clothes. Round his head was a chequered cloth tied in the usual peasant way. His hair was short.

Over stainless steel tumblers of steaming tea, Karnail explained that while his own father had become a sikh, all his uncles and cousins were hindus. 'You see,' said Karnail, 'my grandparents remained childless for many years. Then they made a vow at a *gurdwara* that if they had children the eldest son would be brought up as a sikh. So my father's family are sikhs and my uncles' families are hindus.' He grasped his cousin affectionately round the waist and exclaimed, 'Ever since you moved here to Kahnuwan we've heard nothing of you, king, except that you're getting fatter with each birthday!'

They laughed.

Ten minutes later they were preparing to leave. It was dusk and they still had miles to cover. The market square began to empty. It was not particularly remarkable that shopkeepers were beginning to lock up. In these times everyone tried to get home before dark. An old sikh lady was tottering past them. Karnail's cousin called out, 'Aunty Basant Kaur, wait a bit. I'll help you home.'

'Aye, son, may you live long!' she quavered. 'My eyes are failing me now.'

Just then there was the roar of a number of motorcycles driving up together. A dozen sikh youths, masked and with sten guns hanging from their shoulders, drew up and dismounted. Ten faced into the square. Two faced away.

The old lady peered at them and sighed with a mixture of pride and surprise, 'So many guests for our village! I wonder who they've come to meet.'

Balbir and Karnail exchanged a glance. They both felt a rising sense of alarm.

The villagers were gawking at the new arrivals.

One of the motorcyclists shouted: 'Well then, shall we start it?'

And before anyone realized what was happening, ten sten guns began firing.

There were screams, shouts, shrieks, chaos. People ran pell mell.

The first man to fall yelled even as he crumpled. 'Run brother, run!'

His brother looked in horror then turned and fled to a wall and clawed to get up it. But a spray of bullets dropped him in mid-climb.

They were picking out hindus and the chatter of the guns was sporadic.

A woman wailed: 'Kill me, kill me! You've killed both my sons!'

Hearing her shriek, the old lady near them staggered uncomprehendingly towards the sound, into the line of fire. 'What is it, sister? What is it?'

'No, no!' Karnail's cousin shouted. 'Aunty, come back.' He ran towards her.

Balbir saw one of the masked figures turn and crouch to shoot. He flung himself at Karnail's cousin, bringing him down just as the stutter of the gun began.

People were collapsing and writhing all round. The rattle of the guns was like a clattering railway train.

There was for a while a crescendo of noise—metal objects registering the ricochet of bullets, steel tumblers falling, glass shattering, brickwork and wood absorbing the impact, doors slamming, furniture crashing. There was ping and whistle and whine and thud and smash. And in the melée, the screams of the innocent, dying.

Two of Karnail's men were seasoned fighters but their weapons were in the cab of the truck! They took cover where they could and cursed and were numb with shock. They had never before seen the weapons they dealt in being used. One of these men, tough as he was, vomited where he lay. The other screamed in anguish and frustration.

Just as suddenly as they had come the killers mounted their motorcycles and rode away, leaving behind the smell of cordite, smoke, exhaust fumes and the odour of faeces and urine, for many had lost control over their bowels and bladders in the panic.

After the first seconds of bewildered shock, the cries of the injured and dying were overtaken by the wails of the bereaved, wails that rose from deep in the pit of the stomach and seared through the chest, rending the air as though to tear the fabric of heaven so that it might disgorge a more believable reality.

When those who could rise struggled up out of their dazed

incomprehension, there were still sixteen bodies lying in that market square. Of these, six were corpses.

The next day, at the Golden Temple, Balbir went to Amar Singh and asked, 'Why?'

Amar Singh seemed to be praying for he had his eyes shut and his lips were moving imperceptibly, or perhaps he was memorizing something. He looked up and smiled. 'Why what?'

Balbir felt as though a steel file was grating across his heart. 'Why Kahnuwan? Those are poor peasants, ordinary villagers! And I am told, at the same time yesterday, just a few miles away the same kind of slaughter took place at another village. Why?'

Amar Singh seemed to be thinking.

'Why?' Balbir nearly wept as he repeated it. 'Why?'

Amar Singh frowned. His chin sank to his chest. After a moment he looked up, shook his head and whispered, 'I don't know.'

'What do you gain by making women into widows and children into orphans?'

Amar Singh's face seemed to pale but he said sharply, 'The orders don't originate from me. I just pass them on or carry them out, whatever I am required to do. It is useless to question me.'

'Then . . . then,' Balbir held back a sob. It was not in his throat but somewhere in his chest. 'What does he want with all this?'

'Autonomy. More power for this state to decide its own future. It is for the good of Punjab.'

'But why kill Punjabis? Is killing your own people good for Punjab?'

Amar Singh ran a tongue over his lips, then bit at a flake of chapped skin. 'We are not killing all Punjabis, only some Punjabis.'

Balbir almost shrieked. 'That's no answer! Who gives you the authority to decide which simple persons you should kill?'

'You are overwrought.'

'I am. I should be. I was there.'

'What?'

'Why should that surprise you? Your killers could open fire anywhere, even here!'

Amar Singh smiled. 'Yes.' Then he clenched and unclenched a fist. 'I can understand how you feel—'

'Can you? I don't think so. You have no pity in you, no mercy, no compassion—'

'But it is justice. Justice being meted out. At last.'

'What justice are you talking about, you murderer?'

The pitch and volume of Balbir's voice brought some armed men running into the room. There was already one carbine-carrying guard sitting on the string-bed behind Balbir.

Amar Singh waved them away with the words, 'It's all right. He's in a state of shock. It happens. We're just discussing our political programme. He doesn't quite understand.'

When they left reluctantly, he turned to Balbir. 'You don't fully understand, do you?'

Balbir waited.

Amar Singh glanced at Balbir's quivering hands, the tremors running through his body, the face trying not to tremble with rage. 'Sit down.'

'No.'

'You can lie down for a while on that cot. Many people can't face such an episode. We are sure the government won't be able to.'

'What are you talking about? I don't understand a word of what you are saying.'

Soothingly, Amar Singh said, 'Because you are obviously a non-political person. You see lives as lives, human beings as human beings.'

'Of course I do! How else is one to think?'

'That is not thinking. That is feeling. You are emotional.'

Balbir controlled himself, shut his eyes even as he stood there and felt as though he were rocking on his feet. 'Just tell me,' he gritted, 'what did you mean when you said this was justice?'

Amar Singh said, 'In Kahnuwan, in Bhaini Mian Khan, in the buses we hijacked, we separated the hindus from the sikhs. We killed the hindus.'

Balbir sank down on the rug with his knees under him and faced Amar Singh. 'That is not justice, that is communal brutality.'

'Ah. Now you see the point. We are teaching the hindu government a lesson.'

'But it is not a hindu government. It is a secular democratic government elected by millions of people. Every adult has a right to vote. People of all faiths vote.'

'The hindus are in a majority so it ends up being a hindu government.'

'What nonsense! The parliament is not composed only of hindus. There are—I don't know how many MPs . . .'

'Seven hundred and eighty-seven. In both houses.'

'Right. There are that many members of parliament. Some are muslim, some sikh, some christian, some parsee—'

'The parsees are zoroastrian. That's the religion.'

'Whatever. There are so many of all creeds. And ministers. Ministers are not chosen for their religion but for ability.'

Amar Singh gave a scoffing laugh. 'Ability and religion. But mainly for the votes of the religious community from which they come.'

'There are sikh ministers.'

'Puppets. Tools in the hands of the Prime Minister. The Prime Minister is hindu.'

Balbir said, '*You* don't understand. To an average hindu, religion is not a dogma but a code of behaviour, a way of life. If the people wanted a staunchly right-wing hindu government they would vote for people with RSS backgrounds. They would demand that the Constitution be a religious one. Like Israel's or Iran's or Pakistan's or . . . some others. But we are a democracy like England or the USA.'

Amar Singh came in quickly, 'And the sikhs are like the Irish, fighting for freedom.'

'That parallel is false!' Balbir cried. 'You know as well as I do that Ireland is not part of England, it is part of Great Britain. Ireland is an island. For centuries it had a separate monarchy and history. Ireland was conquered by the English, and now it is up to them to sort it out among themselves. But one thing is clear—from the beginning no one has ever said that an Irishman is an Englishman or vice versa. But a Punjabi is a Punjabi, whether he is a hindu or a sikh. And Punjab is geographically a part of India. You know, Amar, it occurs to me that the more apt parallel is the one from the USA. Your aim is like that of the Southern States during the Civil War. You want to break away to "preserve your culture"—'

'Yes! There is nothing wrong with that.'

'Except that you also want to practise your own version of slavery. You want to suppress every other way of life but your own. Isn't it enough that every morning at 4 a.m.—4 a.m. when most people are still sleeping—*gurdwaras* in the villages of Punjab blast the countryside awake with singing over microphones and loudspeakers? Why can't people pray inside their own temples? Why must the piety of someone with a horrible raucous tuneless voice be inflicted on the privacy of people resting from their labours? When I am rich and independent, I shall soundproof my house! There is so much noise pollution already and the grating voices of untrained village singers are adding to it.'

Amar Singh was a little startled at first. Then one side of his mouth curled in amusement. He began to laugh. 'You are off at a tangent. Hysterical. Relax.'

Balbir thumped the rug with a fist. 'Just you tell me how you would feel if every church and temple and synagogue in the world shattered the peace of the countryside for hours with electronic amplification? You would go beserk. And then there are the weddings and meetings and *melas*—all blasting the nerves with loudspeakers!'

Balbir was not crying but the tears were streaming down his cheeks.

Amar Singh said: 'So it is not the *Gurbani,* the sacred verses, that you are objecting to. I was annoyed for a moment that you might be.'

'No, no. I love poetry. I love hymns, music, songs in praise of life and nature, all kinds of songs. But I will not have bad voices inflicted on me in the name of religion. My point is that, in the name of religion, all kinds of tyranny can be practised including aesthetic tyranny. I go to *gurdwaras* too, and if the singer is good, I sit and listen.'

Amar Singh nodded and suddenly said quietly, 'It is a pleasure to talk to you. So refreshing. Such a relief for me. You know I sometimes feel a pang at having left university for all this, not because I miss other students—some of them have joined me here—but because I miss the arguments I used to have with a couple of my professors. Brilliant men. Even when they couldn't persuade me about something, they showed me another aspect of it. We are all like archaeologists trying to decipher the hieroglyphs of life: each one works out his own kind of answer. For instance in this case I think there is a political solution, you think there is a humanist one. But we are agreed that there is a problem. Let us tackle it from there.'

'You are very clever,' Balbir admitted. Then shook his head. 'But I don't agree with you even there. There is no problem. You are creating it.'

Amar Singh's eyes dilated and flickered but he spoke gently. 'Look here, Balbir, you have ranted on and stood the facts on their head. I was prepared to listen, thinking you must be Einstein coming up with some new theory of relativity—after all, genius is only the ability to gain new insights by a different concatenation of the same facts—but you are a fool conditioned by the platitudes you have absorbed. If you will give me a chance, I shall explain it to your satisfaction from the sikh point of view. You may learn something.'

'I'm waiting,' said Balbir. 'But your attitudes don't represent the sikh point of view. If that were so, your lot would have been voted into power long ago.'

'In short, the sikh masses are not aware. We are trying to make them aware. All right, I'm an extremist. I represent an extreme point of view. It may be the solution to that hieroglyph.'

Balbir was silent.

Amar Singh counted off the points on the fingers of his hand as he said. 'Now then, you spoke of slavery and dominant culture. Do you realize, it is the sikhs who have been enslaved by hindu culture? Guru Nanak himself said that sikhs are neither hindu nor muslim.'

'What he meant was that, during the conflicts of those days, sikhs were intended to be a cementing factor. Guru Nanak too must have longed for peace from communal strife. He meant that sikhs were a bit of both. He wanted the sikhs to represent the common humanity of all religions.'

'That is your interpretation,' said Amar Singh. 'My interpretation is that he wanted them to have a separate identity. Next you will tell me that you have always thought of Guru Nanak as a hindu reformer.'

'I have.'

'That's a typical hindu point of view!' Amar Singh shook his head. 'That's the trouble with you hindus. You want to absorb every creed into your own. If we don't want to live under your tent, why should you force us?'

Balbir shifted and sat cross-legged. 'I thought you were going to explain your politics but you are talking religion.'

'It's the same thing.'

'Anyway, nobody's forcing you to live like a hindu. Nobody's forcing even me. In a secular country you are free to worship as you like. In fact, I don't even pray. Man is not just a religious entity.'

'There is discrimination against sikhs.'

'Ridiculous! Punjabi hindus and sikhs often intermarry. Is that discrimination?'

'There is interference in the religious affairs of sikhs by the government.'

'I don't believe it. The government dares not interfere in a religious practice that does not harm others.'

Amar Singh was still nicking off the points on his fingers. 'For instance, they've applied the Land Ceiling Act to *gurdwaras* in Haryana. The extent of land held in the name of God cannot be curbed as though God were just another citizen. *Gurdwara* land should be beyond government restriction. Another thing is that sikh Personal Law is not recognized by the Constitution. The muslims are allowed their own law according to the Koran, why shouldn't the sikhs have their own form of justice as distinct from other citizens?'

'You know,' Balbir sighed. 'What you are saying is really enough to turn me Marxist, except I fear that that may become another dogma too. Once, in a tonga, I heard a man, a communist, talking. Perhaps he was right. Religion really is the opium of the people. You are hallucinating. You should be trying to ensure one equal law for all rather than—'

'Everyone will be equal as sikhs under the sikh law.'

Balbir held his head in his hands and muttered, 'What else?'

'The government has not cared to ensure sikh control of *gurdwaras* in Pakistan—'

'But,' Balbir protested, 'Pakistan is another country. The government of India can't be responsible for—'

'It can try. It doesn't try hard enough.'

Balbir said, 'But that's like blaming the Indian government for not ensuring that sikhs can carry swords on the aeroplanes of the world!'

'There is that too. It is a matter of faith for a sikh to carry a *kirpan.*'

'But there are international regulations. No one is allowed to carry weapons on a plane. It is a security measure against hijacking.'

'It is a discrimination against our religion.'

'I must be very stupid,' said Balbir, 'but I can't agree.'

'That's because you don't want to see. I tell you it is a hindu government run by a hindu Prime Minister. She is out to destroy us.'

Balbir looked up at the ceiling and sighed. 'As far as I know, she has great respect for sikhs and sikh traditions. She has never discriminated against any religion. She has people of all faiths around her. What is more she was married to a Parsee. For that matter her younger son married a sikh girl and her elder son married an Italian christian. From all that wonderful mish mash, I can only discern that she has very liberal, unbiased opinions.'

'Her security forces are beginning to close in on the Golden Temple.'

'Because you extremists are spreading terror and committing murders.'

Amar Singh got up and went to a tin trunk. Opening it, he took out a pamphlet. 'Here. These are all the forty-five accusations made by the Akali Dal against the government. Read them.' He took out another sheaf of printed material. 'And this is the Anandpur Sahib Resolution. Go through it. Take the material with you. As for the murders you mentioned, we are provoking the deaf hindu government to listen to our demands. Why, look at you. Even you hadn't bothered to know why we are fighting till now—till the violence shocked you! Now you come to me and ask, "why?" I'll tell you why. Because the hindu is a corrupt, trading, money-making, money-grabbing, corpulent, impassive creature. He is the money-lender and middleman in our midst—'

'That's not quite true. Hindus are farmers too and professionals. And there are sikh traders and merchants and—'

'The hindu is an effete, debased type of human being.'

'You are sounding like Hitler.'

Amar Singh sneered. 'Emotional innuendo doesn't wash with me. You can call me anything. I am prepared to act as I think.' He paused and smiled. 'You know Descartes?'

'Who?'

'The philosopher.'

'Ah yes, a bit.'

Amar Singh nodded. 'My version is—I act therefore I am. Action is everything. We will kick the hindu till he responds.'

'But,' Balbir cried, 'the response to violence will only be violence.'

'Of course,' Amar Singh enthused. 'Have you heard of the reaction from Haryana hindus? No? Let me tell you. Mobs are out shouting anti-Bhindranwale slogans, stopping buses and cars, dragging out sikhs as though all sikhs were extremists, beating them, shaving them, sometimes killing them, attacking *gurdwaras*, setting them on fire. In Panipat, eight innocent sikhs, who would never have joined us anyway, were caught in the lanes and lynched. All this will unite the sikhs to our cause.'

Balbir's head was spinning. He said, 'It's madness. Sheer madness!'

'But with a method to it!' Amar Singh exclaimed triumphantly. 'Soon there will only be extremist hindus and extremist sikhs.'

Balbir shook his head. 'Well before that, the army is bound to be called in.'

'Of course the army will be called in!' Amar Singh's glee was extraordinary. 'We're ready for the army. We've kept the police at bay. We've got the arms to handle the CRPF. And we know how to take care of the army.'

'You're mistaken. You forget I know the kind of weapons you have. You can't fight the army. Then, you'll have had it.'

Amar Singh looked at him steadily and exhaled in exasperation. 'You are a simpleton! Do you think the army would dare come in here? This is not a matter of firepower, it's a matter of politics. You're soft in the heart, and therefore in the head.' He laughed and murmured, 'We only have to be on our guard and keep out infiltrators and traitors. The army *cannot* enter the Golden Temple complex for the same reason that the police can't. Of course, the army has the weapons and skill and training to do it. But Mrs Gandhi won't give the order. She can't. It would turn every religious sikh against her. She would lose here standing with sikhs. Look, out there! This beautiful Golden Temple is the Mecca of the sikh religion. It would be intolerable to have it desecrated by invasion and gunfire.'

Balbir waved a hand in exasperation and almost shouted, 'You're wrong! It wouldn't be an invasion. The forces of law and order would come in to clean up the place. There are criminals here. Murders are taking place in the sacred precincts. As for this being a Mecca, you know what happened to the muslim terrorists who took over the holy Kaaba in Mecca. The Saudi Arabian government sent in some commandos and killed every terrorist on the spot. No sensible muslim objected to that.'

Amar Singh pouted and made a gesture of disagreement. 'Whatever the case, whatever the justification, if the army comes in here Mrs Gandhi will be signing her death warrant. She will suffer the same fate as the representative of the last invader of the Golden Temple. He was an Afghan raider named Ahmed Shah Abdali.'

'I know about him,' said Balbir. 'My ancestors fought against his forces and were defeated and pushed down here to Punjab. That was in the eighteenth century.'

'Right. But you don't know what happened to his Governor of Punjab for descecrating the Golden Temple.'

Balbir shook his head.

Amar Singh smiled sarcastically, 'I thought you knew all about the Golden Temple. That's what you told me once.'

'Some things. Not everything.'

'Well, the Governor left behind by the great victor Ahmed Shah Abdali was holding court in Lahore,' Amar Singh licked his lips and continued, 'when two sikhs disguised as pathans came forward to lay their swords at his feet in homage. They *salaamed* him and he bent forward to acknowledge their greeting. Of course, when they got near him, they unsheathed the swords and killed him. Very instructive bit of history. So I don't think she would dare.' After a moment of rumination he added, 'But we are prepared in case she does.'

Seeing Balbir's look of disbelief, he took him by the arm and led him out on to the terrace. Pointing over the heads of some youths, he said, 'You see all those fortifications? More are coming up every day. Our machine guns, stenguns, grenades and carefully thought-out tactics of battle—but I can't tell you those—will hold off the army for at least a week if not a month.'

Balbir couldn't see the sense of it. He snorted. 'Even if you hold out for a year, you'll have to surrender at some point.'

'Perhaps . . .' Amar Singh's eyes had a faraway look. Then he smiled. 'But you really are dull politically. Don't you see that if we hold out long enough and fight with vigour, the sikh masses will be aroused. They will surround the army and come to our rescue. The army will be hemmed in by millions of sikhs. Sikh soldiers will mutiny, desert and come to help us. Civil war will break out. And our aims will be achieved. You see, our strategy is simple and political, the tactics are complex and military. But I can tell you this: militarily we don't need to try and defeat the army. That would be stupid. We can't. All we have to do in order to win is hold out for a few days, and that we can easily do.'

Balbir said nothing. He returned to the room, picked up the printed material he had been given and started to walk away.

'I'm going down too,' murmured Amar Singh near the steps. His escort followed him.

In the gloom of the descending passage, Amar Singh put his arm round Balbir's shoulder. 'Oh by the way, I never thanked you for informing us about Uday the potter. We appreciated that. It took us a bit of time to get round to him. There's so much to be done every day. The movement is attracting more and more young men with every demonstration of our authority. It's hard to keep control on every aspect. Would you like to see him?'

'You mean Kumhareya is here?'

'Of course. Why does that surprise you?'

They were walking along the Parikrama now. Amar Singh still kept his arm round Balbir's shoulder.

'I suppose it doesn't.' Balbir remembered again the conversation he had heard in the barn of the Old Ruin. 'No,' he said again, 'it doesn't surprise me. But I would have expected them to get out of Punjab quickly.'

Amar Singh gave an odd laugh and squeezed Balbir's shoulder warmly. 'You know,' he sighed as he guided Balbir towards another area of the complex, 'it's not easy. I have to keep an eye on so many squads. Incidentally, the ones that carried out the actions in the two villages yesterday were not under me. But of course they all have strict orders. You know what I've heard about one squad? They were returning from the mission when they came upon some women near a temple. One of our boys wanted to shoot them because, he said, "they are the ones who give birth to our enemies". But the leader of the group warned him, "sisters and mothers are common to all religions". You see, we don't kill women unless absolutely necessary. Even on the buses, we shot the men, not the women.'

Some men seated near a manhole moved aside as Amar nodded. The cover was removed. It was actually a trap-door leading to one of the many underground passages in the complex.

'Follow me,' Amar said as he clambered down the iron rungs set in the wall.

Behind Balbir, Amar's carbine-carrying escort came down.

Reaching under his shawl into a pocket, Amar brought out a pencil torch. He hardly needed it though the passage was dark. Not only were there lanterns and naked light bulbs at intervals but he seemed to know his way as if he had practised moving through the maze without illumination. As they came to a room with a string-bed on which an armed man was sitting, Amar chuckled, 'In summer, this is one of the best places to sleep. It's cool.'

There were five men sitting about in the room that held Kumhareya. Like the other rooms this one too had no door or grille. It was open, a sort of enlargement of the passage. Kumhareya seemed to be standing against the farther wall propping up a string-bed with his back. He seemed somehow taller. He had his hands clasped above his head as though he were adjusting his top-knot of hair. He was stripped to the waist and wore only a *kuchchha*, a pair of knickers.

'Uday!' Balbir exclaimed. 'My God, you must be freezing without clothes—'

Balbir had rushed forward to greet him but stopped on seeing that Kumhareya's eyes were closed.

Balbir's mouth fell open as he reached for the torch in Amar's hand and, taking it, examined the condition of his friend.

Kumhareya's wrists were tied to his top-knot and the cord bound him to the bar of the string-bed which was suspended from a couple of steel spikes. The legs of the bed pointed outwards.

No wonder Kumhareya had seemed taller. His feet were a few inches above the floor, tied at the ankles to the frame of the bed. His legs—which he had used so expertly in wrestling and which everyone knew had been strengthened by spinning his father's traditional foot-operated potting wheel—had gone spindly, strangely twisted and oddly indented.

As the beam of the torch followed the contour of the legs, pausing at the marks, Amar Singh said, 'Broken. He'll never run away anywhere again.'

Balbir could hear Kumhareya breathing and each deep intake was punctuated by a clicking sound.

'It's the ribs,' whispered Amar Singh.

Balbir felt like hitting out. Clenching his teeth, he closed his eyes. He cried out softly, 'Uday! My God! Poor Uday.'

Balbir touched the emaciated body which had only a few weeks ago been so healthy. Under his fingers he felt Uday Singh Kumhareya flinch, not with any pain that the hand inflicted but from the dread of it.

'Uday, it's me. Balbir. Uday! Oy Kumhareya!'

The eyes flickered open slowly. A look of recognition came into them. Then they flooded and closed as the brow crinkled with a complex barrage of emotions and the tears rolled down his cheeks, a few drops falling on Balbir's hand.

'Balbir!' It was not even a whisper, only a movement of the lips. Kumhareya was trying to smile but wept instead.

Amar Singh's voice was steady. 'He's now ashamed of what he did. It's an example to the rest. They come and see how he is being punished for breaking up an action group. Girls who join us can see that we protect them. The movement cannot be sullied by lust.'

'But—but he's in love with her!' Balbir pleaded.

'We aren't idiots,' murmured Amar Singh. 'We went there and first talked to both of them. We asked her if she wanted to marry him. She said no. So we brought him here and took appropriate action.'

'But she wouldn't have wanted him to suffer! Did you tell her you would—?'

'What she wants out of the goodness of her heart has nothing to do with preserving the purity of the movement. On one of the buses we hijacked, an old Nihang saved the life of a hindu sitting beside him by insisting that the hindu was really a sikh and his own son. We beat up the hindu for cutting his hair but we let him live. Later we learnt that the old Nihang had lied. He lied out of tenderness but that was a weakness. It was a lie against us. The old man was thwarting the movement. We will find him.'

In the corner were a couple of spears, a sword and some thick sticks. Beside them, a few sacks and a coil of rope.

Seeing his look, an armed man casually interposed himself between Balbir and the corner.

Another came up to Amar and complained, 'I'm sick of cleaning his pee and shit. Can't you depute someone else? The others tease me saying you've given me this job because I'm a mazhabi.'

'Who says that?'

The man had a dark pockmarked face which now clouded with uncertainty. He mumbled lamely, 'Others.'

'Tell them to come and ask me why I've given you this job. I'll give them a better reason than they know.'

The man scowled. Then asked, 'How long before this one goes?'

'A couple of days at most.'

The man seemed relieved. 'Can I be given something else to do upstairs after that?'

'Definitely.'

The man nodded by way of thanks. Then in a sudden flush of anger, he picked up a stick and swung it horizontally striking Kumhareya across the stomach.

'Mother-fucker!' the man shouted.

There was only a gasp from Kumhareya.

Balbir spun on his feet, enraged. He darted towards the man to grab the stick from him but Amar Singh caught him and flung him aside.

The other men were up on their feet and holding Balbir before he could take another step.

Amar Singh began to walk away.

At the start of the passage, he called over his shoulder, 'What're you waiting for? Bring him along.'

They hesitated. One said, 'He's a hindu.'

'We need him,' said Amar. 'He's a gun-runner. Bring him along.'

They propelled him forward.

A few paces on, Amar muttered, 'All right, you can release him. He's not struggling. He'll behave.'

Amar glanced at the armed bodyguard who had his carbine at the ready. Then he sighed, 'Come along Balbir. You mustn't always be an emotional fool. You might get shot.'

'He's my friend.' said Balbir.

'No,' said Amar. 'He was. Till he did that. He has admitted he wanted to seduce her into marriage. Forget him.'

Going along the corridor, Balbir thought it echoed with Kumhareya's voice. He thought he heard it say: Don't worry Balbir, I have killed, I know how to die.

'No, no,' he said aloud.

'What was that?' Amar was solicitous. When he received no answer, Amar nodded and walked on.

When they were out again on the Parikrama, Amar put his arm round Balbir's shoulder. But Balbir withdrew.

Amar nodded and walked on.

Balbir rode that night to Chak Deedar. He wanted to talk to the woman called Fat Aunty. He wanted to know how it happened. He wanted to know where Gulnari was. If she had gone back to her uncle's house, he would go there and talk to her. He had to talk to her. Perhaps get her to intercede. Perhaps even get her to say she would marry Kumhareya, save his life. Perhaps it was still possible, perhaps not. But he had to try.

He rode listening only to his own thoughts, hardly aware of the hammer of hooves under him, not at all concerned that he might be followed. Why should he be followed? He was only an observer on the scene. He had not started anything, he had not stopped anything. He was a powerless nonentity, unable to initiate, unable to prevent. He was flotsam on the tide of time.

The tonga that started off behind him, the cyclists that pedalled furiously from the turning on the main road, the car that must have a curfew pass driving carefully without lights somewhere at his back—nothing mattered. He was impotent. He had nothing to give away. Not even the secret of Chak

Deedar. For the quarry had been whisked away. Kumhareya was paying for his sins at the Golden Temple.

As he approached the village, Balbir became conscious of the pop-pop-pop of one of the illegal flour mills. They were grinding overtime or perhaps they hadn't had electricity all day. This sort of thing happened. It was one of the points on which the extemists battened.

He had had the foresight to carry a torch in the pocket of his suede jacket—a hand-me-down from Raskaan's last visit to India. He fished out the torch and switched it on. He was by the broken mud wall of the settlement when there were a couple of shouts and the bird-like fluting of the mill ceased. They must have seen him coming and thought he was an official.

Lights were on in almost every hut. It was still early. He had no difficulty finding the compound he was looking for. He was glad he had seen Fat Aunty's face that night. Now he would have no problem recognizing her.

There was a flurry of people around him as he dismounted and tied the reins to an unyoked bullock-cart. He ignored the greetings loaded with suspicion and curiosity; he pretended not to hear a question that swung like a sickle at him. He brushed past and strode across the yard to the hut. He pushed at the door gently. It creaked open.

He had conjectured right. There was the dark, middle-aged woman with the face more Dravidian than Aryan. There she was, surrounded by children, rolling maize off the cob for roasting, while a transistor radio, flat on its back on one of the string-beds, blared. She looked up enquiringly but her hands continued working. The beads of maize fell in a steady tattoo on the tray. Balbir felt himself being crowded in in the doorway; the menfolk were curious and worried—a man on a well-groomed horse could be a policeman from Phillaur or even the *tahsildar*.

He said, 'I am Balbir.'

She smiled uncertainly while her eyes searched the faces around him.

He said, 'You are Fat Aunty. I came one night to meet those two. I sat there on that bed and talked to him.'

She really smiled then, showing her two gold teeth, and nodded and, handing the tray to the young girl beside her who went on automatically with the task, she stood up and said to the men, 'It's all right. He's the friend of a friend.'

They withdrew and, in a short while, the staccato whistle of the mill resumed its constant crepitation. It was as though the heart of the area had been stopped and now had begun again with a more vigorous palpitation.

Fat Aunty latched the front door, pulled Balbir by the sleeve and led him out into a lane through the back door.

'Has he sent you to fetch her?'

'Fetch her?' Balbir was startled. 'You mean, she's still here?'

'Of course. Where is she to go, poor child?'

'Why, back to her people naturally.'

'Son, she's unhappy in her uncle's house. Her father is an invalid, her mother is sick in the head. And they were marrying her to a photograph! What kind of wedding is that? Now that she's run away she's got to stay on the run. They'll make life hell for her.' Fat Aunty slapped her forehead. 'Hai, hai! Why did I give them shelter! He never told me he'd turn up with a girl. Why couldn't she have gone with him?'

Balbir said simply, 'They're killing him.'

She gasped. 'It's true then what she says! Two men stayed back that day and told her what they were going to do to him. I didn't believe her.' She thought for a moment and added, 'When they first came on motorcycles and chatted and had tea, I thought they were planning how to disguise her or hide her. She's not easy to disguise with those cat grey eyes. Her grandmother was from Kulu, she says. Those eyes! Hai, they'd give her away every time. But attractive. Very, very attractive. And the police might be looking for her along with her people.'

'They are.'

'Oh God! How stupid of me! We're poor, son, very poor, and I thought we'd make a little money helping that potter boy. When he brought the girl I was a sentimental fool! I thought they were in love. It's not every day that you find love, such strong love. I've never known it, son. And, believe me, I didn't know she was of another caste.'

'Listen, Aunty. You've got to make her go back at first light. It's urgent. She can save him. She's only got to tell them in Amritsar that she wants to marry Uday, that she always wanted to marry him. Otherwise he will end up one of those smashed bodies they find in sacks.'

Her hand flew to her cheek in dismay. 'Son, we're only poor *harijans* and *Mazhabis* here. We *can't* let her go back and tell them where she was hiding all this time. They'll come and kill us all in revenge.'

'I'll protect you. My grandfather will stand by you. He'll find a way. He always does. Uday and she can marry at once in the Golden Temple. Then no one will mind about all this.'

She peered at him incredulously in the dim light. 'Son, you don't know what you're saying. Who are you?'

'I told you, I am Balbir.'

It didn't mean anything to her. She was puzzled and asked, 'What are you?'

'Ah, I understand. I am a Chibber, a Muhiyal.'

'God help us!' She struck her forehead with the palm of her hand. 'Now the brahmins will be upset too! No, son. Just you go and leave us to find our own way.'

Balbir's face went grim as he said, 'Where is Gulnari? Let me talk to her.'

Fat Aunty snorted and her gold teeth flashed as she spoke. 'You can see her. We moved her to another hut. But I don't think you'll get a sensible word out of her. Ever since Uday went, and he went happily, mind you—he even told me he'd send for her in a couple of days—she's begun to behave like a woman in love, pining. She won't eat unless forced. She can't sleep without crying out loud. It's the guilt churning inside her. Uday left thinking he was going to make arrangements for her, but two men stayed back and told her that she had condemned him to death.' Fat Aunty blew her nose on her *dupatta*, shivered as though to clear her head and sighed, 'I hoped she was imagining it. I hoped he would send for her.'

'Does she want to go to him now?' Balbir asked quickly, expectantly.

But Fat Aunty replied dismissively. 'She doesn't know any more what she wants. I fear she's going the way of her mother.'

Gulnari was in the adjoining hut. She had her back to them and was crooning to herself when they entered. At first Balbir didn't realize it was she. He had feared he would find a forlorn, bedraggled, hollow-eyed creature. But here was a young bride dressed in borrowed finery. Red *salwar kameez*, bangles, trinkets, make-up, and she was now intent on applying a matching cutex to her toe-nails. She didn't turn round but continued singing:

> 'Where my love is,
> there is my home.
> Where my love is,
> I have no fear.
> Let him worry for me.
> Where my love is,
> my heart is safe.'

There was another woman in the hut, keeping her company, scrubbing pots and pans by a drain in the corner. She washed her hands quickly with a *lota* of water from the bucket and stood up.

'Don't stop your work, sister-in-law.' Fat Aunty said, flashing her a brilliant, affectionate smile. 'We're just visiting Gulnari.'

At that Gulnari looked over her shoulder. They were the same fathomless grey eyes bruised by wood-smoke but they were rimmed with kohl, even more bewitching now. She held out a hand and exclaimed, 'Wah! Balbir!' They were the same rough palms accustomed to hard work around the house but they were now decorated with a design of *mehndi*. It was the same sugarcane-toughened mouth that spoke but now softened by lipstick. It was the same voice that could tomboyishly, jocularly insult a man that now sounded hushed, subdued as though she had continued with her gentle song.

'I didn't know you could sing,' Balbir said.

She smiled, 'I didn't know a song till I started making them up.'

'That was good.'

'You weren't meant to hear it.'

'I did.'

She frowned. Then jumped up, spun on her feet, dropping the cutex and brush without a care and came laughing towards him. 'Have you brought news? Yes? Have they killed him yet?'

'What?' He took a step back.

'They're going to marry us in heaven. All love is in heaven.' Her eyes were aglow, her cheeks were flushed. But somehow she was unhealthy. She was an imitation of health; her play-acting was a mockery of what she had fled.

'Then they will can him,' she said, 'in a beef factory. Isn't that funny?'

He raised his hand to slap her but instead brought it round to cover his eyes.

'Let me tell you a joke,' she said. 'My heart was buried under despair, till he died for it.'

She seemed to be waiting.

He looked at her steadily and said, 'Do you really want me to laugh?'

She stared back unflinchingly. 'Yes. Otherwise you will only cry.'

An idea occurred to him. 'Do you want to help Kumhareya?' he asked.

'Who?'

'Uday.'

'How?'

'Go home.' As Balbir said this, Fat Aunty caught his arm but his eyes and ears were tuned only to Gulnari.

She simpered in a manner that could not have been her own, fluttered her lashes and gazing down demurely, sang:

'Where my love is,
there is my home.
Where my love is
I have no fear . . .'

Her voice trailed off and when she looked up he saw that the kohl and mascara were splotched.

'Gulnari. Please. Go home and tell them you want to marry Uday. Go to the Golden Temple and say it.'

She said, 'Can you hear the devil bird screeching outside?'

He listened genuinely and told her, 'It's only the flour mill.'

'The devil bird calls out to disaster.'

'Gulnari, you haven't answered me.'

She began to laugh and declaimed with an archaic flair, 'I only want to be free and everywhere they want to marry me. Alas, alas, what good is a woman but to tarry with or marry with.'

He persisted, 'I rode here on a mare. We can both ride out of here. Now. Tonight. You might still save Uday.'

Suddenly she was serious. 'Is he alive?'

He nodded. 'I saw him today.'

'I never liked him in that way. I . . . ' she seemed to be thinking back. 'I detest him. But the movement gave me . . . togetherness, friendship, adventure, yes, a sense of adventure. But no fulfilment, no fulfilment. Now . . . they have abandoned me. I have done wrong too. I have betrayed the squad. I wrote down their names. They will be . . . killed.'

'Not necessarily,' he argued. 'They've been arrested but—'

'They will be killed,' she said with finality. Then she smiled, 'I am the devil bird.'

Outside, there were shouts. The flour mill ceased operation. There was the sound of many people running. A horse whinnied. Was it Rano? Balbir glanced at Fat Aunty. Her eyes were wide with terror. They could hear people hammering at her door.

Someone yelled, 'Open up! Or we'll break it down!'

Other voices were raised in protest. Then a shot rang out. It was a heavy old-fashioned sound—either a twelve bore or a muzzle loader. For a moment it silenced all other noise.

Fat Aunty clutched at her breast. 'My God, it's her people.'

But nevertheless she seemed to have made some preparation for this eventuality. She turned to the woman who had been pottering about doing housework. 'Sister-in-law, take her there! Go on, quick. And make sure she stays hidden.'

As Gulnari was being bundled through another doorway, Fat Aunty poked her in the side and said, 'Keep quiet and you'll be safe. But if they find you, please don't give us away.'

Now she turned to Balbir. 'As for you, come with me. I'll show you how to escape.'

'But the mare is out there! And why should I sneak away like a thief? I haven't done anything wrong. I'm not afraid.'

'Don't play with our lives, young man. It's not you I'm worried about, it's me and my family. There's no way I can explain your presence in my house. For my sake, do as I say. They must have followed you here. They've probably got the settlement surrounded by now.'

The village was coming awake with the hubbub. Weaving through it came the sound of jeeps driving up. Then the deeper roar of a van with a siren that was switched on only perhaps to get through a confusion of villagers.

'Damn it!' Balbir gritted. 'They've brought the police.' He didn't relish a long bout of questions and his name going into a file about eloping extremists. He had his gunrunning activities to keep out of sight.

Fat Aunty sighed, 'Thank heavens, the police are here! The merchants will have to act with care. Come on!'

As she led him along the lane and through a fretwork of alleyways, she hissed, 'I'll say you hitched your horse outside my place but you didn't come to my house. They can't prove anything. No one here will squeal on me. They haven't about the mill.'

'Right. You just get someone to unhitch the mare and give her a slap on the rump. She'll dash off home to her stable.'

They were moving through the slush and muck that laced the little paths between the huts. More vehicles were arriving. The beams of headlights sliced across the colony. In order to move in force during the curfew hours, the merchants had had to summon the police. There was no other way they could surround and comb the entire village.

Jigsaw patterns of illumination sprang and shifted and settled on houses. There was the groan and shuffle of tongas pulling up—the creak of wood, the crackle of harness. The hobnailed boots of policemen could be heard scattering off in various directions, directed by the taut urgency of subdued commands. From one side there rose the sound of argument and protest. The merchants were obviously helping to begin a house-to-house search. Someone must have opened Fat Aunty's door and dashed their expectations.

But the noise receded as Balbir followed Fat Aunty further in. The settlement was larger and more complex than he had realized.

Balbir had a fleeting thought that the police must be upset by the indiscipline of their civilian companions. The hullabaloo was a clear indication of what was going on and which side he should avoid. They were obviously beginning the search from the houses nearest to the road. He could hear a loud drunken voice exclaiming about the lack of a search warrant. Then another voice shouted angrily and there was a general altercation. The police were trying to keep the merchants in control and some people were bellowing about family honour and there was the brief sound of a scuffle and the thud of the drunken man falling, perhaps of his own inebriation, and his curses. Balbir wished the police had not been there. It would have made his escape easier.

He wished that again and more forcefully as Fat Aunty and he stepped out from between the huts and came to an expanse of mud where no doubt during the day the pigs rooted about. She pointed to some brick structures across the ooze and said, 'The other castes live there. Go through and out beyond the wall. May God keep you.'

He stepped into the slime and it sloshed into his shoes. It revolted him. With a shudder, he pressed on.

Just then he heard two rifle bolts click one after the other across the bog. And a voice said firmly, 'Who's that? Identify yourself. This is the police.'

He glanced back and saw that he would be shot before he could retreat. With a felicity of imagination that surprised him later, he said, changing his voice to sound as dull as he could, 'Bhola Ram here. Was just going out for a shit.'

'Come here then,' said a policeman not without a touch of humour, 'and let us see your arse.'

'Right,' said Bhola Ram. 'I think I'll come round. There's too much muck here. What's going on anyway?'

'Never you mind. Just come along and let's see.'

'Right,' said Bhola Ram, 'I'll come round.'

He squidged back to the huts and now a torch had begun playing on his back.

In the spread of light he saw the little alleyway through which he had come but he walked past it a few paces making certain to keep his face averted from the police. Taking a deep breath and uttering a short involuntary prayer he turned, bent and darted back. As he slipped from under the pinning beam and scrambled into the alleyway, there were shouts from across the bog. Two shots rang out and there was a shriek like a cat whose tail has been stepped upon. Perhaps the police had fired into the air, perhaps they had hit someone inside a hut. Balbir wasn't waiting to find out.

He flitted through the phantasmagoria of hovels, scuttling this way and that, trying as best as he could remember to make his way back to Fat Aunty's. Twice he barged into the wrong hut and the startled inhabitants added to the uproar.

Somewhere in mid-scurry he came upon her hurrying to him.

'I turned back when I heard the shots,' she said. 'Come. No, no. This way. If they catch you in my hut, we're all finished.'

An amplified voice rasped over a loud-hailer, 'All right, everyone. This is the police. Get indoors. Everyone indoors. In five minutes we will begin arresting anyone caught outside. Go to your houses. We are doing a house check. You have nothing to fear.'

'In here,' said Fat Aunty, rattling the knocker on a door.

A mousey little man with a thin drooping moustache that gave him the appearance of a darkling Chinese opened the door and yawned and, without a trace of curiosity, stood aside to let them enter. The man shut the door behind them and lay down on the cow-dunged floor and, pulling his soiled old sheet over his face, resumed his interrupted sleep.

In a corner of the room, on a little stool, was a wick-lamp that threw dancing shadows on the walls and ceiling.

Fat Aunty saw Balbir looking at it and whispered, 'There's always a light on in this house.'

'Right,' said Balbir. 'I remember seeing it when I first came looking for your place.' He wondered whether it was some sort of religious place where the eternal light had to be kept burning.

'Stay here,' ordered Fat Aunty. She pushed open a flimsy inner door of plywood planks and went in.

Balbir glanced about the room. There was nothing to sit on. Beside the man on the floor was a *chillum*. The place reeked of the smell of *ganja*. The man yawned again under his sheet and turned over.

Fat Aunty emerged and said to Balbir, 'She's in. And she's alone. This is the house of Gauhar Rand. She's a . . . a widow. Everyone knows about her. The police won't ask questions if they find you with her. She often entertains young men. Sometimes for a small present of a few rupees.'

She saw Balbir's shocked face and smiled with all her gold teeth. 'Don't worry. Just lie down in bed with her and pretend to be asleep.' She indicated the man on the floor and said, 'And don't bother about him. He's her watchdog. He'll open the door and the police will see you with Gauhar Rand and won't ask any questions.'

Just then a heavy-set woman with streaks of grey in her hair and a pockmarked face stepped into the room, grinned and scratched in her tousled hair. She had on a blouse and tattered petticoat and was so round in every way that she was bursting out of her clothes.

'Leave him to me,' she said in a guttural voice. Then she lumbered to the prostrate form on the floor and gave him a prod with her toe, 'Do your job, you lazy crook. Open the door for her.'

Without ado or formality, she then pushed Balbir into the inner room which was really no more than a partitioned off section of the bigger one. He knocked his shin against the string-bed and groaned.

'It's a small place,' she acknowledged as she pulled the plywood door to. Outside, he could hear the main door being opened for Fat Aunty.

Over the top of the partition the leaping light from the wick-lamp pranced on the ceiling.

'Take off your clothes,' said Gauhar Rand.

'Clothes?'

'Of course. You don't sleep with a woman and keep your clothes on, do you?'

There was a waft of garlic and onions when she spoke; the bedding smelt unwashed and was probably bug-ridden.

He had to sit on the bed. There wasn't enough space between

it and the door to remain standing.

'Why are you running from the police?' she asked. 'Kill someone?'

He said, 'No.'

'Rape someone?'

He shook his head and sat thinking of the horror of the merchants finding him here and the word spreading to Jagtara and the reputation of his family being ruined.

'You're not a thief, are you? No, I don't think so. What's your name?'

He was trying to hold his breath. She was sitting so close to him. She put her hand on his lap, letting it fall heavily with a thwack as a man might while assessing a bull at a cattle fair. He shifted a little but she had a firm grip on his thigh.

'What's the matter? You're high caste. I can see that.'

There was a crescendo of noise outside. The clamour came from all round the village. There were sounds of doors being banged upon, things being flung about and shouts and screams and tirades.

'Come on,' said Gauhar Rand, 'if you want to save yourself, you'd better undress.'

He was listening intently now trying to unravel the individual words in the din.

She said, 'They've all lain with me, all kinds of Jats—hindu, muslim, sikh. A few khatri merchants too. And once a brahmin, out in the fields.'

'What . . . what happened to your husband?' asked Balbir as though to stave her off with a loaded question.

'Died,' she said simply but, for a moment, her hand stopped kneading his thigh. 'Killed in the riots.'

'Riots?'

She gave a low laugh and said in her grating voice, 'Before you were even conceived. In forty-seven. I was fifteen, just married, going to Pakistan.'

'You're muslim.'

She gave another low laugh and said, 'I'm nothing anymore.'

'You could still have gone to Pakistan later,' he persisted.

'For what?'

He was quiet. Outside in the village rose the sound of batons and sticks and a sudden fusillade of shots.

After a while she said, 'I was born here. I was only going because he wanted to go. Maybe that's why they looked for him and killed him. They didn't trouble me much.'

'Who?' he asked but he was straining to hear the noises outside. Any moment now, there would come the expected banging on the door. 'Who looked for him to kill him?'

'The Jats,' she said. 'After a while, they let me go.' She paused and then added, 'I didn't really know him. My husband was much older than me.' Suddenly she said with a quiet vehemence, 'Old men disgust me.'

Then with another laugh, as easily as she had moved into the realm of memory, she crossed into the present.

Her voice took on a conspiratorial tone as she said, 'You're a fine young man. You can do it, heh?'

Her hand was over his penis, squeezing it. He tried to brush her hand aside but she chortled and pushed him onto his back. She was trying to get inside his trousers.

A sense of outrage overtook him. She was old enough to be his mother! And she stank and she was filthy and puffy. And, even if it meant getting killed, he was going outside.

With all his strength now he thrust her aside and got up and went out of the plywood door.

She said calmly from inside, 'If you go out they'll catch you.'

The logic was irrefutable. He hesitated.

Now she came into the light of the wick-lamp and folded her arms over her ponderous breasts. 'All right,' she said staring at him in a pitying way. 'Have you got any money?'

He was not sure whether she meant to rob him as well.

'Go on,' she rasped. 'See how much you have.'

He looked in his pockets and answered, 'About forty rupees.'

'More than enough,' she said. 'Give me thirty. Come on, give it to me. I'm trying to help you.'

She was no more the fat woman of the desiring hands. She was a businesswoman quickly putting through a deal. She took the thirty rupees, stuffed twenty inside her blouse between her breasts, then footed awake her 'watchdog' and said, 'Go get Chandu the Gujjar. Give him these ten rupees and say we'll give him ten more. We've got to hide a man in the well. Hurry.'

For a few moments after the 'watchdog' left, the absence of conversation between Gauhar Rand and Balbir was awkward. She glared at him as though he were a pestilent thing that had dropped in to intrude upon her equanimous life. He glanced every which way and kept snagging her eye. It was doubly difficult for him because there was nothing to sit on and his eyes were at the same level as hers. Finally he gave a deep sigh and sat down on the floor.

The commotion outside had developed a character of its own, moving steadily from street to street and hut to hut like a ravening monster that was gradually swallowing all that lay between it and Balbir.

But now suddenly the tumult was made more shrill by the blowing of many whistles in a way that indicated some kind of a signal passed on in relay. Then the muffled tattoo of one pair of hobnailed boots running overlapped with another. There was also the slap and splatter of hurrying shoes and sandals and bare feet. There were explanations and barked commands; it seemed hundreds of people were running, all towards the road. And then there was the roar of cars and jeeps starting and the protesting squeak of tongas, turning, moving . . . away!

The sudden silence was unnerving, as though the entire village outside had been dematerialized in one atomic puff. Then slowly the solitary voices and individual sounds of the village returned.

'That's strange!' said Balbir.

But Gauhar Rand only nodded and said, 'Let me explain what I've arranged. There is a well close to the hut of Chandu the Gujjar. He has some kind of right over it. It has a hole in the side. It's really a cave. It's big enough to take three men comfortably. Sometimes it is necessary to allow people to . . . to stay there for a while. His friends will lower you down to it in a bucket. The rope is strong enough. If people have to stay long, he sends down food too, at regular times. But I'm told its hard sleeping there. One man fell and drowned. There's a saying here that it's haunted but that's because sometimes the fellow down there feels he's been forgotten and he screams.' She gave one of her low, hoarse laughs. 'Chandu once helped one of his enemies. And left him there. He's a crazy fellow. Money is all he cares about. The bucket is always kept rolled up on the pulley.'

'Ah,' said Balbir. He realized she was still waiting for him to say something and mumbled. 'I . . . I am indebted to you.'

She nodded. Then muttered. 'It's very quiet. Do you think they've given up?'

This time Balbir laughed softly. And he wondered whether, in his nervous condition, he had caught the habit from her. 'They're not likely to give up so easily,' he said. 'It's some kind of strategy of the police.'

The 'watchdog' entered in a flurry. He was more animated than Balbir had seen him till now. Behind him came a lanky, glittering-eyed man with long hair that curled out under his haphazard turban almost to his shoulders. He too had a drooping moustache but it was fuller. And he was wearing earrings.

Balbir stood up and his shoes squidged horribly with the slime that had got into them.

Chandu the Gujjar hitched his *tamba* to his crotch with one hand, looked Balbir up and down quickly, then said to Gauhar Rand, 'My fellows have all gone for the night. There's no one to work the rope.'

'We'll do it,' said Gauhar. 'This fellow's in a hurry. It seems he doesn't want the police to catch him here.'

'Then he *can* wait,' said Chandu the Gujjar, 'because the police have just gone.'

'Gone?' Balbir echoed.

'You heard me, fellow. They left.' Then his eyes narrowed and he added, 'Your trouser buttons are still open. No need to dangle your jolly wanker before us.'

Balbir flushed hotly and quickly did up his buttons.

Chandu the Gujjar caressed his moustache and said with a hint of contempt to Gauhar Rand, 'These fellows! A quick one and then they want to hide from the police, eh?'

'Where have they gone?' asked Balbir impatiently.

'How should I know? They were after some runaway girl and her lover, I'm told—'

'Yes, yes, but—'

'Some merchant girl, they say. And the merchants were going to burn this place down. Thought they were hiding here. This is one time I thank the police for coming. Maybe that couple was here. Who knows? So you can relax, fellow, they were not after you.'

'But what made the police leave?'

'Why're you bothered? You mixed up with them?' Then smoothing the ten rupee note he had been given, he asked ingratiatingly, 'Want me to find out what happened?'

'I'd be obliged.'

He shot off like a squirrel. In ten minutes, he was back with the details. 'It seems this girl named Gulnari was hiding in a shelter that some people had cleverly padded up to look like a hay rick. The police and the merchants went past it many times without giving it a thought. Then this dame started singing! Can you beat it? She started singing. And that was it. God, she must be crazy! When they got her out, they found she was dressed like a bride. And you know what she was singing? "Weddings are made in heaven, take me to my wedding!" Can you beat that?'

10

•••

One Man in his Time

'Not at all, Dev, there's nothing to thank me for,' chuckled Lok Raj over the telephone even as he leaned back to blink appreciatively at the multicoloured fur-lined Norwegian long coat that Satyavan had brought him from Europe.

Satyavan was standing in front of him feeling a bit like a salesman though in fact he was laying before him an array of presents which he had been considerate enough to bring for members of the family. One was for Lok Raj; but of course he had to be shown everything—not just because he was the patriarch but because he still had an inquisitive mind that liked to be tickled by strange things.

'What's that?' Lok Raj pointed to an electronic gadget the size of a chocolate box. Then he laughed over the phone, 'No, no, Dev Singhji. I heard what you said. I was talking to Satyavan, my eldest grandson. He's just come back from a tour abroad. What I meant was, you don't need to thank me—why, you're the same age as one of my sons and that's how I consider you, as one of my own. All I did was give you an idea and set up the game. You played it.' He paused, listening, while he adjusted his dentures. 'Inshallah, Balbir will learn a lesson from this. It was good of you not to catch him. It would have been a little . . . embarrassing. What? In the house of a prostitute, was he?' Lok Raj guffawed. 'I suppose that was intended to be a good alibi.' After a moment he sobered and concentrated on what he was being told. 'I'm sorry she underwent such strain. Of course. And the boy? Yes, the potter boy? Is that what she says? Hm. Then it looks like he's got away from you. Why should you disbelieve her? He may really be in the Golden Temple. Yes, he is beyond your reach.' Lok Raj was now completely absorbed in the conversation. He didn't even groan with pleasure as was his wont when he farted. His voice rose slightly as he said, 'There I disagree with you. The onus of the blame is on Gulnari, perhaps even on that young fellow—what's his name?—Uday. But you certainly cannot harbour a grudge against those who sheltered her. She was out in a storm, they let her come in—that's how you should think of it. Why should you think they are still hiding the potter boy?' He cursed under his breath as he slipped back his errant dentures. He sighed. 'The subtlest revenge is total forgiveness.' He listened, and added, 'You're right, I haven't always set a good example. But I try, I try.' He guffawed again at some response that he heard, mumbled, 'It's kind of you to say so,' and in his careful way with all gadgetry replaced the receiver.

Beaming at Satyavan he told him, 'Continue to persuade me that you haven't wasted your money.'

Satyavan had by now rigged up the contents and circuitry of the chocolate box. 'This,' he explained proudly, 'is a paging device. It's a present to myself. The latest model, it has a range of many miles. Works by emitting a coded radio signal. This is the control unit. Compact, isn't it? My men have only to carry these little stamp-sized objects in their pocket and I can beep for any one of them when I like. Actually this model is so sophisticated that any of them can beep a signal back to me from wherever they are.'

'What a luxury!' Lok Raj said sardonically but affectionately. 'Why not just shout? You people have loud voices and good lungs. Anyway I suppose it's a useful toy. Where did you get it?'

Satyavan seemed embarrassed. Then he made an admission. 'Frankly, I first saw a less advanced version in a joint in Germany. It was being used to signal for girls.'

The old man was in good humour. He roared with laughter, 'Oh that Raskaan. He's younger than you but he could still lead you astray!'

Satyavan smiled. 'I'm afraid I indulged myself in my own way. Or, should I say, on behalf of all of us? Because this,' he indicated a small carton, 'is for all of us. It's a very efficient walkie-talkie system with a range of four hundred miles. Actually it's a transceiver, a transmitter-cum-receiver.'

'You'll need a licence for that sort of thing.'

Satyavan gurgled nonchalantly, 'Inspector Dutt owes me a few favours.'

The rest of the few things he had brought were the usual kind of gifts.

The old man rubbed the back of his hand against his chin and said, 'In your bargains with Inspector Dutt, don't forget to make Balbir a clause.'

Satyavan's eyebrows shot up. 'Balbir?'

'Aye. If your information is correct and Balbir's absences from the village have to do with gunrunning for Tarsem, then sooner or later we'll need the help of Inspector Dutt to save him from disgrace.'

'Why? And in what way? We'll get him out ourselves. I have a plan.'

'I don't know,' the old man shrugged. 'It's just a feeling. I like to keep both barrels loaded though I may need to fire only one shot.'

Satyavan nodded. Then murmured, 'Tarsem is getting too big. He's entered into an agreement with an organization called TAT. They ...'

The old man waved the subject aside like so much smoke from his *hookah*. 'That's your part of the forest. I'm not concerned about Tarsem. You can handle him easily enough ...'

'But, Babaji, Tarsem will be protected by TAT and that's one of the big combines.'

The old man's sigh was like a growl. 'Do I need to tell you again that I don't approve of even some of your associations and involvements? But we'll let that pass for the moment. I'm telling you, I'm only concerned about seeing that Balbir is untainted. I've come to a decision about him. We *will* send him abroad.'

'What?' Satyavan couldn't believe his ears. 'I have nothing against it but that's like giving in to him. He's exerting psychological pressure on us. He wants us to kick him out. If he goes, younger uncle will have a heart attack.'

The old man chuckled. 'We'll be giving in to him just enough to throw him off balance. We'll send him abroad only for a while, only for a visit, in such a way that he couldn't stay back there. We'll send him after getting him married. We'll send him abroad on his honeymoon!'

The idea was so startling that Satyavan was about to protest automatically, but he remembered his own resistance to marriage and blushed. He was guilty of remaining a bachelor, depriving the family of the joy of seeing him become a father; he had let the river of inheritance dwindle and disappear in the aridity of his selfishness. He had lapsed in his duty to his elders, for that is what marriage was—a duty to the past and the future.

Not all his ardour in the service of the patriarch could make up for that continuing omission. He kept quiet. Who was he to protest at the marriage of a younger cousin?

'So,' said the patriarch, 'we will see him wed and anchored. If we are preparing for Aadran's marriage, we might as well see her brother married too.'

An hour later, in answer to the summons of the patriarch, Balbir's parents walked into the room.

Satyavan had long before that excused himself and gone about his concerns but now, hearing Balbir's parents arrive, he followed them in.

Lok Raj was neither alone nor busy. He was relaxing in the company of an old sikh, a class-fellow of the village school he had attended. The old sikh, slurping at a glass of hot milk, sat sharing a sense of togetherness and a silence pregnant with memories. For the next half hour he remained there, saying almost nothing but content to be a fixture in a friend's life and in a friend's room. This quiet, contemplative activity common to most old people everywhere seemed so much like inactivity that it distressed Satyavan. 'Good God,' he thought, 'this must be what they call jet-lag! From Europe to here, I'm feeling the distance not in miles but in centuries!'

Satyavan himself remained largely silent but there was the difference of two generations in the quality of that silence.

And then, of course, for Satyavan the international traveller, there was that readjustment to an ancient culture in an ancient ancestral village. When time flows over the land it sometimes leaves behind in nooks and crannies the debris of earlier patterns of behaviour. Satyavan felt he was in a pocket of trapped time. The debris was sometimes as heavy and dull as lead and sometimes as precious as gold.

He remarked how Balbir's mother paused at the threshold and prepared herself. She covered her head with one end of her *saree*, holding the hem close to her mouth. The attempt at demureness was sincere but, at her age, there seemed a tinge of absurdity about it.

Having greeted the patriarch, she said cajolingly, 'Babaji, I'm glad you sent for us. I meant to visit you anyway to ask a favour. You won't refuse me, will you? I know how you scoff at all ritual but ... I would like to hold a *havan* here in the big hall tomorrow, to pray for the well-being of Balbir. I'm so worried about him. He's not his usual self at all.'

Though she had managed to mute her voice, she could not

suppress a twinkle in her eye. The old man was becoming something of a joke in his dotage.

'A *havan*?' he echoed her. 'Here, in our hall? For Balbir?' He was playing at surprise. He left his mouth open so that, when the smoke of the *hookah* had drifted clear, she saw that he had taken out his dentures. For a moment she wondered how he ate whatever was put before him and never asked for anything to be softened or made specially on his account. 'By all means, hold a *havan*,' Lok Raj muttered, 'but how that will help Balbir I don't know.'

'It'll help me,' she admitted softly with a little gasp. Joke the old man might be but if he refused her, she could not go against his decision.

'All right,' he sighed. 'Hold it in the courtyard then. Not in the hall. But I tell you I have as much influence with God as any priest. He may know the ritual prayers and he'll make a good singsong of it, but I know what's to be done about Balbir.'

'Lahh, Babaji,' she said, her mouth still politely behind the hem of her *saree*, 'as if we aren't always asking you what to do about him.'

The old man sucked at his *hookah*, punctuating the gurgle with a cough of pleasure, then he blew out a thin spiral of smoke, all the while dangling his legs thoughtfully under the string-bed on which he sat.

'Marry him off,' he said.

She was about to giggle but Khushi Ram was startled and said, 'What?'

'Why not?' Lok Raj asked. 'He's twenty-four.'

'Yes, but there's Aadran to be married off and—'

'Oh ho! Have I said don't see to Aadran's marriage? You people deliberately try to make me seem senile.'

Balbir's mother said, 'There is a nice girl I've been keeping in mind. Her family lives nearby but I'm afraid the dowry won't be very—'

'Dowry!' the old man roared suddenly. 'What's this talk of dowry in a family of the Muhiyali Chibber clan? We're beginning to talk like *banias*. Soon you'll be talking of commerce and setting up shops. It's one thing to own shops, it's another to sit there cross-legged waiting on the whims of every fool who comes in to do business. No, we will have no talk of dowry. If the girl has been given property in her own right, well and good; if not, we shall neither bargain nor think about it.'

'But . . . ' Khushi Ram began and trailed off into silence.

There were some times when you just couldn't argue with the old man. Khushi Ram had wanted to point out that for years now the Muhiyals had been drifting into the ways of the rest of the world. All the women who had come into the family within his memory had brought with them huge cabin trunks full of fine clothes, gold, jewellery and silver utensils. As in the households of lesser castes these things had been laid open to view so that the groom's relatives might know what the bride's family could afford. But the Muhiyals had their pride and there were injunctions against the acceptance of charity or ceremonial bribes, so the dowry was not laid out neatly and announced item by item as in the merchant classes; it was scattered about and the trunks were left open as though by chance and the men walked in casually with heads held high and cast a quick glance about and then excused themselves as though they had ambled into a ladies' room by mistake.

No mention was ever again made by the men of the objects they had seen but the womenfolk were free to chatter and indulge in the vanity of admiration. In the process, the nervous bride, anxious to please her new home-mates, gave away as presents such portions of the trousseau as particularly caught the fancy of the other women. Khushi Ram had wanted to say all this but it wasn't necessary. The old man knew it too. And resented it. He did not wish to be reminded that the Muhiyals were in danger of becoming as mercenary as the rest.

But Khushi Ram's wife pressed on. She said, 'All I'm trying to tell you is that the family I have in mind are not big landowners, they—'

'Never mind,' Lok Raj interrupted, 'we're not going to marry him to a village girl anyway.'

'No?'

'No. He needs someone who won't bow to his wishes all the time. Someone who will keep him in check. A city girl. A girl who is well-educated. He needs to be a little in awe of his wife. Otherwise he is the sort who'll run away. He can't bear people he can take for granted. I know how the boy is.'

'Old man,' Khushi Ran asked carefully, 'is that why you chose to spend twenty-five years away in Mintgumery?'

'I had to be there,' Lok Raj scowled. 'And I came back whenever I could.'

'But you never took Mother with you. She stayed here. I took my wife with me but you never asked Mother to come.'

'That was a man's world, son. You saw how it was.' But then

the old man fell silent. After a while he opened his mouth with a sort of clicking sound and muttered, 'Son, sometimes you talk too much.'

Now Khushi Ram's wife made her protest. 'If we marry the boy to a city girl, he may begin living there. What will he do? The land is here, we are here. What will he do without us?'

'You mean, what will you do without him?' The old man laughed. 'Don't worry. I also set out once and I came back. But these are details we can go into later when we've decided on a girl.'

'We could ask V.P. Joshi to suggest—' Balbir's mother began.

'Don't you mention that idiot bank clerk to me again. Nor any priest. And I don't want astrology and horoscopes brought into this.'

'But, Babaji, it's his whole life. We can't just—'

'Oh ho, don't start sobbing and crying already. Did I say you couldn't compare the horoscopes afterwards? Did I say you can't see later whether they match or not? But later. First *we* decide on the girl. And you leave the matching of the horoscopes to me. I promise you I'll call a man to do that myself. Don't mistake my laughing. It's not that I'm ready to play free and easy with Balbir's life. It's just that I don't want you consulting fools who don't know what they're talking about. My horoscope was cast. And by that I should have been dead in my twenties of the plague.'

'God preserve you!' She exclaimed quickly, quickly joined her palms, nodded a little reverential bow and made a few staccato spitting noises to ward off the evil of which he had spoken.

She knew the story of his horoscope and the plague. It had been an epidemic of smallpox. The dread goddess had visited the area, smiting young and old. Contrary to usual hindu practice, Lok Raj had not offered prayers for mercy but had gone instead to a muslim *hakim* for the inoculation cure practised from times immemorial in the Punjab. The *hakim* had made a ceremony of it, chanting the name of the fatal disease itself. Lok Raj had insisted on an explanation of everything. Crusts of diseased scab, it seemed, were mixed with powdered grains of rice. And then Lok Raj had held forth his thumb and the *hakim* had made a cut in the base of it with a knife. Into this lesion, he had inserted a few bits of the contaminated rice. Lok Raj insisted that it was the inoculation that saved his life while others were dying around him.

She said, 'Not everything is in the hands of man.'

'No,' the old man nodded, 'but a man must do everything he can.'

'And what do you all propose to do?' Khushi Ram asked with a snigger.

'I've had enough of your lip, Khushi Ram. Stay out of this. Charan Singh will help us find a good girl in Chandigarh. He is going there on a visit to his grandson.'

Charan Singh had remained quiet throughout this crucial family discussion which had grown somehow out of a simple request for the performance of a *havan*. He had even tried to bate the sound of his slurping as he drank the scalding milk. Now he placed the stainless steel tumbler on the stone floor, wiped his white whiskers with his *saafa* and said, 'I shall be very happy to do that. Of course, most people in the cities find it best to put an advertisement in the papers. One of my own grandsons has been married that way, very well too.'

'You do that, Charan, you put in an advertisement for Balbir. Or shall we draft it for you?'

'Damn it, Lok Raj! I know how to make out a simple advertisement.'

Lok Raj laughed and slapped his thigh. 'I didn't mean to remind you of your reputation as a duffer at school!'

Charan Singh shook with laughter too.

Balbir's mother signalled discreetly to her husband to follow her out and said to Lok Raj in the customary way. 'I'll be going then, Babaji.'

Babaji was what almost everyone now called him. The appellation rang with affection and respect. And he took advantage of both, wielding his whims like a sword and his demands were treated as decrees. Yet he must have missed the easy camaraderie of his peers. Only the odd octogenarian or contemporary still called him Lok Raj. And there weren't many men of his age around.

Sometimes when a visitor, like Charan Singh, dropped by and did call him Lok Raj, it had the effect of an elixir of youth, not only on him but also on all who happened to observe. It was a marvel to see the transformation that took place. His chuckle would become as light as the tickle of a feather, his face would glow with a cherubic radiance and the conversation, like dice rolled on a gambler's cloth, would tumble out of the past such stories, anecdotes and incidents that you forgot you were in the presence of a towering old man who wore his ordinary shawl like a mantle; you felt instead that you were listening to an argumentative youngster full of wonder at the absurdities of the world.

But he had remained argumentative at all times. This quality he had in even greater measure than his sons. He had a manner of speaking as though he were ready to quarrel. He had his way of looking at things, his interpretations and his self-deduced philosophy of life. He welcomed disagreement but could not brook not having his say. That is probably why he was litigious. He fought for every boundary and right as though it represented his last breath. But with all that, he was a direct man. He had a few pragmatic assumptions and he tested these on every occasion he could as though his entire life were a proving ground. He believed, for instance, that a law remained supreme only because it was deemed good by the largest number of people. That belief had its corollary; a law was not merely ineffective but it was bad if the largest number of people wished to rebel against it. This meant that he was always prepared to hear arguments in favour of breaking a law but he had somehow to assess for himself whether society, as he knew it, was for the law or against it. Yet he was aware that in his own area he was a shaper of opinion and could, to a large extent, work it to his will.

Lok Raj believed in two other specifics besides the law—the family and the land. You could tell him that India was now a democracy but he based all his practice on the idea that it was run by a family. Next to the law it was these two things that were most important—family and land. If there was no recourse through law for the redressal of a grievance then he considered it necessary to find some means, however indirect, of gaining the ear of the ruling family.

You could tell him convincingly enough that the days of the family as an institution were numbered. He would rejoin that he saw the vitality of the family, whether for good or bad, everywhere. He would point to the biggest business houses in India of which he heard constant mention—the Tatas, the Dalmias, the Birlas, the Jains, the Kirloskars, the Bhandarkars, they were really family houses. And the smaller tradespeople were the same, right down to the *banias* in the village. He pronounced no judgement, he took in the situation as it was. He saw simply that in politics too the server of the people became the ruler of their will and gradually the family crept in after him. It was an animal condition, a basic animal condition; all animals looked to their family first even when they had been tamed away from the larger community of the species.

As for the land, it was the only stable source of economic security and he was prepared to fight over it as any animal did over its accustomed territory.

Sometimes, Lok Raj's pragmatic assumptions intermeshed, at other times they diverged and once or twice they had actually clashed and these clashes constituted the major tragedies of his life.

Poor Lok Raj. He had been beggared twice by the politicians. They had fiddled the law twice to the detriment of millions. First, they had deprived him of his land through Partition, then they had tried to deprive him of his sense of belonging by redividing and re-constituting Punjab on the basis, again really, of religion. Haryana for the hindus, Punjab for the sikhs. But he knew he belonged to the Punjab just as much as the *vedas* or the five rivers did. The land belonged to those who tilled the soil and made it produce. He really had no religion except the land and making it yield grain. Punjab belonged to him in his blood and bones and hard work. And Punjab had no meaning if it did not contain all its peoples and five rivers. He continued to believe in the old undivided, perhaps re-united, Punjab where a man knew a man for his ability not for his mere profession of a religious belief.

Lok Raj sighed.

He said, 'It'll never be the same again.'

Charan Singh sighed too but he assumed that Lok Raj was thinking of their schooldays and the open compound in which they had had to study, sitting cross-legged on the ground in rows before the teacher.

'Hm,' Lok Raj muttered and sighed again and said, 'I was thinking, Charnaa, that the three best and most troublesome things in the world are the law, the family and the land.'

Charan Singh was startled at the way the subject seemed to have veered from that of their schooldays. Lok Raj is beginning to feel his age, he thought to himself, his mind is slipping like a cart on a monsoon road.

'The family and the land can raise a lot of problems,' Charan Singh agreed, 'but what's wrong with the law?'

'The politicians change it to suit themselves. Partition.'

'Ah,' Charan Singh nodded and he felt as though he had heard the deafening roll of a thunderbolt.

There was no conversation now. There was nothing to be said.

Each man had known his tragedies at the time. Each man was alone now, fighting back his memories. Charan Singh's brother had been killed on the road out of Lahore, two nieces whom he considered his daughters had been abducted, raped, killed, who knows what . . . Charan Singh saw himself scanning the refugee columns, searching among the tens of thousands of sorrow-scarred faces for the ones he knew. He heard himself asking those he knew for the whereabouts of those he loved. He saw the refugee camps, the trains as they came in, bulging at the seams, carrying on their carriage-tops bundles and human beings, and amid it all the stink of fear and sweat and urine. He saw bodies on the roadside, decomposing, headless, limbless, being eaten by crows and stray dogs. He saw himself shuddering and shaking and weeping. And he saw himself quiet, lost, bewildered amid the wailing and agony of those who had suffered more. He saw himself, at the age of forty-six, mount his bicycle, *kirpan* in hand, and go careering with tear-blinded eyes down the road. Suddenly he was among others rushing the same way and all restraint was lost as he merged with the roaring mob of hindus and sikhs bearing down on a few escaping muslims. The racing mob shattered and split against the clump of muslims and, as they broke and scattered, they were overwhelmed and cut down. Suddenly one of the group, with his right arm severed at the shoulder and his face gashed and spurting blood, came towards him screaming for mercy in the name of Allah. He skewered him on the point of his *kirpan*. The man was lifted off the ground for a second and his writhing weight brought Charan Singh crashing down. The blade of the *kirpan* broke in the man's stomach. Charan Singh wrenched the remaining piece out by the hilt. The man was still crying for mercy and grappling with his one arm. As the man gasped his last appeal, 'O brother . . .', Charan Singh cut off his head. Now many years later, that 'O brother . . .' still rang in his ears and he could feel the dying clutch of that grappling hand. Charan Singh leaned forward and spat slowly into the brass spittoon.

Sitting there, eavesdropping casually on the old men, unwinding from his hectic trip abroad, Satyavan was aware only of the long silences that seemed to him to be empty.

It was good to be back among these gentle retiring souls who seemed never to have known a hot-headed moment. For ten minutes after his grandfather had mentioned Partition, there had been a vacant, fathomless pause. Satyavan had listened to the sparrows cheeping in the rafters. How was he to know that

Lok Raj's mind, far from being empty, was full of a time when he was younger and that his brain was crowding with images of a dread day when his faith in the law had been shaken? That is how it had seemed to him then. It had seemed to him that the law had gone mad for it was the law that suddenly, unexpectedly agreed with the politicians and proclaimed that all lands held by non-muslims in the newly-declared Pakistan were to be forfeit for a meagre compensation. He had been bewildered and had argued about it, refusing at first to leave. He had been unable to bring himself to believe that it was a good ruling, yet all around him he saw that it held true for all. Then with a shock he heard the timely warning of his friend, Khan Ahmed Rasool: a group of fanatics was preparing to get him. He had reached immediately for his old twelve-bore and loaded it. Come, said Ahmed Rasool, we will go together to the border, I will not see you killed while I live, it's your duty to your children to stay alive, and there's Khushi Ram at the other *dera*, he'll be killed too if you don't take him away, he'll stay too and die, think of his family, think what you owe them. He thought all that and he thought too of his acres and acres of scrubland, land which he had made green in patches, land which had crumbled in his fingers at first and then stuck to them, land over which he had stood feet apart and head bent—digging, digging between his legs till his sweat mingled with the water trickling in channels from the Ravi river. He had forced the water, he had built his little bunds and dams, he had employed men but led them by example. Yes, he thought of his sons and their families, his families; he thought too of this, their land that he was greening for them. And what was to become of the hundreds of sheep that grazed on the scrub, the sheep among which he had often slept caring for their being born and dying? And the hacks stabled in the various *deras*—who would ride them in relay, who would see to their feed and massage and to the milking of the cows and the calving of the one that would tomorrow deliver? There were debts and relationships, bonds and transactions, friendships and little ties that could not suddenly be forgotten, held in abeyance, nullified. At one stroke of the law-makers' pen, his life's work was to be cut away from him. Who decided this thrusting of oblivion at him? It was like sentencing a man to death. What was his crime? Who had told him in advance not to go to Montgomery? Who had told him then that the incentives held out for the settling of the scrub were a bait and the vagaries of the law a trap? Who could he rail against, who kill? He had a great, overwhelming desire to prove his right by taking blood for blood; but whose blood? Bewildered and only half aware of what he was doing, he mounted Shaitaan and rode out to the *dera* of his son, Khushi Ram. Somewhere along the way, with Ahmed Rasool leading and arguing with groups and guiding, they had been joined by Sardar Harminder. Sardar Harminder with the revolver at his hip and Lok Raj brandishing his gun and then they were at the *dera* of Khushi Ram and Khushi Ram was laughing and saying what frightened middle-aged men they already were and Lok Raj shouting at him without bothering to explain or argue, ordering him, yelling at him almost violently as though he would kill his own son for being the first one to mock at him in any way, for this entire development in their lives was a mockery of what they had believed. They had believed that the law protected human life.

At first they moved towards the Sutlej. The journey to Jalandhar would be no more than a couple of hundred miles. Each of them was mounted, each of them was armed; they would in a few days be across the Sutlej in safer territory. They had ridden this way before and Ferozepur did not seem all that far away. But now they found every road blocked and prepared for ambush. Every way they turned, they seemed to hear crowds. They turned off into the fields and Khushi Ram who had less love for horses than his father cursed his miserable pony as it stumbled and jogged and its spine cut into his for he rode without a saddle and had chosen the least venturesome animal thinking they would amble along as they usually did. But now he could not keep pace with the others and the beast bogged down in mud or scrabbled painfully forward while the others galloped. Over this undulating ground he felt he was in constant danger of falling off and this animal it seemed had never learned to lift its hooves over scrub and stone. Skirting all habitation and human noise, they were back on the road and the dust of it choked Khushi Ram as he followed the others. He wound the end of his turban round the lower part of his face as the others had done. Then suddenly before they knew it they were against a bank of bullock carts and, out of these, men leaped with bloodcurdling cries. Khan Ahmed Rasool wheeled on the spot as they surrounded him and shouted out his name and called the wrath of God down upon the fools. They hung back, surprised. Ahmed Rasool pressed his initiative, berating them for blocking the road as though he were yelling invective at some oafish bullock cart driver in a narrow village lane. But now some of the men lit kerosene lanterns and holding them up came closer to scan their faces. Sardar Harminder did not move as someone reached up and unwound the shawl from about his face. There were exclamations. Lok Raj and Khushi Ram were recognized too. By the light of the lanterns, they also recognized some of the faces in the crowd; a few persons they had always called 'our own men', men who had worked beside them and for them. Lok Raj addressed himself to these, talking to them by name and chiding them half-jocularly for finding no better occupation on a cold night than highway brigandage.

'In the name of Allah, Panditji, we mean no harm to you or Sardar sahib. You are our friends. On either side of this road the land belongs to you. It's not you we were waiting for but . . . others. And what do you do yourself out on a night like this? In the few days since Partition, men have lost their sense of friend and foe. It is no longer safe on the roads.'

'Aye,' said Sardar Harminder Singh closing the gap in the exchange as Lok Raj seemed at a loss for words, 'you're right to say it's no longer safe on the roads but we fear nothing on our own land and from our own men. We are on our way to the *dera* of Mohammed Yakoob this side of Dipalpur. He is to celebrate the wedding of his daughter. It would be wrong not to attend.'

'But why travel at night?' asked a voice.

Lok Raj looked at the man.

'Why, it's you, Ghulam Hussein! Are you demanding to know why we choose to ride and when? You would do better to ask your mother why you were born at a particular time or born at all!'

The man Ghulam Hussein started angrily but whatever it was he said was lost in the laughter of his companions.

Sardar Harminder said, 'We ride at night because the invitation reached us too late. You know what times these are! We must be at Yakoob's *dera* by dawn.'

'Impossible!' one of the men exclaimed, 'Sardar sahib, with your long hair and your beard you'll be spotted at once no matter what turban and shawl you use. There are bands of men waiting all along the way.'

'What would you advise then?'

'Turn back.'

The men on horses looked at each other; the men on the ground seemed immediately to understand what they were thinking.

'Have no fear,' one of them said, 'none of us will trouble you. We could have raided your houses before this.'

'If you did,' said Khan Ahmed Rasool, 'you would have to answer to me.'

'And you would have to answer to this,' said Lok Raj holding up his gun.

'That's a good gun,' one of the men muttered and Lok Raj could sense the edge of covetousness in his voice.

'A fine horse too,' said another.

'And there's some dead land that I've brought to life with my sweat and urine!' Lok Raj suddenly roared. 'Would you have that, too, you greedy—?'

'Elder brother!' Khan Ahmed Rasool said sharply.

Lok Raj controlled himself then mumbled almost like a child, 'I don't know these two men.'

'Don't worry,' said one of them, 'you'll get to know us. We'll come and see you.'

'Welcome,' said Lok Raj, 'but come without your greed or I'll prepare a feast of bullets for you.'

'You wouldn't shoot them,' said the man called Ghulam Hussein, 'they're also one of us.'

'Lo, Ghulam, the mouse has learnt to roar! No, I wouldn't shoot them because I don't like shooting men in the bum!'

There was a ripple of laughter.

One of the strange faces said with an undertone of ugly sarcasm, 'You mean we would run from you?'

Lok Raj cocked both barrels of his gun and heeled Shaitaan forward. It was mere bravado but it did the work it was meant to do. The man who had spoken retreated hurriedly. Lok Raj reined in his horse. There was laughter from the crowd.

'Go home, Panditaa,' said one of the men quietly, 'there will be no weddings these days, only funerals.'

'Aye, Shafeek, what you say is true,' Lok Raj sighed and wheeled his horse round and they returned the way they had come.

They spent the remaining portion of the night and the next day at the *dera* of Khan Ahmed Rasool. Sardar Harminder Singh cut his hair and for the first time in his life shaved and made a bitter joke to console himself in his anger, saying, 'This is the least of what I am losing: the hair will grow back again.'

They rested as best as they could knowing now that a long journey lay ahead. They had decided to move in the opposite direction from the way they had intended to go. That would allay suspicions about them. They would go across the river Ravi and merge into anonymity and moving north recross the river weeks later after the first flush of crazy bloodshed was over. Little did they realize then that they would be homeless for three months and would be forced to trace a jagged, frightening course covering hundreds of miles.

But already the next day they were aware of the inroads into their emotions made by the horrendous mental epidemic spread by Partition. There were moments when they even began to doubt the intentions of Khan Ahmed Rasool. He was three times called out during the day and twice they listened to the voices of men asking about their whereabouts. When the men moved away accompanied by Ahmed Rasool and his answers became indistinct, they glanced at each other unspeaking and held their firearms in readiness and one of them always looked into the inner rooms to make sure that Rasool's family had not slipped out leaving them there, trapped, unsafeguarded.

That night they set out again. They tried to persuade Ahmed Rasool not to risk his life on their behalf but he insisted on accompanying them at least till the bridge on the river Ravi. Khushi Ram now had a better horse under him and in addition to the primed muzzle-loader he also carried a sword borrowed from Ahmed Rasool.

Crossing the bridge presented a problem. It was glutted with pillage, murder and havoc. Little groups of hindu and sikh refugees were trying to come over from the other side. They were perhaps from the Rechna Doab, the Chaj Doab, the Sind Sagar Doab or perhaps even from the North West Frontier Province, though people said that the NWFP was comparatively quiet. There was no time or possibility of talking to any of them to ask how conditions were beyond the Ravi, the Chenab, the Jhelum or around the Indus. The river was dotted with floating bodies and the river was in spate. There was no alternative but to cross over the bridge. What an irony, thought Lok Raj, that they were heading the way the refugees had come. In that split second he wondered how many of these straggling bands would ever see the river Sutlej towards which they were so directly heading.

It was a dark cloudy night. The moon struggled out from behind moving wisps of black and then was swallowed again. A chill wind seemed to encircle them, howling and whining and obliterating some of the shrieks and cries that rose from the bridge. At the farther end a lorry loaded with people was moving onto the bridge. Its headlights illuminated a nightmare.

Harminder Singh felt the wind nip strangely at his hairless face. It was a new sensation to him. He looked up and said 'I think it's going to rain.'

'Aye,' Lok Raj nodded. He looked across the river. The hillock on the right which he knew so well seemed deserted. He said, 'If we get separated on the bridge, we'll meet by the tomb on the hillock. I can't see it very well from here but I don't think we'll find anyone else there.'

There was no talk of the possibility that they might not get across. There was no mention of the dread that one or all of them might not live through the next ten minutes. They dismounted and bade Ahmed Rasool goodbye with an embrace. Then they embraced each other. After that there was a hesitation and a silence. They were all waiting for one of the others to say something.

Finally, Ahmed Rasool said, 'We shall all meet after this is over, Inshallah!'

'Inshallah!' they murmured acknowledging the same hope.

There was another akward silence. Ahmed Rasool knew they wanted to thank him but were at a loss for words. He deflected the moment with a joke. He said, 'The christians say that Samson lost his strength with his hair, but Harminder, you've lost some years. You look as young as Khushi Ram. The women will chase you now.'

The laughter was forced and unsteady. They were all thinking of other things. Ahmed Rasool turned away and there were tears running down his cheeks. He did not raise his hand to wipe his face. He did not want them to know he was crying. But they knew. He mounted his horse and said quickly, 'I won't stay to watch. Khuda hafiz.' He spun his animal round and rode away.

They mounted and trotted slowly to the foot of the bridge.

Thirty-seven years later, which seemed only a wink away in time, Charan Singh leaned forward and said to the old patriarch slumped in thought, 'Lok Raj, are you asleep? Wake up!'

Lok Raj straightened up and ran his tongue over his lips slowly. Then he smiled, 'Charneya, tell me again about our days in school.'

And as Charan Singh opened again the floodgates of anecdote and repartee, it seemed to Satyavan that these old men were children again and had known nothing beyond the joys of mischievous childhood.

When the telephone rang, Lok Raj was so pleasantly absorbed

in conversation with his friend that Satyavan took the message for him.

It was Dev Singh, Gulnari's uncle. He sounded most distressed. He said that the *panchayat*, the council of elders, of the village of Maina had unofficially conveyed to him that they disapproved of any attempt now to send Gulnari to Canada to be married to a man who ran a beef-canning factory. Hearing this, Satyavan's heart fell. He himself had often eaten beef, crabs, frogs legs, heaven-knows-what! But Dev Singh went on to clarify that he thought it was a subtle way of saying that, as long as the potter boy was alive, she was tied to him by common law for she had eloped with him. The only way to free her was to ensure that the potter was dead. As for the unofficial decision and stricture of the *panchayat*, once Uday was dead, perhaps Lok Raj could use his influence to have the social stigma erased by putting in a word with the relevant elders.

'Where is Uday?' Satyavan asked.

'Gulnari says he went with some of his extremist friends to the Golden Temple. But, frankly, I don't believe it. After abducting her, why should he leave her there on her own? I suspect he has been hidden somewhere by that woman called Fat Aunty. I've sent some men to fetch her here.'

Satyavan said, 'Perhaps it would be better to persuade Gulnari to tell the truth, since you don't believe her.'

'It's not only that,' sighed Dev Singh. There was a short pause. Then he said, 'She's in . . . a state of shock. It's impossible to get one coherent sentence out of her.' There was another pause. Then he added, 'I'm glad you're back. Babaji won't let us talk to Balbir. He's trying to keep him out of this. And we quite understand his feelings. Some of us are more than upset by what has happened. We realize Balbir was carried away by misplaced sympathy. But perhaps you should speak to him. Things are very tense here. I'm having difficulty restraining some of my relatives. If Balbir were to come voluntarily and speak to us . . .'

'I'll try.'

'We'd be obliged to you.'

Satyavan replaced the receiver and muttered with distaste, 'That Balbir! As if we didn't have enough troubles in Punjab without his stupidity!'

'Oy!' said Lok Raj affectionately, 'don't speak ill of my grandson.'

'That's the trouble with you, Babaji,' Satyavan frowned. 'You protect him so much that he fears no danger.'

'It's better than beating him. He's headstrong.'

'Then he needs to be cooled down with a good lesson.'

'Just you try teaching him, Satyavan. You try.'

Satyavan nodded. Then waited till Charan Singh had left before passing on the message. He was, by nature and experience, secretive.

11

•••

The Little Dove

A group of Dev Singh's relatives were standing in the courtyard of his house when the woman called Fat Aunty was brought and flung at his feet.

She touched her forehead to Dev Singh's shoes and begged for mercy. He averted his eyes. The others could see that the whole proceeding was repugnant to him. He was a man of some feeling and refinement.

Seeing his discomfiture, a bull-like man stepped forward with a martyred look. He was a pawn broker and hardware merchant. Under normal circumstances the two men had very little to do with each other; they were poles apart. Dev Singh considered the hardware merchant crass, dull and the epitome of all that he loathed. Furthermore, the man was known to be a blatant cheat who ruthlessly expoited those who came to him. He had not a tenth of the wealth of Dev Singh and yet wished to be considered on a par with him. At his approach, Dev Singh wanted to withdraw all the more like a turtle into his shell.

'Leave this to me, Dev,' said the hardware merchant in a sorrowful tone.

Gulnari's uncle nodded with a sick look on his face, the corners of his mouth turning down in a grimace though he had meant to reciprocate with a smile. He pulled back the matting of bamboo strips over an inner doorway and went in. Already, he could hear the woman's cries as the hardware merchant kicked her in the side.

The ladies of his household had a separate drawing room to themselves and now as he found himself sitting in one of the worn sofa chairs that adorned it, he was relieved that he was alone and the rest of the family was outside watching the torture that was being meted out. With each cry that he heard, he rocked back and forth involuntarily and eventually to prevent the nausea from erupting through his mouth, he gritted his teeth, and smacked his forehead with the side of his clenched fists. No one could see him now—a respected cloth merchant, a respected rich man—in a consternation of grief. For surely, this old woman could not survive such treatment. Outside, the younger men had joined in and were now threatening to apply a heated iron to her hands so that she could not work for a long time. An even more enthusiastic elder suggested that her feet and forehead be branded so that she could neither move nor be seen without the stigma of her involvement in the crime against the community. At the top of this hysteria of voices, he heard his wife scream, 'No, no, no!'

Suddenly there was silence and in the midst of it there was the crack of bones and he knew without being told that the hardware merchant had proceeded whilst the others were debating and threatening. He knew that the hardware merchant had acted, had perpetrated something of which he, Dev Singh, could never absolutely absolve himself no matter that he was not there when the deed was done. In the unexpected stillness that had cut through with the sharpness of a knife he had heard the crack of two bones, no louder than the report of a child's firecrackers, and he feared even as he knew that something had been done.

His wife burst in screaming, wailing that the woman had been maimed. Two fingers of her right hand had been broken.

Dev Singh stared at his wife. Though she fell heavily into another of the sofas, he seemed to see her like a ghost. But now, even as he looked, half in disbelief, she came alive, not as she was but as he had known and loved her many years before, when she was hurt by things like birds with broken wings. What a ninniness that had been to him! She had changed over the years and become distant and removed behind her household chores and he had drifted into his books of accounts and the daily newspaper. Now, this woman—his wife—whose sensitivity he had scoffed at till it had hardened into a stiffness from which he himself retreated, was splitting herself open and showing her raw inside. He loved her for that. Now, at this time, again, after many years, because perhaps it suddenly made her young and all those years ago again.

He went and sat beside her and held her hand and shut his eyes.

'It has to be done I suppose,' he whispered. And even as he said it he was aware that he really had no control over what was being done. It was being done in his name. In order that there may be respect for his name.

Fat Aunty's screams stitched the din of the other voices into a nightmare of sound. She cursed the day she was born, she bewailed her sins not of this but a previous birth for there was nothing in this life that she had done to deserve such retribution.

She moaned, she gasped, she sobbed. She cried out that she had been paid to provide shelter and that was all she had done. She beseeched them to spare her. She swore that Uday Singh the potter had fled with his friends to the Golden Temple. She did not know why he had not come back.

Suddenly she screamed, 'Ask that *brahmin* boy, Balbir. He'll tell you. He's been there. He has seen Uday in the Golden Temple! Ask him. Then you'll believe I'm telling you the truth.'

Listening in horror and amazement from within, Dev Singh found his hands trembling at his forehead. His turban was pushed askew. As he clutched his head to stop it from aching, the turban fell off onto the cotton rug and lay there upturned. The cheap local black hair-dye he used had left a dark ring along the rim where the sweat had settled.

At this moment, overriding the noise from the courtyard came a prolonged shriek from an adjoining room. Fat Aunty continued her lamentation, oblivious to everything but her own predicament. But those who were standing in Dev Singh's house for the first time in years were frozen in a chill panic. The jagged cry that had cut so unexpectedly into their angry concentration now seemed to convolute itself into a spiralling screeching and squawking like a squabble of birds at high pitch. The chattering rose and fell and broke and rose again. The petrified men stood looking in the direction of the room. Even the hardware merchant seemed unaware of Fat Aunty clawing at his feet, begging for mercy.

'That,' said one of Dev Singh's sons quietly, 'is Gulnari's mother. She's off her head. We confine her to that room.'

The men looked at the young man and then slowly lowered their gaze. One among them voiced their thoughts as he muttered, 'Your father is a good man.'

Dev Singh's son nodded. In turning aside, his glance brushed against a man on crutches who nodded too and, in acute embarrassment, began to hobble across the courtyard towards the women's sitting room. They watched pityingly as Gulnari's father made his slow way across. This paralytic was a familiar sight about the village. Everyone knew him, and liked him. He was generous with his smiles but he rarely spoke. And he never went to the cloth shop which had gone by default to Dev Singh.

Gulnari's father was halfway to the door when the screeching from the other room ceased.

'The fits come and go,' he said. And the men nodded again with understanding.

In the deadening silence, the tapping of the crutches seemed to glow and burn like blobs of molten steel.

As the cripple reached out to pull back the curtain of bamboo strips, he stumbled. One of the crutches slipped on the stone flagging. An involuntary gasp escaped from the men but he quickly steadied himself. Then turning to them, he nodded. His eyes were very sad and his brow was puckered in a frown; but he smiled. Retreating from the barrage of stares, he went indoors.

There, he was taken unawares to find Dev Singh with his head in his hands, studying the turban that had fallen on the floor. It was quite unlike Dev to be in the ladies' sitting room. Dev Singh's hair was a youthful black but he had been experimenting with a cheaper dye than the one he normally used and now perspiration was making it run in small grey streams.

The cripple smiled awkwardly and sat down carefully opposite his younger brother.

Dev Singh's wife immediately got up and went out. She had never got on with the cripple or that part of the family. They were a bother and a burden.

'I'm sorry about all this,' said the cripple to his younger brother.

Dev Singh returned a similar, awkward smile in acknowledgement. They were brothers after all. They shared some of the same traits and mannerisms and features. And, whatever happened, they would stand together.

'Where is Gulnari, Dev?' the cripple asked.

'Upstairs. In her room. I locked her in. Didn't want her to see all this. Or do anything silly. She's not herself at the moment.'

'Like her mother. Like her mother.'

'No, no,' Dev Singh said quickly. Then he sighed and leaned his head back against the sofa. The dye soiled the Victoriana of lace that protected the headrest. These antimacassars were affected by his wife in the gentle rustic way that clings to fashions after they have fled.

The cripple wondered how the stain on the family honour could be erased.

He said, 'Give me the key, Dev. I want to talk to my daughter.'

Dev Singh hesitated.

'She's my daughter, Dev. I want to see her.'

'As you say, elder brother.' Dev Singh took the key out of his pocket and gave it to Gulnari's father.

Then he stood up with determination, and putting the turban on his head pushed aside the cane matting and went out.

In the courtyard, Fat Aunty was sitting up, cradling her broken fingers. The hardware merchant kicked her in the ribs and she began writhing on the floor, out of breath.

The hardware merchant gritted out the demand, 'If he is in the Golden Temple, how do we find him there? Is he hiding? Who is hiding him? Many of us have been there in the last few weeks. We didn't see him. Where is he? Tell us.'

A chant of 'Tell us! Tell us! Tell!' rose from the throats of the other men. One or two prodded her with staves as though she were a wriggling unclean thing, a snake. They were trying to control their inner frenzy which could break out in hysteria. They were too few in the courtyard to constitute a mob. They could be identified and blamed later if anything too serious happened to Fat Aunty. They held themselves in but with difficulty.

Dev Singh raised a hand and called out, 'Brothers!'

They stopped at his decisive tone.

He said, 'Let us gather the other merchants, sikh and hindu. After all, that Uday has misused Kulwanti's good nature too. Let us gather the village, for it has been an insult to Maina itself! Let us take this woman back to Chak Deedar and show them how we feel! Let us search for Uday the potter. I have just vowed to myself that I will not change this turban for a clean one till I see Uday Singh dead!'

The men shouted, 'Aye!'

The hardware merchant held up a fist and turned to the men. 'We'll raze Chak Deedar to the ground! And if we don't find the potter, we'll take his father and go to the Golden Temple itself! I say: we contribute and announce a reward of ten thousand rupees for the person who brings us Uday Singh's head!'

He thrust his hand into a pocket and brought out a ball of crumpled currency notes. Flinging the lot into a bucket, he shouted, 'There, I've started the fund!'

Others dipped into their wallets and pockets.

The bucket was soon brimming with coins and currency notes. A second bucket was put beside it. The news spread through the village. A crowd gathered outside.

Kulwanti's father came, wearing a stiff black *topee*, a silk *kurta*, white *dhoti* and a streak of vermillion on his forehead. He added a wad of notes to the fund. Other merchants came.

More villagers gathered outside. Whatever transport could be commandeered was obtained.

Tractors with trolleys crammed with men carrying sticks, swords, knives, sickles or just a length of sugar-cane. Tongas. Three or four cars. An old lorry.

In the sparkling afternoon sun, they left like a procession of doom.

The house had emptied quickly. The reward money had been locked into the steel cupboard that did as a safe. Only the women of the house remained. And the cripple.

Slowly, painstakingly, he hobbled up the steps to the door of his beloved daughter's room.

She hardly heard him over the noise from the street. She was standing at the window, still in those ridiculous bridal clothes, peering down through the grille but she could not see into the street. A compound wall thwarted her as it had Uday whenever he had attempted to communicate with her from the street.

'My little dove,' the cripple said, as he pushed the door shut behind him.

As she turned, the red glass bangles tinkled and clinked.

He took her face in his hands, propping himself on the crutches at the armpits.

'You have grown very beautiful,' he said. 'But we neglected you. Don't blame us too much.'

She shook her head and looked down and away.

He said again, 'My little dove. You know when you were a baby that's what I called you. I wanted to name you like that. But your mother thought of you as the rose of paradise. And that's how we named you Gulnari. But to me you are still my little dove. We have failed you. The world has failed you, my little dove. And you must fly away.'

She looked at him, almost with relief. And comprehension.

'Fly away, little dove,' he said as tears welled in his eyes and he choked them back. 'Your uncle has been good to us, and we must not disgrace him or ourselves. Fly away, my dove.'

He turned and stumbled hazily out of the door.

He left it open but she knew that that was not the kind of flight he had meant.

She sat on her bed, thinking a long time. She had read other people's death warrants to Uday Singh. She knew how people were 'put on trains'. And she searched again in all that, in all her life, for love, for more than love, for tenderness.

She thought of Kulwanti. She was a friend. She loved her. But that was not quite that tenderness.

Suddenly she thought of Balbir. Balbir who had helped Uday. Balbir—Uday's friend. In his eyes, once, in Fat Aunty's hut, as she sat up, she had seen a softness, an appreciation. There had been a hint of something. What? Was that tenderness?

It escaped her.

She began a letter to her mother. Then to Kulwanti. She wrenched the sheets out of the exercise book she was using. She crumpled the sheets and flung them in a corner.

Placing the exercise book on the floor, she put beside it the stone that was used as a doorstop.

Then she took off her red bridal bangles and piled them on the open exercise book. She did not know how many she would need. She had no experience of this. This could not be experienced twice. Only once.

It would take time. Patiently, dilligently, using the stone, she began to crush the glass bangles to powder.

She wondered how she would swallow the powdered glass. Would it stick in her throat? By her bed was a silver tumbler of water. That was the mug from which she had drunk milk as a child. She put the mug of water by the exercise book, then continued grinding the bangles to powder.

After she was gone the silver tumbler would remain. She wondered who would drink from it hereafter.

12

◆◆◆

A Way of Life and Death

Among those who were killed in the attack on Chak Deedar was
the woman known generally as Fat Aunty. It was said that she
had been used like a human torch to set fire to the colony. They
had doused her hut and then her clothes with kerosene and set
her ablaze. Simultaneously fires were begun in other corners of
the colony. The poor inhabitants were unable to concentrate
their attention and the few who tried to repel the arsonists were
clubbed back or frightened away by shots. A man who came
rushing out with a sword was riddled with bullets before he
could raise it; his body was consigned to the flames. The cluster
of hutments became an inferno within seconds. Many were
injured in the stampede towards the bog at the rear. A couple of
attackers too suffered severe burns in the panic. The third
person to die in the blaze was not a victim of burns but of
suffocation. He was a notorious criminal of the region on the
run from the police; he had mistaken the commotion for a
well-organized manhunt and had taken shelter in the supposedly safest place in the centre of the colony. His body was
recovered later from the small cavern in the side of the smoke-
filled well belonging to Chandu the Gujjar.

Besides these, there were other casualties—cattle and poultry
and stabled tonga horses. Most personal belongings were engulfed in the conflagration. However, it would be wrong and
inaccurate to assume that all those who set fire to Chak Deedar
were of the merchant caste and that this was another one of the
many atrocities aimed specifically at *harijans* as are reported
sporadically from other parts of the sub-continent. In the
Punjab, fortunately, caste does not carry with it the bigotry and
vehemence that it does in the more backward, less intermixed
populations of some other states. In the Punjab, while caste and

creed and origin still serve as easy means of identification they are not hemmed in by daily discriminations and barriers. The Punjab has suffered too many invasions, too much strife and rapacity to bother with petty social stigma when life, liberty and property have themselves so often been at stake. Furthermore, the moment a religious dogma has tried to straitjacket the Punjab, out of its own adherents has grown a reform movement to balance it; and the followers of other creeds have learnt from it and incorporated some of its beliefs into their own.

The basic fact of the matter is that despite the romance in folklore, despite the great popularity of the meretricious cinema with its fairy tale heroes and heroines, the 'love-marriage' as it is called is generally abhorred in rural society. A 'love-marriage' often crosses not only caste and creed and economic disparities but, certainly, it by-passes the authority of the elders. Then everyone rallies to abominate and thwart it. They rush to stem the rot before it touches them.

So it is not surprising that the merchants who attacked Chak Deedar were accompanied by belligerents of other castes and included both hindus and sikhs. It would not be fair either to assume that the sikhs who participated in the incident were motivated by the sort of prejudice that had erupted in a violent clash earlier in Amritsar between two factions over the question of whether or not untouchable castes of sikhs could enter the Golden Temple at all times or be restricted to a discriminatory hour. The hindus and sikhs were friends, relatives—for sometimes one brother may be a hindu, the other sikh—neighbours from the same *mohalla*, street or colleagues in trade. They were villagers conscious of their respectability and anxious to preserve the status quo. But there is no denying that their indignation was stoked by the thought of the temerity of a family of *harijans* in giving shelter to a potter who had abducted a merchant girl. And it gave their anger an edge to think that *chuhras*, *chamars*, *jamadars*, *harijans* had so dared to presume.

In the midst of such raging retribution and its aftermath no one could speak well of Uday Singh. It was impossible even to say that he had been a good field-hand or had occasionally put in a creditable stint at his father's potting wheel. It was as if the boy had been bad to start with and doomed at birth. He was a traitor to society and had tried to break with his place in it. The most charitable assessment that was ventured shrugged off his memory with the phrases 'that fool Uday' or 'that mad fellow'.

When Balbir heard of the catastrophe at Chak Deedar, he

knew that now there was no easy way out. A corridor of hell was stretching out before him. He shuddered to think of the manner in which the woman called Fat Aunty had been killed and he couldn't help thinking also how fortunate he had been that earlier night when he had almost taken shelter in the well of Chandu the Gujjar. If the police hadn't been there, the merchants would certainly have set fire to the village then. And Balbir imagined how horrible it must have been, both for Fat Aunty and the man who ended up being suffocated in the well.

Satyavan had already spoken to him earlier in the day. Balbir was convinced that he had to go and talk to Gulnari's uncle. He had to tell him flatly that Uday Singh Kumhareya was as good as dead. That Uday was in the Golden Temple but hardly alive and probably by now just a body in a sack fished out by the police from some manhole.

Satyavan had immediately telephoned to say that he was coming with Balbir but he was told that Dev Singh was out. He left a message saying they would come at 6.00 pm. Little did they realize then that Dev Singh and the villagers of Maina were at that moment on a rampage in Chak Deedar.

But do not think this was one of those ironies that, had it been otherwise, might have changed the course of events. No. The fact is, Balbir was utterly powerless to stop it though he might have been able to postpone it by diverting their attention for a few hours. The merchants of Maina would have avenged themselves on Fat Aunty and her people anyway. The whole social structure encouraged and demanded it.

Of course, later in the afternoon, when Balbir heard of the fate of Chak Deedar, he *needed* to feel that he could have prevented it. His horror at the outrage was exacerbated by a sense of shared responsibility. Had he not at that point felt that he could have interceded, intervened, altered, he would have succumbed to despair—for himself and for all life. If he did not have the power to prevent, he had to assume he had it. And since he had not used the power he had assumed, he bore guilt. Guilt gave his existence meaning.

At 5.30 in the evening Satyavan came for him and they drove to Maina. Beside the driver, who was armed, was another armed man. Satyavan himself was wearing a .38 revolver under his *kurta*. And on the floor of the Fiat was a sten gun covered by a travelling rug. These were not unusual precautions for Satyavan; this was his accustomed mode in Punjab.

Throughout the drive Balbir made no mention of his dilemma. Would he be betraying Kumhareya somehow by leading the Ahluwalias to him? But Kumhareya was probably dead already! He should have told them earlier, before they raided Chak Deedar this afternoon. It might have saved so many lives. Would he be saving life now by telling them, perhaps even taking them there? Was he doing it because he feared for his own life? He had to admit that he was afraid that they might—rashly—come for him unless he went to them. Perhaps even now he could persuade them that their best course was to get Gulnari to marry Kumhareya. He hated the prospect of dealing with an angry, bloodthirsty Dev Singh. And, yes, he was afraid.

But the dreaded interview lasted less than a minute.

Dev Singh and a small group of men were standing outside the house.

As they drew up, they could hear the sounds of wailing and crying and lamentation. Satyavan frowned as he waited for his bodyguard to come round to his side.

Dev Singh shook hands with Satyavan and said, 'Thank you. Thank you for bringing Balbir.'

Then he turned to Balbir and asked, 'Can you take me to Uday tomorrow? I can't leave here now. I'll come for you by seven in the morning.'

Satyavan interposed himself gently. 'He'll take you. But come alone.'

'Of course, brother. You have my word.'

'They . . . they're killing him,' said Balbir. 'We might still be . . .' Balbir tried to control his trembling lips, to speak despite a dry airless throat. 'We might still be able to save him if . . . if Gulnari agrees to—'

'She's dead,' said Dev Singh. 'We're preparing for her cremation.'

It was Dev Singh who turned away, his podgy features trying to control the tears.

'O God!' Balbir automatically reached out and touched Dev Singh on the arm. 'I'm sorry, uncle.'

Dev Singh could not speak. He nodded.

That night Balbir went to Tarsem's *chabara* and was so crazily drunk that he smashed every bottle he could break, and no one could restrain him.

13

•••

The Thread and the Sword

At seven in the morning, Dev Singh came for Balbir. He was dressed in a suit over which he wore a short ceremonial *kirpan*, no bigger than a dagger.

At that very hour, in the ancestral village of Chamkalan a *havan*, a *puja*, a prayer was being offered for the welfare of Balbir. His mother, unable to communicate with him, was relying on spiritual forces to help her get through to him. The patriarch humoured her. A number of relatives gathered.

As Balbir sat in the car, Dev Singh murmured apologetically, 'I'm sorry to be taking you away today. I hear some sort of ceremony is going on at Chamkalan. I just spoke to your grandfather on the telephone. He shouldn't worry. He's an old man. Old people need to be reassured.'

'That's thoughtful of you,' Balbir said quietly. Neither of them was really in the mood for conversation.

Dev Singh eased the car into gear. 'You understand, I just want to see this scoundrel Uday for myself. I've never seen him.'

A few miles later, he said, 'You realize there's a reward for anyone who locates the potter . . . or takes me to him.'

'Please—' Balbir began angrily and then leaned out of the window to vomit. He was sick, with the liquor of the night before and the thought that Dev Singh had ventured to offer him money for what he was doing with the best intentions in the world. In his mind he heard Kumhareya's voice snicker: 'Blood money!'

He gestured to Dev Singh to stop.

He had to get out and retch it all up and clear his head.

Dev Singh said kindly, but with a tinge of surprise, 'You're only a kid.'

Balbir replied sharply, 'I'm twenty-four.'

Dev Singh smiled.

They drove on without talking.

In Chamkalan, out in the vast yard beside the house of Lok Raj, a regular pandit was chanting a string of *shlokas*. About him were a couple of hundred men, women and children sitting on rugs or milling about greeting each other. The gentle hubbub was continuous, broken now and again by the priest's loudly audible intake of breath as he launched afresh on a new tangent of chanting. Before the priest were various metal utensils including a *lota* and a ladle, there were petals too and grains of rice and wheat and some turmeric; neither the priest's paraphernalia nor prayers were signifying much to the audience but when he struck sparks with the start of a slightly familiar mantra, a few men and women intoned a phrase along with him.

Seated directly in front of the priest was a little boy of about four and a half. The child was dressed in the sort of gaudy finery that is dear to the hearts of northern villagers. Printed silk shirt, green corduroy shorts, a purple velvet jacket spangled with silver *zari*-embroidery, yellow socks, red shoes. His eyes stared wonderingly out through rims of antimony. He looked scrubbed and brushed and obviously thought the priest's ceremonial implements and ingredients were toys and he was playing with whatever he could lay his hands on. His parents were trying to keep him from upsetting things.

Khushi Ram arrived, saw that the prayers were well underway, looked about for the old man and, not seeing him, went into the hall.

Lok Raj was sitting there, in conversation with Satyavan.

'I fall at your feet, old fellow,' muttered Khushi Ram.

'Live on!' responded Lok Raj in the traditional manner.

He was seated in a straight-backed chair smoking a *hookah*. Around him were five or six others sipping glasses of iced fresh lemon juice.

Satyavan was saying, 'Babaji, all said and done, we've got to admit that Western-style loos are better than our traditional ones.'

One of the men said, 'I prefer to go out into the fields myself. Can't bear being cramped in a bathroom.'

'You should see Raskaan's toilets in Berlin,' insisted Satyavan. 'A delight, an absolute delight.'

'I hope you didn't tell him,' Lok Raj muttered. 'He's already got a swollen head, it'll give him a swollen bum.'

There was general laughter.

Satyavan pressed on. 'There's only one modern bathroom in this region and that is in Jagtara—in the house of Karnail Singh's mistress.'

'Who?'

But Satyavan ignored him and went on. 'That is really a garish monstrosity. What we need are practical, efficient, sensible toilets not those shit-between-bricks lavatories we have up there.'

He spoke so forcefully and pointed so definitely that everyone looked up.

Above them was a grille of about ten feet by five set in the high brick ceiling. Through it could be seen some children and women moving around it on the first floor. Occasionally some-one stepped carefully along or across the grille—the children for fun, the adults in order to take a shortcut—and if the movement attracted attention to itself, the men seated below would look up and exchange an informal word.

The real function of the grille was, of course, a military one. From there it was possible to observe who entered the hall; from there it was possible to shoot down intruders. This house in Chamkalan was a classic, bearing evidence of the chief concerns of big landlords in Punjab. The area had lain in the path of too many invaders; it was natural that the architecture of this ancient village should display signs of preparedness. Like the streets outside, the interior of this great house too was designed for ambush.

Through the grille it was possible to glimpse the steps mounting up from the first floor to the two terraces with their miniature turrets and battlements. On each of these terraces was a screened off corner providing the privacy needed for function-al toilets. Inside were two footrests of raised bricks set in the flooring. There was no flush system, of course; the sweeper-woman did a long haul up each morning to clean and carry away the accumulation. This was one of the unhallowed chores of the untouchables and still is, in most parts of India.

Naughty-minded visitors to this ancient village could, if they positioned themselves at an appropriate angle somewhere in the environs at street-level, look up and through the serrations and drain-hole catch a glimpse of high-caste male or female bum. The village folk were themselves not bothered by this. The women had over the centuries and under the strong impact of Islam in the north begun to observe *purdah*—to veil their faces—but the natural functions were accepted routinely. So, if a young woman suspected the presence of a peeping-tom below, she cautiously veiled her identity before exposing her derrière.

Perhaps some of this passed through Lok Raj's mind too, for he chuckled and said, 'Very well. Have a couple of modern bathrooms installed. But you can't put them up there. Difficult plumbing. What about down there?'

He meant the basement. A series of steps led down from the hall to a cool, cavernous, semi-furnished room and storage places in the cellar. That was also where the family's stock of guns was kept.

Satyavan said quickly, 'No!'

He didn't want everyone going down there and visitors getting a chance to spot the concealed armoury.

'No,' he repeated. 'We'll build them off this hall. Here. And here.'

One of the men grumbled, 'What a thing to be talking about while prayers are going on!'

'Why,' argued Lok Raj, 'what's wrong with that? I pray best in the toilet. It relieves me both ways.'

There were roars of laughter.

A middle-aged man wondered tentatively whether he could ask the priest to conduct the sacred thread ceremony of his twelve-year-old son. It would save calling all these relatives again.

'By all means,' said Lok Raj. 'Go ahead. It's a day for children and womenfolk anyway. All this hooha! Just gives them a chance to meet, that's all.'

'Aye,' agreed the man, with pleasure. He went off to add to the ceremonies.

'So!' said Lok Raj a trifle sarcastically, 'the head of the Jagtara family is here. But where is his younger son.'

'You know better than I, old man,' replied Khushi Ram. Then he muttered, 'But I do think we should go out, otherwise it will be taken amiss.'

'Amiss? By whom? The gods? Don't be silly! Ah, you mean we should let everyone see that we are concerned about Balbir. But we are. I don't need to show anything.'

'No, old man,' said Khushi Ram patiently, 'but if anything should happen to Balbir, they'll have an excuse to say it was your fault.'

Lok Raj shook his head and moaned, 'All right then, out we go.'

Just as he was about to heave himself from his chair something thick and turdy plopped on the floor before him. The other men stared at it without comment and one or two looked up uneasily at the grille. Lok Raj sat back and shielding his eyes saw a little three-year-old with his bottom bared squatting atop the grille.

'Oy!' Lok Raj roared. He had somehow got his thick curved walking-stick in his right hand and he shook it at the terrified little visage that peered down awkwardly. 'Is that the place to do your nonsense? Whose little brat are you?'

The little fellow said nothing, whether out of fear or because he was absorbed in studying the curious upturned faces it was impossible to say.

Lok Raj bellowed again, 'Speak up, won't you? Whose child are you? Who looks after you?'

After only the slightest hesitation now, the child answered in all innocence, 'You do.'

The old man's anger dissolved and he began to laugh. 'Right, right,' he nodded. 'You are all my children.' Then he looked down at the lump on the floor and muttered, 'But I'm damned if I begin clearing up this stuff at this age! Satyavan, you'll not only have to build your loos but also teach people to use them.'

The men laughed. Upstairs there was a great deal of hurrying and scurrying like a bevy of birds agitated; a woman who may have been the child's mother came down quickly, her face veiled in a *ghund*, with two pieces of cardboard in her hands.

'We're just leaving', said Lok Raj and led the men out to the yard.

On the road to Amritsar, the silence in the car was intolerable. Dev Singh switched on the radio. It was time for the morning news. Punjab dominated the bulletin. Balbir cringed as a roll call of victims was announced. The arson and deaths at Chak Deedar faded into insignificance. The extremists had many times that number to their excruciating credit. Names and places ceased to register. In the two and a half days since the butchery at Kahnuwan, the figures had mounted like a rash spreading in patches.

Two persons fired at. A bomb exploded. A man murdered. Two shot dead, a third injured seriously. One person shot dead. Four riddled with bullets and two hurt. One killed, another injured. Three killed, four injured. A body found and identified. Four injured. A man and his son and grandson of eighteen months murdered. Four killed, six injured, including a woman and child, in a shooting spree at a grain market. One man shot dead. A bomb exploded, killing one, injuring ten. Two persons shot at, one succumbed to injuries. Two people injured by gunfire. A shopkeeper fired at. A man robbed. One man shot dead and two seriously hurt. Two persons attacked and injured. A village shopkeeper shot and killed. Another man murdered.

Almost invariably, the extremists vanished, fled, escaped, took refuge in *gurdwaras*.

Dev Singh turned off the radio and muttered, 'It's sickening. And to think that Gulnari let herself be drawn into this!'

Balbir said nothing. He was not expected to. Dev Singh was going through a hell of his own.

Out of the corner of his eye, Balbir looked at the bulbous features, the gold-ringed hand on the wheel, the beard showing grey where the dye had worn off, the perspiration glistening at the pores as the hands alternately gripped and thumped the steering wheel.

He was so avuncular, this dear Dev Singh, and he was suffering. He had seen brutality in his own courtyard, carnage in a village and the devastation of his peaceful life—all for 'duty'. Perhaps the most horrible, loveless word in the world.

Dev Singh thought of all that he had forced himself to do in the name of duty. 'It was my duty to look after my paralyzed elder brother, my duty to adjust to his insane wife, my duty to run the shop so that it could support the tribe and pay for the treatments of its ill, my duty to see to the girl's education, my duty to put the happiness of my wife and sons second to my duty to my brother. My duty to avenge the honour of a foolish niece—may her soul rest in peace! —with lies and murder and destruction, and perhaps murder with my own hands. No pawn-broker here, no hardware merchant to ease my way with his crassness. My duty not to enjoy peace and prosperity and good living. Those are for men who have no sense of duty.'

Suddenly, for some reason, he thought of his wife's fondness for antimacassers.

And he glanced at Balbir. And caught him looking. And he wondered—but it wasn't possible! —did he understand?

In Chamkalan there was killing too—of a ceremonial kind. A pure white lamb had been tethered near a sapling of an auspicious tree. A clay lamp was lit and a basket inverted over it. A number of earthern pots were placed on the ground, mouth down. The head of the lamb was washed and a dollop of curd rubbed about its ears. Then, with a razor, a vein in one of the ears was cut. The blood began to trickle out.

The Muhiyals had prayed for Balbir. They were now into the initiation ceremony of the twelve-year-old child.

Suddenly Lok Raj interrupted loudly. Everyone turned to look where he stood, tall and erect, not resting on his stick but holding it before him. Someone had obviously brought him his turban for it was now on his head and even with its careless unstarched cockade he seemed to tower over the tallest around him. Without his turban and Peshawari sandals he stood a good six feet four inches anyway.

'Oy, holy man! What is the use of this mumbo-jumbo if we don't understand its meaning?'

'Yes, yes, Panditji, I was going to explain at the end.'

'Too late, holy one. By then the fun will be stale and everyone will rush off to eat a bit of the delicious *halwa* that I can smell already.'

'Yes, Panditji. Well . . .' said the priest turning to the gathering, 'Among you Muhiyals, the blood of a lamb is used for marking the forehead of the child. Normally I would have used vermillion colour. That would be for scholarship which is the calling of *brahmins* and with this ceremony today the initiate launches on a life of study. But, among you Muhiyals,' and here a tone of apology bordering on disapproval tainted his voice, 'the mark of blood signifies the start of studying the military arts.'

The priest now snipped a lock of the boy's hair and handed it to the mother. Then a barber, engaged for the occasion and spruced for his public performance, stepped forward and with the razor shaved the child's head clean leaving just one curl of hair at the back. The child was asked to jump on the earthern pots and break them. He did so with gusto and began to like the game.

The priest cleared his throat and declared, 'This breaking of the pots signifies the destruction by the boy of his enemies.'

There were exclamations of approval from the audience and some hearty shouts of encouragement to the child who was now enjoying himself hugely.

The priest pointed to the sapling and said, 'May he embody the tenacity and strength of a tree and remember to plant trees in the land he owns or conquers, for a warrior may ravage the land only if he makes it yield again.'

As the *halwa* was distributed, the priest said, 'This is symbolic of the eating together of friends and sharing.' Then he added with a sigh which provoked some laughter, 'But there is one part of the eating which I cannot share in.'

Most people understood what he meant but so that his disapproval was not unnoticed, he indicated the lamb with a nod and grimaced.

Amid the laughter, someone said, 'Get on with the bloody sacred thread!'

'Ah yes,' acknowledged the priest, 'the sacred thread. I must confess it is different with you all. Do not mistake me. The sacred thread normally has to do with scholarship but with the Muhiyals . . .' he shuddered despite his attempt at benevolence, 'it has to do with the sword. This boy is a Chibber. Among the ancestors of the Chibbers was the renowned Parashuram who dethroned every tyrant king in India to see justice done—'

'Enough!' shouted Lok Raj. 'You've earned your rupees. Drape the thread over his shoulders and be done with it!'

The priest's discomfort at being interrupted was received with a murmur; but loud encouragement among a group of men resulted in a jocular improvisation. A youth was sent racing off and returned with a sword in its scabbard. The cross-belt was slung over the shoulder of the boy and the sword dangled at his side.

Amid the shouting and laughter and applause, someone said, 'It suits him.'

And indeed it did for though the scabbard and hilt were not ornamented with precious stones, it was a sturdy weapon with an emblem carved on the guard. The scabbard was covered with deep blue velvet and embossed with little spangles of gold.

The boy drew the sword out with some difficulty.

'Keep it. You need practice,' some wag called, and a number of 'ayes' were heard.

'Not on your life!' Lok Raj bellowed. 'That was my grand-father's sword and his father's before that. It is steel and workmanship you don't get nowadays.'

The boy looked disappointed and began putting the blade back in its scabbard.

There were protests from the gathering and murmurs of sympathy for the boy.

Lok Raj said somewhat hesitantly, 'It's not that I am attached to it. Why, I'm now an old man. And . . . and you are all my children and have a right to anything that is mine. But,' he bellowed again, 'that is a sword that has drawn blood in the passes down from Kabul. It is not a toy.'

There was silence. Suddenly the lamb tied to its stake bleated and there was a relieved burst of laughter.

Lok Raj was blinking furiously and his tongue was running over his gums when someone called out, 'So all this girding of a sword is nonsense. Poor boy! It makes a mockery of his initiation!'

Lok Raj dropped his walking-stick, strode forward and whisked the cross-belt off the child.

'Initiation?' he roared. 'You youngsters don't know what it means. To you now it is just symbolic. In my day you had to prepare for it. Like others learn scriptures, we learnt how to use a weapon. Only when we proved our ability were we allowed to strut about with a cross-belt and sword. The test was simple. While the priest said two holy words—'om shanti'—you had to make three strokes. Like this.' He turned to the priest. 'Say the words.'

The priest began to intone the two words.

In one swift movement, Lok Raj unsheathed the sword. It glinted in the overhead sun but already in a continuous motion it was swishing down in an arc, cutting through the rope at the stake and upward again slicing through the lamb's neck. Even as the severed head was falling and the animal remained standing, the tip of the sword jabbed into its trunk and raised the body aloft. Only now did the blood begin to spurt from the jugular.

There was not a sound as Lok Raj flung down the skewered lamb and wiped the blade on the end of his turban.

He said quietly, 'That is how we were bathed in the blood of the lamb.'

He studied the blade for a moment. He was upset with himself for the sentimental attachment to a family heirloom. Even a hint of such attachment was disgusting.

With a flick he dropped the sword into its scabbard. And draped the cross-belt over the boy.

'It's yours,' he muttered. 'Better learn to use it.'

Taking his walking-stick from the man who had picked it up, he waved a path open for himself through the gathering and went off towards the fields, muttering, 'Bastards! Bastards, the whole lot!'

A gabbling hubbub broke out behind him.

In the car, Dev Singh said, 'It is most distressing that sikhs and hindus are being pushed apart like this. It goes against the example of the gurus. Just look at the gurus.'

He meant that literally. The dashboard of his car had colourful holy pictures of the ten gurus. Balbir had not really noticed the portraits before. The practice of adorning a dashboard with the pictures of revered persons is as common in India as the practice among christians in Europe of sticking a medal of St Christopher near the instrument panel of a vehicle. Now he looked.

Dev Singh said, 'Only the Tenth Guru had long hair, with a top-knot under the turban. And even that is like some hindu *sadhus*. But look at the others. Some of them were clean-shaven. I think of all this every day when I drive.'

After a while he added, 'And the Ninth Guru gave up his life to persuade a muslim emperor that hindus should be allowed to wear the sacred thread.'

He pulled up outside the Golden Temple and parked.

'You'll have to cover your head,' he reminded Balbir.

'I know.'

'You should've brought one of your father's turbans. Or your grandfather's. Please lock your door. Yes, put up the glass.' He laughed, 'Maybe you don't know how to tie a turban.'

'I do. Have to wear one for ceremonial occasions. Not much different from wrapping a muffler on the head. Or a bandage.'

Dev Singh looked at him but he was not being facetious. Dev Singh sighed, 'It means something.'

Balbir stepped out. 'To people like my father and grandfather.'

'To me too.'

They walked towards the entrance.

Balbir gave a short laugh. 'I used to wind a muffler round my head. Then I lost it somewhere. Now Satyavan's given me this.' He reached towards his pocket and pulled out a rolled-up cloth cap. It was olive green and had a sunshade. He put it on. 'How's that?'

Dev Singh smiled. 'Be careful. It makes you look like an army officer on holiday.'

Sure enough, after they had taken off their shoes and walked in, a gun-toting extremist sentry eyed the cap and approached.

Balbir said, 'I'm a friend of Amar Singh. We're going to meet him.'

The gun-toter followed them.

They had to wait a while till Amar Singh was found and fetched.

To Balbir's surprise he didn't smile on seeing him but said glumly, 'So he did send you. At least he didn't cheat us on that.'

Balbir was puzzled but introduced Dev Singh, explaining that he was Gulnari's uncle.

'Sardar sahib, my deepest apologies,' said Amar Singh, sincerely joining his palms and bringing them to his forehead. 'One of our boys has misbehaved and he must pay the price for it.'

When he learnt that Gulnari was dead, he was moved and dismayed. He took Dev Singh's hand in both his and condoled with him. 'Believe me, I have no words to tell you how much I regret what happened.'

He led them down to see Uday.

'Thank God, he's still alive!' Balbir murmured but Amar Singh ignored him.

Uday had been moved to a proper room where he was being kept under guard. To Balbir's astonishment, he was lying in bed propped up and though he didn't seem much better than before, someone was actually spoon-feeding him a vegetable broth.

'Kumhareya!' he exclaimed and rushed towards the bed.

Uday stared at him, recognizing him with some difficulty. Perhaps it was the new cap.

Then he hissed, 'Get away. Get out.' Slowly, Uday turned his gaze on Amar Singh. 'I told you, he must have done it. Ask him. I am not guilty.' He closed his eyes. The effort of speech exhausted him.

'So this is Uday!' said Gulnari's uncle. His forehead was glistening with perspiration. He had spat out the phrase as though he were saying 'So this is my tormentor!' His mouth stayed open, curving downwards. His right hand reached across his bulging paunch. It gripped the hilt of the *kirpan*. But, somehow, though the hand clenched and unclenched, the mind hesitated.

'No,' said Balbir softly. 'Please, uncle, no.'

Amar Singh had held up his hand to forestall any reaction from the guards.

'Go ahead,' he nodded. 'It is your right.'

Dev Singh was breathing heavily. He turned to Amar Singh, his mouth still open, his hand still on the hilt of the short dagger.

'Go on,' said Amar Singh gently with a smile. 'Do as you wish.'

Dev Singh bit his lower lip, turned again towards the bed.

Uday's eyes flickered open. 'I've seen you in the shop. Used to watch you,' he whispered. 'You're Dev Singh.' He frowned, swallowed and then smiled. 'Gulnari . . .? Has she come?'

Dev Singh brought his hand to his forehead. The action pushed back his turban slightly. He turned and walked to the door.

Amar Singh went after him and restrained him gently. They began to talk softly.

Balbir knelt by Uday's bed. 'Uday? Oy, Kumhareya!'

'Has . . . Gulnari come?'

Balbir shook his head. He tried but couldn't tell him.

Then he asked, 'Hey, what did you mean—I did it? Did what?'

Uday opened his mouth but the effort to explain seemed too much. He said briefly, 'The guns.' And he fell into a sleep.

The man who had been feeding him tried to continue. Uday stirred, turned his head to Balbir. 'I want . . . to die. Unless . . . she comes. Let me . . . die.'

'Come with me!' said Amar Singh sharply.

Balbir was a little offended by Amar Singh's brusqueness. He hesitated for a moment, then got up and followed him. 'Will he live? It looks like he might.'

'No. Definitely not,' said Amar Singh curtly. 'It's only your criminal actions that have delayed his death. You forced us to revive him.'

'I?' Balbir felt like thanking him.

'But that's temporary. We needed him to be sensible enough to support our identification.'

'What are you talking about?'

'You know well enough.'

'I don't.'

'You've been cheating us. But we'll discuss that among ourselves.' Amar Singh caught up with Gulnari's uncle who was moving somnolently towards the main shrine. 'After your prayers, Sardar sahib, you may go. Balbir will be staying back.'

Dev Singh turned to him in surprise. 'But he came with me. His people will worry if—'

'That is our affair.'

'But—'

'Sardar sahib, please. You may go. We have some things to discuss.'

Dev Singh looked at Balbir.

Balbir had gone pale. He said, 'There must be some misunderstanding. I'll . . . I'll clear it up.'

'Are you sure?' Dev Singh was uncertain what to think. He was concerned.

Balbir indicated the armed men with a glance and shrugged, 'There's no choice.'

Dev Singh took out a handkerchief and began to wipe his palms. 'If you're sure ... but only if you're sure ...'

Amar Singh said, 'He is sure.'

Taking Balbir firmly by the elbow, he began to lead him away. The armed escort followed.

Dev Singh remained standing where he was.

At some distance, Amar Singh turned and called out, 'As for Uday. You may depend on us. We keep our word. And thank you for the donation. You may send it any time. It will be much appreciated.'

Balbir was taken to what appeared to be an office. It had a desk, files, a telephone, a typewriter, some rubber stamps. But it also had a rack for guns, some large trunks and a string-bed standing on its side against the wall.

'Well,' sighed Amar Singh sitting down behind the desk, 'I had begun to trust you but it seems you're just another greedy cheat, after all! I'm afraid our relationship must change now. It cannot be helped. You have no understanding of our cause. You are not even a genuine sympathizer. You are just a money-grabbing mercenary with a criminal inclination. I should have borne that in mind. By the way, would you like some sugar-cane juice? Or buttermilk perhaps? The afternoons are getting warmer.'

Balbir shook his head. 'I'd like a chair to sit on. And I'd like to get this over with quickly so I can go home.'

'The chair you can have, of course.' Amar Singh nodded to one of the men on guard. 'As for going home, I fear that depends on what we decide. Didn't Tarsem tell you?'

'Tarsem? I was with him last night. I told him I was coming here. He didn't warn me about anything.'

'Oh?' Amar Singh readjusted his ever-present carbine and tapped the table thoughtfully. 'I thought Tarsem had sent you to us with some explanation. Or money. But apparently he preferred to let you walk in here unprepared. Do sit down.' He indicated the chair that had been brought. 'Now then, I sent some boys to talk to Tarsem. He denied any hand in the cheating and, from what has been reported ...' He opened a file and studied it, '... after due thought, he blamed it on you.'

'Oh me? What did he blame on me?'

Amar Singh signalled to a bespectacled man who had come in discreetly and seemed to be taking notes. The man opened one of the trunks and took out a carbine. He checked that it had no magazine in it and then placed it on the table.

Amar Singh said, 'This is an army issue carbine. Do you recognize it?'

Balbir glanced at it and shook his head.

Amar Singh snorted. 'Obviously you haven't been long enough in the trade. Or perhaps you are playing the innocent. Anyway, you know of course that every gun carries an identification number and manufacturer's mark.'

Balbir nodded.

'Good. You are aware that we are buying a lot of guns of various makes and calibres. General Shahbeg is very particular about checking each one.'

'We haven't sold you any bad ones, as far as I know,' Balbir protested. 'Unless Tarsem tried something funny and decided to pin it on me.'

'That's what we want to find out. You have nothing to fear, unless you are guilty.'

Balbir had a faint suspicion of what was coming but he restrained the impulse to blurt out anything he may regret.

'What you perhaps don't realize,' continued Amar Singh, 'is that General Shahbeg has instituted a system of noting down the identification number of each weapon we possess. That is sound military practice. It also helps to prevent conflicting claims to the same weapon. We issue specific weapons to each squad and they are responsible for those. Now, with the quantity of arms we are buying, this sort of book-keeping takes time and cross-checking takes even longer.' He laughed, 'Perhaps we should buy a computer. Now the crux of the matter is this: we have on occasion got back a revolver or two that was lost in a skirmish. Sometimes some of our boys get killed during missions. Now and again, through the black market, a weapon may find its way back to us. Usually these are small arms, like pistols, that can be pocketed by some greedy fellow. If he is a peace-loving man, he usually sells it. By degrees it reaches a gunrunner . . .' Amar Singh's face contorted with contempt, '. . . the scavenging small-time kind of gunrunner, and we buy it back happily enough.' Then his voice went hard. 'But we don't encourage cheats to steal our guns and sell them back to us! When we brought Uday Singh here, he only had his revolver with him. He told us where we could recover the other weapons. But when our boys went there, they found the weapons missing. We thought the police might have found and taken them, or one of the other squad members could have. Then just the day before yesterday while cross-checking our list of weapons, we discovered that Tarsem's group had re-sold us the carbine issued to Uday Singh. We also found that a .38 pistol had been re-sold to us.' With some satisfaction and glancing complimentarily at the bespectacled man, he said, 'That was good detection!'

Balbir said nothing. He felt trapped.

Amar Singh went to an earthern pot and, with the aid of a mug, drank some water. Smacking his lips, he said, 'That same night some of my boys collared Tarsem.' He added as though by way of explanation, 'We don't like anyone to take advantage of our generosity. We pay well. But we don't want to pay twice over. He might have done it in other things too—bombs, timers, grenades, explosives. We had to threaten him, frighten him, make sure.'

Amar Singh was a natural talker. He liked his own fluency. He pouted, raised an eyebrow and tapped the table for emphasis. 'We also had to find out just how corrupt in spirit Uday was. Yes, Uday. We had to know if he had himself sold the material to Tarsem. We began reviving Uday in order to question him about this. That has been done. We are satisfied. Tarsem says *you* sold this carbine and the pistol and even some grenades to him. Is that true?'

Balbir looked at the table. There were whorls in the grain of the wood—a locally made table. He didn't know what to say.

'Did Uday sell them to you? That is possible too. You see, I want to give you every possible way out.'

But Balbir sensed a snare. And he remembered the time his father beat him for riding the mare without permission, for stealing the mare at night. He had said, 'You have the blood of a young lion. Be bold. Admit what you have done. Don't be afraid.'

Balbir looked straight at Amar and said, 'I did it. I found the stuff and sold it.'

'You didn't find it, you stole it.'

'I saw where it was and took it.'

'You stole it!'

'All right,' Balbir almost shouted. 'I stole it, if that is how you want to think of it. But I had no intention of cheating anyone. I was merely trying to earn the money to get out of India.'

'Ah. And how much were you paid?'

Again Balbir hesitated. But surely Tarsem had told them.

'Twenty thousand,' he said.

'To begin with, we would like you to give us back that money.'

'To begin with? Surely that is enough.'

Amar Singh shook his head. 'You are in no position to bargain. Tarsem assures us that this is a stroke of luck. He says, if we hold you hostage here, he can use that as a lever to get your relative Satyavan to put him in touch with a bigger pipeline. We need a vast quantity of guns. The matter is quite intricate. Tarsem wouldn't dare touch you. He hasn't the infrastructure. But we have. We are not afraid of Satyavan or whoever. We just want to advance our cause.'

'Tarsem only wants to advance his greed.'

Amar Singh smiled. 'We are aware of that. We have to put up with it.'

'Satyavan won't be blackmailed.'

Amar Singh brushed that aside. 'We have every reason to deal strictly with you. Money alone can't buy you out. We need more guns.'

Amar Singh called someone and ordered him to bring a shawl or blanket for Balbir. It was getting on to evening. He also asked that a bed be prepared for him in what he called 'the D room'.

Balbir glanced at the telephone. 'Can I speak to elder brother Satyavan?'

'No. Tarsem will do that.'

'Then I'd like a word with Tarsem.'

Amar looked at the bespectacled man, then said doubtfully, 'My instructions are to hold you hostage till we hear something positive. Tarsem will communicate with us. But not by telephone. All our phones are tapped. The police listen in.'

'Don't you want the twenty thousand back?'

'Of course.'

'I would have brought it if Tarsem had told me.'

Amar Singh snorted. 'You wouldn't have come. You would've run. Tarsem was expected to bring you here—under some pretext or by force if necessary. It seems you saved him the trouble. I would say your *kismet* is against you.'

'How long do you intend to keep me here?'

'Till we have some positive response.'

'If the response is negative?'

'I cannot imagine it will be. But if it is, then I'm sorry. I'm rather fond of you.'

Balbir fiddled with a paperweight.

Amar tapped the table. 'Please don't touch any objects in the room. Keep your hands still.'

'I'm not suicidal,' said Balbir, a trifle mockingly. 'I won't attempt hitting you with a paperweight.'

Amar laughed. 'You're right. Well, I must admit I enjoy your company. A pity about all this.' He sighed and added, 'You know, we hesitated to pull you in. Didn't want to spoil relations with Tarsem. We need him to keep running guns. We just didn't want to be cheated—by him or you or anyone. But Tarsem supported this action. The boys I sent to him were surprised, till he explained the plan. It seems this fits in with something he had in mind.'

'He's really desperate for an opportunity to force Satyavan, isn't he?' said Balbir wrily. 'But you won't need Tarsem once Satyavan agrees to supply you.'

'We need as many as we can get. We're not concerned with gang rivalry.'

'You mean, business rivalry.'

'Whatever.'

With an attempt at humour, Balbir muttered, 'I hope you'll continue to need me—though I'm only a petty functionary.'

He was trying to maintain rapport with his captor. Instinctively he sensed that that might be his only chance of emerging from this ordeal alive and without too much discomfort.

Amar saw through his tactic. He smiled, 'Yes, you'll be keeping us company for some time. The kind of response we want cannot be arranged overnight. Satyavan has to provide Tarsem with a really big consignment and put him in touch with the right people. When we take delivery and Tarsem gives us the signal, we release you. You'll be well cared for here.' Then he laughed, 'But of course we won't give you blades or a shaving kit. We might even make a sikh out of you.'

Balbir grinned, 'That's the least of my worries.'

Amar turned and spoke to the bespectacled man, in whispers. The man nodded and slipped out.

Amar explained, 'I've sent him to find out if we can send a message to Tarsem.'

After a moment of pacing the floor, he frowned and murmured, 'Has it ever occured to you that there is no sikh film-star in India? And we have the biggest film industry in the world! Now isn't that discrimination?'

Balbir thought about it. He had to keep at least the spirit of debate going between them. He said: 'The film industry is largely Punjabi controlled. Most of the stars are Punjabi. So are the producers and directors. India's film culture is largely based on Punjabi culture. There are plenty of shaven sikhs in the industry.'

'Lapsed sikhs, failed sikhs, they are not proper sikhs. A *mona* is not a sikh. He becomes a hindu.'

'Really? Why don't you say he becomes a muslim or a christian?'

Amar Singh rapped the table. 'This is no time for cleverness.' He saw Balbir smile and shake his head. 'What's the joke?'

'You must have got that habit for those professors you miss over here. When you can't answer, you use your authority to stop debate.'

Amar Singh paced the room. 'You're right. I'm sorry. Actually I began thinking of something else. I've got other things to do.' He looked at his watch and stepped out briefly, leaving Balbir under guard. Returning in a few minutes, he patted Balbir's shoulder casually. 'All right. But why is there no proper sikh actor in films?'

'Because there are not enough stories with sikh characters. You should encourage writers to write some. But then, some sikhs are so hypersensitive they object to any portrayal of a sikh.'

Amar Singh sighed bitterly, 'The film industry portrays us as buffoons and clowns. A sikh, to be acceptable, has to be in line with *sardarji* jokes! The media discriminates against us. We must change that. That's part of our demands! Have you read the papers I gave you?' Without waiting for an answer, he spun round and with a wave of the hand included the surroundings. 'Look at all this! Isn't what's happening deadly serious?'

He patted his carbine. 'These guns will stop people laughing.'

He resumed his pacing. 'And some sikh journalists pander to it too.'

The bespectacled man returned. There were a couple of small feathers sticking to his blue dress. He whispered something to Amar.

Amar turned to Balbir. 'It may take longer but it's safer. You see, we don't send messages on our transmitter if we can avoid it. Our liaison with Tarsem prefers us to use an older, safer system—carrier pigeons. You can send a one-line message. That will serve our purpose. Tarsem will know we have you here. Understood?'

Balbir nodded.

'What are you going to say? No tricks, mind. Nothing will get you out of here'. He laughed. 'In fact, I have no objection to your using the phone if you want to call the police. But I'm afraid that won't help.'

'I know.'

'Good. What do you have to say to Tarsem?'

'I want to tell him where the twenty thousand rupees is kept so he can fetch it for you.'

'Really? You haven't spent it in all this time?' Amar was suspicious. 'Why do you want to do that?'

'Obviously in order to pay off my debt to you so that whatever happens you'll know I didn't cheat you.'

Amar considered that then shook his head. 'You *are* a fool, but a good-hearted fool. All right. Phrase your sentence.'

The bespectacled man got ready to write it in his note book.

Balbir said slowly, carefully, 'Ask Babaji for my twenty thousand from the storage bin.'

'No, no,' said Amar. 'That'll puzzle him. Our man won't know who the message is for or from. The correct way is to say: "Tell Tarsem to ask Babaji for *Balbir's* twenty thousand from the storage bin." Right? Got that?'

The bespectacled man nodded and withdrew.

'Now, Balbir,' said Amar with a sign to the escort, 'let me show you to your room.'

Outside, Balbir could hear the murmur of worshippers and pilgrims returning from the shrine, ambling towards the exit, on their way home.

14

•••

The European Gambit

Raskaan was attempting to sing a German *lieder*, Renate was playing the piano and a party was in progress, when the call came from Satyavan.

Some of the hundred and forty guests had joined in the vocalization and, under its own momentum and the encouragement of the piano, the singing continued with gusto as Raskaan bent an attentive ear to the buxom little maid who had tiptoed to his side to inform him. She was one of four engaged for the evening, along with a chef and assistant, to see to the wining and dining of his guests. His own restaurants were closed today. It was a holiday. In any case he never made use of his regular employees when catering for European-style revels at home. His waiters wouldn't know what to serve when. He lived not between but in two cultures simultaneously with one foot in each and never made a scrimmage of the two. Each had its own delights; he didn't want to change either, he wanted to be able to appreciate both.

Perhaps as a perverse concession to that ideal, when he spoke to India from the privacy of an adjoining anteroom, he dipped one hand into the giggling maid's frilled neckline to assure himself that she was all there. He accompanied the action with a wink that was not so much conspiratorial as convivial. She took no offence but sensibly looked about her, withdrew his hand, smacked it smartly as she blushed and, tittering, went off with a flattered flounce in her step.

The conversation was only a little odd.

'Hullo?'

'Raskaan?'

'Yes, elder brother.'

'Come.'

'I'll be on the first flight tomorrow.'

'By the way, got anything for me?'

'Yes. I was going to send but I'll bring.'

Satyavan's voice, metallic over the wire, became commanding and cautionary. 'In your head.'

'In my head, of course.'

'Good. And I need a European. Can you bring one?'

'Renate?'

'No. A man.'

'I can bring a plane load. There's a party going on here. A big bash. But if I charter a plane and invite them sight-seeing, they'll all have to come. Can't break up the shindig. So there'll also be two Arabs, three Jews, one Vietnamese—'

'Shut up! Be serious. I don't want the United Nations.'

Raskaan began laughing.

Satyavan's gurgle responded, albeit reluctantly. He cut into the cachinnation. 'Raskaan, you're a shit-head—being jolly at the worst of times!'

'Best thing to be at the worst of times.'

'You don't know how bad it is.'

Raskaan sobered. 'OK. I'll bring a man.'

'Not a toughie. And not a sophisticate.'

'Oh?'

'One of your café hippies. A vagrant type.'

'The restaurants are shut. Today's a holiday.'

'Find one.'

'It's late.'

'That's your headache.'

Raskaan sighed. Then a thought struck him and he convulsed with laughter.

'What's so funny?'

'Elder brother, now I know why you never married! Do you require any particular size of arsehole?'

Satyavan nearly choked. 'I'll break every bone in your sinful body!' But he chortled. 'Don't you know every trunkline operator is listening in? Don't spoil their morals! Oh, by the way, you remember how impressed I was by the bathrooms you have in your house.'

'Well? What now?'

'I've persuaded Babaji to let us build a modern one in Chamkalan.'

'One—just one—for the whole family?'

Satyavan sounded a little irked. 'He said we could make some.

But I thought we'd start with one, a really big one, and see how popular it is. Then we'll make more. When you're here, I want you to see to the building of it.'

'Good God! You mean I'll be there that long?'

Satyavan's voice replied equivocally, 'Perhaps.'

'And you want me to bring the plumbing and fixtures when I come!'

Satyavan burst into laughter. 'Of course not, you idiot. You can buy anything in Punjab now. Why, some farmers even use their washing machines to churn out gallons of buttermilk. That gives them time to watch TV and video and play with their calculators!'

Raskaan was still grinning when he rejoined his guests, many of whom had linked arms and were swaying as they sang. He saw that his glass had been cleared off the top of the piano, nodded to another maid, decided to stick to lighter liquor, picked a glass of Beaujolais off the tray she carried, pinched her cheek affectionately, then eyed his invitees for possible transportation to India. At the same time he thought, that elder brother of mine is really peculiar in his demands! But *ç'est la vie*!

The request had come at an awkward time. Most of the men and women gathered here tonight were *très elegant*, mostly middle and highbrow—the sort of people Renate could discuss books and paintings with. Unlike him, she read a lot. Indeed, in her spare time, of which there was little anyway, she had begun to do some research and put together a thesis on Indian architecture.

He wrinkled his nose at the uniformity of status and talent around him: Baron something, Count the other, this von that, and if there was no title before the name they had degrees behind or honours and honorifics and achievements that raised them above the common pale. No wonder he had started them singing! Anything to break the monotony of unflappable self-esteem. It occurred to him that somehow this party was neither his nor Renate's, it was his father-in-law's, and that too in absentia. Renate had called the sort of people her parents adored. Her father, with his vast vineyards and vintner's particularity, chose guests with care so that they matured smoothly through the evening. Raskaan preferred not so much to blend his guests as to jostle them together in an extraordinary divergence of spirits in the hope of discovering a new cocktail and he was not averse, like all pioneering persons with a proclivity for scientific enquiry, if on occasion there was an explosive combination.

Yet Raskaan got on excellently with his parents-in-law. They saw that he was brutally discerning. He knew that Renate's father did not have a family history as he did, and therefore no ancestral or inherited confidence. Her father had only his wealth and wine, and he called the sort of people who he hoped would grow to appreciate both. Raskaan couldn't have cared a damn. He called people who could entertain and enlighten him at the same time. He enjoyed people.

While all this was going on in his mind, he was also responding automatically to various conversational ploys and pitfalls around him. He still managed to flirt with the women— no matter how old—and cajole and caress the egos of the men. But all the time too he was wondering if he could overnight convert any of these primping, mincing men into a passably destitute hippie.

He decided that none of them had the insouciance, the acting ability and the motivation to carry it off. What he needed was a natural. Let me, he thought, scout the kitchen.

But the chef and his assistant were as refined as the meals they were trained to produce.

The house was now buzzing with conversation punctuated by the tinkle of bracelets and glasses.

He caught Renate's eye. She was in the grip of an awe-stricken denouement being delivered by a doddering old collector of art. Even at this distance, Raskaan could see that what the collector really wanted was to win over the wife so that she might help persuade the husband to smuggle out some antiques from India.

He flicked his hand near his beard as though to scratch it but in doing so he signalled her to join him. She did, having seen that the collector was satisfied with the end of his earnest gabble.

Raskaan said to her, 'Please book me on the morning flight to Delhi, with an onward connection if possible to Chandigarh. Also reserve a second seat for a male companion. Then ring Chikku at his residence in Bonn. Tell him that even if the Indian Embassy is shut, we need a visa tonight for one male German national. If he comes up with something officious like "the rubber stamp is locked away somewhere and sleeping", tell him to phone Delhi and have a man deliver the visa at the airport on arrival. Say it's an emergency. Give him any cock-and-bull reason you like.' He snapped his fingers. 'We Indians are sentimental. Tell him this German's mother is dying in

Chandigarh, and she runs an orphanage. Also make it practical. Say the publicity of the orphanage is one of the factors that gets India considerable aid from West Germany.'

Renate shook her head, tightened her lips, adjusted her spectacles and still managed to smile. She loved her unpredictable Raskaan.

As she turned to go, he said, '*Mein Liebling*, one more thing. Trunk call the Soaltee Hotel in Kathmandu. See if Wilhelm has reached there with the Rolls. If he is there, tell him to park the car somewhere safe and fly to India. Give him the address. I want him to meet me in Jagtara.'

Her eyes went wide. But she nodded and, with a friendly touch here and a charming word there, made her way through clusters of courteous carousers to the quiet of the bedroom telephone.

A few minutes later as Raskaan formed part of one the congeries, half-listening to an Arab and a Jew trying to solve the Middle East crisis by reference to German opinion, he heard the siren of his other Rolls going off in the basement garage. He knew the shutter of the garage had been left open to enable a couple of other cars to use the available space. The screaming siren rolling towards full pitch indicated that someone was trying to unscrew the solid gold statuette from the bonnet of his car. He had rehearsed his reaction before, so he was quick.

The garage door could be activated by inserting the correct key in either of two electronic switches, one outside the basement and one within the house at the top of the steps that led down to the garage. The switches also controlled the lights in the basement. In a flash he was at the top of the steps. He flicked the key in the switch and, along with the siren, he heard a hoarse muffled shout as the garage door rattled shut. The intruder was trapped in the dark of the basement garage.

Raskaan whistled. Jackie the Schaeferhund who had been happily basking in the admiration of a gaggle of guests came bounding to him. Only a few people had realized what the wailing sound was and even they were loathe to disengage themselves. But one of them did call out, '*Was ist los?*'

Raskaan waved reassuringly. '*Nichts*. It's probably just another guest who leaned against my car.' Then, irrepressible as ever, he added, 'Or maybe a couple making love against the radiator!'

There was laughter. The evening was well into that stage of

relaxation when barriers begin to slide down. And, anyway, nobody could take offence at Raskaan's jaunty vulgarity.

Raskaan stood aside to let Jackie go down. He hissed, 'OK, Jackie, get 'im!'

Jackie snuffled down, wagging his tail, hackles up.

For a few seconds, only the caterwauling siren could be heard and then there was a scrambling sound as of someone climbing onto a bonnet. A rasping voice pleaded, '*Nein, nein!*' And Jackie was snarling and barking furiously.

Raskaan switched on the basement light and descended.

Schneider the tramp was scrabbling from the bonnet to the roof of the car.

'You never give up, do you, Schneider?' sighed Raskaan. 'I should've guessed it was you. Who else could be stupid enough to keep trying for the same bit of gold when he's been caught at it before?'

'Get your hound away, you bloody *Gastarbeiter*! You owe me something for all the nights I gave you food and the times I told you where to sleep without getting picked up!'

'I've given you enough. More than enough.'

'You would've died of cold if I hadn't—Get your hound away! I'm an old man! You can't frighten me like this. I'll ... I'll sue you for setting that dog on me. You don't know me. I'll—'

Raskaan whistled and said firmly, 'Right, Jackie. Go up. Go on, go up!'

Jackie, with a few gruff protests and a hesitant manner, obeyed. Raskaan opened the car door and switched off the siren.

'That's better,' rasped Schneider. 'I was coming up to see you anyway. Then I saw this light on and the garage open, and I thought, well, maybe this is the best way up. Who knows, nowadays, whether old friends object to you coming to the front door? The fact is I thought you might lend me ... a little something to tide me over the next few—'

'Shall I help you get down from there?'

'What? Ah, yes. But don't ... don't hit me. Don't—'

'Why should I hit you?'

'I don't know. People are funny. They set their dogs on you, they ... forget old friends.'

'Look here, Schneider. How much do you want?'

Schneider's eyes darted about suspiciously.

Raskaan held out the wine glass that he was still holding.

'What's that? You trying to poison me? Everyone's trying to get rid of me.'

'Here, Schneider, watch this.' Raskaan took a sip of the red wine. Then he offered Schneider the glass again. 'Go on, it's yours.'

Schneider snatched it, in case Raskaan should change his mind, and swallowed the wine and smacked his lips. 'Good stuff! You're really up in the world, eh? Rasky the rascal has come up in the world! Wouldn't know him from another *Gastarbeiter* but he's Rasky the rascal with a lot of gold.'

'If you go on singing my praises,' said Raskaan, helping him clamber down, 'I might even invite you up to join a lot of fine folks at the party.'

'Huh? What?' He laughed bringing up phlegm. 'Ah, you and your jokes!'

'I mean it, Herr Schneider. I'm proud of you. Most people in your place would've given up and taken a job. But not you. I admire your independence of spirit, your ability to scrape by without compromising, your faithfulness to old friends.'

'You always made fine speeches, Rasky. But you're a bloody crook! It's you who forget what you owe to old friends.'

'I know what I owe,' sighed Raskaan, his eyes almost misting over, 'I owe you a good drink, a hot bath, a warm bed. I owe you—hell, I'll think out how much and what I owe you, upstairs. Come on up. I'll introduce you . . . to some other friends.'

On the steps, Schneider paused and took off his shabby felt hat. 'I've got manners,' he said.

Schneider's belated debut into high society had a catalytic effect on the party. It would have been ridiculous for anyone to make the effort to impress a tramp. The result was, people stopped trying to impress and began enjoying themselves. They stepped off their high horses and frolicked on their own feet. Schneider was an instant hit.

An hour later he was regaling them with how, one chilly night, he had shown Raskaan an exhaust vent on the pavement and how they had sat round it as though at a fireside.

Of course he also sent some of Raskaan's stock lower with one or two persons—particularly the collector of antiques. It seems Raskaan had, in his days of penury, sold his last discardable possessions—his tatty old shoes which had worn through so you could see the sky if you held them up—to a gullible buyer. Schneider, playing the father figure, had advised Raskaan that no one would buy his old shoes in a country like Germany where everyone could afford at least one pair of new shoes. Raskaan had responded that these were special gold-*zari*-embroidered village shoes and, while no one would want his footwear, someone would surely want the hallowed favourite shoes once worn to shreds by the great Maharaja Ranjit Singh himself: shoes that had been handed down as heirlooms and smuggled out by a nobleman now fallen on bad days. And so, at the local flea market, placed on a crate covered in borrowed velvet, the shoes had fetched the fancy price of DM 1600.

'Good heavens!' cried the collector of antiques who was attending the party. 'Then those are the shoes for which I paid eight thousand Deutsche Marks. They are in a glass box in the centre of my drawing room. They're lovely enough to have been the Maharajah's. And to think they are only Raskaan's old shoes! I have been tricked.'

'Not at all, sir,' said Raskaan kindly. 'You have been taught to appreciate India's village handicrafts.'

But the gathering pressed Schneider to reveal more about the con man, Raskaan. Schneider had prepared for years to blackmail Raskaan with his past. Now he found that his preparations had made him, for the nonce, a socially-acceptable raconteur.

'His next business venture, after he despaired of selling samosas from a tray strapped to his neck, was the Indian horse cart.'

'Horse cart?' That was Renate who had joined the audience. 'I didn't know he drove a horse cart.'

'He didn't drive it,' said Schneider smugly. 'He made others pay him to let *them* drive it.'

Savouring the delicacies that were being proffered him and sipping wine, Schneider told the story of how Raskaan had imported a ramshackle tonga from Delhi for less than DM 500. He had had the buggy painted white and hired a white horse. Then he had let it be known that the horse and buggy were available on a rental of DM 1000 a drive, especially for weddings. Soon there was not a couple in the vicinity who didn't want to take a romantic ride round the park, or drive from church to reception, in that exotic transport. Brides clamoured to book the buggy and bridegrooms handled the reins, dressed in top hat and tails. Raskaan soon bought the horse, and later sold the whole ensemble to a dazzled entrepreneur for DM 15,000.

The other guests loved the anecdotes, and they loved Schneider. And Schneider loved them for loving him. On that wave of euphoria he was led to dinner. Waving his knife and fork in the air, with his mouth dripping gravy, he gave in to their importunings and told them how Raskaan had really started his travel agency. With authority he declared that that was another Raskaan enterprise which had its beginnings in a crooked but adventurous deal. For a small fee, Raskaan used to take groups of students on ticketless tours of Europe. The students were delighted with his techniques for evading checkers and the police.

While Schneider was holding forth, Raskaan asked casually whether he had travelled much. Schneider was chagrined, 'Me? Travel? Why, I've been to Turkey and Greece. I went to Egypt years ago. And just last year I went across the Mediterranean on a steamer to Morocco. But,' he sighed, 'I always come back to Berlin. This is my home.'

'But how could you go to Morocco without a passport?' Raskaan asked in disbelief.

'I've got me a passport,' said Schneider proudly. 'Now that's stupid of you, Rasky! We've all got passports. You couldn't get out of Berlin without proper travel papers. You've got to go through East Germany. Every sensible Berliner has a passport. Me? I never know where I might go tomorrow ...' Raskaan exchanged a glance with Renate and gave a slight nod, as Schneider continued, '... So I always carry my identity papers and travel papers with me.'

'But Morocco,' prodded Raskaan, 'that's a bit far-fetched. They wouldn't have let you in. I know Singapore wouldn't!'

'Nasty Rasky! That's the other side of you I can't stand. Bloody ...' He was going to say *Gastarbeiter* but restrained himself. Pushing aside his plate and remembering delicately to dab at his mouth with the serviette, he pulled a wad of papers wrapped in grubby cellophane from his coat pocket. 'There, look in my passport, you'll see the stamp for yourself.'

The next morning Schneider was on the plane to India with Raskaan. He couldn't believe his good fortune. A free trip to the East. Everything paid for. He adjusted the string that he used as a belt through the loops of his baggy trousers. Then he wiped his face with the eau-de-cologne drenched paper napkin that the hostess gave him. He leaned back and waited for breakfast to be served. This was the life, at last.

He glanced at Raskaan beside him. Bloody *Gastarbeiter*. This was the least he could do. Thank heavens it was still possible to shame him into gratitude.

15

◆◆◆

A Plan and Preparation

The message from Satyavan was clear. He had requested an urgent meeting. Inspector Dutt glanced at his watch. Sixteen hundred hours. He still had an hour, time enough for him to file a quick report in the office he had been allotted and get to the meeting.

The jeep swung left off the main road into the Police Headquarters at Phillaur. He drove past the shining brass cannon and the sentries at the gate of the massive old Rohilla fortress. It was kept in better repair than perhaps any other war monument in the country. He couldn't help thinking again of the anachronism of a modern police force functioning from within walls that were seven feet thick. And yet a fortress represented a traditional seat of authority, a source of popular confidence or hated tyranny, depending on who occupied it. Furthermore it was the safest place to barrack your men, keep your armoury, garage your vehicles and headquarter your offices. And it was a quiet, clean place, quite suitable for stabling the horses of the mounted constabulary. Yes, and he smiled to himself again as he waved in answer to the clicked heels and salutes of a scattering of men who saw his jeep pull up before the verandah of his office, horses still in use in the last quarter of the twentieth century!

What a pleasant change to be posted here in the guise of an inspector of police in the mounted constabulary! Such a relief from the years he had spent as a spy in Pakistan, pretending to be a snivelling pimp. The only joy in that was finding out which women were patronized by high army officials from Yahya Khan down. Now here he was pretending to be a Dutt, a Muhiyal, so that he could more easily establish contact with Satyavan the biggest wheeler-dealer in the region. And it had worked! As a fellow-clansman he had been able to reach Satyavan's heart. That was an Indian weakness—the head is ruled by the heart, and the heart belongs to the family, and the family extends through caste-bound kinship. So Inspector Dutt was a fellow Muhiyal, and therefore to be helped in his endeavours. Of course, he had had to make concessions too. But that was all in the game. He had managed to prevent any bigger inflow of arms. He had managed to tap an underground network and receive international intelligence.

And all he had had to do was read up a few books and articles about the Muhiyals! He glanced at the quotations he had culled and kept prominently under the glass top of his desk. One was from the Civil and Military Gazette of India dated 23 March 1911. It said: 'The Muhiyals are one of the most interesting peoples in India, who figured as ruling kings in bygone epochs beyond the threshold of which history hesitates to follow.'

But history had not hesitated to follow for quite some distance, thanks to the diligent research of British administrators and India-hands like T.P. Russell Stracy who, in the 1930s, had published a book entitled *The History of the Muhiyals, The Militant Brahman Race of India*.

Inspector Dutt shifted some papers and, to make sure he wasn't going to say the wrong thing at the imminent meeting, examined the Stracy quotation again.

'They have also figured at some early period in the affairs of Arabia, Central Asia, Afghanistan and Persia. They are still found in Afghanistan . . . The Muhiyals are a fighting class of Brahmans as opposed to the ordinary Brahmans whose functions are restricted to more peaceful pursuits or the practice of austerities . . . The fact that nearly fifty percent of the commissioned Muhiyal officers were decorated for meritorious services by awards coveted by those entering the Army proves that they are amenable to the severer discipline of military service and that they possess those higher qualities which make for success on the battlefield. Kings in their own right of Kabul and kingdoms in India during the earliest Hindu rule . . .'

On an impulse he put through a lightning call to his mentor in the Intelligence Bureau. While he waited he quickly made out his daily report and locked it away. Just as he was putting the key in his pocket, the call came through.

'It's QX2, sir.'

'Yes?'

'Chief S has requested an urgent meeting, sir.'

'So?'

'He's actually risking visibility.'

'Dangerous.'

'Sir.'

'Couldn't you go to him in the usual way?'

'That takes a day of preparation, sir. He seemed agitated. Said it was . . . a family matter.'

'Oh?'

'Yes sir.'

'Are you sure of your family background? Did he imply you'd blown your cover? You might have made some slip.'

'No, sir. None that I know of. In any case, he is now sympathetic to our target. Has been sympathetic for some time.'

'But if you had slipped on background, he might resent the deception.'

Inspector Dutt hesitated then said, 'I think I probably know more about the background than he does.'

'Don't be arrogant. You've had to study it. He *is* it.'

'I think it's something else, sir. I think he wants to request some major action—not a concession, not favours.'

'Hm. We aren't geared for anything like that. Yet.'

'No sir. Not yet.'

There was a pause. Then: 'I'll leave it to your discretion. A small limited action, yes. Major action, no. Our main target must not be jeopardised. We can't risk all the eggs in our basket for the descendant of some petty brigands!'

'Sir?'

'You heard what I said.'

'Yes sir.'

'Report back afterwards.'

'I will.'

Inspector Dutt replaced the receiver, bent to see that no one was coming in through the swing doors, reached for his hip-flask and took a stiff tot. He had acquired the habit as a trainee in England. It was all very difficult this, giving Satyavan the impression that he was in a position to make major decisions, strike long-term bargains, aid him fully in any crisis . . . all very, very difficult. It militated against his sense of fair-play, ate into his equanimity. He took another swig and thought how strange it was that his superior should have used the very words that they had picked up from the tap on Tarsem's telephone. Tarsem hardly ever used the telephone but someone had rung him three evenings back from a post-office, saying, 'The message is this, tell Tarsem to ask Babaji for Balbir's twenty thousand from the storage bin.'

And Tarsem had blustered like a slightly inebriated man trying to screw his courage to the sticking place, 'OK, OK, OK. I'm not afraid of the descendants of petty brigands!'

Yes, Tarsem was getting big obviously, but how, and why? There was no way of pinning anything on him. He was clean. It was just a waiting game till he made some mistake, or Satyavan helped in bagging the whole set-up. If Tarsem was detained on suspicion, he'd be out in a day.

Inspector Dutt looked at his watch. Fifteen minutes more. The meeting was to take place just across the road. Seven minutes before I saunter across, he thought. The descendant of brigands! Do I know the background really? Can I pass as a Muhiyal, react as one in this 'family matter'? And yet stall if the request is for major action!

He thought again of the Muhiyals and the impersonation he had done, the part he had assumed in order to gain Satyavan's confidence. Yes, his director was right. He had to *be* a Muhiyal and think like a Muhiyal so that he would respond like one, and yet place limits on the promises he could make or fulfil.

One time early in their acquaintance, he had almost failed the test. They had met in a completely safe place and Satyavan had exclaimed, 'Wah, Dutt Sultan!' and the otherwise well-prepared Inspector Dutt had responded simply with 'Hullo!' A totally wrong response.

Satyavan's brow had puckered and he had immediately become wary.

By the next meeting, Inspector Dutt was aware of the mistake he had made. What he had taken to be Satyavan's greeting was in fact part of a well-known saying about the Dutts which the Inspector, as a Muhiyal clansman, had been expected to complete.

This is how the exchange should have gone in Hindustani.

> Satyavan: *'Wah, Dutt Sultan!'*
> Insp. Dutt: *'Hindu ka dharam,*
> *Mussalman ka iman.'*
> Satyavan: *'Wah, Dutt Sultan!'*
> Insp. Dutt: *'Adha Hindu, adha Mussalman!'*

In other words:

Satyavan:	'Hail, Dutt King!'
Insp. Dutt:	'The religion of the Hindu,
	The respect of the Muslim.'
Satyavan:	'Hail, Dutt King!'
Insp. Dutt:	'Half Hindu, half Muslim.'

It referred to the fact that, in the past, Dutt chieftains—and indeed the Muhiyals—had never discriminated on the basis of creed but had fought on the side of those who sought justice. The old saying also had a historical connotation, for a Dutt chieftain known as Sultan Rehab, despite being a non-muslim, had fought on the side of the Prophet Mohammed's sons in the famous Karbala War in Arabia.

Yes, there was much that Inspector Dutt had to bear in mind. Indeed, he had to go beyond thinking and *be* one of the tribe.

These were men descended from the warrior brahmin kingdoms encountered and praised by the Chinese travellers Fa Hien and Huen Tsang in the 7th century AD. He had to remember too the legends around Muhiyal kings and the great Chibber Chhaj. With another quick swig at his flask he reminded himself that Maharaja Chhaj had repelled the Huns and his dominion ranged from Persia to Kabul and Kashmir. His clansmen at various times had held sway over large areas of the North. Till today, the area around Bhera in Punjab is known as Chibberan Di Rajdhani, the Kingdom of the Chibbers.

A lesser man's head might had reeled with the facts it had to hold but Inspector Dutt was a professional, an impersonator par excellence. The details he had studied were the mere foundation of the personality he had built in order to gather other facts of more immediate consequence. He had to be as close to his role as a snake to its skin and shed it only when the season was ripe.

His natural, shy, retiring demeanour and nail-biting uncertainties would not do—indeed, he had forced himself to stop biting his nails so that the character's credibility was not undermined!

He got up now to go to the meeting but in a sudden private reversion to anxiety he stepped into the toilet and examined himself in the full-length mirror. Good God! In writing his report he had worn his glasses and forgotten to take them off. Somehow it wasn't right for an officer of the mounted constabulary to be seen wearing spectacles. He put them away and remembered to pick up his riding crop. Sticking it under his left arm, he clicked his heels and saluted. Yes, that's it. Stand straight, no slouching. Spread your legs out at the thighs when you walk. Sailors and horsemen have a similar stance but a different gait. Sailors keep their toes out, horsemen keep them straight almost to the point of seeming pigeon-toed. It helped that he was in jodhpurs and breeches and wore a frontier-style khaki turban, the cockade of which was stiff with starch. His cleanshaven face was reddened by the after effects of his regular evening tipple but it gave him the look of a hardy, outdoor man who had spent time in the sun. The sideburns that peeped out from under his turban were white and gave his ruddy complexion a burnished glow. He told himself: I am a handsome, confident, dashing son-of-a-bitch and I can negotiate any deal with aplomb. Now all I have to do is step across to the training ground, beyond the road outside the fort where the mounted drill is in progress. Much as I detest horses and the smell of their sweat, I must now look with benign satisfaction at the ridiculous exercises that the men will be performing. I must enjoy them with smug justification.

When he had first arrived at this posting, he had been mildly amused to see the care taken over the mounted drill.

Now as he crossed the road towards the *maidan* or playing field, he thought it wasn't a bad place at all to hold an emergency meeting. He didn't even need to change out of uniform. All he had to do was light a cigarette, lean against the wooden fencing and wait. Making contact was up to Satyavan. Since this was the Grand Truck Road that ran all the way from the border, through Phillaur, to Delhi and beyond, traffic along this premier artery often slowed to watch and many people disembarked to have their flasks of tea while enjoying the free exhibition. The comments of the bystanders, and perhaps the bets they laid on various riders' abilities, were easily drowned by the roars of the drill sergeants; the equestrian jumping, lancing, wheeling and charging, tent-pegging and pig-sticking were carried out with much flourish. It did not matter that the days of lances were over, the lancers were still here; it did not matter that there were no wild boar left in the countryside to pig-stick, the idea was to deter human swine; it did not matter that it was no longer possible in the era of rapid-firing weapons to approach close enough to any enemy's tents to lance the pegs out of the ground in one swift charge and drop the canvas ignominiously over the surprised enemy, it was the awesome skill and horsemanship that were on display. The aim was not just to win the trophies they did in competition with the few remaining non-mechanised units of the Army's Cavalry and the scattering of riding clubs in the country, the object was more practical and utilitarian: to instil confidence in the mounted police and simultaneously generate respect among the population for these otherwise unprotected men in their saddles. Horses, as Inspector Dutt could not deny, were still the best means of patrolling the dusty tracks and fields of the hinterland.

He was only vaguely aware of another car pulling up somewhere behind him. To his right was a squabbling bunch of children interspersed with exclaiming parents. To his left a small convention of yokels gaping and commenting. Directly opposite, standing inside the paddock, was a group of horse-dealers eyeing the animals and discussing possible prices with the Chief Sergeant; this was in anticipation of the auction when some police horses were sold and others purchased.

To his surprise he saw Satyavan, dressed in a loose *kurta* pyjama with his licensed revolver bulging in its hip-holster under the flapping cloth, going towards the group of horse-traders. He was now speaking to the Chief Sergeant. Suddenly Satyavan seemed to point in his direction and the whole group began to approach, but he realized to his relief that Satyavan was referring to someone who was now getting out of the car behind him. He turned casually to look.

A towering old man was struggling out of the Fiat. His voice boomed, 'Damn these little cars they make! A man has to sit scrunched up! All these years I've kept the cockade of my turban erect against any dishonour and now a mere car threatens to crush it! I'll have no more of cars, I say. It's either a horse for me or nothing!'

The group of traders had advanced well within earshot and they responded with indulgent laughter and a few comments but they were respectful. Each one seemed anxious to encourage the old man's idiosyncracy. The idea, after all, was to make money by selling a horse or two.

Satyavan said to the Chief Sergeant, 'This is my grandfather.' Then to the old man, he communicated an opinion, 'I do agree with the Sergeant. These horses are too volatile for us. Perhaps we should tell these traders to find more suitable ones.'

'Volatile? For us? What do you mean?' Lok Raj's normal bellow had some riders reigning in as though a parade ground command had been issued.

There were smiles all round at the old man's incomprehension.

The Chief Sergeant grinned politely. 'My father was a great admirer of yours, sir. He used to tell me about your vast knowledge of horses but these are . . .'

'Trained, aren't they? Therefore a little more expensive perhaps, but so what? It makes them more sensible. They understand the knee, the heel, the bit and the way a man sits.'

'Of course, sir, but we only sell the ones that are . . . difficult. I think you would do better at your age to—'

Lok Raj turned, blinking in a puzzled way, to Satyavan. 'Difficult? My age? What is all this? I say we want to buy two horses. A sixteen or seventeen hand for me and another for Khushi Ram who has a bad leg. It'll be easier for him to be carried about by a horse than to torture that leg walking in the fields. Gyan Chand already has a nag to ride so we won't bother with one for him.'

'Babaji,' pleaded Satyavan, 'you're eighty-four!'

'Yes?' the old man paused. 'Go on, I thought you were going to tell me something I didn't know.' Then he almost roared, 'Look here, boy. A man is only as old as the horse he rides. I may be eighty-four here on the ground but once in that saddle the horse gives me his strength, his energy, his youth. Then I am the horse and he is me. He is my strength, I am his will.'

'Babaji, we're only trying to warn you of the risk.'

'Come here to me, boy.' Lok Raj put his arm on Satyavan's shoulder like a confidant. 'My father died riding. So did my grandfather. They were both old but neither of them was thrown. One died in a storm when a branch fell on his head, the other was hit by a bullet from a nervous hunter's gun. You can't blame the poor horses.'

'You haven't ridden in a long time.'

'Aye. But does one forget how to walk or run or drink a glass of refreshing water?'

'All right,' relented Satyavan. 'You choose the animals and we'll leave our bid with the Chief Sergeant.'

'Sorry, sir, but that's not allowed since I conduct the auction. You'll have to come yourself.'

'Ah, but the day and time don't suit us. Perhaps I could ask one of your officers to stand in for us.' Satyavan looked around. The only officer in the vicinity was Inspector Dutt. 'Perhaps you, sir, would—'

'Delighted,' nodded the officer. 'The name is Dutt. Inspector Dutt.'

'As soon as Babaji decides, we'll discuss the range of the bids.'

'Fine,' agreed the Inspector.

'Now then,' said Lok Raj to the Chief Sergeant, 'which are the ones going on sale?'

'Since you want a seventeen hander, there's that one,' the Chief Sergeant pointed out somewhat ruefully, 'but he's too obstreperous. The other day he—'

'Mettlesome, is he? Good. I like an animal with spirit. It means he has something to give. But I'm afraid you'll have to help me up. Or bring him to a mounting platform.'

'You don't mean to ride him now?'

'How else can I find out what he is like?'

They helped him into the saddle. And that was the beginning of the miracle.

The police riders slowed and stopped, partly out of respect for an old man, partly out of curiosity. And then they were rivetted in amazement. And there were exclamations from the onlookers. They had not seen such an exhibition of riding before. The old man was, of course, enjoying himself—but so was the horse!

And then a rather frightening thing happened. To the horror of bystanders, the horse came straight at the fencing of the paddock and cleared it in a fluent leap. Horse and rider came down all right. No one noticed as Lok Raj winked at Satyavan. Now it seemed the old man was struggling to control the animal which was managing to inch his way, snorting and rearing and bucking, across the road towards his stable.

'Go on,' Satyavan hissed near the Inspector. 'Go and stop the horse.'

The Inspector paled. 'But . . . but I hate horses!'

'Then follow me. Quick!' Satyavan rasped as he ran after the horse.

By then another gallant policeman had stopped the horse. And by then Lok Raj was well inside the fort.

A number of people had followed Satyavan and the Inspector.

The Chief Sergeant was there too. He shook his head, 'I told him the horse was dangerous.'

Lok Raj was eased out of the saddle and the horse was led back to the grounds. The old man was clutching his chest and gasping, 'Oh my heart, my heart.' He had put his arms round Satyavan and the Inspector.

'Isn't there somewhere he can lie down, Inspector?' Satyavan asked.

'Ah yes, of course,' said the Inspector with sudden understanding. 'My office is right there. He can lie down on the bench. Let's take him there.'

When they had draped him on the bench, the Inspector turned to those who had come in out of curiosity. 'All right, all of you, get back to your own work. The old fellow just needs a rest and a bit of air. Leave him alone. Out. Out.'

The policemen withdrew, shooing the civilians before them. There were remarks about the foolishness of the old man.

When all was quiet, Lok Raj opened his eyes, winked at Satyavan and asked, 'OK?'

'Perfect,' he responded.

Lok Raj sighed and closed his eyes. 'I might as well rest anyway.'

'What a hullabaloo!' exclaimed the Inspector.

Satyavan gurgled with his kind of laughter. 'Only two ways to keep a meeting secret—either it should be unseen or above suspicion. This was Babaji's idea. His Trojan Horse scheme!'

The Inspector nodded. 'Did you get the names of the officers running the camps in Pakistan?'

'Of course. Plus other interesting details. But first, there is this family matter, Dutt sahib.'

The Inspector tried not to squirm. 'Family matters can be gone into when the country's problem is solved.'

'Not this one. You'll understand, as a Dutt, a Muhiyal. It's urgent. Tarsem is trying to force my hand. He has entangled my younger brother in such a way that—'

'I didn't know you had a brother.'

'Balbir.'

'Ah. Isn't he your uncle's son—?'

'Yes, my younger brother.'

'Go on. What about Balbir? Be brief. We can't spend too much time alone. It's dangerous for you. And for me.'

'Balbir has to be rescued from some clients of Tarsem. They are holding him hostage.'

'Is that all?' the Inspector was relieved. 'That's not a problem. I can send as many men as you like. Where?'

'In the Golden Temple.'

'What?' The Inspector sank down into his chair.

'Impossible. We can't send the police in there. We couldn't when the DIG was killed. We couldn't when—'

'This is my brother. Your brother.'

Inspector Dutt bit his lip. 'We ... we'll have to find some other way.'

'There is one. If I put Tarsem in touch with a big pipeline for arms, they'll let Balbir go.'

'No! You promised you wouldn't supply arms in this kind of situation.'

Satyavan said carefully, 'Just in case you are recording this conversation, let me put it to you straight. I don't supply arms, never have and don't know where to get them.'

'On my oath, this is not being recorded. I wouldn't risk complications.'

'Right. I only have to blow your cover and you'd be a dead man.'

'Thank you,' said the Inspector sarcastically. Then cracked a joke. 'As a lisping Englishman might put it: "I'd be a dead Dutt." You wouldn't like that, would you?'

'No,' Satyavan's eyes narrowed. 'But I've never known a Dutt who was afraid of horses.'

'It's . . . it's an allergy I have to horse sweat.'

Lok Raj interjected firmly from the bench, 'Get on with it. Tell him the plan.'

The Inspector said, 'Let me make one thing clear. Honestly. No major action is possible. In fact, no limited action is possible . . . at this stage in the political scene.'

'We are not talking politics,' said Satyavan. 'We are talking about saving a young man, a boy.'

'All right,' nodded the Inspector. 'I can get the police to take any indirect action you require. But, mind you, it can only be indirect.'

'It'll do,' agreed Satyavan. 'Now this is what we're going to do. I am going to provide Tarsem with one big consignment, a really whopping one, to reassure him and whet his appetite.'

The Inspector exploded but managed to keep his voice down, 'You'll give us more problems! Tarsem will become the biggest gunrunner in the East. We'll be—'

'Don't worry. Leave Tarsem to us.'

'We want him in the bag, the whole ring.'

Satyavan said gently, 'Leave Tarsem to us.' He pulled out a folded sheet of paper. 'Here is a typed list of the actions we want from your people. You'll notice that each point is headed a,b,c etcetera. I have a copy. When we want a specific action, I'll send you a message, merely giving the alphabetical reference and the date and time we need it. For instance, b is the longest item. Read it.'

The Inspector held it before his eyes but it seemed out of focus.

'For heaven's sake,' gritted Satyavan, 'wear your glasses and read it.'

'Glasses? But—? How did you know I wear glasses?'

'There's a mark on the bridge of your nose. You just rubbed at it automatically. And there are two small channels between the turban and your ears. Plus your glasses are lying on the table.'

'Right you are, right you are. I was wondering where I had put them,' the Inspector gulped but managed to smile with, he hoped, aplomb and panache. He hadn't expected that the meeting would gravitate to his office! All round him were the preparations of his Muhiyal-hood, indeed his brahmin-hood!

He put on his spectacles and began to read aloud. 'Item b says: Kitchen side of Golden Temple complex. Challenge truck carrying persons with turbans coloured 1) red, 2) green, 3) yellow. On being challenged, they will fire and run. Police/CRPF to return fire but with no, repeat no, casualties to red, green and yellow who will dart into Golden Temple complex. Arrest/shoot at/kill any other passenger of truck. Seize truck. It contains arms. Hold truck and contents in safe place till return process is communicated.' The Inspector finished reading and looked up.

Satyavan said, 'I may send you a message stating b 3031015. That means b is to be carried out on the thirtieth of the third month, that is March, at ten fifteen in the morning.'

'Ingenious!' exclaimed Inspector Dutt.

'And short and sweet,' admitted Satyavan. 'Now item a is simple. It merely states: Allow old European into free feeding kitchen.'

'Exactly, but I must warn you,' the Inspector cautioned, 'that we are thinking of banning all foreigners from Punjab. It's a Disturbed Area. We don't want persons of other nationalities wandering about here. Furthermore, it's a risk, diplomatically. We don't want international repercussions over an internal matter.'

'Quite,' Satyavan affirmed, 'but that sort of rule is not yet in force. There are lots of students here from other countries, especially agricultural university students. Also, there are jour-nalists.'

'True. But the regulation may come into force any day.'

'In that case we'll send Schneider in tomorrow.'

'Schneider?'

'He's an old, down-at-heel vagrant. A German. Friend of

Raskaan's. I phoned him three nights ago. They reached Delhi yesterday and have arrived in Jagtara today.'

'What is all this? What're you hoping to achieve?' The Inspector didn't want his own clean, clear, streamlined operations to be obfuscated by machinations concerning a mere boy.

Satyavan said, 'Many hippies and tramps go to the free feeding kitchen of the Temple. Some of them sleep there in the dormitory. No one would suspect an old foreigner like Schneider. We'll send him in with a long-range walkie-talkie.'

The Inspector sneered, 'He'll never be allowed anywhere near Balbir. He'll never find him.'

Satyavan agreed. 'He's not expected to. If I was holding someone hostage, I wouldn't allow a bumbling old foreigner to get past my armed guards.'

'Quite. So what's the point?' The Inspector took off his glasses and began to play with them.

'The point is, no one would suspect him of relaying messages to us. No one would search him for a walkie-talkie. It looks like a transistor radio anyway. He'd just be another foreign bum living off holy hospitality. Actually we're in luck. When I saw the specimen Raskaan had brought, I was delighted.'

The Inspector clicked his tongue sardonically. 'He wouldn't pick up any information worth relaying, not in the dormitory and the free feeding kitchen.'

'But don't forget, everyone eats in the same dining area—bums, pilgrims, terrorists, everyone. Everyone, that is, except those who are being held prisoner. So Schneider will be in a good place for collection and transmission. Now these are our two objectives: one, keep up Balbir's morale by getting in touch with him; two, get him out.'

The Inspector laughed outright. 'My dear Satyavan, much as I respect your brilliance—and, mind you, we are very pleased with all that you have done and are doing for us—I must tell you that nearly every plainclothes policeman or intelligence man who has gone in and tried to get pally with the terrorists has ended up a corpse in the gutter. Sometimes they've just been hacked to pieces and distributed over the countryside.'

Satyavan nodded. 'All of them went in like any pilgrim through the front door. But our men—red, green and yellow—will come in on the run from gunfire. They'll be terrorist sympathizers, gunrunners. Furthermore, they'll be Tarsem's men, not mine. As far as Balbir's captors are concerned, they are Tarsem's men, against me and therefore against the escape of

Balbir. They'll continue to take orders from Tarsem till they receive the signal from me.'

The Inspector's lip twitched. He thought for a moment then shook his head. 'It's too late to start infiltrating Tarsem's set-up. It's an excellent plan but it's too late. You can't begin now to get three men into Tarsem's organization.'

'I'll be frank with you,' Satyavan acknowledged, 'I haven't got three men there but I already have one in place. He is one of the truckers working for Tarsem. Each trucker uses his own men. So if I short circuit the chain of command and divert the trucker, his men become my men too.'

'Hm. Possibly. But there could be a hitch there. If one or both of the trucker's fellows is even mildly well-inclined towards the terrorists, you could be faced with disaster. As you know yourself, gunrunning is not always done for just money; sometimes sympathies are involved too.'

'You have a very good point, Inspector Dutt. We'll try and ensure he takes the right men but . . .' He sighed. '. . . there is an element of risk.'

'Who is this trucker?'

Satyavan smiled and shook his head. 'No. I can't tell you that. You must forgive me for withholding this detail. But I'm sure you understand. While I trust you implicitly because you're not only an accommodating government officer but also a Muhiyal, I must place the safety of my man above all else. He is crucial to the entire scheme. And he is a good man in his own way. You know yourself that there have been leaks in the past. Your own department has lost—'

'We won't go into all that,' said the Inspector curtly. 'It's been very awkward for us and that's one of the things we are chasing up. You're right. Keep the name to yourself. So we're agreed. We'll give you the indirect help you need. But one more caution—we've thought of infiltrating commandos into the Golden Temple and surprising the terrorists from within. It wouldn't work. They are too heavily armed and the complex is too big.'

Satyavan clarified the difference. 'Your aim would be to rout the terrorists and take over the entire complex of the Golden Temple. Our aim is simply to get one person out. We would concentrate on the small group that is holding him, attack that and get Balbir out by a subterfuge.'

'What subterfuge?'

'Again, I must apologize. That detail is not material to our discussion.'

'Very well,' nodded the Inspector. 'Now give me the international intelligence that's come in.'

Satyavan sauntered about the room, looking at various fixtures and clippings.

'Raskaan hasn't had time to put it all down in a typewritten report. Most of the details are still in his head.'

'You mean,' said the Inspector cannily, 'you're stalling some of the information? But our agreement is clear. We'll abide by the terms we set out at the start.'

'Of course. I'll give you the most vital information now and some other interesting details after this little family matter is concluded properly.'

The Inspector laughed. 'All right. I understand. You want to ensure our cooperation—'

'Absolutely.' Satyavan now went to the map on the wall. 'Fortunately, Raskaan could send a man into Pakistan as a tourist. All he had to do was some efficient spadework and write airmail letters in German. About those training camps across our borders. The biggest one is at Kasur. Extremists are flocking there for training in guerrilla tactics. My information is that the administration of this camp is under the command of a Pakistani Deputy Superintendent of Police from the Special Branch. His name is Samar Gul Afreidi. An inspector of the Special Branch, called Mohammad Hassan Khan, assists Afreidi. The actual training in weapons and guerrilla combat is imparted by former army personnel of the Sutlej Rangers. Each course runs for a period of one to three weeks. I have similar details about the other camps, all of them clearly written out for you in this report.' Satyavan straightened out the folded sheets of typewritten foolscap that he had taken from his pocket and handed them to Inspector Dutt. He added, 'By the way, we have also been able to identify the chief recruiter for these camps. He travels a great deal between Pakistan and England. We have also included a short biographical sketch. We cross-checked with our sources in Kenya. He used to be in the Kenyan police some years ago. Though he is a Pakistani, he holds a British passport and is a highly mobile agent.' Satyavan withdrew another sheet of paper from his pocket. 'I've already told you all that I did while I was abroad. Here are some other snippets that have come in through business channels. The list of free-loaders flying to Pakistan is on its way. There is some background also on the treatment of the hijackers who have gone there.'

'Thank you. That's a good haul of material, especially after what you've given me previously. I look forward to those remaining details.'

Lok Raj sat up and rubbed his eyes. 'Don't forget about the horses.'

'Horses?' the Inspector looked at Satyavan. 'Don't tell me you're serious about purchasing horses!'

Satyavan gurgled with amusement. 'I'm afraid so, yes. My grandfather selected the ones he wanted on sight. He didn't really need to go through that exercise. He just couldn't resist the temptation to ride—'

'And show off!' rumbled Lok Raj with a laugh. 'Can't help it. Anyway, it got you both together in privacy. Now make a note of this, Inspector, we want the seventeen hander I rode and the fifteen hander chestnut with the long mane.'

The Inspector wrote it down.

Lok Raj added, 'As for the price, we'll pay five hundred more than the highest bid for each horse.'

The Inspector nodded. 'I think you're crazy. Why on earth do you want horses at all?'

Satyavan explained, somewhat embarrassed, 'It's hard to keep Babaji out of something like this. He vows that, if our plan fails, he'll go in himself—dressed as a Nihang and made up appropriately. They're always riding about the countryside, even the old ones. Well, he'll take a slow ride to Amritsar and see what he can do.'

The Inspector was so jolted he couldn't speak. Then he exploded, 'I forbid it. I absolutely forbid it.'

'So do I,' said Satyavan quietly. 'That's why I'm hoping all the more that our plan will work. I don't want to have to worry about Babaji too!'

As they left the Inspector and drove back, past the shops of the township, both of them were absorbed in their own thoughts. Satyavan re-examined the plan for possible flaws. Lok Raj ruminated on the number of times he had been reminded today that he was old. But then the land itself was old, yet it yielded something to each generation that loved it and cared for it. Sometimes he felt the land was watching him, fitting him into a pocket of its vast unfathomable history.

He adjusted his turban against the low ceiling of the car and vowed that he would not leave alive the man who had snatched at his grandson. He would prepare himself and deal one day with Tarsem.

16

•••

Setting it Up

Raskaan used all his considerable powers of persuasion—more like temptation and seduction really—on Schneider and the next day he hobbled, gawking and bumbling, into the environs of the Golden Temple.

In the beginning he had no messages to communicate but spoke only of his own welfare. Raskaan manned the receiver, for though Schneider could manage a passable variant which they dubbed 'hobo English' the brief monologues were in German. Between the appointed hours each day, Schneider would call. He was an adaptable breed of person. He was not unhappy where he was and was even starting to understand the politics of the situation. Everyone seemed anxious to proseletize the crabby, eccentric foreigner to their point of view!

But there was one contingency they had not foreseen: the big consignment that Satyavan had to deliver to Tarsem took some time to arrange. Satyavan had blocked off his pipeline. To restart it and bring in a major shipment required not days but weeks. Schneider the tramp had to curb his yen for movement and stay where he was.

He began to complain that though he was comfortable and well-fed, he was missing booze! Three days later he relayed the news that he had found a source of supply and drinking companions among some masons and labourers. From then on he began not only to attend various functions that seemed to take place in different parts of the premises but also attended a press conference among a group of foreign journalists. In the same way he had drifted into a harangue being delivered by Bhindranwale.

Whenever anyone asked politely how long he intended to stay, he would answer vaguely, 'Till my situation improves.'

One day he stumbled upon a terrorist who had visited Germany as a student. The terrorist spoke a Hamburg version of German. From casual conversations with him, Schneider heard of a young gunrunner named Balbir who was being held hostage in a room. On his own initiative Schneider bumbled along and exchanged tourist chat with the men who were obviously guarding the unshaven hollow-eyed youth. He was sitting on a rug, reading some tracts in which he seemed to have little interest. But he glanced up at seeing the shuffling old fellow who appeared completely ignorant of the predicament he was witnessing.

That was when Schneider did a clever thing. He waved to the youth, while still attempting to chat to the grinning guards, and nodded a word of casual greeting, 'Raskaan!' The guards assumed it was German. He followed it up with a friendly wink. That was all. But he saw the captive's face light up for a moment. And Schneider strolled away.

In Chamkalan there was jubilation in the family. Contact had been made with Balbir! But only three people knew who had made the contact. Raskaan, Satyavan and Lok Raj kept the identity of their man secret. No one guessed it was Schneider. Though everyone had met him when he had arrived with Raskaan, they had assumed that he had left to wander through India.

In the dormitory for pilgrims, people came and went after staying a day or two. Schneider and a few hippie diehards hung on as long as they could. He never risked seeing Balbir again. He concentrated on maintaining his popularity in the dormitory and the dining room.

He was to remain there three months. But each day it gave him solace to know that he would live like a lord afterwards. What were even a few months in a comfortable place when he had spent longer spans in jail elsewhere?

Raskaan, of course, remained in Chamkalan though he would rather have had more time with his parents in Jagtara. But the villages were only three miles apart and his parents came often, sometimes spending nights at the ancestral home. They knew it was all necessary for the rescue of their beloved, wayward, worrisome Balbir.

Raskaan was also in touch with Renate and with his six enterprises in Germany. Renate was efficient. And they ran smoothly anyway. She could handle them. There was no problem on that score.

But an unexpected development was the arrival in Jagtara of Wilhelm. He had responded to Renate's initial request to fly to India from Kathmandu. That request had been made before Schneider was caught in their basement garage.

Typically, Satyavan seized the opportunity to put Wilhelm to use. Within a few days, Wilhem was ready to face Tarsem as though he was a representative sent by a major international gunrunning network. With his tough, blond, steely looks Wilhelm was utterly believable.

For Satyavan this was a relief. It meant that, in fact, Tarsem would be dealing with a dummy. He would never really make direct contact with what he called the big pipeline.

Wilhelm was ensconced in the best suite in a five-star hotel in Chandigarh and the meeting was set up. Satyavan introduced the two and left.

Tarsem was delighted. Here was the first big contact and they were totally alone to work out the future.

Wilhelm had trimmed his ginger blond moustache, discarded his leather jacket and other familiar accoutrements and donned a suit and dark glasses and a couple of rings on his fingers. He had also decided on a pipe and a tin of the finest tobacco. A silk scarf peeped from his breast pocket; Satyavan had checked that 'No hardened gunrunner of international repute allows his silk handkerchief to flop out in an effete manner.'

And the meeting had gone beautifully.

Wilhelm had sat back in his deep comfortable sofa, crossed his legs, kept his coat buttons open and allowed a shoulder holster to show. He had merely nodded when introduced to Tarsem. After Satyavan left, he had haughtily signalled with the stem of his pipe for the two bodyguards who Tarsem had recently acquired to get out of the room. At Tarsem's nod, they obeyed.

Tarsem too had dressed in his best. He was in a rather tight suit. And his taste in ties was atrocious. But he had his wits about him.

'So,' he began. 'I believe you were seen in Jagtara. How do you like our village?'

Satyavan had prepared him for this. Wilhelm answered, '*Ja*, I went there briefly because Satyavan called me. But I am not used to villages. Still—you understand?—it is necessary to see where the man you will be talking to comes from, eh? I was actually scouting you. Yes, I like what I saw.'

The trolley of drinks and ice was ready and waiting. Tarsem glanced at it.

'Please,' said Wilhelm sucking at his pipe, 'you must help yourself. We are here to talk business not bog ourselves down in formalities, *nicht wahr*? Ach, these formalities bore me!'

Tarsem helped himself to Scotch and a dash of soda. Wilhelm pulled the trolley near and without getting up poured himself a snifter of brandy.

They spent the next hour going through a list of weapons. Wilhelm told him when and where and how the armament could be collected. 'And you will pay of course in . . . dollars? Ah, rupees. Ah so! But only this time. We do not need rupees.' He laughed. 'No one needs rupees.'

At some point Wilhelm said, looking over the top of his dark glasses, 'And you will make sure there is no—how you say?—fuck up? No fuck up from your side. Our consignments have never been caught. We deal only with those who have friends in the right places. You understand? I will tell you how to be in touch with us. But if you are in trouble, we do not know you, you do not know us.'

Tarsem's lips, blubbery, shining, wet, kissed the arms list. 'No one will take these from us. I normally have three look-outs. This time I'll keep five. It's a big job.' Then he took a large gulp of whiskey and his head bobbed as he smiled, 'But we must think in the long-term. It is a good relationship we are establishing, friend. I have many customers, major clients. If ever something goes wrong with one load, we must be ready with another. After all, we are beginning a fruitful relationship. There will be a lot of business. We must keep together.'

'*Ja, ja*, if the clients are big, one or two consignments don't matter. *Ja*, let us drink to that, eh? A good business relationship!'

Tarsem drank and in his mind's eye saw himself owning an illegal plane service carrying people and cargo from a hidden airfield. The big time was here.

Half an hour later, he was telling Wilhelm to advise his network to sever connections with Satyavan.

He said, 'They are a set of fallen bad-tempered brahmins—'

'What is this word brahmins?' Wilhelm asked.

'You don't know what that is?' Tarsem seemed aghast. 'And you have been dealing with them!' Tarsem now cautioned him. 'They are supposed to be men of learning but these ones have gone rotten. They are called Muhiyals. Their forefathers were dacoits and brigands. They come from the mountains. Even now some of their kind are fighting like barbarians in the passes of Kafirstan. You know Kafirstan? It's north of Afghanistan, deep in the Hindu Kush mountains. Their thinking is soaked in blood. Even the Afghans hesitate to go there.'

'I did not know!' exclaimed Wilhelm. 'You mean they are savages?'

'Yes. With them it is not an eye for an eye and a tooth for a tooth, it is a bucket of blood for a drop!'

'No!' Wilhelm was softly horrified.

'But I'm not afraid of them. See how Satyavan led me to you. They can't say no to me. The other day I went to his grandfather and demanded a small amount—twenty thousand rupees— which they owed to some people and, you know what, it was handed over in five minutes! Anyway, little by little as you and I get to know each other better, we can work something out.'

'Of course,' said Wilhelm. 'You give us an idea and we will follow it through. Frankly, I do not understand fully your concern with all this stuff about Muhiyal, brahmin, caste and so on. We have got over all that in Europe. You are telling me that these people are Aryan savages—OK, it does not bother us. But I will tell you one thing that has been worrying us about Satyavan . . .' Here, he leaned forward conspiratorially and lowered his voice.

Tarsem automatically looked about to make sure his body-guards were out of earshot and outside the room. He edged forward to hear.

Wilhelm enunciated in slow, clear whispers, 'We are not pleased with him because he has stopped the pipeline, cut off all our profits, robbed us of a vast income just when the situation was ripe. He has doublecrossed us for mere sentiment. He has let us down. It is most frustrating. We had built up an infrastructure and he chokes it off at the root!'

Tarsem's head bobbed as the realization dawned on him that he had a willing ally in Wilhelm. The pipeline itself had a grudge against Satyavan!

He ran a hand over his close cropped hair and grinned, 'We will deal with Satyavan whenever you say.'

'Not yet. I'll give you the word.'

Tarsem nodded. 'He could be dangerous if he is not dealt with. Some months ago a man shot him in the shoulder—a few inches off the mark. We won't make that mistake.'

Wilhelm tapped the ash out of his pipe. 'For the moment,

don't do anything. It would be rash. The big consignment must come through. What do your people feel about it?'

'They do as I say.'

'I mean your organization, your bosses, this TAT as you call it.'

'Ah,' Tarsem leaned back and sighed. 'I have informed them. Their representatives will be coming to take a major decision on collaboration with your set-up.'

'When?'

Tarsem leered cannily, 'Only after they are sure I can handle matters. After the first big consignment. They are very careful people. Bombay people. Not like us from these parts.' He laughed. 'They don't let emotions come into their decisions. They go by figures, statistics. Their computer tells them what to do.'

They talked then of the big consignment, the mode of its collection and transportation, and they fixed a date for the job and a time precisely to the minute in late May.

In all their discussion, there was no mention of Balbir.

For Balbir, in his captivity, time had gone slowly, punctuated by moments of such horror that he felt certain he would never emerge alive from this traumatic situation. Indeed, he had despaired and considered suicide. But how?

If he made a dash for freedom in the hope that his guards would shoot him, he could not be sure they would kill him quickly. They had reason to keep him alive.

If he smashed the mirror on the wall that daily showed his growing beard, and tried to use a sliver of the glass to cut a vein, he would be prevented at the first sound. He was never alone. The sheer lack of privacy was destroying his nerves.

He was in a room that was not even locked all the time. And when it was, a couple of armed youths kept him company inside. Their motivation was so strong and morale so high that there was no lapse on their part. It was worse than being in jail.

He read whatever he was given and, more infrequently now, Amar Singh dropped in for a futile one-sided discussion. The spark had gone out of Balbir's arguments though, somewhat like his grandfather and father, he remained by nature argumentative.

He wore the clothes given him by Amar Singh. Day by day, he seemed to be turning into a reflection of Amar Singh.

But the worst shock he endured was served him just two days

after he became a reluctant guest. He had, at the morning hour of prayer, been allowed to sit out on a terrace and listen to the singing that welled up from below.

He sat huddled in a blanket, shivering against the nip in the air, his senses coming awake to the beauty around him that no distress ever seemed to dilute. The sky like a concave shell of mother-of-pearl. The sparrows and pigeons and parakeets rising and wheeling and rummaging in the glory of dawn. There was a smile inside him. He loved the morning sounds, even those of people being roused from their slumbers and the usual coughing and hawking and spitting and washing and rinsing. It was a symphony of thanksgiving.

Amar Singh had come and stood beside him. A grim-faced man approached with what appeared to be a hat box.

Amar Singh said, 'We're sending a small present to the Ahluwalias. It will be delivered to Dev Singh in the village of Maina. But the box is too conspicuous, don't you think?'

Without waiting for an answer he turned to the man with the box. 'Better use the cane basket, the one with the handle. It will look like you're going on a picnic. Take a couple of women with you. Go by bus. It should seem like a family outing. No one will notice you then. Just leave the basket outside his door.'

The man nodded, left the hat box near Balbir and went away. By the time he returned with what seemed a small picnic hamper lined with a sheet of plastic, the sky was bloodshot and the sun was beginning to glare over the Sindhi Hotel and the Langar building.

Amar Singh remained standing as though at an inspection.

The man squatted down and undid the cord on the hat box and transferred the present to the wicker basket, pausing with it in his hands just long enough for Amar Singh to give a nod of approval.

It was the severed head of Uday Singh Kumhareya. Somehow it seemed wizened and smaller in the man's hands.

Balbir could not remember later whether he cried out or gasped but the morning tilted and rolled under him as he passed out.

From that point on, death became his constant companion, an intimate he did not fear and one he almost loved.

He became impervious to the effect of news about more murders and explosions and outrages.

He heard how negotiations were progressing between Tarsem and Satyavan. His captors did not wish to deprive him of hope.

But even hope seemed painful to him, like a pebble in his shoe as he trudged wearily on through the desert of day to day.

And then that grizzled old European had shuffled up outside the open door of the room and winked and waved as though in greeting, 'Raskaan!'

Though he had later dismissed it as an aberration of his mind, it had sunk in and raised his spirits. On a few abstracted occasions he had caught himself humming.

Twice he had had to speak a few sentences into a cassette recorder. They had explained that this was to assure Satyavan that he was alive and well.

Meanwhile the dimensions of the political power struggle were growing. Its effects were most obvious in the environs of the Golden Temple. The Bhindranwale faction was well-entrenched and ascendant; now even venerable religious persons could be bumped off with impunity. The retired head priest of the Akal Takht, who had often protested about the violence and attitudes of the extremists, was mercilessly gunned down at his residence. Earlier, such a killing would have drawn vigorous protest and retaliation from the sikh masses. But now it passed with a shudder in the fearful silence.

The extremists in the Golden Temple became more strident. This tore at the last shred of the polite relationship between Balbir and Amar Singh. But in that very moment of its destruction they realized the existence of another, perhaps unhappier one.

Amar Singh was no longer concerned to persuade, he only stated. 'You are a waste of time,' he declared one day. 'If after all the books and printed matter I have given you to read you can't digest the truth then I abhor you as I do the Arya Samajis! You have seen for yourself how the Arya Samaj under the guise of a reform movement among hindus is sapping at the sikh religion. The hindus had no conversion ceremony till the Arya Samaj introduced it. Why? In order to lure the sikhs back to hinduism! They scoff at all other ways of worship. They are the fanatics. We are fighting their aggression. We are defending an identity. You say that all sensible hindus of Punjab support the demand for Chandigarh to be declared the capital of the state but even Indira Gandhi said she agreed and then, under pressure from Haryana, withdrew her decision. You say that the demand for more river water and more electricity for Punjab is supported by all Punjabis. Then why do the hindus not also support our demand for naming a railway train after the Golden Temple or a street after one of the gurus? You see the discrimination against sikhs in the recruitment quota of the Armed Forces. It used to be about forty-eight percent. No one denies that the sikhs belong to a martial religion. The British saw that and encouraged us to join the Armed Forces. But this hindu government under the pretext of being democratic has ruled that recruitment should be proportionate to population figures. So the sikhs are reduced to a mere two percent. Do you not see what havoc this causes to our morale and to our employment prospects? Since the time of the Tenth Guru, the sikhs have been like a standing army anyway. Most of our young men are wondering why they wear all the signs of warriors without a chance to go to war. You cannot condition people to fight and not give them a cause or an outlet!'

'Now you are doing that,' Balbir nodded quietly.

'For two hundred years at every prayer meeting we sikhs have been yelling "*Raj karega Khalsa*". What is the point of our shouting that "The Khalsa will rule" if we do not set about to make it a reality?' Then with a fiery vehemence that seemed by its own adamance to expect contradiction, Amar quoted the entire couplet.

'*Raj karega Khalsa, baqi rahe na koe
Khwar hoye sab milenge, baje saran jo hoye*'

Balbir silently considered the significance of the well-known refrain.

'The Khalsa will rule, no distress shall remain
The worried shall unite, relieved by grace from pain.'

Amar seemed to be waiting, as though out of an old habit, for an attempt at refutation. Balbir said nothing.

Suddenly Amar said quite gently, 'Why don't you join us?'

Balbir's mouth twisted in a bitter smile. 'I am too much under threat here to think.' He ran his hand over his unkempt growing beard and glanced at the armed men lounging about.

A wave of something that might have been remorse or regret passed over Amar's face. After a moment's hesitation he shooed the guards out and sat down beside Balbir.

'Now,' he murmured with a hand resting on Balbir's thigh, 'let me ask you something. Why is our point of view so hard to understand? It bothers me. I must confess that some nights I toss about, wondering. The killing of our enemies does not trouble me as it does you. It has to be done. I am not too perturbed about the infighting in our ranks or the many factions we have to subdue. That is part of political growth. What nags me is that I can't seem to get across even to someone like you. What is the barrier?'

Balbir thought about that. Then said, 'Fear.'

'Fear?'

Balbir nodded. 'I am only afraid of the gun you are carrying but you . . .'

'Go on, say it.'

Balbir shook his head. 'You won't like what I am going to say.'

'Never mind.'

'You are afraid of me.'

Amar laughed. 'That's ridiculous. Why should I be afraid of you?'

'You are afraid of my mind. You don't really want to discuss, you want to dominate. You don't want to debate, you want to dogmatize. It's even possible that you are not quite sure of what you are doing.'

'I have faith in what I am doing.'

'Exactly. But do you have reason?' Balbir saw the flash of anger on Amar's face. 'If it will placate you, let me say that, emotionally at least, I have begun to understand some of your fears, the fears that are making you fight.'

'Really? Well, that is an advance.' The tone was sarcastic.

'Yes,' Balbir agreed. 'That is a step forward. And I was able to take it only when I stopped being afraid of the guns around me. That was from the day I decided that I was ready to die, ready to be killed.'

'Wonderful!' exclaimed Amar. 'That's like the time Guru Gobind selected the Five Faithful. He asked for five men willing to die immediately by his sword. There was hesitation, dread and dismay. Eventually five men stood up prepared to sacrifice themselves. Guru Gobind did not kill them. He blessed them and gave them charge of defending the faith. After that many stood up who were prepared to die.'

Balbir sighed and said sardonically, 'But of course I am afraid of being wounded.'

'Anyway, you crossed your fear.'

'Yes. Why don't you cross yours?'

Amar Singh's pale, good-looking, baby-like face broke into its customary smile. 'I don't know what fear you are talking about.'

Balbir said, 'Do you remember the day you first led me up to the terrace of the Langar building?'

'Indeed. That was when you first heard Santji speaking.'

'Right. Now when we sat there I looked out at the fields and saw the billboard, the hoarding that depicted the historical sequence of oppression against the sikhs. First there was a muslim with a sword torturing the sardars, then there was a Britisher doing the same with a gun and finally a hindu with a raised stick. You know, I was puzzled. I thought, that is strange. The hindu has no real weapon in his hand. The natural progression from the sword of the Mughals and the gun of the British might have been a machine gun or a tank or something. But the hindu was shown oppressing sikhs with nothing but a stick. What is a stick compared to the sword with which every sikh is armed? I thought that the author of that depiction had made a mistake. I thought that, ironically, he had ended up pointing out the hollowness of Bhindranwale's holy war. The poor hindu was being maligned. But now I understand better. You are afraid of the hindu mind. It is clever. It can tie you in knots. It can frustrate you emotionally because all your reasoned arguments are answered by better reasons. Your anger is answered by affection. All of it is sincere.'

Amar Singh's expression had been that of a flower opening to the sun but now suddenly it closed upon itself. 'No, none of it is sincere. It is hypocritical.'

'I am sincere,' Balbir almost whispered. 'And I am a hindu. True, I am not a practising, worshipping hindu. But, in accordance with your thinking, since I am not a sikh and not of any other religion but the one I was born into, I am a hindu. What I am trying to say is that I understand you and your cause now. Not with the mind but with the heart. My mind rejects all these stupid theses.' He waved a hand over the pile of books and pamphlets. 'But my heart declares that Amar and I are psychological kin.'

'Now what the hell do you mean by that?' Amar was intrigued but he was also suspicious.

'Amar,' said Balbir standing up and walking about the room, 'you want to be free of the warm embrace of hinduism just as I want to be free of my family. I want to get away, where I don't know or really care, but somewhere where I can grow on my own, learn on my own, be on my own. Yet every time I've tried to break free, the family has answered me with good reasons that keep me trapped. Maybe I'll come back—who knows?—but I want to have that choice. Everywhere I go, the family supports and protects—and frustrates—me. I don't want to be absorbed within the family, I want to be myself. I want my identity and independence just as you want yours.'

Amar got up swiftly and clasped Balbir's hands in both his. 'Thank God, you've understood that.'

Balbir nodded sadly and resumed his pacing. 'But I also understand that you and I are criminals, each in our own way. Because we are frustrated we do "bad things". We hope that, if nothing else, we'll be kicked out.'

'That's it! Let them kick us out of the hindu fold. We've been burning Article 25 of the Constitution! We are not going to be effaced into being a so-called branch of hinduism.'

'The torment for me,' Balbir continued as though he had not heard Amar, 'is that no matter how unreasonable my action, the family responds with an equally unreasonable affection. I am a prisoner to their love.' He stopped and with a mischievous grin added, 'And here, I am a prisoner to your hate.'

Amar's mouth hung open. There was a pause. Then he blinked as though in disbelief. 'We are talking at last! Really talking.'

Balbir shook his head. 'We are feeling at last, really feeling each other's predicament. Now I understand the high morale and fierce motivation of all these armed fellows.' He took a few more paces and said, 'But I still disagree with almost everything you say.'

'For instance?'

'My major point. Religion and politics should never mix; if they do, they lead each other astray. Look what happened when the British used the sikh religion for political purposes. They not only got diktats or *hukumnamas* issued by the loyal high priests condemning the organizers of the Komagata Maru and the Ghaddar movement, they even got them to honour the Butcher of Jallianwala Bagh—General Dyer—soon after the massacre which he supervised not far from this very Golden Temple.'

Amar Singh was stung. He snapped, 'Show me where you read that.'

Balbir sifted through the disorder of books and pulled out *The Akali Movement* by Mohinder Singh. He said, 'You'll find details of it there too. But it's better to get it straight from the horse's mouth. Here it is—*The Life of General Dyer* by Ian Colvin.'

He began looking for the relevant page.

Amar said, 'Ah yes, I remember. But that's why the Akali Dal came into being, to free the *gurdwaras* from British stooges.'

'Of course. I've read how Nehru supported the Akalis and went to jail. And I know that Mahatma Gandhi sent a telegram of congratulations saying "First battle for India's freedom won." But after the Akalis got back the keys of the Golden Temple from the British, they should have disbanded. Their job was done. Any form of political control of *gurdwaras* is wrong, whether it is by the British or the Indian government or the Akali Dal. It corrupts even holy men, for they are men after all. Look again at how low they sank before General Dyer. Read it.' He held out the book to Amar.

Amar was about to protest but Balbir said insistently, 'Please.' Amar Singh bent his eyes to the page and read.

> . . . *he and his Brigade-Major, Captain Briggs, were summoned to the Golden Temple, and found themselves in the presence of the chief priests and leaders of the sect.*
>
> *'Sahib,' they said, 'you must become a Sikh even as Nikalseyn Sahib became a Sikh.'*
>
> *The General thanked them for the honour, but he objected that he could not as a British officer let his hair grow long.*
>
> *Arur Singh laughed. 'We will let you off the long hair,' he said.*
>
> *General Dyer offered another objection, 'But I cannot give up smoking.'*
>
> *'That you must do,' said Arur Singh.*
>
> *'No,' said the General, 'I am very sorry, but I cannot give up smoking.'*
>
> *The priest conceded, 'We will let you give it up gradually.'*
>
> *'That I promise you,' said the General, 'at the rate of one cigarette a year.'*
>
> *The Sikhs, chuckling, proceeded with the initiation. General Dyer and Captain Briggs were invested with the five* kakas, *the sacred emblems of that war-like brotherhood, and so became Sikhs. Moreover, a shrine was built to General Dyer at their holy place, Guru Sat Sultani. . .*

While Amar was reading, Balbir was studying his own gaunt visage in the mirror, a rectangle of glass in a rusty metal frame hanging on the wall. Beside it on a peg was a deep blue turban.

Most of the men preferred to sit about without their turbans; the afternoons were hot. Summer was approaching.

Balbir took the turban and placed it on his own head. It settled comfortably round his ears. With his ragged beard that was now beginning to tickle his chest just as it had once made him scratch at his chin, he looked like any fierce extremist biding his time in the temple.

'It suits you,' said Amar Singh, glancing up from the page.

But Balbir replied, 'I was thinking how they honoured Dyer with a turban and a sword. And that for a crime which I gather, disgusted even that arch-imperialist Churchill.'

Amar shut the book with a snap and strode up to Balbir.

'Are you trying,' he gritted, 'to humiliate me?'

'No,' Balbir's voice was even. 'I am only pointing out that there is no holiness in a temple that is under political control. You know yourself that when the *mahants* enjoying the support of the British government were in charge, the *gurdwaras* were often places of lechery and licence. Women were cautioned not to come for their own safety. Some *mahants* had many wives and mistresses. They were pleased to entertain themselves with prostitutes, drugs, nautch girls. They had only one real care—to toe the expected political line. The Akali movement began because it wanted to change that. Many Akalis lost their lives. Many were killed inside *gurdwaras*. That is how degenerate the holy places had become. The Akali Dal managed to free the *gurdwaras* from British government control. But who will free the temple from control by the Akali Dal? And who will free the Akali Dal from the extremists who have taken control of it?'

Uncertainly at first and then with increasing assurance, Amar began to laugh. 'However cynically you may say it, I see it as a compliment. Yes, we are in control. And I admit things are bad now. Some things are very bad, especially since this is a temple. But we have taken over the structure in order to lead it to improvement. First we must have power and then we shall see to that. Why do you snigger? Don't you believe me?'

Balbir said, 'I really feel for you.'

Amar's eyes narrowed. 'I resent that,' he muttered. 'And what the hell makes you think yourself so superior?'

Facetiously, Balbir tapped the side of his own forehead with a finger, 'The same thing,' he grinned, 'that makes you hate me.'

A red curtain seemed to drop behind Amar's eyes. He snarled, 'Swine!' And struck out with an open palm.

Balbir was numbed and bewildered by the slap. He had not expected it.

An expression of sadness spread like a web over his face. The centre of that web was the tingling sensation on his cheek. He looked down at the floor. He had made a mistake. It was too optimistic of him to have hoped. You cannot joke with a fanatic. The gulf between them seemed to have widened and was growing with every second.

Just then, to his surprise, Amar leaped over the chasm effortlessly.

Clasping him close, his eyes shut tight in genuine pain, Amar kissed him on the cheek, over his beard. 'I'm sorry,' he muttered. 'I'm very, very sorry. I . . . I don't hate you at all.'

Balbir stood there uncomprehending. And slowly, as Amar remained clinging to him, he became aware of a strange warmth between them that disturbed him.

He heard Amar say, 'It's . . . it's very lonely here.' Then he added, 'For someone like me.'

And he thought: Amar is not as tough as the men he directs or those he obeys. Maybe that's why he tries to be tougher.

A few days later the first consignment of arms arranged through Satyavan drew up outside the Golden Temple. Amar Singh was delighted. Balbir seemed relieved at learning that he might soon be ransomed out.

But just as the men started to unload the sacks of 'food-stuff' from the truck, they were challenged by the police. The trucker Karnail Singh and his two men—wearing turbans of red, green and yellow—fired wildly in the air and bolted into the precincts of the Temple. Two others were not quick enough. They were gunned down in the answering fusillade.

Amar Singh was disappointed but not suspicious. After all, two men had been killed in the attempt. Tarsem would just have to try again with another consignment using a less conspicuous mode of delivery. But he was annoyed at the delay. It meant another wait for the next attempt.

The waiting was worse for Balbir. Unaware that this was part of a plan for his rescue, he began to despair. His inner defences dropped. He became vulnerable to suggestion and persuasion.

More than a week passed before he could be clearly told what was afoot. By then he was almost another person.

'It's a man's world here,' said one of the gunrunners who had slipped in along with the trucker Karnail Singh in order to rescue Balbir. 'And you've got to prove yourself a man among men. We've done that. We came in under a hail of bullets. Two men were shot, probably died. But they were the extra look-outs who Tarsem had attached to our truck. It was scary, all right. How were we to know that the cops and the CRPF wouldn't make a mistake and shoot us?'

The three men had been allowed to visit Balbir. They were above suspicion. If anything they were trusted. They had come in at the risk of their lives. The circumstances were unequivocal. Furthermore, they were, as far as everyone was concerned, Tarsem's men. They had a stake in keeping Balbir where he was. They stood to gain by holding him to ransom. If the first big consignment from Satyavan's pipeline had been nabbed, another load would surely come through. Tarsem would see to that. He was now in direct touch with the Pipeline.

On their first visit, the men sauntered in to see Balbir as though he were an animal at the zoo or an object kept for exhibition. They commented about him and made jocular or rude remarks as though his plight pleased them. Karnail Singh, spruce as ever, shocked him by spitting out a stream of invective against Satyavan and the family. This so enraged Balbir that he sprang at him, calling him a betrayer, a doublecrosser, a cuckold. The last insult was particularly hurtful to Karnail since there was some truth to it: rumour had it that his adopted son, grown into a young man now, was carrying on with his wife. But Balbir was not content with words. He lashed out with his fists. The men soon pummelled him into a corner from where he was saved only by the intervention of the guards.

It was only on their third visit that Karnail Singh and his men, all armed with sten guns, were left to lounge about and chat with Balbir, out of earshot but within sight. That was when they told Balbir of the plan for his rescue.

The guards were on the terrace absorbed in some commotion that was taking place. Commotions had become quite frequent here ever since the extremists had been tipped off by a sympathizer in the Intelligence Bureau that a plot was afoot to kill Bhindranwale. That was before the Spring Festival, early in April. Indeed, the thirteenth had been specified as the targeted date. That date came and went with calamitous consequences for the plotters who were caught. But the tension continued. Another attempt might be made any day. The terrorists were sure that it was the moderates in the Akali Dal who were trying to get rid of their leader.

While the extremists were keyed up and geared to protecting the Sant, their interest in more mundane duties naturally declined. The priority of guarding the kingpin of the movement was infused with intense urgency when the rival faction succeeded in killing Bhindranwale's right hand man, the commander in charge of all the murder squads.

The extremists learnt that a secret deal had been struck between the secretary of the Akali Dal and three Bhindranwale adherents, Surinder Singh Chhinda, his lady-love Baljit Kaur and Malik Singh Bhatia. The three were prepared to kill the Sant. The first two agreed to a reward of four hundred thousand rupees, of which they received two hundred thousand in advance.

Later, Amar Singh swore that he had noticed how nervous Baljit Kaur seemd as she sat for near on a couple of hours directly across from Bhindranwale as he addressed his followers on the roof of the Langar building. She clutched her bag to her. Inside it was a pistol. She either lost her nerve or some detail of the plan went awry for she sweated through the ordeal and went off to another meeting with the secretary of the Akali Dal, Gurcharan Singh.

The extremists believed that it was only their heavy guard round Bindranwale and their hawkeye, hair-trigger look-out for any suspicious movement among the small audience that prevented her from making an attempt. Be that as it may, they were certain that she and her paramour were then instructed to strike against the second-in-command, S.S. Sodhi.

In pursuance of that, Chhinda lured Sodhi to the tea shop known as the Sindhi Hotel just outside the eastern exit of the Golden Temple. There, Baljit Kaur was waiting.

Whether or not Sodhi was liable to the charms of Baljit Kaur no one knows for sure. But what did transpire was that Baljit Kaur let him hold her hand in both his. The excuse was a bandage round her thumb. She asked him to retie it since it was coming loose. While his hands were busy doing this and at a safe distance from his automatic carbine, Chhinda shot him from under the table with a pistol.

Baljit Kaur was naturally grilled intensively by Bhindranwale's men. She declared that Chhinda, who had run off and managed to reach his village, had killed Sodhi because he had tried to rape her. The extremists suspected that statement just as much as she was sure that it would protect her. Bhindranwale was known to be harsh in his punishment of anyone accused of such misbehaviour. They had before them numerous examples, including that of Uday Singh Kumhareya who had suffered a slow death for his lapse. If Sodhi had indeed made an unwarranted pass at Baljit Kaur, no matter how important to the movement he was, he deserved to die. But. And this was the big but, had he in fact been guilty of trying to carry her away, abduct her, seduce her or rape her?

Unfortunately for her, Baljit Kaur's spirit snapped under interrogation in the Golden Temple. She blurted it all out in a taped confession: the trio had been paid by Gurcharan Singh to kill Bhindranwale and failing that to get S.S. Sodhi.

Chhinda's name was placed on top of the hit list. It also appeared on a blackboard outside the Langar building. He was located in his village that very night and killed. The name was rubbed off the blackboard.

Beside that same blackboard in the premises of the temple, the third conspirator Malik Singh Bhatia was publicly hacked to pieces, first one limb then the other, by a sword-wielding Nihang. Still crying for mercy, his blood-spurting body was dragged away and given the coup de grace.

Baljit Kaur's was another body that ended up in a sack dumped on the streets of the city. Her breasts had been sliced off and she had obviously been given the third degree.

Gurcharan Singh had to resign as the secretary of the Akali Dal and a number of shocked members went over to the militant camp of Bhindranwale. Gurcharan Singh insisted till the day he died in a grenade explosion, that he had had nothing to do with the plot. He maintained that all the persons involved were known to have been smugglers and the killing of Sodhi was the outcome of gang rivalry.

So gang rivalry was an accepted part of smuggling activity in the temple. And Balbir was a useful pawn to stimulate such gang rivalry for the benefit of the movement. The interests of the extremists and Tarsem's men converged in that they both wanted to keep Balbir alive and hostage. Therefore, Tarsem's men were not disarmed of their sten guns and revolvers when they sat about chewing the cud in Balbir's room. It was understandable that they should drop in now and again; what else was there to do? Captives and captors were all restricted to the same area. Outside, the police patrolled and there had also been a tip off that, till recently, some of India's five hundred élite paracommandos had been snooping about, hoping to get in and snuff out the extremists. According to the informant, it was only the government's disinclination to risk the loss of such highly-trained men that had led to their withdrawal to the more important task of guarding the lives of VIPs in Delhi who were on Bhindranwale's hit list.

The task of the commandos would have been infinitely more complicated than that of Satyavan's men who had managed to infiltrate the defences of the extremists with the simple objective of liberating one person at whatever cost. The commandos would have had to take over not one room but numerous rooms and fortifications in a vast complex of buildings. One alarm and the commandos would have been decimated by the well-entrenched fire power of the extremists.

The men who dropped in on Balbir were, gang rivalry and expediency notwithstanding, smugglers after all. They were bound to flock together.

Thus, Balbir received news of his family, even to the extent of how the harvest had gone. But it had been no festival at all this spring. Everyone was morose. His father, who usually planned the cropping as though it were a strategy of war, did not bother this time if the tractor swung the harvester so that it left the corners unreaped. He did not even shout and fume. He missed Balbir.

And Balbir heard also, with some amusement, of the bath-room that Raskaan had built.

17

❖❖❖

The Bathroom that Raskaan Built

Any outsider observing the activities at Chamkalan would hardly have believed that Raskaan was there in order to participate in a plan for the rescue of Balbir. It seemed his entire concentration was on building a bathroom for the ancestral home, a bathroom as odd and extravagant as he.

And yet it was not as if he had immediately on arrival flung himself into this endeavour. No, he had waited, anxious with concern for Balbir, till he had been reassured by the patriarch that the old man and Satyavan had indeed devised a scheme which, if executed precisely, would result—and the old man chuckled as he said it—'in the ejection of Balbir from the Golden Temple. He will be spat out like the bitter pip of an orange.'

But, simple and daring though the plan was, it entailed the fitting together of a few components over a period of time. Raskaan groaned at the prospect of twiddling his thumbs in the village. He was a man of action—quick, decisive, impulsive and inclined to be impatient of long-term strategies. That indeed was how he had left the village to begin with. He had plunged abroad without a plan, diving as though into a pool without ascertaining its depth, uncaring whether he hurt himself or touched bottom and came up with his fists full of gold. His unexpected success had made him both more adventurous and more religious. He cavilled at delay and was cavalier with matters requiring careful concatenation.

'You would make a bad chess player,' Lok Raj had said when Raskaan protested at all the factors that the old man seemed to be assessing and reassessing.

'Aye, Babaji,' Raskaan admitted with a mischievous twinkle in his eye, 'chess was never my game. I'd rather be at flush, rummy, blackjack or poker. And I'd win money too.'

'Here the stake is not money but your brother Balbir.' The old man had growled and Raskaan had felt Satyavan lean forward beside him, hanging on every word of the patriarch. It made him a little scornful of Satyavan. Satyavan was a hero-worshipper, Raskaan was his own hero. The old man had tugged at his *hookah* and added, 'It is not a matter of taking a chance but of eliminating all chance.'

Satyavan had nodded and turned to Raskaan like an interpreter who has received his cue, 'What he means is that all the gears have to mesh at the right moment. We have to make sure that every aspect of the plan is in place and functions correctly.'

Raskaan sighed and raised his eyebrows. His eyes seemed to grow bigger like juicy ripe *liichis*. 'What more are we waiting for? I've brought you Schneider and Wilhelm. They've both done what we want. Elder brother Satyavan has now got Karnail Singh's group into place and they're ready to go into action. We're only waiting for you to give the word.'

'And for me,' said Lok Raj with just a hint of a chuckle as he leaned back, 'to grow a beard.'

'A beard? Why should you—?' Raskaan looked from his grandfather to his cousin.

Satyavan was beginning to gurgle with his deep belly-laugh. These two still had some aspect of the plan that was secret even from him! How alike these two are in that, he thought, they will always hold something back till the very end, they will always keep some precaution even to their caution.

Lok Raj might have been reading his mind for he now muttered, 'You and Balbir are too impulsive, Raskaan. You are like your father, quick to be charmed and quick to anger. But Satyavan has fortunately inherited patience from his father.' Then the old man couldn't resist a jibe, for he added, 'Perhaps the only good quality my elder son has.' He took another pull on his *hookah* and a faraway look settled on his face. 'When I am gone, Satyavan,' he said, 'help your father to run things. Don't leave it all to his judgement. He lives . . . in his own world. He spends all day in the stables though nearly all our horses are gone. What kind of man is that?'

It really was a question but Satyavan winced and had no intention of answering. This was the one area of their relationship that he did not enjoy. The old man expected him to subscribe to the taunts and badinage against his own father. He could never bring himself to say anything. He suffered such moments to pass in silence. Satyavan knew his father to be a kind, gentle, brave but rather impractical and totally unambitious man. He was happy to be led anywhere, even to the death, but he was happiest left alone to care for animals and to attend to daily chores. He had quietly abdicated from major decisions long ago. He had been content to live dependent on the wishes first of his father and then of his son. There was some mystery there that Satyavan had never pierced. Perhaps his father had been in love once with some woman who may have scorned him for his high-pitched voice and rather effeminate light complexion which betrayed every small embarrassment with a rush of colour. Perhaps there was something more complex than that in the days before Satyavan was born. He only knew that Gyan Chand did not figure as prominently in the uproarious Montgomery days of Lok Raj as did the younger son Khushi Ram. Gyan Chand had always fulfilled without fuss the responsibilities allotted to him. He had, in a sense, held the fort in Chamkalan while his father and brother had been adventuring. He was somehow the taken-for-granted factor in all their roistering.

Looked at another way, it was Satyavan who had been commandeered away from his father by the domineering love and demands of Lok Raj. But the old man had not been able to wean him away from his mother. Fond as he was of his father, Satyavan was a slave to the care of his mother. He waited on her every breath and would cancel all appointments if she so much as mentioned a headache or a pain. For her sake, Satyavan would buck even the will of Lok Raj. Fortunately for his peace of mind such a situation had never arisen. Lok Raj was careful never to belittle Satyavan's mother. Indeed he respected her status as the eldest woman in the family, his own wife having died long ago, and often praised her good-humoured efficiency in running the household and administering the domestic chain of command that ran through all the ramifications of the family.

She often came and sat on a chair before Lok Raj without even the formal politeness of covering her white-haired head with the end of her *saree*. She gave him no accounts of expenses and could demand what money was needed. Her face seemed always illumined by the glow of cheerfulness but she had a rather raucous voice that she used teasingly. Once Satyavan had even heard her chide the old man saying, 'Don't be such a fool!' and Lok Raj's jaw had gone slack for a second before he had sought refuge in laughter. Yes, he needed, her, not only to see to the smooth functioning of all the related households, but also for advice on family matters and for whatever information she gathered from the servants and the listening posts of kitchens and drawing rooms and sewing circles. She was a small-built, beautiful, ageing woman with a ready smile that displayed two large rabbit teeth, and she was clever. Lok Raj ran Satyavan but she could, if she wished, sway both.

Now with Lok Raj preparing to indulge in more unwarranted ridicule of his own eldest son, Satyavan took the bit between his teeth and carried Lok Raj away from the subject. He said, 'Babaji, why talk of when you are gone? Mother says you are so strong that you'll probably outlive us all.'

The old man chuckled but said, 'God forbid. I have lived a full life and am not afraid to go. That stupid Balbir with his troubles is forcing me back to ways I had renounced long ago. But let us see, let us see. I must be prepared, that is all.' Then he looked at Raskaan and winked, 'First, let my beard grow . . .'

Raskaan sounded a little irritated as he asked, 'And what shall I do in the meantime? Shall I go back to Germany and return when you are ready? I don't know what you intend, with your beard and all, but I think you should leave such matters to us. If you are thinking of risking your own life in any way—'

'Raskaan,' muttered the patriarch, clamping a hand on his shoulder, 'stay. We never know when we may need to move suddenly dropping all our plans. As for your affairs in Germany, you have a sensible woman in Renate. Have faith in her.'

'I do. She's an excellent . . .' Raskaan swallowed as he said it, '. . . secretary but—'

'She is an able woman, a fine person,' said Lok Raj with finality.

Raskaan got up and paced the room. 'You don't understand.'

'I do, better than you realize.'

'If I am not there to control the business—'

'Business lost can be regained but a brother killed can never be brought to life.'

Raskaan stopped. His black trimmed beard touched his chest. It was a nod but it seemed like a bow. 'You're right, Babaji,' he agreed. 'Renate will handle things there very well. It's just that I regret being idle.'

'Why be idle?' the old man chuckled. 'You can employ yourself building that bathroom.'

Raskaan seemed about to have a fit. His cheeks ballooned with air. Then suddenly he saw the funny side of it and burst out laughing. Satyavan's gurgle welled up and joined in. Lok Raj rocked back and forth, guffawing.

And so Raskaan began building a bathroom, partly in exasperation, partly in fun and largely, of course, so that it could be utilized by the family. However, a psychoanalyst examining it might have seen much in it that revealed not only the personality of its builder but also the desire of Raskaan to cock a snook at the demands of Satyavan and the dictates of the patriarch.

For weeks, when he was not busy on the transceiver to Schneider, Raskaan supervised a string of masons, carpenters and plumbers. Fittings were brought from Ludhiana and Jalandhar, some from as far away as Chandigarh. It was a large bathroom, the size of a small hall. Raskaan designed it as though he intended someone to live in it all his life.

There were shelves for books and a row of containers for magazines. There were articles of decor—not in the best taste admittedly since Renate was not there to advise Raskaan—and potted plants and some amazing contrivances, the sole function of which was to surprise. In one corner was an escritoire with a chair that revealed itself to be a commode. Another corner was devised like a changing room in a tailor's establishment, with mirrors that angled to display every fall and drape and trick of stitch.

Another section was dominated by a dressing table laden with cosmetics and lit by a garland of bulbs like a filmstar's make-up room.

Each area was demarcated by distinct tiling but the whole place was dominated by the white paving of the main section which ran up the walls to waist height. It seemed to make the entire room grin, perhaps like Lok Raj's false teeth lying disembodiedly in a glass of disinfectant. But there was great generosity here. Two types of commodes, Eastern and Western, both fitted with flushing cisterns. A shower, a bathtub and taps that gleamed like silver decorations or awards won in competition. There was a surplus of urinals, three of them, standing like marble memorials commemorating the three elders of the family. Raskaan was obviously considerate of the companionable herd instincts of the family. He seemed to be saying, 'Aye, we shall all stand or fall together.'

'It's like a cinema hall!' villagers exclaimed when they trooped in to examine this new gift that Raskaan had contrived with which to awe them.

'My Taj Mahal,' Raskaan nodded benignly. 'A symbol of the

love I bear the family.'

And they marvelled at the bidet, the function of which no one knew. They washed their feet in it as though in preparation for entering a holy place. At such moments Raskaan could not restrain his puckish nature. 'No, no, no!' he would cry and brushing them aside he would set an example by bending down and drinking water from the shooting jet.

Everyone loved the switchboard on the nearer wall. It was set at eye level and had about thirty switches and a corresponding arrangement of varicoloured bulbs. Flick a switch, a coloured bulb lights up and simultaneously something else happens in the room: a neon light comes on, soft music starts playing, the geyser's ruby indication glows or a voice guffaws in imitation of the patriarch. At the same time outside the bathroom a red signboard lights up. The signboards seemed to have been collected at random for they carried a variety of messages, such as 'Engaged', 'No trespassing', 'Alert', 'Reserved', 'Silence', 'Danger', 'On the Air', 'Sale', 'No smoking', 'Fasten Seat-Belts', 'Emergency', 'Exit', 'On Display', 'Service', 'Enquiry', 'Work in Progress', 'No Parking', 'Security Zone', 'Explosives' and 'Fire'.

Altogether the bathroom with its gadgetry and polished menace had the atmosphere of a place you entered for a surgical operation. And yet it had the festivity of a carnival. The villagers, accustomed to going out into the fields or making do with two bricks set ten inches apart, were delighted. This crazy son of the grand old zamindar had brought refinement and hilarity to basic unmentionable needs.

Lok Raj and Satyavan were indulgent but not amused. That rapscallion Raskaan was up to his jokes again!

Meanwhile Raskaan dallied pleasantly with the groups that came to admire and laugh.

He had launched it all by inviting his father Khushi Ram to inaugurate the surreal bathroom when it was complete. Khushi Ram had churned his way to the door expecting to cut a ribbon or pull a cord but, much to his chagrin, Raskaan said, 'No, no, father. Go in and have a bath. See the difference between this and bathing from a hand-pump in the courtyard.'

Grumbling that he had never suffered such levity at his expense in public, Khushi Ram stripped to his underpants and stepped into a bubble bath for the first time in his life.

Now Raskaan switched on the jacuzzi. When it started Khushi Ram leapt out with a yell thinking he was going to be electrocuted.

'That,' nodded Raskaan proudly, 'has been smuggled in specially from Germany.'

'What is the good of that!' Khushi Ram shouted. It was a rhetorial question and its implication was obvious.

But Raskaan answered it, enjoying the perversity of the moment.

'It is for wrestlers and exercise fanatics like elder brother Satyavan so that, when they bathe, their tired muscles will be massaged.'

'Heaven help us!' Khushi Ram yelled. 'What are we coming to? First its machine guns and washing machines and then this ... this madness!'

Thus the debate on the new technology of luxury was started in the village. The distinction between what aided progress and what represented decadence became blurred. Nobody wanted to throw out tractors and threshers and washing machines and TV sets along with sten guns and battery-powered toothbrushes and jacuzzis. Punjab grabs the future, it does not wait for it.

The bathroom that Raskaan built played its part in other ways in other people's lives.

Clusters of young women came shyly and were fascinated by the allowance it made to personal vanity. Those who had individual access to it spent hours in there addressing their thoughts to a mirror or simply preening.

Raskaan's own sister, Aadran, spent more time in Chamkalan. She had come often enough to spend an hour or two with her brother and to goad them all on to more effort over their dearly beloved Balbir. But now she also came to retreat into that region of privacy and to wonder, with the aid of the unfamiliar cosmetics that Raskaan had stocked on the dressing table, what the projected marriage to Harmesh, the Bank Manager's son, might mean for her. He lived in England and dealt in real estate. He had come and visited them and been approved, even by Lok Raj.

She had only conversed with him twice and that briefly. He was quite handsome with his clipped military-style moustache and wavy hair, though his ears fanned out a little. She must persuade him to grow his hair longer in the manner of the filmstar Amitabh Bachchan; that would hide his ears and suit him better.

But would she suit him? She was a little afraid that she would be caught out with her rustic ways. He was only a dealer in real estate and she came from a powerful land-owning family but still he was accustomed to a wider world and she was not used to life in a city, and that too abroad. Would she be able to adjust? To what would she have to adjust? Did this bathroom represent life abroad?

She grimaced at her image in the mirror. Face too broad, nose too wide at the base. She stuck her tongue out at herself. Silly goose! How had he approved *her*?

She felt she didn't look as inspiring in the flesh as she did in the carefully retouched photograph that had been despatched to him.

Well, she told herself, don't fool yourself. Moving from country to country means nothing to a woman; it's just a transfer from one kitchen to another.

But surely they would go out. They would go to the cinema and to events and they would have friends to visit. And between them all those things would happen like in novels. She read a lot, mainly in Hindi but also in Punjabi.

Every time she came to Chamkalan, the chore of reading newspapers to Lok Raj would fall to her. His eyes were really bothering him. But he insisted on knowing as much as he could. She shook her head and gave a half-laugh.

Yes, perhaps she should be like Balbir and rebel against the wishes of the family. Perhaps she should rebel and fall in love not with the husband chosen for her but with someone unexpected. But who? How? Here?

She made an incredulous gesture and sighed and reached for lipstick and powder. She was unused to make-up. Should the powder be unnoticeable or should it be like icing on a cake? She tried eye-shadow and liner, remembering the instructions in magazines, but they made her look as though she had woken from the dead.

Her hair. She would have to do something about her hair that hung like coir rope in two plaits. She would like to have it all squiggled and wriggled up like an upturned conical basket. High fashion. Yes, she would have to venture into high fashion. She slapped her thigh in amusement.

No, that won't do. That was a village girl's action. She must not slap her thigh or her forehead. She must not stick out her tongue for emphasis or in mockery. She must make small mincing movements with her lipsticked mouth.

She did. And burst out laughing.

No, no, no. That won't do at all. She must be proper, even prim.

Suddenly she wondered if she was attractive in herself. Would he find her . . . desirable?

She bit her finger. No, that won't do either. No biting fingers like an immature girl. She was going to be married. A married lady. But first, a married woman.

She took off her clothes and looked. She propped up her breasts and looked. She raised her eyebrows, tilted up her head and looked.

She didn't particularly like herself but she admitted that he might. And she dropped all play-acting and slapped her thigh and laughed.

No, she told herself, that won't do. No slapping the thigh.

Someone rang the bell. That was another perversity of Raskaan—a doorbell to demand entrance to the bathroom.

She jumped at the sound. Then quickly began flinging on her clothes.

Suddenly a voice said close to her ear, 'Come on, come on, hurry up!'

'Haw!' she exclaimed in horror, clutching her garments about her, certain that she had been observed. 'Who's that? How dare you! Where are you?'

The voice bubbled with laughter, 'It's your elder brother Raskaan here. I'm outside, speaking to you on the intercom.'

She had now traced the origin of the voice. It came from a little metal box attached to the wall.

'Can you see me?' she asked with annoyance.

'Of course not, you silly village frump.'

'Thank God!' she sighed, then muttered, 'You're shameless. I'll tell your *mem* about it. I'll tell Renate. She'll really pull your ears for scaring people like this!'

He laughed. 'In the West it's called "invasion of privacy". Presidents of countries do it, so why can't I?'

'Shut up, elder brother.'

'OK. But I only wanted to tell you that a gaggle of girls is here to see you.'

'Me?'

'They didn't find you in Jagtara so they came here.'

'Oh.'

'They want to congratulate you on your engagement to be married. And I'm sure they want to see the photograph you have of Harmesh. One of the girls is a real giggler. They'll titter over the handsome bridegroom.'

'Stop it, elder brother. I couldn't care less about him.'

'Oh ho, is that really so? Then why carry that picture of him wherever you go?'

'I don't.'

'It's in your handbag.'

She was aghast. 'How do you know?'

'I looked in it.'

'In my purse! You . . . you . . .!'

'Be careful. Whatever you call me will reflect on you. I'm your brother.'

'You . . . filthy dog!'

'Now you know what that makes you,' he laughed. 'Come on out. They've been waiting half an hour.'

The girls were waiting in the courtyard of an outhouse. There, over the barking and furore of the chained dogs belonging to the family, they gushed their best wishes and clung to Aadran asking for more details about her husband-to-be. Aadran deflected the questions with swift recourse to hospitality, urging them to have tea or buttermilk or sugarcane juice. She sent one of the servants for sweetmeats, another for tumblers of water, a third for oranges gathered from the orchard.

But then she had to show the photograph and tell all she knew, not only about him but about his family. And she thought, with a tremor, yes, I am marrying not a man but a family. And it put a jab of nervousness in her. Will I get on with my mother-in-law and the others? And what are they like? It was as if she were entering a black hole of the universe. A sense of dread overcame her. She was pleased to be getting married, she didn't want to spend her life as an ageing spinster, she was old enough already. But she knew now that she too would cry like all brides of arranged marriages do when they leave home in the ceremonial palanquin. And she knew her mother would weep too. And her father; in her mind's eye she saw him throwing back his head as though to scan the sky while swallowing back his tears.

She hardly heard what the girls said. The one with the fuzz on her upper lip was indulging in conjecture about the wedding night. The dumpy one with the slight squint was remarking on the bridegroom's hairline which she was sure would recede with the years. They were all very merry. The one with the aquiline features reached out and took Aadran by the hand. 'There's something I want to say to you,' she giggled as she led Aadran up the steps to the roof-top terrace.

There was a sort of rest room, a sun room, on the terrace. In front of it, on a string-bed spread with a cotton rug, red chillies had been set out to dry. Near the string-bed were three spinning wheels, marking the gossip station of older women.

'You may not remember me,' the girl suggested.

'Oh but I do, Kulwanti,' nodded Aadran. 'We studied together for the Prabhakar degree in Hindi.'

'And we learnt embroidery together—'

Aadran laughed, 'From that garlic-chewing hunchback in Jagtara.'

'Twice a week between two and four in the afternoon. And no excuses. God, she was a witch! I was sure her feet turned backwards at night.'

'But you stopped coming after a month.' Aadran's tone was accusing. 'We knew you didn't have to work in the kitchen making meals for the labourers. You don't have land. You people are shopkeepers, aren't you? We wondered why you'd stopped coming.'

Kulwanti giggled. 'My father . . .'

'He objected? To what?'

'No, no. He wanted me to learn music instead.' She giggled again. 'Better marriage prospects if a girl can do something entertaining and elegant like playing the *sitar*.'

Aadran frowned. 'Don't talk to me of marriage. I'm sick of the subject.'

'But I do want to talk of it,' Kulwanti insisted. 'That's why I came. Oh I envy you! You're so lucky not to love anyone else.'

'You call that lucky? I wish I did love someone else like . . . like in the movies. Then I could—'

'I do. I love someone and want to marry him.'

Aadran gazed at Kulwanti in amazement. 'You do?'

Kulwanti nodded and bit back a giggle. 'His hands are gentle but his voice is rough. He has the frightened eyes of a deer but he feeds on danger.'

'Who is this?' Aadran asked conspiratorially.

Kulwanti seemed to be biting back another giggle but her eyes brimmed with tears. She spoke in a sudden rush. 'You must help me be strong, Aadran. We must give each other comfort. Oh, we are both unfortunate in the loss of Balbir.'

'Balbir? Balbir who?' Aadran's mouth remained open. She searched Kulwanti's eyes. 'You don't mean . . . our Balbir. My younger brother. My kid brother!' As Kulwanti nodded slowly, Aadran spat out the words, 'No! Never! Impossible!'

She now saw Kulwanti in another light, couldn't think of her as an aquaintance who had shared hours of instruction in Hindi and embroidery, couldn't see her as anything but a greedy monster attempting to swallow her brother.

Kulwanti was saying, 'I think he cares for me.'

Aadran found herself laughing. 'Whatever gave you such a whimsical idea? What gives you such notions about . . .' Politeness was stopping her but she broke through it for her brother's sake '. . . about yourself? How can you presume?'

Kulwanti wanted to say something about fate but couldn't. She wasn't sure how it worked anyway. She looked at the spinning wheels sitting idle on the terrace. No, fate was not just a thread spun by an old woman. There were too many old women—and young ones—spinning at their wheels in Jagtara, Chamkalan and Maina. The sight was too familiar for awe or fantasy. From deep in her childhood rose the memory of a business trip her father had made to Kasauli. She and her mother had been taken along. Since then Kasauli had remained unreal for her though she knew it existed in the foothills of the Himalayas just a short run by bus from here. The sense of ethereal mystery had been stirred during a walk in the woods. They had suddenly come upon three wizened old men ringing birds. She couldn't remember now whose hand she was clinging to or who interpreted for her over the viaduct of centuries that seemed to lie between the old men and them. But she saw that the professorial men were catching birds in an almost invisible net, then attaching little metal strips to their legs and releasing them. The metal strips bore numbers and inscriptions, and an eternally bent man with a perpetually trim little goatee was writing destinies in a book as each creature winged away. They knew what would happen to those birds. She remembered being told, 'That one will die in Central America' and 'These will go with the flock to Siberia' and 'This one is headed for Japan'. The places were exotic and the authority irrevocable.

She heard herself saying, 'I am ringed for Balbir.'

'What?'

'I met him with Uday the Kumhareya.'

'I see.' Aadran felt like crushing the dry chillies and throwing the powder in Kulwanti's eyes. She picked up a handful and flung them back on the string-bed. 'Sluts, that's what the two of you have been. You and that Gulnari.' She turned to Kulwanti, her eyes blazing but her voice a hiss, 'Get out! Get out of our house.'

18

•••

The Panicking Ploy

The plan for the rescue of Balbir was audacious and brilliant. It was to be executed in broad daylight. The sheer finesse of it carried the signature of Lok Raj's handiwork. But it had taken the patriarch a long time to set it in motion. Satyavan and Raskaan had indeed fretted.

Meanwhile the old man seemed to go to seed. It was obvious he was worried. He began to look shabby, scruffy, glum. He stopped shaving. The village barber who came daily, stropping his razor and working up a lather with the old-style soap-stick and brush, was dismayed. Lok Raj had never before abstained from this morning ritual, not even when he was down with a bout of flu. It was as much a part of his style as, say, the shawl draped over his shoulders. He loved being attended to. In that sense he was spoilt. Where ordinary matters were concerned, he never did anything himself that he could get others to do for him. He had never owned a shaving kit, and the electric razor that Satyavan had once given him was rusting somewhere in some cupboard. He was fixed in his habits to the extent that he never even used the battery-operated toothbrush that Raskaan foisted on him. For that matter he didn't use a toothbrush at all but preferred a twig of the neem tree, one end of which he chewed to a brush and rubbed on his teeth like any villager. He did this even with his dentures.

Something was definitely wrong with him, the barber opined. Not only did the old man refuse shave, massage, manicure and the clipping of the hair growing out of his ears, he had no interest in the gossip that the barber usually brought him. He seemed to have vowed not to care about himself till he saw his youngest grandson again. At least that is how the barber interpreted Lok Raj's puzzling statement: 'Only when you know what to live for do you discover what is worth dying for.' The barber was certain the old man was sliding towards his funeral pyre, for surely the old man would never see his youngest grandson again.

But Satyavan and Raskaan, still clinging to their sense of humour, knew that the old man was up to something. As for the statement about living and dying, why the old man had always been a ready martyr to the moment, risking all at the drop of a turban. He was a natural celebrant of the bold life. The only thing that kept him from tempting death now was, ironically, the restrictions imposed by old age.

Lok Raj grew a bushy, wiry white beard. His eyebrows unsnipped by the diligent barber, burgeoned thickly curving upwards like scimitars. He had always had an authoritative demeanour but now it was garbed in what he had never chosen to display—an appearance of ferocity.

Casual visitors said he was wasting. But in fact he was girding whatever remained of his loins. As usual he had decided that he had lived long and happily enough and it was time to go—not with grace, but with abandon. He had taken this sort of decision many times before, even as a callow stripling, and it had always seemed to him that some great joy was beckoning. That is why he hated heights, because he was always tempted to fling himself down for the sheer exultation of it. And that is why, when his feet were firmly on the ground, his spirit was always soaring upwards: there was no other direction it seemed, only up or down, and either way there was joy. So he would fly or fling himself but there was no place in his thinking for the stumble, the hesitant step, the fall.

'Now, then,' he said to Satyavan and Raskaan, 'let's mull over it again. Check it for flaws. First, our entire scheme is based on Schneider's information that there is no competent doctor in the Golden Temple. The medical facilities they have are basic. They couldn't handle a major disease. Short of that, they are ready for anything.'

'That's right,' said Satyavan. 'If the police or the army ever laid siege to the temple they wouldn't succeed for years, because the terrorists have everything there. There is plenty of water in the tank and there are fish too. There are also wells in the complex. And they have stores of food grains, plus there are underground tunnels leading to houses outside. What's more, jumping from roof to roof is easy. The whole area would have to be surrounded and blocked off. But . . .' he paused and looked at Raskaan and Lok Raj, '. . . the one thing that they have no provision against is the outbreak of an epidemic. If one case of cholera or smallpox occurs there, they've had it.'

'What would you do if that happened and you were in charge of the situation?' Lok Raj watched every flexion of Satyavan's face.

Satyavan replied, 'It would depend on who fell ill. Don't forget we are talking of a deadly contagious illness in an enclosed atmosphere. For instance if it happened to a dog, although dogs don't get smallpox they can contract other contagious diseases, you'd immediately have him put to sleep.'

'Euthanasia,' murmured Raskaan. 'And prevention.'

'Exactly. Similarly if the patient was of a rival faction or a mere captive, I would place the health of my men above all else and have the patient shot and his body cremated to destroy the germs.'

'Why wouldn't you send him out to a doctor?'

'Because if he was an opponent I couldn't care less and if he was an important prisoner then obviously I wouldn't want to be thwarted in my control over him. Furthermore the prisoner is probably slated to be shot anyway once his usefulness is over.'

'So if Balbir fell ill . . .? Really fell ill?'

Satyavan's lip quivered, his eyes flickered. In a split second there was a moist glisten in the furrow of his brow. 'He would be shot.'

Lok Raj nodded and sighed. 'So Balbir cannot afford to be ill.'

'Oh he'd be permitted a cough and cold, a stomach-ache, a headache, even a little fever. But nothing serious.'

'And what we require as our ally is a serious contagious disease that could create the dread of an epidemic.'

'Yes, preferably smallpox.'

Lok Raj cleared his throat, spat into the spitoon and asked, 'So, since Balbir cannot be allowed to have smallpox, who can we use? What would you order if an inconsequential criminal, a smuggler on the run from the police, a real sympathizer of the extremists, developed smallpox? Would you have him shot?'

'I think that would demoralize all the other smugglers and petty criminals aiding the general effort. They would resent it. They might even rebel against it.'

'What would the smugglers propose?'

'That the man be taken to a hospital. After all, the choice for him is clear: his life could be saved at the cost of a few years in prison.'

'Hm. Was Karnail properly briefed? Did he take the right tint of lipstick with him?'

'Yes, and we tried it out too. From anything beyond three feet, the spots look deadly. By then no one will dare to stand near the victim anyway.'

'Hopefully,' muttered Lok Raj.

They waited.

A minute later, Lok Raj asked, 'Did you explain that we want no bloodshed if possible? The minimum, if necessary. Violence only calls down upon itself more violence. It brutalizes. We must use technique, skill, intelligence, daring to loosen the grip of brutality. Anyone can use brute force. We have to be better than that.' Suddenly he frowned, 'Did they remember to take the little bottles of chloroform?'

Satyavan nodded. 'Karnail is also carrying a beeper in his pocket.'

'Huh!' Lok Raj chuckled. 'One of your playthings!'

'It might help. It'll alert us to standby.'

Lok Raj smiled. 'These gadgets!'

A full five minutes elapsed. At last, Lok Raj grunted, '*Hai Rubba*! *Bismillah*! All right. Send out the signal—Shivaji.'

Shivaji was the code word. It was the name of the famous seventeenth century Maratha warrior who was perhaps the first real guerrilla tactician in the world. He had led small bands of soldiers in successful forays against massive Moghul armies. Among his numerous exploits was the manner in which he had escaped from captivity in Delhi. He had been sneaked out, hidden inside a hamper of sweets.

The final part of Lok Raj's plan owed its inspiration to Shivaji. Balbir would be spirited out not in a basket but under the double quilt of a patient suffering from highly contagious smallpox.

In the Golden Temple, Schneider received the signal and passed it on. Shivaji was in action. The three stages of the plan would proceed automatically.

First, the slimmer of Karnail Singh's men put a raw, skinned onion in his own armpit and kept it there throughout the day. Whether or not this ancient method of inducing fever really worked is difficult to say. But the man not only began to think he had fever, he actually developed a rising temperature.

Meanwhile, Karnail Singh and his assistant cut out a man-size jigsaw piece in a quilt and sewed the edges. With another quilt over it, Balbir was less likely to be noticed. There would only be a gentle undulation beside the patient on the stretcher. The stretcher would be the string-bed. It was broad enough to accommodate two persons. And the justification was simple: every object belonging to the victim of the disease was bound to be a source of contagion and therefore it was best to carry him out on the bed. In any case it was quite a common practice to use the light string-beds as stretchers.

Karnail Singh and his colleague would carry the patient out. They had already risked contamination; they too needed to go to a clinic for vaccination. They would stand by their friend through thick and thin. They would all give themselves up and face prison sentences together.

For Schneider the launching of Shivaji signalled reprieve. He could leave the premises and check into the best hotel in the city. There, in comfort, he would listen without let for three days awaiting just one word that would indicate a sudden cancellation of Shivaji. That word was Aurangzeb. In the event of his receiving such a message, he was to go back to the Golden Temple and halt the process. Meanwhile he could drink, have a hot bath in a tub, eat the western meals that he was longing for and generally luxuriate.

In the area occupied by the smugglers and other denizens of the associated underworld, the patient began to perspire, shiver and rage with fever. By dint of furious scrubbing at his stomach he developed a red rash. And with the help of a quantity of water and a surreptitious finger down his throat, he began to vomit a yellowish liquid.

Those who felt his forehead were sure he had at least a little temperature.

By now the man was well-swaddled under the two quilts. Not only was he perspiring but he kept shivering with the cold he professed to feel. People offered what help they could. Someone produced a thermometer, another lent a bottle of balm, a third brought out a cough syrup and a fourth rubbed the patient's feet with a linament for sprains. In the result, the room began to reek of medicine and its corollary, illness.

Karnail Singh put it about that he suspected the worst. The man had confessed to having eaten some delectable sweetmeats despite having found the torn packet near a gutter. Indeed rats and other vermin had scampered away when he had bent to pick it up.

'A cockroach or two I can understand,' Karnail Singh had

muttered to the persons who had gathered round, 'but rats and flies, ugh!'

On the second day, the man was delirious. Karnail informed Amar, Balbir's guards and Balbir sadly that the symptoms were clearly those of smallpox.

Amar came to have a look. But he stood at a distance. There was no need to caution him. He knew how awful the consequences of contact could be.

Karnail eased down the quilt and bared the patient's belly. It was splotched and red. A murmur of horror rippled through the observers. Just then the patient moaned, made a distasteful noise and with a weak attempt at avoiding the bedclothes retched up a thin trickle. His throat was already sore with his earlier efforts and now he was quite adept at using it to bring up whatever possible.

'Poor fellow,' Karnail Singh mumbled. 'I hope he doesn't die before we can get him to hospital. Better that than—'

'Yes, yes,' agreed Amar Singh. 'But we have a doctor. Actually I think he's only a medical student. I don't know. Anyway, let him take a look.'

Karnail's heart sank. Someone was sent to fetch the doctor.

Karnail's eyes misted with tears of anxiety—and these were easily come by—as he turned to Amar. 'But it's not just a doctor he needs, he needs injections, medicines, a glucose drip, proper nursing. We could have a doctor brought in from outside but that's not enough. He's got to be isolated from the rest otherwise everyone here will catch it and die like flies.'

The gathered listeners broke apart visibly.

Amar Singh said, 'I'll send the doctor myself. I must inform Santji. It could be serious.'

Sometimes a person has what people commonly term a 'brainwave'—an idea that seems to strike like lightning out of the blue. Karnail Singh had one just then.

As soon as Amar turned on his heel, Karnail casually asked his colleague to prepare some tea on the little primus stove. Then he requested everyone to move out of the room to give the patient some peace and also to protect them from contagion. He pulled the door to.

Taking out the thermometer lent by a good samaritan, Karnail dipped it briefly in the warming water on the stove. Screwing up his eyes he read the temperature. 105°. Perfect. He wiped the water off the instrument and placed it on the stool beside the patient's bed.

They were just having tea when the doctor, who might have been an ex-medical student, a compounder or a quack, knocked. He was an old-looking young man with flecks of white in his beard and spectacles on his thin hook nose. He was carrying a medical kit but it was soon apparent that he was prepared only for rendering first aid and rudimentary surgical assistance to those injured in violence.

Karnail Singh's first question was, 'Doctor, have you any medicines for smallpox?'

'Smallpox?' The voice was thin and querulous. 'The correct medical term is variola. You know something about it?'

'Aye. I've seen it before. My younger sister died of it. We weren't allowed to touch her after it was diagnosed.' He then told the doctor about the sweetmeats and the rats.

'Fever?' The doctor was examining the patient from a distance.

'It goes up and down,' admitted Karnail. 'He's delirious now. Risky to shove a thermometer into him. He's broken one—'

'Don't put it in his mouth,' said the doctor. 'Under his arm. Anyone knows that.'

'We did,' said Karnail. 'He broke it when he twisted to vomit. Then an hour ago we got another thermometer and held him still long enough to take his temperature. It was . . .' he picked up the instrument and squinted at it, '. . . 105°.'

'105!' The doctor studied it worriedly, without touching it. 'But he has no rash.'

'On his stomach. It's there. Look, there it is.'

Despite Karnail's enthusiastic diagnosis, the doctor had one objection. 'He should have it on his face,' he insisted.

'And he does!' exclaimed Karnail triumphantly, 'I've checked under his beard. 'It's spreading. By tomorrow you'll see red spots all over his forehead and hands. Tomorrow is the third day. That happens on the third day.'

'Yes, you're right,' agreed the doctor. 'The rash really breaks out on the third day. I think we should isolate the patient immediately. There's danger in even handling articles touched by him. The germs can be breathed in too, so people should stay well away.'

Ten minutes later, things were moving so well that Karnail had to slow the pace a bit. Everyone was inclined to pack them off at once. But stage three of Shivaji was scheduled for the morning of the third day.

Karnail held out determinedly against the tide that sought to shove them out. He pleaded for one more night in which to nurse his friend back to health by dint of sheer affection.

That night they had the room to themselves. No one came near them. The portion of terrace directly outside the room was untenanted. People preferred to stay at the farther ends and talk in whispers. The dread of smallpox overrode even the news of fresh killings outside.

By the morning, the room was smelling of the man's faeces too for he had refrained from going to the communal toilet and instead had peed and shat in a bucket. It all added to the odour of disease.

Now Karnail wielded the lipstick and created a sprinkle of awful pink-red pustules on the victim's hands and face.

Stage three. The crucial stage. The last phase of the plan. 10.30 a.m. The period when Balbir was kept locked in his room with two armed guards inside. The door was bolted from the outside so even if the men dozed, Balbir could not get out.

They were passing Balbir's door when the patient moaned and sighed weakly for the stretcher bearers to stop. They put the bed down. Groups of people were watching them. Amar was standing there too, looking rather distressed.

Karnail bent his ear close to the patient's mouth and nodded as he understood what the poor fellow was trying to say.

Straightening up and sighing as he shook his head with regret, Karnail went to Amar and informed him that the patient was sure he was dying. If he did die he didn't want the curses of Balbir to accompany him into the other world. He wanted to ask Balbir's forgiveness for the doublecross they had all done. Whether Balbir forgave him or not, he would die at peace knowing that he had cleared his conscience by showing his repentance.

Amar frowned and murmured, 'Poor man. Do you think he will . . .?'

'I'm afraid so,' said Karnail solemnly. 'There's not much chance of his surviving unless the hospital works a miracle.'

'All right,' nodded Amar taking the key of the padlock from one of the guards on the terrace. 'We'll bring Balbir out.'

'No, no,' said Karnail quickly. 'That would defeat the purpose. Balbir must not come to him. He must go to Balbir.'

'Very well,' said Amar. 'Come with me.'

He unlocked the door and told the guards inside what was happening. Then he stepped back, well away from the path of the stretcher-bearers, retreating carefully to where the others stood on the terrace at a safe distance. It was fortunate for him that he did so. Karnail had reckoned that he would come in too to watch. But, naturally, his fear of the disease was greater than his curiosity.

Karnail suffered a moment of trepidation as he and his partner carried the bed towards the door. Would it go through or not? Of course he had, on an earlier occasion, measured the width of the doorway roughly by the simple expedient of yawning and stretching his arms wide against it.

He had done the same with the stairways and passages they would later have to negotiate. He had spent a couple of hours one morning carefully yawning all over the place. If all went well, he would laugh about it. But now every moment was a test of the attention they had paid to detail.

It went through!

He put down his end of the bed and turned and pulled the door shut.

In the room there were two guards but their eyes were rivetted on the poor patient who was moaning and gasping, crying out horrendously about the sins he had committed and the double-crossing of Balbir to which he had been a party.

Balbir was sitting cross-legged on his own bed, staring stonily ahead.

Karnail exchanged a glance with his help-mate. Their thoughts were the same. There were only two guards in the room. It was four against two. But the two were armed and could call on reinforcements with one shot or shout. It had all been planned up to this moment. Now the choice of action was Karnail's.

They could use their *kirpans* to kill silently, unexpectedly. The daggers had been honed for this. Even the patient had one ready to hand under the covers.

Or they could use the chloroform to snuff them into sleep. The chloroform might take a fraction longer to be effective. There would be a struggle. But there would be no blood.

With the dagger you could strike from any angle but a chloroform pad necessitated getting behind the quarry for a proper clamping over the mouth and nose.

It didn't seem possible that they could get behind the two guards simultaneously. They were standing on either side of the room, looking rather cramped. It was not a large room.

Karnail thought how ridiculous it was that he and his colleague couldn't use the sten guns hanging from their shoulders to blast out.

He positioned himself near one of the guards. His colleague was ready by the other, the one Balbir had once sneeringly described to them as Curd-face.

Karnail reached for the hilt of his *kirpan*.

'No, no, no!' Balbir shuddered. And began to tremble where he sat. 'No more violence. Please. Please! I can't take it. Please.'

Karnail froze. The guards were perplexed. Balbir's response was at variance with the entreaties of the dying man.

Balbir had shut his eyes tight and was shaking like a leaf.

Karnail looked at his men. They were wondering too. Balbir seemed to have snapped under the strain.

Balbir was saying. 'Let me be. I don't want to go anywhere.'

Curd-face spoke for the first time, with a short laugh, 'You're not going anywhere.'

'That's right,' said Karnail. He pointed at the patient. 'It's he who's going to hospital. Not you.'

'No, no,' Balbir shook his head, his eyes still shut tight. 'Let me be.'

The patient was astounded too. He began to sit up. In doing so, he grasped the arm of the person standing nearest him. It was Curd-face.

The guard drew back in horror. 'He touched me!' he gasped, the muscles of his jaw working. His mouth shut firmly in the set scowl he always wore. At the same time, he raised his carbine slightly. It seemed likely he would riddle the patient with an angry burst. Then he looked jerkily about the room like a bewildered bull, caught the eye of the other guard, snorted, 'I'm going to wash myself . . . with disinfectant!' and stomped out of the room.

Karnail Singh again pulled the door to. And smiled. This goddess of smallpox was working overtime!

Outside, Curd-face could be heard snarling sullenly as he walked away, 'The mother fucker touched me. I'll kill him if I fall ill.'

Karnail could visualize the small crowd at the far end of the terrace parting quickly to let him through.

But his own concern now was to get as close as possible to the remaining guard. The other man was sidling towards him too. Balbir was of no use. He seemed to be succumbing to the pressures he had been under just at the moment when he should have been most alert. That often happens; a climber feels the greatest weariness just as he nears the summit, as though the mountain were overwhelming him from within.

Was Balbir displaying nervousness? Fear? The will to fail?

'They're right, they must be right,' Balbir was saying, his eyes open now but staring into the middle distance. 'Amar must have reason to be so determined, so motivated. There must be logic beneath the emotion.' His eyes travelled to the books in the corner. He dug the phrases out of his mind slowly like a man sifting for gold. 'It can't just be the lust for power—'

'Balbir,' interrupted Karnail gently, 'we can think this out later.'

'Later? But it's urgent. They killed nearly eighty people last week. It can't just be for medieval ideas. Punjab is one of the most progressive states. The sikhs are a progressive community—'

'I'm a sikh too,' said Karnail. 'There are only about two thousand extremists. But there are fourteen million sikhs. You've been brainwashed.'

The guard straightened up. He sensed that something odd was going on. It was Karnail Singh's rejoinder that sounded an inner alarm. That other smuggler fellow was also too close for comfort. And the damned patient was beginning to rise from his sick-bed.

Karnail gestured to the patient to stay where he was. Then he called across to the other gunrunner. 'I think you'd better take out the medicine pad. Sprinkle some of that stuff on it. We may need to use it on him. Never thought it would be like this. We could be in real trouble if he doesn't cooperate.'

'What are you talking about?' asked the guard with a suspicious glower.

'The patient,' Karnail assured him. 'He should be . . .' He shrugged and glanced at the others. 'He should be prepared to lie down in bed. But now I see that he may not. He may be delirious. So we've got a pad of cooling medicine to apply to his forehead. I never expected that we'd have to use it this way.' He looked at his assistant. 'You understand?'

'Of course.' The man nodded and took out a pad of cloth and a small bottle. As he pulled out the stopper, a sickly sweet smell began to pervade the room.

'He doesn't look delirious,' said the guard testily.

'He could become delirious,' insisted Karnail. He dreaded the possibility that, any moment now, Curd-face might return.

Karnail had practised his movements for just this moment.

His knee rising up caught the guard in the crotch, his left hand struck away the sten gun and his right thrust up at the heart with the short-bladed *kirpan*. He twisted the hilt and the blade broke inside.

It was not the guard who yelled but Balbir.

The other gunrunner leapt at Balbir and grabbed him back by the hair and tried to smother him with the chloroformed pad. But it was the patient who succeeded in knocking the breath out of him with a blow to the stomach. As he inhaled deep, the chloroform took effect.

They stuck him in the bed, threw the quilts over him pushing his body down so that it curled smaller like a babe in the womb and the patient climbed in, lying down in position. Over the covers, they scattered the few other belongings of the patient. Balbir was invisible.

Karnail washed his hands quickly in the pot of drinking water while the other man carefully hefted the guard's corpse onto Balbir's string-bed. It looked like someone sleeping face down. But the blood was dripping onto the floor.

Karnail opened the door slowly. No one was close enough to look in. With a start he realized that even Curd-face was standing on the terrace. He hadn't wanted to come in again.

But that meant Curd-face might go in at once as soon as they brought the bed out. They wouldn't stand a chance.

'*Wahe Guru!*' muttered Karnail and uttered a quick prayer.

They picked up the bed and carried the patient out. At the end of the terrace, the spectators murmured.

Curd-face began to move reluctantly in their direction. Amar Singh was not there.

Karnail put the bed down, turned and shut the door. He pulled the bolt across and taking the padlock from its loop inserted it so that the bolt was in place. But it didn't have the key.

Curd-face was about ten feet away. He stopped and cursed. 'You shouldn't have done that. You've been handling the patient. You're putting smallpox germs on the lock and bolt. Now we'll have to clean those with phenyl.'

'Sorry, I forgot.'

'What was that shout?'

'What shout?'

'Sounded like Balbir.'

'Ah yes, that . . .'

'Did he agree?'

'To what?' Karnail almost collapsed.

'To forgive him.'

'That's what the shout was about. He couldn't bear to but he did.'

'Good. Dying is not as easy as living.'

'No.'

'Now if this fellow dies he'll go with a clear conscience.'

'Right.'

'Oy!' Curd-face beckoned to a child who was standing by the wall picking snot from his nose. 'Go and call the sweeper, that *Mazhabi* fellow, and tell him to bring a bottle of phenyl.' He turned to Karnail. 'Only one *Mazhabi* in our lot. They don't join. Most of them are pro-Congress.'

Karnail picked up his end of the bed.

Something seemed to be bothering Curd-face. He was more loquacious than he had ever been. 'By the way,' he mumbled. 'Amar asked me to slip out this evening and get vaccinated. Would that help?'

'Oh definitely.'

Curd-face was relieved. He said apologetically as though it was impolite of him not to see them off to the exit, 'I'll stay here and see that no one touches this till it's cleaned.'

At the end of the terrace the onlookers scattered as they approached.

Going down the passage, the patient muttered, 'Karnail, you forgot to beep.'

'What?'

'The beeper. You were supposed to let them know. They must be worried sick. We're half an hour late.'

'Damn!'

Just then two old Nihangs began to ascend the steps. They gave off a terribly horsey smell.

Karnail cautioned them. 'Smallpox case here. Give us room.'

The first Nihang grunted and retreated taking his companion with him. When the bed passed them the Nihangs instead of going up as they had intended, turned and followed.

Karnail and his companions didn't have much time to wonder. They had just set the bed down briefly and Karnail had reached into his pocket and pressed the beeper when someone called out, 'Hey you! Just a minute.' It was Amar Singh.

He approached to within a couple of yards.

'I'd take you out through one of the tunnels but we can't risk your spreading the illness in the houses. We've taken over quite a number now. For tactical reasons. But what I came to say was, you can't go out carrying those sten guns.'

'They're ours.'

'Of course. But the police will take them from you. They're bound to arrest you as soon as you step out of our territory. You'd better leave them behind. We'll pay Tarsem for them.'

'These are contaminated.'

The two Nihangs were hovering near Amar Singh. The taller one was stroking his beard and had his left hand resting on the hilt of his sword. Both of them were decked with baubles and quaint insignia.

Amar glanced at them and ignored them. Some pilgrims going to the shrine stopped and enquired what was wrong with the man in bed.

'Smallpox,' grimaced one of the Nihangs.

'You'd better leave the guns there,' continued Amar. 'We'll have them disinfected.'

Karnail shrugged and unstrapped his gun. His companion followed suit.

'Where's his gun?' Amar indicated the patient.

'He didn't have one. Came in with a revolver.'

'Where's that?'

Karnail wasn't going to start searching in the bedclothes.

'He sold it to one of the gang who came to visit.'

'Right.'

They propped their guns against the wall of the Parikrama. It was a splendid morning despite the heat. The dome of the Golden Temple shone brilliant in the sun. The pool of nectar reflected the surrounding architecture with not a shimmer of wind. Some armed men were sitting by the tree known as Budda Baba Ber.

Karnail was about to pick up the bed and move on when he saw that Amar was staring in amazement at the patient's face.

'His . . . his spots are like smudges. They're leaving stains on the pillow.' He was moving closer.

Suddenly the tall Nihang pulled him back effortlessly. 'That's when it's dangerous,' he said. In the same instant, somehow with just a swish like a gust of air, the sword was unscabbarded and in his hand and the tip of the blade had flicked the quilt over the patient's face.

'Take him away,' said the old fellow to the stretcher-bearers.

Amar Singh was shocked by the Nihang's presumption in pulling him back.

'I mean,' said the old Nihang with an ambiguous chuckle, 'it's dangerous to go near a patient when he's at that stage. It's when the pustules break and spread, and the blood smears the clothes, that anything could happen. You could be killed with a breath. It's the most contagious stage. It's absolute death.'

'But it looked like—'

The old Nihang held him firmly with an arm draped over his shoulder. The sword was in his right hand. The other Nihang had come round now and was standing in front, looking mournfully at Amar and nodding.

'Yes,' sighed the second Nihang. 'I've seen men drop like threshed wheat. In my time we called it the plague. That's when you have a lot of people die. But now you've stopped it. Good thing you sent the bed and everything out. Let the hospital handle that.'

Amar Singh was pouting and frowning uncertainly. The bed and its attendants had climbed up and out of the main exit.

'Aye,' said the tall Nihang. 'Some things are better sent out than kept.'

Amar freed himself, a little rudely, without a word. He ran to the exit.

The bed was being carried down the lane. Armed youths were patrolling as usual. Some were looking down from fortifications.

In front, by the verandah of a shop, two horses were tethered. These obviously belonged to the cranky old Nihangs.

The two old fellows came past him now and went to the horses. The taller fellow was clearly the older of the two. He had difficulty mounting. Even from the plinth of the shop. But he managed. With help.

They wheeled on their horses and went down the lane, blocking the patient and his companions from view.

19

◆◆◆

An Old Man's Old Ways

Life does not settle easily around one incident. It spreads like a fungus in many directions.

Balbir was out but he had left part of himself in the Golden Temple.

Karnail had helped in the escape and shown that he had played a double game with Tarsem.

Tarsem, thwarted in his ambition and realizing that he had been duped all round, did not flee. Where could he go? Though he had the whole world before him and had engineered the flight of others to distant places, he had no desire to leave. This was his village. This was where he wanted to be big. His ambition centred on this place. It was his home as much as it was that of Lok Raj and his family. Tarsem stayed. He would dig in and fight for supremacy. He would yet be more powerful than Satyavan. And he would revenge himself on Karnail.

But there was not much time for all that. That he did not know.

Nor did the extremists know as they exchanged fire from the Golden Temple fortifications with the security forces ringing the complex that soon the army would be called in to flush them out. They were secure in their stronghold, almost certain that, by the rules and tradition, their sanctuary was above direct physical assault. So they fired down upon a unit of the Border Security Force, exulting that they had killed three persons outside and injured nine but unconcerned that the return of fire had killed seven inside and injured sixteen. The terrorists were nearly all holed up in one nest. As Lok Raj might have put it: their strength was their weakness. They were vulnerable to being wiped out in one swoop.

Balbir said: 'I am going to become a sikh.'

'Very well,' smiled Lok Raj rubbing a hand over his face which had just been shaved by the barber. 'You keep your beard and knot your hair. You're still my grandson.'

'What's the catch?'

As Balbir asked that, even Raskaan and Satyavan looked quickly at the old man echoing the same thought.

'No catch,' chuckled the patriarch. 'Why should there be a catch?'

'There always is with you,' muttered Balbir so woefully that everyone laughed.

'Look here, Balbir, what you believe is your own business. How you act is mine.'

'What does that mean?'

'It means that you can be a communist, a buddhist, a christian, a sikh—it doesn't bother me. You can even become a puja-doing brahmin priest, it wouldn't irritate me too much. But, whatever you are, you can't behave in a way that may disgrace the family. I won't have you being a petty crook or a petty gunrunner.'

'What about being a big crook and big gunrunner?' Balbir cast a loaded glance at Satyavan.

To his surprise, the old man answered, 'Aye, it's all a matter of size. And heart. No one says to the elephant, don't take this path. But they brush ants aside.'

'I don't understand, Babaji.'

'Is there time for me to explain?' Lok Raj asked Satyavan.

'Yes, Babaji,' he replied. 'Karnail will come up and let us know when the guns have been distributed. He's noting down the names and calibres.'

'How many have you given him?'

'Only fifty. Should be enough.'

'Aye.'

'What's going on?' Balbir asked in bewilderment.

'Oh just some villagers going out with your father and your uncle to see to some work in Jagtara.'

'But why the guns?'

'They won't use them. But these are troubled times. There's a lot of turbulence around. It's better to be safe. Now then, you were asking how you should behave.' He paused as he placed the cockaded turban on his head. 'Big. Big-hearted. If you're a sikh, be a big-hearted sikh, not a sneaky little fellow going around shooting innocent people in their moral bum. We're Muhiyals. We don't disgrace what we do, we elevate it. That's all.' He turned to go downstairs, then added. 'Oh, by the way, my friend Charan Singh came to see me the other day. He came to say that he's found a very fine bride for you in Delhi.'

'Bride? For me? But I—!'

'Yes, she's pretty and smart and . . . Raskaan is the specialist in that department. He's approved her on your behalf.'

'What? Babaji, you people can't just—'

'He's got her photograph to show you. Go on, Raskaan. Relieve him of the suspense.'

'No!' Balbir stood up and stamped his foot. 'No, I tell you. You can't ride all over me as you please. Not any more. I won't be—'

'But there was one hitch. I had to tell Charan Singh that you were likely to be unavailable because you were busy being hostage in a bit of gang rivalry. Your brother Satyavan was being blackmailed to distraction. We were all struggling to save your silly piddling life. And you know Charan Singh was most disappointed that you might miss your own marriage. He was sorry you were not here. He said, why don't we go and get him? And I said that we were trying. So he stayed back to help. You know Charan Singh has done a lot in his lifetime. He's seen many things. He's only a few years younger than me. But we had neither of us ever been Nihangs.' He began to laugh. 'I was going to take Khushi Ram but he's never been able to overcome that painful leg of his. It slows him down. We might have needed to move fast. So I said to Charan Singh, let us—you and I—be the Nihangs.'

'Nihangs?'

'Aye,' said the old man laughing. 'Only Satyavan and Raskaan knew. Even Karnail was surprised. That look in his eye when he caught on!'

'I don't know what you're talking about,' Balbir frowned in perplexity.

'Sure. How could you know? You were under chloroform. Never mind. Just don't disappoint old Charan Singh. You owe him your life.'

'I don't owe anybody anything!'

Satyavan and Raskaan were aghast at Balbir's effrontery and made as though to rebuke him. But the old man chuckled.

'That's the spirit! That's what I like about you. You're quite right too. You could spend your life being a bonded slave to other people. Like to your mother and father who gave you birth.'

'Yes!' said Balbir vehemently.

'You see I understand how you feel. You feel it so strongly that even now, rather than being happy to be back with—'

'Babaji,' Balbir gritted, 'all I ever wanted was to get away for a while, to stand on my own feet, to find out about things for myself, to—'

'Balbir,' the patriarch soothed him gently like a man petting an excited animal, 'we're going to send you abroad.'

'Abroad?'

'Yes. On your honeymoon.'

'On my—? No!'

'Very well. We won't.'

'You won't?' The wind went out of Balbir's sails. He was like a toy in the old man's hands being pushed along with a touch, a nudge, a block. But always without being cornered so that he had a way to go.

'Not if you don't agree to marry the girl Charan Singh has found with so much care. Then we'll just have to settle for Kundan Mal's proposal.'

'Kundan Mal's proposal?'

'Aye. His daughter Kulwanti swears you've won her heart.'

'That's nonsense.'

'Are you sure?'

Raskaan, subdued as he was before the patriarch couldn't resist a crack. 'He means, it's not her heart he won.'

'Easy, easy,' smiled Lok Raj. 'You cannot trifle with a man who knows his daughter has a good match. He's a very wily shopkeeper.'

Balbir went pale. His head spun. He sat down. A vision of Kundan Mal the wily shopkeeper sprang up before his eyes: a short, rotund man with a *paan*-stained mouth, a *tikka* like a vertical streak of menstrual blood on his forehead, a gold chain about his neck, a silk *kurta* on his back, a black *topi* on his head and a *dhoti* between his legs—merchant, money-lender, Kulwanti's father. And Kulwanti—grasping, grabbing lustfully without love, giggling without humour.

He knew he was tamed for the moment. Broken in. He could think of nothing to say. He wanted to get away. And he was being extricated and sent away. He remained silent.

'You have my blessings,' said the old man. 'As for Kundan Mal, there are a couple of places in the bazaar that he's always wanted to rent from me. He wants to expand into Chamkalan. I think he'll be pleased with a counter-proposal I have to make.'

Karnail Singh appeared in the doorway and said, 'Babaji, it's getting dark outside.'

'Good. Have the men gone?'

'Long ago.'

'Have you explained to them where I shall be?'

Karnail nodded.

The old man opened a cupboard, took out a tough khaki canvas holster with a light .38 Enfield in it. He loaded all six chambers, weighed its 750 grams in his hand then strapped the holster on his right hip and put the revolver in so that its butt faced forward. He reached across with his left hand once and drew the weapon and put it back. Then from the cupboard he took a sword and slung it on his left side. He made a quick movement with his right hand without looking down and the sword was out. He sheathed it as quickly, with a flick of the wrist. The action was as unselfconscious as that of an experienced driver shifting gears in a car.

Satyavan and Raskaan had stood up.

Karnail said, 'I'll come with you.'

'No, none of you.'

'We'll just see you off,' mumbled Satyavan.

'As you wish.'

The old man searched in the cupboard and took out a long electric torch. He turned to Raskaan and Satyavan. 'Well, I must admit one of your presents will be useful to me.'

He checked the battery cells.

Balbir asked worriedly, 'Where're you going?'

'Out.'

'But where to? You can't be driven around at night. There's a curfew on, you know.'

'I'm going riding.'

'With your eyes, at your age!'

'It's a good age to go anywhere, son. And my eyes see better in the moonlight. It's the sunlight that bothers the cataract in one eye.'

Balbir shook his head in exasperation. And found himself speaking with the impertinence of his father. 'You're a crazy old man.'

'With a crazy grandson,' said Lok Raj, and winked.

For some reason Balbir's eyes filled with tears as he watched the old man preparing to leave. But Balbir remained sitting as he watched. Some months ago he might have stood up out of habit and traditional respect. Now he understood why his own father

Khushi Ram treated the old man so familiarly. He had seen the patriarch in action, he had seen him in his prime in his element, he had seen him close. He knew him not only as his father but as a loyal friend.

But with all that, the old man could be a bastard, twisting you, moulding you, punishing you.

Raskaan and Satyavan went down with Karnail Singh to the stable to see the old man off.

When they came back, Balbir said, 'At least he took the torch. He'll need it on the road.'

'That's not an ordinary torch,' said Raskaan. 'It's a stun-light. If you shine it at someone in the dark, it blinds for a few seconds.'

Balbir turned to Satyavan and scolded him, 'Elder brother, how could you let him go out alone like that? He might hurt himself!'

'You can't stop him,' complained Satyavan. 'He'd rather die doing the things he wants to do. If you try to retire him, he rebels. He's impossible! And, you know, he's sent his own sons out ahead of him to Jagtara. My father went on his old nag and your father's gone on the pony which Babaji got him from Phillaur and the villagers all walked. Now he's trotted off to join them.'

Raskaan laughed softly. 'You sound like you want to be there yourself.'

'Of course,' Satyavan admitted. 'It's my battle he's fighting. I should be sorting out matters with Tarsem.'

'Tarsem?' Balbir looked up from studying his hands and the thoughts of marriage that were distracting him. He said, 'But Tarsem is my affair. I was the one who fell in with him. He tricked me!'

'Forget it,' Raskaan sighed. 'The old man has made it his problem. He says it's gone beyond business rivalry and touched his family responsibility.' He grinned, 'Personally I think he's off his head. But he's got a point. The police can't do much with an old man of eighty-four. By the time the case drags to a hearing in court, he'll probably have passed on anyway. He might as well go, as he says, with his cockade high.'

Satyavan's gurgle joined in his laughter. Balbir played with his beard and thought, I've been born into a crazy, crazy family.

The village that Tarsem loved and wished to conquer with power and popularity seemed to have risen against him. The mob out there seemed a thousand strong. He wondered where the police was. One man or two, or even a gang, he could handle. But a thousand villagers, and some of them were probably armed. He couldn't even shoot at them. His two bodyguards and Hazara were with him. But what could four do against the village? They'd massacre him, burn his place down and roast him along with his men. No, he had to get out. There was no point phoning the rest of the gang and the truckers who worked for him; they'd never get here in time.

He thought of his wife and children. And he cursed. Goddamit, she was right, he should never have let things come to this pass. Now she must be listening from the house to all this yelling outside the *chabara*, and she must be shaking with fear and crying.

He had turned the lights off in the room and now peered down quickly. It seemed everyone was out there in the street yelling for his blood. Those fellows who had sold their land and belongings to go abroad but been turned back from Heathrow, they were there hoping for revenge. They wouldn't have dared individually or even together but now with such a crowd. . .

He thought of sending Hazara down to explain that it hadn't been his fault. That Heathrow affair had to do with Banta Singh. But Banta had gone underground and then vanished.

There were others down there shouting about other things— blackmarket cement and God knows what! But, of course, it was clear: this was all the doing of that Satyavan, perhaps even of Lok Raj. They had roused the mob, raised it, sent it to do their dirty work. Well, they had another think coming.

Luckily he had taken to locking the big corrugated iron doors that led into the courtyard. He could hear them banging and cursing and shouting to be let in. Did they think he was stupid?

His own men were looking rueful.

Someone shouted up, 'We only want Tarsem the racketeer! Let us in. We have no quarrel with anyone else!'

Bastards! Most of the villagers seemed to be carrying sticks and bamboo staves. He could hear the sound they made on the street. What the hell did they think they could do against four armed men? In the last resort they might have to use guns to defend themselves. His old double-barrel was in his hands. He'd never thought he'd have to use it. His bodyguards had sten guns which they'd taken out of the discreet bags he preferred them to use. Hazara had that knife strapped to his leg and the revolver under his shawl. But what the hell! What could they do against a village? They'd be lynched if they shot anyone.

But maybe a few shots in the air to scare them.

He nodded to one of his bodyguards, 'Fire a burst into the sky.'

The man did. The stutter of the sten was answered by a fusilade of shots that thundered, whined and splattered against the brickwork. A few bullets whizzed in through the window. There was a yell. One of his bodyguards was hit in the shoulder, probably by the ricochet of a slug.

'They're armed!' hissed Hazara in astonishment.

'That settles it,' muttered Tarsem. 'You fellows stay here. They won't harm you. They're looking for me. I'll use the ladder and go over the courtyard wall into the fields. Ten minutes from now, you can let them in.'

But Hazara and the bodyguards wouldn't stay behind. They were not disciplined to implicit obedience. They refused to be left to the mercy of a mob.

'We'll come with you,' insisted Hazara.

There was no point arguing. The mob was battering and levering the corrugated iron doors of the courtyard.

He said, 'All right. We'll go over the wall one by one.'

The injured bodyguard was clutching his shoulder. 'There's no shelter out there,' he grumbled. 'We'll be seen in the moonlight. The crops have been harvested. It's all flat and treeless at the back.'

Tarsem said, 'Two hundred yards away is the field of a Jat called Sohan Singh. His brothers have quarrelled with him and are disputing his claim to the crop. So the sugarcane is still standing. We'll separate and make for that clump. In any case, it's not likely that Sohan Singh will be out in the fields at this time. Everyone is on the street. We'll be safe.'

He went over the wall, throwing his gun into a patch of dry grass, then lowered himself and dropped with a thud. Practised wrestler that he was, he rolled over on his shoulder to absorb the impact. The ground was hard. The earth had been baked all day by the sun and now exhaled its pent-up distress. A hot wind was building up and blowing straight at him. This was the first of the summer blasts that scald Punjab. It felt like a dragon's breath. And the dust was swirling up and engulfing him.

He picked up his gun, and without waiting, he began to run towards the large rectangle of standing sugarcane. He bent as low as he could while he moved. Behind him he could hear the thump of his companions' feet as they spread out and circled towards the field of Sohan Singh.

And then he heard a horse neigh shrilly. The sound seemed to come from the direction of the sugarcane. He tried to see but the dust was flailing at his vision. For a moment it cleared and, in the brilliant moonlight, he saw the three men on horseback moving calmly towards him, not hurrying, their cockades flapping in the wind, their turban ends wrapped across their faces. Only their eyes were visible but he didn't need to guess at their identity. He knew who they were.

He shouted in alarm. He heard his men hesitate and stop and scatter.

The hooves of the horses were adding to the dust and it was blowing towards him. Now they were breaking into a trot. All three were heading for him, converging on him. He couldn't turn and out-run them. He was too heavy anyway. He thought of falling flat on the earth but he didn't want to be trampled to death. He fell onto one knee and raised his gun. The wind whistled across the barrels.

Just then there was a blinding dazzle as though a thousand flash bulbs had exploded before his eyes. Automatically his finger tightened on the first of the two triggers on his gun. The gun started to roar. A horse started to gallop. It was the beginning without end.

He neither saw nor heard the sword.

20

A Time of Blooding and Becoming

The shot that Tarsem managed to fire missed Lok Raj but it killed the second horseman, Gyan Chand, the eldest son of the patriarch. In keeping with tradition there were thirteen days of mourning for Satyavan's late father. On the fourteenth day, Satyavan ceremonially wore the turban of his father and into its tail flap the gathered Muhiyal clansmen dropped currency notes signifying the paying of tribute to the new head of that house.

The police case arising out of the killing of Tarsem was complicated by the fact that he had fired first and mortally wounded one of the three gentlemen who had been out riding in the fields. Lok Raj did not deny that he had used his sword. But there were convolutions of argument involving pleas of self-defence and provocation. Legal brains went to work picking at the details. It was not possible to keep a man of Lok Raj's stature in jail without arousing the ire of the local population. He stayed out on bail, pending further investigation.

Amar Singh and his fellow terrorists were upset at the death of Tarsem only because it had suddenly deprived them of an important gunrunning source. But even as Satyavan proceeded to take his precautions, he heard from Inspector Dutt that the army had been called out to surround the Golden Temple. The Inspector hinted that the army would probably move in without too much delay.

On the same day that the army took up its positions, the presence of foreigners was prohibited in Punjab. Schneider and Wilhelm were flown back to Germany by a materially grateful Raskaan.

In the Golden Temple area, repeated appeals to the terrorists were made by army officers over the public address system. One hundred and twenty nine persons surrendered, many of whom were probably pilgrims and uninvolved worshippers. But there were more than two thousand terrorists still in the temple, armed with Light Machine Guns, sten guns, rifles, revolvers, grenades, anti-tank weapons, mortars, mines and explosives.

Under the overall command of Lieutenant General Sunderji and the tactical advice of Major General Dayal (incidentally, a sikh), the Division Commander Major General K.S. Brar (a shaven sikh Jat) prepared his troops for storming the temple with restrictions that must surely be unique in the world. Even if fired upon from within the sacred central shrine of the Golden Temple, they were not to return the fire. No damage must be inflicted on the main sanctum.

'I know,' said General Brar in his precise but dulcet manner of speech, 'this amounts to sending somebody into the boxing ring with one hand tied behind his back. But here, this will have to be done.'

Also the soldiers were to go in without their boots and other leather accoutrements since these would violate the sanctity of the environs.

At the same time the extremists were being led by an experienced general too. Shahbeg Singh had had a number of machine gun emplacements set up behind exhaust ducts and ventilators at floor level. Some of these were alongside the descending steps of the main entrance.

The result was that, soon after the army assault began, many soldiers were crippled in their feet by gunfire. Along the Parikrama, these floor level positions prevented the soldiers from crawling to the attack. Their only method was to dart behind pillars and hope to get past crossfire, some of which came from less than twenty feet away. It was a deadly undertaking.

But most terrible of all was the square of area in front of the Akal Takht which drew fire from all directions. 'It was,' as General Brar described it, 'a veritable hell hole.' The Akal Takht was tactically significant to the terrorists as it housed Bhindranwale and was the headquarters of their operations. The approach to it from the two frontal sides bristled like a porcupine with armament.

The army had been assigned two main tasks: to clear the Punjab of terrorists in order to provide security to the people, and to help stop smuggling and gunrunning across the Indo-Pak border.

The first of these tasks entailed taking the Golden Temple.

But the terrorists were very ably led; anticipating such an eventuality they had been preparing for many months. They had taken over and fortified a number of houses in the area surrounding and overlooking the entire complex.

The official report described this and the events that followed in precise military terms without flourish or exaggeration.

'Seventeen houses in the civilian residential areas had been selected by the terrorists at distances of 500 to 800 metres from the outer periphery of the temple complex and held by approximately ten men each. These look-out and early warning posts were veritable arsenals of Light Machine Guns and other automatic weapons with huge caches of ammunition. The posts had been given common communication equipment to be in instant touch with their command posts.

'At 1900 hours on June 5, the Army commenced preliminary operations to secure dominating buildings on the periphery of the area occupied by terrorists around the Golden Temple.

'From 2230 hours, Army units commenced moving to the Golden Temple precincts. This drew a very heavy volume of fire from the terrorists into the narrow streets at close range. A large number of tear gas shells were fired by the troops into the terrorist positions including the Akal Takht but these were not effective since all windows and doors had been heavily barricaded with bricks and mortar as well as sandbags. Despite casualties, the troops gradually closed in and commenced movement into the area around the Temple, after overcoming very heavy and organised resistance.

'Intensive fire had to be faced from the Akal Takht, which stood like a fortress, covering all avenues of approach with a deadly and concentrated volume of machine gun fire, causing heavy casualties.

'Starting from the basement upwards, gun placements had been planned out and sited at every level including the floor level, the window level, the roof ventilators, on to the first floor and the upper storeys. The terrorists had cut holes in the walls and the marble façade like a pillbox for the positioning of weapons.

'The terrorists from their outer line positions also reinforced the fire from the Akal Takht and made it a bastion of automatic weapons. Machine guns from Harminder Sahib (the main shrine located like an island in the tank) simultaneously raked the Parikrama (path around the sanctum sanctorum) and surrounding buildings from where the troops had forced back the terrorists. In spite of this the troops exercised great restraint and refrained from directing any fire at Harminder Sahib.'

Under these conditions and unable to get the soldiers through the furious gunfire raining down on the 'killing ground' in front of the Akal Takht, the army urgently requested Delhi around midnight for permission to use armoured firepower against Bhindranwale's headquarters.

In Delhi, Prime Minister Indira Gandhi must have devoted much worry and agitated thought to this request. It could have political consequences. The use of a tank's armament against any of the buildings in the complex would leave it seriously damaged. Four hours later, she granted permission.

'At about 0410 hours on June 6 some troops attempting to close in on the Akal Takht in an Armoured Personnel Carrier (APC) were fired at by anti-tank rockets from the Akal Takht.'

A tank then moved into position on the farther side and, approaching the Akal Takht, fired a shell that tore through the building, demolishing part of the structure.

'By the morning of June 6, the troops had effectively engaged all gun positions at the Akal Takht. After engagement with and silencing of some machine gun positions of the Akal Takht, the troops effected entry into the Akal Takht. Room-to-room engagement commenced. Some extremists were then observed rushing down towards the first and ground floors, where shortly thereafter an explosion took place and a fire started. The troops also heard an exchange of fire among the extremists themselves on the ground floor and in the basement.

'Some terrorists at this stage attempted to rush out of the Akal Takht to clear some areas held by the troops, but were beaten off. A group of ten terrorists surrendered with a white flag. Room-to-room fighting, however, continued in the Akal Takht till it was cleared by 1230 hours on June 6, except for resistance continuing from the ground floor and basements.

'The continued resistance from the ground floor and the basement of the Akal Takht was tackled during the night of June 6/7. When this resistance was finally overcome the troops commenced a thorough search of the ground floor and the basement. The bodies of Shri Bhindranwale and Amrik Singh were found among thirty-four bodies on the ground floor of the Akal Takht.

'Some terrorists remained active in the morning hours of June 7 using the surrounding buildings and number of tunnels in the area of the Golden Temple. It required a few days of careful search to winkle out the last of the terrorists who inflicted brutal casualties on troops.

'The terrorists also tortured in a most inhuman manner and brutally murdered two Junior Commissioned Officers whom they had captured. They strapped explosives on to the body of one of the Junior Commissioned Officers after having skinned him alive, and blew him up as he was thrown from the upper floor of the Akal Takht. On 8 June 1984 they hacked to death an unarmed army doctor who had entered a basement to treat some casualties.'

92 soldiers had died and nearly 300 had been injured. 554 terrorists had been killed, 121 wounded and 1592 persons had been apprehended.

Bhindranwale's body was identified among a pile of others. Shahbeg Singh too was dead.

In the village of Jagtara, the days and nights of sudden curfew were over.

Balbir never heard of Amar Singh again and was probably right in assuming that he was among those killed and cremated. Amar Singh was unlikely to have surrendered or been among those who fled.

More than ever, Balbir wanted to leave. He wanted to be free of Punjab and its blood-letting, bloodthirsty concerns. He wanted to be free, of course, of his family. And the only avenue he could see now was the one offered by it—marriage.

But in this at last he thought he would outwit the patriarch. Yes, he would marry the girl they had chosen for him; he was obliged to do so after all they had endured on his behalf. He would go abroad on his honeymoon. And there he would strike out for himself! He would ditch the girl in some luxury hotel, leaving her the return ticket. Or he would disappear from some European airport just before emplaning for India. He would leave the family in a fix from which it would never recover. He would be not just the black sheep but completely disavowed. He would be disinherited, discredited, damned. He would be free.

Autumn and spring are the seasons of marriage in India. His own marriage was set for December. In the second week of the same month, his sister Aadran was to be wed.

It was a long wait but he put a patient face on it. He became seemingly more amenable, more pliant, more prepared to live, die and marry at the will of the patriarch.

And in that time he gave some thought to the pattern of his own behaviour. He was, he realized, an 'emotional fellow-traveller.' For that he despised himself. It was surely a weakness to be that easily swayed by feeling. He liked it better when he thought of himself as a rebel of the heart.

But was it not heartless of him to think of deserting his bride-to-be? He excused that after much consideration. He was after all revolting against the whole system and, whatever she may turn out to be like, she was part of the system from which he was breaking away.

The wait was more eventful than he had anticipated. For India, as for him, it was to be a time of blooding and becoming.

On 31 October, even as the season of weddings approached, Indira Gandhi the Prime Minister, walking across the lawn from her residence to the annexe that housed her office, was gunned down by two sikhs of her trusted security guards. They were there to protect her against extremists. They were policemen. The had both been on leave in Punjab. They were both now extremists. Perhaps they had had friends or relatives who died in the attack on the Golden Temple. Perhaps they were indoctrinated, enticed, bribed, or suborned by interests beyond local political extremism. Perhaps it was just fanatical revenge. It was for the investigators to go into all that and come up with the answers.

The public only knew that a sikh officer whom she considered loyal had shot her with his revolver at the very moment that she was responding politely to his greeting. He had then stepped aside and the sikh constable near him had pumped an entire magazine of rounds into her prone body. Indira Gandhi was nineteen days short of her sixty-seventh birthday.

Both the assassins threw down their weapons and gave themselves up. They were taken to the guardroom on the premises. There, it is said, one of them tried to snatch a loaded sten gun from a guard and the other drew a dagger from inside his turban. In the spray of gunfire that followed, one of the killers was shot dead and the other was seriously wounded, though he survived to stand trial.

But the sense of outrage that surged through most of India was calamitous.

Anger, shock, disgust and distrust sizzled through the country like a charge of electricity.

The least of the occurrences was that in an access of disillusionment and revulsion, Balbir renounced his espousal of a beard and unshorn hair, though he retained his respect for the teachings of the gurus.

He just didn't want to be associated with the madness around him. But it seemed there was madness everywhere.

Hindu Jats and Gujjars swarmed into the outskirts of Delhi from surrounding areas and began butchering hapless sikhs, burning their vehicles and houses and looting. In the centre of the city, other hindus went on the rampage setting fire to sikh shops and property. Mobs attacked colonies in other parts of the capital, dragged out sikhs, beat them up, murdered them and then set the bodies aflame with the aid of kerosene or petrol. Almost always the mobs came from other areas and were strangers to those they attacked. Hindu neighbours stood by their sikh friends and many saved entire families even under threat to their own lives and property. The bonds of affection and kinship were as always stronger than the madness.

Many transport operators are sikhs. Neither they nor their vehicles were safe for the four days that the fury raged. Corpses were seen burning on roads and railway platforms. The shells of trucks, taxis, tempos, scooter-rickshaws and scooters dotted the streets. Clouds of black smoke rose from various parts of Delhi. There were accusations of police culpability.

The new Prime Minister, Rajiv Gandhi, the slain woman's son, appealed for peace and vowed to put down all communal violence firmly. The army was called out to restore law and order. Refugee camps were set up. A considerable amount of looted property was recovered and restored.

During those four days, havoc rode the railway tracks and the terror of mob violence reigned in other cities such as Kanpur, Lucknow and Allahabad. Groups of youths searched trains for sikhs to slaughter. Many survived only by dint of hasty barbering.

A number of sikh families fled temporarily to Punjab.

Punjab was silent and still. Perhaps stunned by the enormity of the violent reprisal. Perhaps held to peace by the stern hand of military administration.

But a day, no matter how hellish, passes in twenty four hours; so the four passed in their accustomed ninety-six. The sun rose and dropped, no bloodier for having seen so much crime. The birds sang as usual. The stars sparkled at night.

People fixed their eyes on the future and hoped.

Aadran was married with much fanfare.

Balbir's turn came too. The wedding was in Delhi since the bride was from there. Traditionally the bride's parents play host and foot the bill for all wedding expenses. There was feasting and dancing for many days. The wedding pandal glittered with lights and strings of marigold. The surrounding trees were lit with thousands of little blue and green electric lights. The bridegroom rode to his wedding, as tradition insisted, on a gaily caparisoned white charger, his head wreathed in a cockaded turban bedecked with a veil of flowers. The procession escorting the groom was led by men carrying hissing petromax lamps and a brass band playing lilting tunes. As the procession wended its way to the bride's house, the younger celebrants danced the *bhangra*, prancing about vigorously and rending the air with ululating whoops.

At the bride's house, before the huge *shamiana* as big as a circus tent, the elders of the two families met formally. The hereditary family poet of Balbir's clan read out a specially composed epithalamium.

It was like being in a fairyland. There was no bitter after taste of rioting here. Guests of all communities—hindu, sikh, muslim, christian—mingled exchanging compliments and pleasantries. But sometimes, despite the necessity for merriment, a few gathered round a topic and briefly discussed the searing events that had stained the year. The wounds would heal but would the scars? For a while then, even the most determined merrymaker would look glum and thoughtful.

Balbir's father crunched towards him, smiling for a change.

'Come,' he said, 'your grandfather wants a word with you before the nuptials begin.'

Lok Raj was seated on a sofa playing the magnificent landowner and powerful zamindar to the hilt. He was showing off for the sake of his grandson. The only concession to his normal, simple village ways and peasant style was the presence of his well-thumbed *hookah* which somehow trailed him everywhere. He took a deep gurgle of smoke, coughed a little, muttered '*Bismillah!*' to the consternation of a few puritan high society hindu ladies near him and then said, 'Balbir, be gentle with her, eh? I've just been talking to her. She can put you through the hoop. She's an MA in Political Philosophy. You can talk any of your nonsense to her and she'll straighten you out. But she hasn't lived the life you have. She doesn't know what ideas mean in terms of death and destruction. She only knows ideas as words. She's innocent, sensitive, vulnerable. I'm not so worried for you as for her.'

He could see that the girl had won the old man's heart. Balbir had only seen her photograph and now briefly he had seen her. She had dazzled him. She was more than pretty, she was enchanting. But, as was his wont, he had told himself that brides are not always as attractive as they are made up to be. She had an advantage now in all that jewellery and ornamentation and the build-up of ceremonial that accompanied their introduction. He would wait and see. Later.

All through the wedding ceremony as he sat by her in the *pandal*, he was aware of the smirks on the faces of Raskaan and Satyavan. Renate was here too, being secretary again. And he thought, it's really cowardly of Raskaan not to admit he's married to her, and if he isn't, it's about time he did. At least he could feel smug about one thing—he had taken the plunge.

He cast a glance at his bride. She was looking down at the fire and—damn!—she was crying. Something wrenched at his heart. Poor thing, being married to me, not knowing at all what I am like, risking her entire life and future at her family's beck. Pity. Maybe he should look a little more into all this about Women's Lib. But this was hardly the time to think of all that.

Anyway he wasn't really concerned. He was going to ditch her. Just to fix the family.

He felt his feet going cold under him though the sacred fire was roasting his face. Awful to think that he might hurt this helpless creature.

Two days later they were on a plane to Europe. Again she was, of course, sitting beside him. From now it would be all of course. He glanced at her again. She was not at all like Kulwanti or Gulnari. She was quite fine. Yes, quite fine.

He didn't even know what to call her. Of course he knew her name. But do you call your wife—wife!—by her name or some endearment? But endearments have to develop. It seemed that much might develop between them.

The thrill of going abroad was lost in the thrill of knowing her. Who is she, apart from being her parents' daughter? What is she like as a person?

His arm touched hers on the armrest. She withdrew hers quickly out of habit. Then was embarrassed that she did.

He chuckled. That was a family habit. They developed a sense of humour as their sense of responsibility increased. Odd but that's the way it was. He felt somehow on the threshold of a new maturity.

He looked over his shoulder, over the backrest, at the other passengers on the plane. It struck him that there was not another person on the plane with a turban on his head. He was still wearing his cockaded ceremonial one.

He smiled at her and sheepishly he began to take it off. The days of the turban were over.

'Keep it on,' she said softly. 'It looks nice on you.'

He shrugged in the old one-shoulder Kumhareya way and took the turban off anyway.

'I carry it in here,' he said tapping his heart, thinking of all that the turban signified to his grandfather. 'I carry everything here.'

He said it so seriously that she laughed. Not mockingly. Not even shyly. Just laughed.

And he laughed too. It was such a long time since he had really laughed.

And neither of them knew really what the joke was. But they seemed on the threshold of knowing.

Acknowledgements

More persons that I can name have helped me with constructive suggestions and encouragement in the researching for and writing of this book. Among them are: B.C. Dutt, Abdul Mulla, Pritam Singh Arshi, Vinod Advani, Vinod Sharma, P.K. Dave, my wife Susan, the typist Jane D'Cunha, Laura Cecil, the late Charlotte Wolfers, John Wolfers, Maggie Hanbury and Chris Holifield. An especial thanks to Mary Lutyens for permission to quote a phrase she used in conversation.

My debt to printed sources of information, eye-witnesses and those who were embroiled in the events that overtook Punjab in 1984 is too great for me to detail. I was also enabled to interview many people—high and low, combatants and observers, soldiers and civilians—during the course of making a documentary film in June 1984 in Amritsar. I am thankful to all those who opened their hearts to me.

P.S

LEFT OF NORTH

JAMES FRIEL

'His sense of dialogue and detail verges on the wicked . . . uniting kitchen sinker and satire, it's a mischievously compulsive read' – *Time Out*

This story begins in the North. It begins on the day that Denise Monton and her best friend, Deborah Ridley, had a fight up on the Rucks – and the Rucks opened up and swallowed Deborah whole. It ends – if ends it does – somewhere to the left of North.

For though it was Deborah who died and Denise who lived, Deborah's ghost would not be put to rest. Soon Denise believed that she had killed Deborah; and not long after, the rest of the town believed it as well. Ostracized and harassed, the Montons fled the slag heaps of Little Atherton for the tower blocks of Angel, Islington. And there things, as they will, went from pretty bad to truly awful. As Denise's mother said, philosophically, 'We're fated, cruelly fated. We're like the Kennedys or the Barlows off *Coronation Street*. Tragedy stalks us.' Except , of course, that neither the Kennedys nor the Barlows had Deborah Ridley's ghost stalking them as well.

LEFT OF NORTH

James Friel's brilliant brew of black humour and sharp-edged satire.

FUTURA PUBLICATIONS
FICTION
0 7088 3667 4

Futura

SQUARE DANCE

ALAN HINES

A beautifully written novel of the South in the tradition of *To Kill a Mockingbird* and *A Member of the Wedding*.

Set in rural Texas in the early 1950s, *Square Dance* is a compassionate and humorous novel about a young girl's coming of age and her cantankerous grandfather's letting go of his past.

Old Homer Dillard is the ornery but ineffectual eggman in the little town of Twilight. Deserted by his wife and daughter he lives with his eleven-year-old granddaughter, the bright but wilful Gemma. Although devoted to each other they balk at saying so, and confine themselves to a round of daily wars. Incensed by Homer's cussedness, Gemma leaves the ramshackle chicken farm for the supposed glamour of Forth Worth, where her mother lives a life of tawdry failure as a hairdresser.

But, as humanity triumphs over pettiness, events conspire to re-unite Gemma and her grandfather once more.

'*Square Dance* is that rarity: a first novel startling in concept and execution, introducing an auspicious new talent' Leonard Sanders

'Hines writes lovingly and convincingly about rural Texas, creating a strong sense of place and some wonderfully complex characters' *Publishers Weekly*

Square Dance has been made into a film starring Jason Robards and Rob Lowe.

FUTURA PUBLICATIONS
FICTION
0 7088 3656 9

Futura

PLAYING FIELDS IN WINTER

HELEN HARRIS

Sarah Livingstone and Ravi Kaul meet at Oxford.
She is English, sensing a chance to evade the pattern
of conventional middle-class life to which her
experience has so far conformed. The more
sophisticated Ravi, too, wishes to sample another way
of life – if only temporarily. Against a quintessential
Oxford background of gloomy winters and hesitant
summers, of tea and ginger-nuts eaten beside
electric bar fires, of other people's lovemaking
overheard through thin walls, of sherry parties and
suicide attempts, of girls in long cotton skirts and
evening punting expeditions, their affair blossoms
for two academic years. Until the inevitable time
when Ravi must depart for Lucknow, Sarah for job-
hunting in London – and their expectations clash
head on.

'So well does Miss Harris handle this story, so
convincingly and passionately does she write, that we
get to know the hero and heroine, fear for them,
feel for them . . . an accomplished first novel'
Susan Hill, *Good Housekeeping*

'The relationship between Sarah and Ravi is very
nicely, perceptively and credibly handled. Miss
Harris has got a real subject, she can tell a story and
create character.' Allan Massie, *The Scotsman*

'Helen Harris has drawn a painfully accurate picture
of the difficulty of holding on to a love in the face of
society's prejudice' *Over 21*

'An unbridgeable gap is the theme movingly
explored in talented Helen Harris's first novel'
Daily Express

FUTURA PUBLICATIONS
FICTION
0 7088 3370 5

Futura

Futura now offers an exciting range of quality fiction and non-fiction by both established and new authors. All of the books in this series are available from good bookshops, or can be ordered from the following address:

Futura Books
Cash Sales Department
P.O. Box 11
Falmouth
Cornwall TR10 9EN.

Please send cheque or postal order (no currency), and allow 60p for postage and packing for the first book plus 25p for the second book and 15p for each additional book ordered up to a maximum charge of £1.50 in U.K.

B.F.P.O. customers please allow 60p for the first book, 25p for the second book plus 15p per copy for the next 7 books, thereafter 9p per book.

Overseas customers including Eire please allow £1.25 for postage and packing for the first book, 75p for the second book and 28p for each subsequent title ordered.

B.F.P.O. customers please allow 60p for the first book, 25p for the second book plus 15p per copy for the next 7 books, thereafter 9p per book.

Overseas customers including Eire please allow £1.25 for postage and packing for the first book, 75p for the second book and 28p for each subsequent title ordered.

Futura